THREE WOMEN LOST IN LONDON

Emanuela Cooper

DEDICATION

I dedicate this book to Joya Hope, my beautiful granddaughter, with hope for a better future, where people and their environment are respected and treasured.

'There are all sorts of revolutions: political revolutions, economic revolutions, industrial revolutions, scientific revolutions, artistic revolutions . . . but no matter what one changes, the world will never get any better as long as people themselves remain selfish and lacking in compassion. In that respect, human revolution is the most fundamental of all revolutions, and at the same time, the most necessary revolution for humankind.'

(Daisaku Ikeda)

CONTENTS

ACKNOWLEDGMENTS

Thank you so much to all the lovely friends who helped me: To my daughter Robyn for the first editing; her invaluable insight and suggestions have hugely enhanced both content and language. To Tanya Myers for patiently reading whole chapters aloud and taking me through sound, rhythm and language. To my husband Richard for his keen insight and art work. To Tanzie Oliver, Mary-Lynne Stadler, Dez Lewis, Helen Porter-Smith and Susan Shephard for their thorough proof-reading and gentle corrections. To Peter Buckle for his encouraging feedback. Thank you to Stephen Lowe for his guidance, and to Ludwig Engl for the design of the book cover. Thank you to Jean Stanley for sharing with me her memories of Hackney of the past eighty years and to Marietta Ramaer for her memories of World War II. And to all those friends who have encouraged me all along. Thank you!

PART ONE

Chapter 1

THE FORTUNE TELLER

As Lina locked the front door of her terraced house, she had no inkling whatsoever that this was going to be the last day of the uneventful, comfortable life she knew so well.

As always before going out she carefully brushed her greying hair, pushing it neatly behind her ears, and applied a thin layer of pink lipstick. She selected a light straw summer hat with a checked band and picked up her fold-up shopping bag.

She decided to walk to the local supermarket, just a couple of streets away. There wasn't really any shopping she needed but, rather than staying at home all morning, going out would help her fill the time and keep the fluttering butterflies in her stomach at bay. Lina always felt that way before an imminent journey and had never managed to get used to the uncomfortable sensation. It made her fidgety and more than a little anxious.

After the supermarket she would maybe take a short stroll and make her outing last a little bit longer, across the park not far from the Sherwood shopping area, where she had lived for the past fifty years. The friendly undulating green grounds of the park made for a relaxed, easy walk.

Pushing her empty trolley, slowly browsing through the Co-op shelves for any special offer, she caught sight of Mavis, by far her favourite neighbour, a little further down the aisle.

The most striking feature about Mavis was her sparse hair which she insisted on dying raven black. There was definitely something a little ridiculous about this, because she was closer to eighty than seventy and at that age nobody still had black hair. She gathered it in a bun at the nape of her neck and decorated it with artificial flowers that matched the colour of the cardigan she was wearing; today it was a bright turquoise.

Seeing her old neighbour, the lonely feeling nestling at the bottom of Lina's heart disappeared instantly. 'Look who it is! Hello Mavis, I haven't seen you for a few days,' she exclaimed enthusiastically.

'Fancy that!' a surprised Mavis burst out in her slightly hoarse voice, slapping her hand on the trolley handlebar and looking equally pleased to see her: 'I was just thinking about you!'

Lina felt immediately more alive: 'Were you now? What a coincidence! I'm going away tomorrow, for a week. Had you guessed it?'

'I sort of *felt* that there was something going on,' confirmed Mavis; her opaque eyes studied Lina closely. 'I'm just getting sugar and bread before I pop and see an old friend down the road, but I am free this afternoon,' she added quickly. 'Why don't you come over for a cup of tea, around four o'clock? I'll do you a reading.'

'That would be lovely Mavis! I look forward to it.'

'Me too. I'm sorry I have to rush now, but I'll see you later.'

'That's quite all right, my dear! I have a lot to do too,' Lina lied. 'I'll see you at four!'

'Cheerio then Lina!'

'Cheerio my dear.'

Lina watched Mavis push her trolley down the aisle, walking briskly despite a limp. Her heart lighter, her lips upturned, she stopped in front of the sweet counter, scouring through the vast selection, musing upon her meeting.

Mavis was not just any old neighbour. Over the past fifty

years that Lina had known her, she had become a famous clairvoyant who now demanded a handsome sum of money in return for her services. Little by little, her fame had grown and now innumerable people consulted her, travelling from far and wide, booking their appointments well in advance.

When people in their street saw a luxury car parked outside Mavis's small terraced house – a two up two down, from which she had never wanted to move – everyone knew some rich celebrity was inside hanging on Mavis's every word. One time a very famous person arrived by helicopter. Those who had recognized the elegant lady could not quite believe it was actually *her*. She was accompanied by a man – friend or body guard – who walked with her from the landing patch in the park over to Mavis's door. By the time word got around, the eminent guest was departing in a flurry of dust and spinning helicopter blades, leaving them wondering whether they had all been dreaming. Mavis refused to go into any details; she only said it wasn't the first time the lady had consulted her and that she was sworn to secrecy. She told them to keep an eye on the national tabloids and, sure enough, two days later there she was.

You could have knocked the whole neighbourhood down with a feather!

Lina didn't really believe in the sort of things that Mavis was famous for: tarot cards, tea leaves and all that – it seemed a bit silly – but she never said anything. She was a polite person who didn't want to offend. When she was a child her mother used to tell her to treat everyone with kindness, because one never knew whom one might need help from in life. Lina had always put this teaching into practice and it had served her well. Besides, living alone, there were days when she didn't speak to anyone at all, and when she did, her voice came out all croaky. She enjoyed people's company and now, after years of taking care of her husband, bringing up four children, working all the hours God sent, these days her house felt definitely too quiet;

exchanging a few words with someone, especially Mavis, was precious.

After some dithering, she chose a packet of chocolate chip biscuits to share later on and, with a new sense of purpose, she paid for them and headed for the park. Now she really *was* busy if she wanted to go for a walk, finish her packing and have her 'fortune' told.

At four o'clock on the dot, biscuits in hand, Lina rang her neighbour's doorbell.

When she expected clients, Mavis put on her eye makeup and painted her lips red, but today she opened the door wearing a faded blue and red flowery pinafore with two big pockets at the front.

'Come on in, come on in,' she invited Lina, holding the door open, stepping to one side to let her through.

As always, the house had its own unique smell of weak lavender and old dusty carpet, mixed with a stale odour which seeped down from upstairs where nobody, apart from Mavis herself, had ever set foot. Lina thought it would do well to open the windows and circulate some air, but the old magnolia-coloured sash windows – which opened from the bottom upwards – had been painted closed.

'So, back to London, Lina?'

'I'm going to visit Sofia and the family. They have *so* insisted that I go to see their new house.'

'Of course! They'll be so happy to have you there for a week... and it will do you good to get away for a while.' Mavis hobbled towards the kitchen, shuffling her feet. 'Take a seat,' she pointed to the chairs around the table. 'Did you know that the young couple three doors up are expecting their first child?' Mavis gossiped, as she filled the kettle.

'Oh! That's nice. They are both good looking; they'll have a beautiful baby.' Lina sat herself down on the wooden chair.

'That's right. It will be nice to have a new baby in the street,' Mavis agreed, moving carefully towards the gas stove. 'And you must know that Dick, next door, is struggling to recover from a nasty bout of flu.'

'Well, he ought to stop smoking,' Lina replied. 'He's always outside his front door with a fag in his mouth. It can't do him any good. He hasn't been looking after himself since he's been a widower.'

'It's been fifteen years since Freda died, you know?'

'Is it really? It seems like yesterday!' Lina mused.

'It does; the years have flown by! Dick has been smoking like a chimney for far too long. He'll probably die with a fag in his mouth,' commented Mavis as a matter of fact, turning the gas on and placing the kettle on the ring. She turned around and looked at Lina with an amused smile: 'You know what he told me the other day?'

'What did he tell you?' Lina's small brown eyes were bright and sparkling with curiosity.

'That he has ordered a coffin for his own funeral!'

'Oh no! Why would he do that?' Lina asked in disbelief.

The neighbour continued: 'Apparently there is a special offer. The funeral directors on the main road are giving fifty per cent off to those pensioners who buy by the end of the month. He said it was such a bargain, he jumped at it.' Mavis burst out laughing. She opened a cupboard door and handed Lina a small plate. 'Put the biscuits on here Lina, we'll have them later. He also suggested that I, *and you*, ought to take advantage of it, while we can!'

'I would never do that!' Lina declared with a shocked expression. 'I've done enough for my children, bringing them into this world, bringing them up. They'll have to sort those things out when I'm gone.' She carefully opened the packet by pulling on the little tag and laid four biscuits on the plate. 'Actually, I never think about my own death; it hardly ever crosses my mind. I much prefer to think about what to do with my days.' She paused, reflecting. 'Do you, Mavis... think about your own death?'

Mavis set out two porcelain cups on their saucers and, out of a round tin box with the scene of a pond and flying ducks, ceremoniously extracted a teaspoon full of tea leaves, which she divided equally between the two cups. 'With my work, looking into people's lives, death is always a possibility, but I don't talk about it. I see change all the time, as you can imagine, but rarely do I see someone's death... and even if I thought I did, I could never be sure,' she explained with confidence. 'Besides, it wouldn't be good for business.'

'No, I suppose not!' Lina agreed thoughtfully. 'Who wants to pay good money to be told they're going to snuff it?'

'Too right!' said Mavis with a giggle and a mischievous look on her face. 'You hit the nail right on the head there, Lina.'

As soon as the kettle started to whistle, Mavis poured in enough water to half fill the cups.

'To answer your question,' she said, 'I don't think of my own death often; like you, I am too busy with my life.' She sat down heavily opposite Lina. With her elbow resting on the table, she lifted herself just enough to grab the chair with her hand between her legs and drag herself closer to the table. 'Now let's see what this journey is going to be like,' she declared, giving Lina an encouraging look.

'Let's hope everything will go smoothly,' Lina said. From the pocket of her cardigan she pulled out the penny she had prepared – a symbolic but necessary payment – and placed it with her arthritic hand onto the plastic tablecloth with its print of a dark, mysterious landscape. Despite not believing in this 'tea leaves business' she felt a nervous shiver.

As a rule she took her tea with a teaspoon of sugar and a dash of milk, but today nothing was to be added.

Mavis encouraged her: 'Drink the tea but leave a few drops.'

'Yes, yes, as usual.' Lina prudently sipped the hot bitter drink until only a few drops were left in the cup, trying to prevent the leaves from going into her mouth. She then passed it to Mavis.

Mavis stared into the cup. Her expression changed; she became serious. She closed her eyes, whilst breathing in deeply through her nose. After a while she opened her eyes, rolled the cup counter-clockwise three times (Lina knew it had to be done with the left hand) and proceeded to turn it over onto the saucer. She lightly tapped on the base of the cup, letting the last drops run off before reversing it one last time. Next, she studied the leaves strewn up the sides and across the bottom of the cup.

Lina knew that, from now on, the fortune teller was not to be interrupted; no questions were to be asked until the end of the reading. She shuffled uncomfortably on her chair. Then she saw Mavis frown.

Chapter 2

THE DAY AFTER - 5TH AUGUST 2011

Dragging her wheeled suitcase, ticket in hand, wearing her purple hat with the two red flowers, Lina reached platform one and looked for coach F. The train to London was patiently waiting for everyone to board.

With a little difficulty she placed the heavy suitcase in the storage area reserved for luggage next to the door and walked more freely along the corridor, looking for her seat: 32A, near the window. She removed her red jacket and folded it carefully. Tiptoeing, she just managed to reach the luggage rack; then, satisfied, she sat down and settled her travel bag carefully next to her on the seat.

She loved travelling by train. Her father, born and raised in Italy, had been the station master of their small village, and loved by all for his kindness. Lina was sure she had inherited from him her fondness for trains, railway cafes, speaker announcements and the on-board trolleys selling snacks and drinks.

More and more people were now boarding and walking along the corridor, checking their reservations. A white haired gentleman with a newspaper in his hand smiled and greeted her politely, before sitting down next to her. A moment later a young woman arrived, placed a cup full of steaming coffee and a sandwich on the table, and then sat down opposite her. From a green leather bag she pulled out her computer, and finally smiled at Lina saying 'Good morning'.

'Good morning' Lina replied with a smile, and thought: what a pretty young lady.

She pulled out of her travel bag the snack she had prepared at home. Wrapped in cling film there was a ham and cheese sandwich and, separately, a slice of apple & raisin cake; a small bottle, filled with water from the kitchen tap, and a little carton of fruit juice. She had promised herself a cup of tea from the trolley when it came by. It was expensive of course – almost two pounds for a bit of hot water and a tea bag – but it was a little luxury she allowed herself when travelling. Having picnics on the train was an English custom, one of those she liked the best.

Every time she embarked on this journey to visit her daughter it felt like an adventure. She couldn't wait to embrace Sofia, Steve - her son-in-law whom she loved dearly - and her wonderful grandchildren Claudia and Micky. She didn't yet know which of them would be coming to fetch her from the station. They were all very excited about their new house and kept telling her that it was beautiful. It had a large garden, ideal for Steve, who loved plants. If they were lucky and the weather held they would be able to have a barbecue. After all, it was August and the sun might just make an appearance. The Italian sunshine was the one thing she really missed. Apart from that, she had become accustomed to living in England - her home for over sixty years - and it had become her country. English people were polite and friendly, often sparked up a conversation with people they didn't know and Lina liked that. She felt comfortable here.

As soon as the train moved, Lina unwrapped her sandwich and opened her water bottle. The woman sitting opposite did the same, and began to munch her own sandwich distractedly, whilst concentrating on her computer screen, earphones in. She certainly wasn't looking for conversation. Lina took a first small bite and chewed slowly. She brushed away any crumbs from her lips with a paper napkin and listened carefully to the announcements describing the route – Nottingham, East Midlands Parkway, Leicester, Market Harborough, London Saint Pancras – and surrendered herself, gazing out of the window.

The suburbs of Nottingham flashed past her eyes: the terraced houses, gardens with slides for the children, and the conservatories where people could sit even if cold or raining outside, enjoying the light and the flowers in the garden. The passing trains offered further entertainment.

Finally she could reflect upon what had been simmering in her mind since Mavis had read the tea leaves the day before. Ever since, she hadn't been able to sleep properly. Mavis had started her reading by saying 'I see tears'. That hadn't worried Lina much. Tears and laughter, with women and teen-agers around, were bound to be plentiful. Italians expressed their emotions freely and she was comfortable with that. Tears often turned to laughter. She just hoped that Mavis wasn't predicting *too* many tears, if any at all. What kept nagging at her was the memory of the frown that never left Mavis's face. After studying the leaves for a long time, she proceeded to share what she saw: A handbag and money. At this point Lina felt excited and thought it might be a positive occurrence of some kind. Maybe she would find money in the street? But Mavis's face didn't bode well. 'Someone will take it away from you' she stated. Whether that was the handbag or the money she hadn't specified. 'I want to check something', her old friend said standing up and limping out of the kitchen.

She returned with a pack of tarot cards, from which she asked Lina to choose ten cards.

Lina was beginning to feel uneasy. She had anticipated a bit of light-hearted time with her neighbour; instead it had become quite serious, but... Lina was curious. Warily, she selected ten cards and watched Mavis lay them out as a spread. She hoped to see Mavis's expression relax. Quite the opposite happened. The fortune teller's face darkened. Now, Lina was dreading what Mavis was going to say next. Quite rightly so, as out of the old woman's mouth came the words 'I see danger, confusion'. At that point Lina became annoyed. What confusion? What danger? She wanted to say 'I'm not enjoying this, Mavis. Can we drop it?' but out of politeness she couldn't, could she? She had to remind herself that she didn't believe these silly things, so why get so wound up? She would sit it out quietly. The next time Mavis suggested doing a reading for her, Lina would remember to say she was too busy.

Out of the train window the houses gave way to warehouses and local industries. The ugly industrial zone finally faded away to be replaced by a more interesting landscape: the pointed bell tower of a distant village; the river and lakes of the Attenborough nature reserve; a closed level crossing where bicycles and cars waited for the passing of the train. She nibbled at her sandwich and observed, letting her thoughts flow one after the other, along with the passing fields.

Mavis stood up again, hobbled out of the kitchen and returned, carefully carrying in both hands a very fragile, sacred object – her crystal ball. Lina gasped. This was the first time Mavis had brought out the crystal ball for her. On one hand Lina could have run a mile - although of course she wasn't going to - and on the other she was definitely intrigued. Sitting stiffly, her hands started to sweat in her lap.

'Let's see what this has got to say,' Mavis declared, as she placed delicately her psychic tool on the table. She plopped herself into her chair, held her wrinkly hands near the ball, her eyes closed, inhaling deeply. Eventually, she opened her eyes, looking into the ball with a soft gaze. 'I see a lot of smoke and fire. Danger, there is danger', she stated dramatically.

At that point Lina had felt both nervous and irritated. She fidgeted uncomfortably, fighting her impulse to get up and leave.

Fortunately things started to improve and the final part of Mavis's reading offered good news, even too good to be true. 'You will sing... and you will dance...' she promised.

Singing, Lina could easily believe. She used to sing all the time, suddenly realizing she hadn't sung so much recently, but dancing?... that was not so very likely at her age. It just proved how unreliable Mavis's reading were.

To wrap it all up and send her client home happy, her fortune-teller neighbour declared that her forthcoming trip was going to be life-changing and things would never be the same again. Now, that was clever! – Lina thought. – When do things ever stay the same? She couldn't remember a single trip in her life when something hadn't changed, one way or the other.

Glad to be back in her own house, Lina tried to brush aside all she'd heard and concentrated instead on checking her luggage one last time. It had been sitting in her bedroom, almost ready and waiting, for the past few days. Later, she had eaten a bowl of soup while watching Coronation Street and gone to bed earlier than usual. But sleep hadn't come easily.

'We are now approaching Leicester station.' The announcement brought her back to the present moment. Lina ate the last morsel of her sandwich, brushing a few little crumbs from her lips. She folded her napkin neatly and put it back into a see-through bag. She had no appetite for cake, not just yet.

The gentleman next to her held his newspaper wide open. Lina noticed his fine hands.

She had always had an uncontrollable desire to take a peek at what the person next to her was reading. She couldn't control herself, and the irresistible curiosity always won, even when she had bought herself an interesting magazine. She could read that later – she would tell herself.

The gentleman looked at her sideways, perplexed.

'Please forgive me,' Lina addressed him. 'I have this terrible habit of reading other people's newspaper. I can't control myself. I've always done so, since I was a little girl.'

The gentleman smiled. 'Maybe you are still a young girl at heart,' he observed with a mixture of irony and reserve. 'What have you seen that has caught your attention?'

'The article about the four-year-old boy who got lost in the centre of Manchester. His parents were worried sick.'

'Indeed! All it took was a moment of inattention and he disappeared,' the gentleman turned to her. 'He was 'adopted' by a couple of young girls who took him to the fair in the main square. They must have got bored and left, leaving him there.'

'Oh my God!' Lina brought her good hand to her mouth.

'Indeed,' the gentleman empathized. 'He walked over to an elderly couple and started talking to them, as if they were his grandparents. They spent almost an hour together, waiting for someone to come and fetch him and eventually, since no one showed up, they went to a pub and called the police.'

'Well done!' Lina said with relief. 'Do *you* have any children?'

'I have two grown up children, a boy and a girl; and two grandchildren. And you?'

'Four, but only three alive. Vittorio lives in America, Marcello in Lisbon and Sofia, the youngest, is in London. She is the only one who lives in England... All my children have names of Italian actors or actresses,' she added with a giggle. 'I chose them. The one who is no longer with us was called Anna, like Anna Magnani, but we used to call her Anita... and then I have two grandchildren. I'm going to London to see them. I've been widowed for five years and my children are beginning to think that I'm too old to live alone.'

'You are not at all old, on the contrary.' The gentleman turned to look at her and studied her carefully. 'You look very well.'

Lina laughed, flattered: 'That's what I say. When I look in the mirror I see a mature woman, not an old one. But for young people it's different. For those who are forty or fifty, a person of seventy is quite old, but for people in their twenties we are ancient.'

'What matters is how one feels inside,' asserted the gentleman. 'I'm seventy-three years old and I do a lot of things. I have an active role in my family, mainly as a grandfather, and in the village where I live. I work for a charity as a volunteer; they always need people who can help. I am also part of a choir; we go around singing in schools, in residences for the elderly and at village festivals. As well as having fun, we raise a lot of money that we donate to different causes. For example, we have just delivered three thousand pounds to a family with a child who suffers from a rare heart condition and can now go abroad for surgery.' He turned to look at her again and added: 'Age is a relative thing. I know people much younger than me who feel and behave as if they were old men or women; they have no enthusiasm, or energy, or they are selfish and only care about themselves. Instead, when you actively contribute to society you feel young... and in a way we are!' he concluded with conviction.

'You are so right!' Lina agreed. What the gentleman had just said made her think. She reflected on how much she contributed to society, or the welfare of others. It was with a disturbing sense of guilt that she had to conclude that she was not doing much and ought to do more.

The trolley arrived, pulled by a smiling friendly young woman in uniform: 'Tea, coffee, wine, beer, gin, whiskey, cake, chocolate, sweets?'

The gentleman had gone back to reading his paper.

Lina ordered a cup of tea and began to sip it slowly as she watched the landscape go by: old houses with pointed roofs and an area of allotments; an old bridge with partially buried arcades; fields with grazing sheep and then those horrible giant smoke-spitting towers that, as a child, Anita had nicknamed 'the cloud-making towers'. Imposing and squalid, broad at the base and narrower at the top, they were flanked by expanses of pylons that extended endlessly into the bright yellow rapeseed fields. The yellow fields were quite a new addition; when she was young there were very few. She found them movingly beautiful, the flamboyant warm and heartening colour as bright as the sun; they gave light even when the sky was overcast. That intense yellow extended into the horizon and mingled with the open countryside, undulating on one side, flat on the other, with trees standing out against the pale blue sky, the roof of this very special country. And again, as far as the eye could see, expanses of green fields mixed with yellow ones, a crane here and there in the inhabited areas.

She wondered who would come to pick her up at the station. She hoped it would be Claudia. The last time they were on the phone, she had the strong impression that her granddaughter needed to talk to her. They always enjoyed a close relationship, as if they were friends instead of grandmother and granddaughter and, when something worried the young woman, she perceived it immediately. Who knew what was bothering her just now?

Her grandson, on the other hand, was the opposite: cheerful and carefree, he seemed to go through life as if he were gliding on ice, without any effort. It was a joy to have him around. And Sofia, her daughter. She couldn't wait to see her and give her some help. She worked a lot, maybe too much, but her husband supported and loved her, and this comforted Lina. Not everyone had the luck to find a life partner they were happy with. Soon they would all be together again.

As they approached the capital she recognized the names of the stations they were passing through: Mill Hill Broadway, Hendon – her heart swelled as the distance shortened – Cricklewood, West Hampstead. An excited smile curled her lips. The train went through a tunnel and her ears suddenly blocked up. It was a sign they were almost there. And finally here were the London suburbs.

As the train slowed down the passengers got up, took their suitcases from the luggage rack, turned their computers off and put things back in their bags. The gentleman asked her to identify her jacket, extended his arm and pulled it down. Then, with a discreet smile and holding it by the shoulders, he invited her to turn around and put her arms inside the sleeves.

Moved by such kindness Lina thanked him, buttoned it up and put her hat on. Now that she had arrived her heart was a whirlwind of emotion. The train stopped with a slight jolt and soon the queue in the corridor began to move toward the exit. The gentleman had his backpack on his shoulder and invited her to step in front of him. Once they reached the luggage compartment near the door, having found out which one was her suitcase, he grabbed it and took it down the two steps leading to the platform. Then he turned around and held out his hand to help her down, with all the grace of a true gentleman.

The noise of the station made it difficult to exchange the last words of farewell. They walked side by side, but they had already said goodbye. Approaching the clerk who would ask to see her travel ticket, Lina recognized Claudia among the crowd of people waiting and, with a jump of joy, greeted her waving her hand.

Finally, her granddaughter hugged her and held her tight. She was taller than her by a whole head. 'I'm so happy to see you, Nonna! I took a couple of hours off work to come and meet you. But... look at you,' she said with an affectionate smile, pulling her slightly away and studying her. Claudia unbuttoned her jacket saying: 'You've buttoned it up wrong and one side is higher than the other. There you go... that's better!' she concluded with satisfaction and hugged her again, holding her close. 'So lovely to feel your comforting hug Nonna, I missed you!'

'I missed you too, darling. Couldn't wait to see you.' Lina

declared.

'I need to talk to you.' Claudia changed tone and became suddenly serious. 'Let's go and have a cup of tea, then I'll take you home. You'll see how beautiful it is!'

They stopped in a café on the ground floor of the station and, seated at a small round table, ordered scones with butter and jam and a milky tea.

Claudia had lost weight and wore a tense expression that she tried to disguise with a smile. Her wavy brown hair was longer than usual and gathered with a clip over her ear. The makeup couldn't fully hide the pallor of her face and the dark circles under her eyes. Lina perceived the anxiety that troubled her granddaughter, a beautiful girl with an olive complexion, full mouth and slightly prominent nose. She had inherited her complexion and features from the Italian family, her height and build from the English one. Her undeniable charm came from the mixture of the two stocks.

'Tell me everything,' Lina encouraged her, leaning towards her.

'I don't know what to do!' the young woman blurted out, restlessly twirling a button on her beige linen jacket. 'Since we set the date for the wedding, everything has started to change. Tom seems distracted, far away, always engaged in something more important...'. She took a deep breath to control her trembling voice. 'I see him very little and now he's talking about going to work to Saudi Arabia.'

'To *Saudi Arabia*?' Lina was shocked. 'But it's very far... and besides it's a very strict, Muslim country. What would he be doing in Saudi Arabia?'

'They offered him a contract in a construction company,' Claudia replied, a disconsolate expression on her pretty face. 'The salary is very good and he says that in two or three years he would be able to save enough money to buy a house.'

'But... if you get married and he goes to Saudi Arabia, would you go with him?' Fear squeezed her heart.

'I don't know! He told me about the offer but didn't ask for my opinion. It seems as if the decision is only down to him. He takes it for granted that I'll go with him... I think.' Claudia was on the verge of tears.

'Oh come on! That's not right!' Lina protested. 'Even your grandfather would have consulted me before taking such an important decision... and he always did whatever he wanted!' She was bursting with indignation. 'What did your mother say?'

Claudia's dejected expression became even more intense and tears began to fill her eyes. 'I can't talk to her...'. She buried her trembling hand in her jacket pocket and pulled out a packet of tissues. 'She'll just shout at me!'

Lina stared at her open-mouthed: 'You are afraid of your mother? But... you've never been afraid of her... How come?'

'When I mentioned it, she jumped at me. She said that Tom had gone crazy and that if I had any common sense I'd stand up for myself and make him change his mind.' Now the tears were falling one after the other, wetting her pale cheeks and melting her mascara. 'She made me feel even worse. Like a stupid child. We haven't talked about it since. We speak very little.' Now Claudia was crying freely. She mopped her tears with a tissue now soaked in black stripes, put it on the saucer and extracted a dry one from the plastic packet.

Lina knew that mother and daughter usually had a very close relationship and this distance must be making them both suffer. 'Let's think about this for a moment,' she said, leaning forward and stroking Claudia's arm. 'Your mother's reaction was probably because *she* was afraid! Don't you think?'

'Afraid of what?' Claudia looked up at her while pressing her handkerchief on the tip of her stuffed nose.

'That you might go to Saudi Arabia, that she won't see you for months, that you will be far away, that something might happen to you,' Lina explained with emotion, putting herself in Sofia's shoes. She knew well what it meant to have a child a long way away. Hers was in America; she heard very little from him and hardly ever saw him. Looking carefully at her granddaughter she asked: 'Would you go there... to Saudi Arabia?'

Claudia struggled to breathe. She was in a painful state. She opened her mouth to inhale some air; her chest rising and lowering to absorb some oxygen.

It broke Lina's heart to see her like that. It was obvious that she was physically unwell and suffering greatly.

'*No*! I want to stay in London.' There was desperation in her voice. 'I have my friends here, my job... my family...' She hesitated and Lina waited for her to say that something else she was holding back. 'Danny also said that it is a terrible idea, and he's travelled a lot,' Claudia finally added, while her cheeks turned suddenly pink.

'Who's Danny?' Lina asked cautiously.

'My boss. We have been working together for eight months and we talk often,' Claudia confided. 'He was in the Middle East and said I wouldn't like it one little bit. Foreigners are kind of segregated and, as it is very hot, life takes place almost always indoors, where there is air conditioning; and you have to be careful how you behave, because you risk going to jail if you make a false move.' There was some anger in her voice. 'I don't want to go there! I like living in London, with the cold, the fog, the rain... everything,' she concluded with frustration.

Lina looked at her with understanding. 'Tell me more about Danny. People who have travelled extensively are interesting,' she encouraged her.

'He is definitely interesting, and very nice, too. He's kind... and makes me laugh,' Claudia brightened up. 'When I get to work I always have to go past his desk. He asks me how I am, if I slept well, if I'm ready for a new day of challenges and victories.' She broke into a little smile at the memory. 'Sometimes we go for a sandwich together. If it doesn't rain we sit in the park for half an hour and talk.' She paused and then added: 'He's the only person I feel I can be myself with and say what is closest to my heart. He listens to me.'

'It's nice to have a friend like that,' Lina remarked. 'You're lucky.' She would have liked to know if Danny was married, but decided it was best not to ask. She would find out later and the most burning problem for Claudia was deciding what to do about her relationship with Tom. 'Don't be in a hurry to get married,' she reached out to her granddaughter. 'There is always time for that.'

'But we have already set the date, I've chosen the dress I want... and now everyone knows about it! What would we say to people?' the young woman groaned, her eyes full of anxiety.

Lina took a deep breath, love in her eyes: 'These things are not as important as they may seem to you now. A date can be changed, a dress can wait and people understand.' She looked at Claudia straight in the face, covered her smooth hand with hers, her fingers deformed by arthritis, the skin marked by time and housework, her palm rough and warm. 'We are talking about your future Claudia, about the rest of your life. Hurry is a bad advisor and... as for what others think, well...'. She looked at the young woman with empathy. 'People think about us a lot less than we think, you know? Everyone has their own life, problems and aspirations, like you, like me. Your parents only want your happiness, and so do your real friends. Don't think about other people now, or even about Tom. Think of yourself at this time, of what *you* want. Otherwise you will be unhappy.'

Claudia squeezed her hand with hers, thin and wet. 'I love you Nonna,' her eyes veiled with tears, the beginning of a smile on her full lips. 'Come! I'll take you home. Dad is waiting for you. You'll love the house!'

She drove her nippy white car through the streets of London. The monotone voice of the sat nav – nicknamed Judith – telling her where and when to turn.

Lina looked around. The streets were not very different from those in Nottingham: the same terraced houses, perhaps here they were larger; the shops run by Indians that sold everything, with mountains of fruit and vegetables on display; take-away restaurants; the lush trees filling the space between road and sky; the August flowers that brightened the windowsills with red, pink and green. In London people lived in basement rooms whose windows could be seen at street level. Surely they were dark and damp, and expensive? London rents were twice those of Nottingham. The streets followed one after another as Judith's voice continued to guide them.

'How is your father?'

'He is well, happy with the new house,' Claudia replied with a pale smile. 'It's very big and full of light. Dad has organized an office for himself in the small room, but now he has moved it to his bedroom so you can have your own room while you're staying. Every now and then he empties some boxes, but he doesn't know where to put things, so he leaves them on the floor,' she chuckled. Claudia got on well with her father and cheered up when talking about him. 'With Mum always at the shop, sometimes he prepares dinner but, otherwise, getting the house sorted is taking forever.'

'Now that I'm here I can help.'

'There's plenty for everyone to do, that's for sure.' Claudia gave her a quick glance as she drove. 'If you cook we'll all be delighted!'

Lina was happy to be of help. She smiled as she went back to watching this huge London that seemed like nothing but a series of villages running into each other, a huge expanse of houses, pubs, shops and people.

Cyclists wearing helmets sped by.

On the pavements, busy people wove their way between mothers with pushchairs.

At bus stops were women dressed in saris, others with headscarves, men with long beards and a cap, girls in miniskirts and boots, boys in t-shirts and tattoos painted on their arms.

This culture of tattoos was weird – Lina reflected. In Italy only people who went to prison had them done and then, when they came out, everyone knew that they had been in jail. She had never liked them then, and didn't like them now. Large trees lined the streets and swayed in the midday breeze.

'We're almost there,' Claudia announced, more serene than before. 'I'll drop you off and go straight back to work. I'll see you tonight. Meanwhile you settle in. Micky comes home from college at around four o'clock.'

'How is he?'

'He's fine, you'll see. He's happy with his college course and spends all his time playing the guitar, the keyboard and the flute. He can play any instrument he picks up and composes music. He would be popular with the girls, if he wanted to, but he doesn't seem very interested. Maybe he's gay!'

'What do you mean? That he likes men instead of women?' Lina asked turning to her.

Claudia laughed: 'No, I don't think so, but I tease him because he seems to be more interested in his friends than in girls.'

'When he finds the right one, he'll change his mind.'

'Whether it is a man or a woman?' Claudia turned to look at her with a cheeky smile.

'Whatever makes him happy, love.' Lina took a deep breath. 'We didn't have these things when I was young. Men liked women, and that was that.' She shrugged her shoulders. 'But times have changed.'

'I'm sure there were gay people in your days, too. It's not as if it is a passing fashion; that's the way it is for some of the men, and women.' Claudia briefly turned to look at her grandmother. 'Maybe they just kept quiet about it. They were persecuted, weren't they?'

'Yes, I suppose you are right, darling. In Italy they would have had a very hard time... they must have had to keep it a secret, for their whole life.'

'I'm glad things have changed, and are still changing...'

Claudia stated, slowing down and turning right. 'This is our street, the house is at the end, on the left,' she announced. 'And here it is!' She parked the car in front of a small garden. She hurried to open her grandmother's door, held out her hand and helped her get out. Then, from the boot, she unloaded Lina's wheeled suitcase.

Chapter 3

STEVE AND MICKY

Steve opened the front door and calmly ambled down the stone path next to a small garden. He was still a handsome man and looked impressive with his blond hair, green eyes and considerable height.

Every time Lina saw him her heart filled with joy. There was something special about her son-in-law. He exuded the kind of charm that calm good people possess. With him she felt immediately at ease. She had liked him straight away when she first saw him, twenty five or so years ago, with Sofia at Victoria station in London.

Sofia had been sitting on his lap on the only available chair outside a closed pub. When her daughter had spotted them she had sprung to her feet and Steve had rushed – in his own quiet, caring way – to welcome them. He had greeted them with a 'hello' and a few words in Italian. Among the errors and the odd pronunciation, they hadn't understood anything at all, except that those words were coming from the heart. He had bent down, embraced her and kissed her with a natural spontaneity that had made him immediately endearing. Then, instead of shaking his hand, he had embraced and kissed Bruno too, who definitely was not expecting that.

'What a handsome man' he said on that occasion. It was the only time she heard Bruno make such a comment about a man. Strongly impressed with his future son-in-law, he had also liked him straight away. Full of himself as he was, convinced he was more intelligent than anyone else, Bruno immediately appreciated the respect shown to him by Steve.

Steve was a man of few words, spoke in broken Italian and smoked marijuana discreetly. They realized it quite quickly, but never said anything because they too had fallen in love with him and liked him the way he was. He inspired trust, security, and cared about Sofia, his every gesture said so. He treated her with love and respect, better than anyone in their family ever treated her. Perhaps because of this, they too began to look at her with new eyes and appreciate her more.

Before leaving to get back to work, Claudia hugged Lina affectionately and kissed her on the cheek: 'Thank you for everything Nonna! I'll see you this evening.' She got into her car and waved with her hand, throwing her a kiss from the open window.

Steve greeted her with a big smile. She could see that he was happy to see her. 'How are you Lina? Have you had a good trip?' He bent down to embrace her and she melted into that comforting hug. He took her suitcase and was about to take her other bag, too.
'I can carry this one,' Lina prevented him picking it up. 'How is your back?'
'Not too bad today, thank you. It varies. I never know how I am going to be from one day to the next,' he said, trying to sound light-hearted. 'Come! I'll show you the house. I'm sure you'll like it.' He stepped aside to let her through the door first.

Lina put the bag down and looked around the spacious living room. A lot of light came in through a large rounded bay window which, from the outside, looked like a protruding pregnant woman's belly. On the right hand side there was a fireplace — she loved fireplaces but never had the pleasure to live in a house with one — and on the left were the stairs that led to the upper floor. One more large window let in even more light. Being in such a large open space made her feel that she could breathe easily and this, for an asthmatic like her, was most reassuring. 'It's beautiful!' she declared, 'even as it is, with all the boxes.'

'We've just arrived and there is still a lot to do,' Steve explained. 'Come and see the dining room.' He walked ahead of her into a spacious room with another fireplace and a large window overlooking a long garden, far below.

'The garden is so big!' Lina exclaimed looking out. 'And so many trees! But... is there another floor below?'

'Yes. You can't tell from the road, can you? It's because we are on a hill, so the back of the house is lower than the front.' He was clearly enthusiastic about their new home. 'Now I'll show you the kitchen and the upper floor and then I'll take you downstairs.'

The kitchen was small and it was going to be difficult to have two people in it at the same time. You'd definitely need to be alone to move around and cook – Lina thought. In the corner there was the red stool that someone could sit on to keep the chef company, just like in their old house where it had become a tradition.

Steve seemed to read her mind: 'It is small but it has everything we need.'

'That's all that matters,' Lina reassured him. As soon as she had had a rest, or maybe tomorrow, she would prepare a bean soup, Sofia's favourite dish, the lasagne that Claudia adored, and aubergine with parmesan for Micky and gnocchi for Steve.

Her son-in-law preceded her up the wide stairs and, brushing aside her objections, insisted on carrying her suitcase.

Arranged around the landing were four bedrooms and a bathroom. In the master bedroom a corner was taken by a large desk with Steve's computer and a printer.

'Is this where you work? I'm sorry you had to move your office,' she apologized.

'Not at all, Lina, I am really glad you're here,' Steve stated warmly. 'I'll show you Claudia's room. It's quite messy,' he warned her before opening the door. His words were confirmed by what she saw: the bed was unmade; clothes strewn on the floor; the wardrobe doors were open and showed a chaotic array of clothes piled into a bundle. 'Sofia has given up tidying up Claudia's room,' he said, closing the door quickly.

'Well, she shouldn't need to. Claudia is a woman and surely it's up to her to keep her room tidy.'

'Quite right!' agreed Steve. 'I think I'll leave Micky's room for now. Not sure I can face another messy room.' He gave her an amused smile. 'He'll show it to you, no doubt. I'll take you to your room instead. I think you'll like it.'

In the smaller room there was a single bed near a large window. A small vase of fresh flowers on the table made her smile: 'Flowers, too! How kind!'

'From the garden, for you,' he confided. 'I know you like flowers.'

'You are such a gentleman!' How could anyone not love him?

'You deserve them.' He gave her a smile and stroked her shoulder. 'Now let's go downstairs and I'll show you the basement floor.'

As they went down to the ground floor Steve launched into a detailed explanation that, for a man of few words like him, was quite unusual: 'The basement is huge. For now there is only one habitable room but, with some work, we can convert the other room and double the living space. At the moment it's a bit damp. There is also a toilet that eventually can be made into a proper bathroom.'

Steep and narrow stairs led to the floor below: 'Come, be careful climbing down. Hold on tight to the handrail. Let me step in front of you so, if you slip, you'll at least land on me.'

Lina smiled to herself. She had no intention of slipping down the stairs and made her way with the utmost attention, but Steve always thought of all eventualities and took the necessary measures. He was wise and this was a good quality, surely.

The basement was spread out over the same area as the entire floor above. A large French window, as wide as the whole wall, gave onto a huge garden enclosed by harmoniously arranged bushes and large pines.

'It was designed by a landscape gardener,' Steve said, clearly pleased.

'It's stunning!' Lina was very impressed. It was at least forty metres long and fifteen wide, luxuriant, private and with fertile-looking soil. 'There is enough land to build another house, if you wanted to.'

'Indeed! But first we want to renovate the basement and make it liveable. I think the kids would love it and it would be an ideal space for Micky to play his music in,' Steve elaborated. 'A little at a time.'

Walking over the thick grass Lina recognized a huge rosemary plant. She squeezed a twig between her fingers and brought them to her nose to inhale the fresh pungent essence. Looking up at the trees, she exclaimed full of admiration: 'These pines are beautiful. It feels like being in the mountains!' She gazed around. 'It would be nice to plant more flowers, to give more colour to the garden.'

'Sofia said the same thing,' Steve remarked. 'Maybe you can do it together.'

There was also a wooden shed with some tools inside and plants that Steve was cultivating. From the small window Lina recognized the five-star leaves, but pretended she hadn't seen them.

They went back upstairs, into the small kitchen and, while her son-in-law was preparing a cup of tea, she asked him about his job. Fine, he said, a little frugal with words. She had to ask specific questions if she wanted to know more. She discovered that he was designing a new software system for a client and now, in this new big house, he thoroughly appreciated the independence that working from home gave him. He didn't miss having colleagues. 'I see my family during the week and enough people at the weekend. Micky often brings his friends, who sometimes stay a couple of days. When I'm working I'm fine on my own, in fact I need to be alone... and if I feel like lying down I can do so.'

They sat on the couch with their cups of tea.

Steve sipped the hot tea from his large black mug. 'Sometimes my friends come to see me, Stuart or Nick. Do you remember them?'

She remembered one of them well: 'I've seen Stuart many times, he is the tall one. I'm not so sure about Nick. Which one is he?'

Steve smiled: 'Nick is the one who walked fifteen miles to get to our wedding, after missing the bus!'

'That's right! Yes, I know who you mean. What good friends you have.' Lina was most impressed at the time, when she heard that the young man had walked all that way.

'Indeed. They are always there for me if I need any help,' Steve confirmed, with gratitude in his voice. 'Sofia likes to surround herself with people and in that respect her job is perfect. But I think she works too much, she's always rushing... and lately she has become very stressed... There's something wrong,' he confided, releasing part of his worries, and sighed. After some hesitation, turning towards her, Steve added: 'I could do with your support, Lina. Sofia is no longer the cheerful woman she used to be. I hope you can understand what's going on. She is often sad, absent, locked up in herself... sometimes she pushes me away. I don't know what the problem is, or what to do to help.' His concern was written all over his face. 'I am happy you have arrived. Women understand each other better, at least I hope so.'

She covered his hand with hers: 'I will do my best, Steve. Maybe it is her age, the midlife crisis. I went through it. It wasn't easy, but it's one of those things women have to face. It comes as a shock though, as I well remember.'

They ate a salad together and then, taking a cup of coffee with him, Steve went back upstairs to continue his work.

In her little room Lina undid her suitcase and arranged her clothes in the wardrobe. She laid her numerous necklaces, earrings and bracelets on a tray, while her thoughts turned to the conversations with Claudia and Steve. The love she felt for her daughter and granddaughter gave her such a desire to see them happy that it filled her heart to the brim. She was an uneducated woman, but hopefully she would be able to find the necessary words, the wisdom, to help them... at least a little.

Inside the first drawer of the chest of drawers she placed her medicines: one for high blood pressure, one for her asthma – that had almost disappeared since Bruno had died – gastric protector, tablets for sleeping and those for digestion. From her bag she pulled out the magazine she had bought in Nottingham and settled on her bed with two pillows behind her back but, instead of leafing through its pages, Lina looked out the window. She could see people walking on the pavement, trees swaying and cars passing by. It was like being at the cinema and, without realizing, she slipped into a deep sleep.

She woke up when the front door slammed and she heard Micky's voice. She could tell he was busy in the kitchen while talking and laughing on the phone. The fridge door closed with a thud and the grill bell rang. He was having a snack, no doubt. Micky was always hungry and ate like a wolf. Lina got up slowly and, still half asleep, went down the stairs while the smell of cheese melting under the grill spread throughout the house.

'My gran!' Micky exclaimed when he saw her.

Lina was surprised, to see that he was considerably taller than when she had last seen him. His blond hair was longer, curling in a fetching way into ringlets just under his ears. She observed him, fascinated. His face had changed, it was slimmer, but his jaw line seemed stronger. His cheekbones were more evident and his green eyes more piercing. Micky, who had always been an angelic-looking child, and then a very attractive teen-ager, was now turning into a stunning young man.

He ran to hug her and lifted her off the floor: 'Granny! You're here!'

'Don't squeeze me so hard, Micky; I can hardly breathe!' Lina complained, chuckling with delight. When her feet touched the floor again, still held in his embrace, Lina realised that her head only reached his chest. This confirmed that he was now as tall as his father, perhaps even a little taller.

Micky was as cheerful and carefree as a child. He didn't seem to have suffered during adolescence as so many other boys of his age did, and displayed a cordial, easy-going nature.

'I am so happy to see you!' he cried out. 'Will you make me your aubergine with parmesan cheese?'

Lina laughed. Aubergine, lasagne, tortellini, ravioli, she would prepare him anything he wanted. 'Take this, put it away,' she instructed him, stuffing a sealed envelope into his hand. 'Buy yourself whatever you want.' The trousers he was wearing fell way below his waist, leaving half of his bottom uncovered.

'Oh Gran,' Micky protested, embarrassed. 'You always give me money, every time I see you.'

'It makes me happy,' Lina replied unassumingly. 'The others have a job and earn money, but it's different for you and remember... whatever you need, you just have to ask me, okay? Buy yourself a pair of new trousers, maybe, that will stay up.'

'It's the fashion, Gran,' he laughed. 'And you!... You talk as if you were a millionaire.'

'I don't have a big pension, but I have what I need and I feel like a lady.'

'Because you are! You're the most elegant grandmother I know,' Micky declared, bending down to embrace her. 'I must have learnt everything from you!'

They giggled, happy to be together.

Lina told him what Claudia had said, that he could play any instrument he put his hands on and composed music. She would like to hear it.

'I'll play you a piece I'm working on, but it's rap, I don't know if you'll like it.'

'Is it that style where they talk non-stop with music underneath?'

'Yup. What a modern granny!' Micky was surprised to hear that she knew what rap was.

Lina didn't like this kind of music at all and hoped the trend would soon change and they would start once again to write songs as they ought to be, that sang melodically of love. But she was too shy to say what she thought. 'It depends on the lyrics. If the words are good, I like it.'

Micky took her into his room – which was tidier than she had expected – and started getting busy with his electronic keyboard. There were dozens of spray cans in a box near an empty bookcase.

'Do you still do graffiti?' she asked, looking around and taking in the shape and size of the room.

'Sometimes. I did a shop shutter at the owner's request,' Micky said, unplugging something with great concentration and plugging it into something else. 'Can you believe that he asked Mum if I was the one going around graffitiing and she said yes! She should have said no, that she didn't know anything about it, because they can give you a hefty fine, they can even put you in prison, and instead she goes and says yes!' He snickered at Lina's surprised expression and continued: 'And then the shopkeeper said: Ask your son if he can draw on my shutter. I'll pay him'.'

'What a surprise! And did he pay you?' Lina was excited at the unusual development.

'Yup, a hundred pounds! One of these days I'll take you after he's closed the shop and show you.'

He handed her a sheet of paper with the words of a song and turned on the recording on the keyboard. The music started and a male voice recited a rap at full speed that, from what she could understand, spoke of social inequality, racism against black youth, freedom of expression and injustice in repressing the harmless smoking of marijuana. Shifting her weight from one foot to the other – not quite dancing as the piece didn't have a proper music, or rhythm – Lina tried to follow the words written on the page and found the tune less unpleasant than she had feared. 'Is that you that 'sings'... so to speak?' she asked in amazement.

Micky nodded while he hummed the song and looked at her with a smile on his face.

'I hadn't recognized your voice.' Lina was buying time as she focused on the words that kept coming out at full throttle. After what seemed like an eternity the track stopped and she saw that her grandson was confidently waiting for her compliments.

'It's interesting... the words are... interesting,' Lina muttered, and thought that if he had inserted some real music she would have liked it better. 'You're good! Have you thought about using some classical music?' she suggested timidly. 'I heard songs where they used sections by Mozart, or Beethoven, as a pretext to develop some very modern compositions and they seemed catchy to me.'

The young man smiled: 'For now this is my style, maybe later... I'll give it a thought.' His eyes suddenly lit up. 'Gran, have you ever heard a bomb fall?'

Lina sat down carefully on the bed. Of course she had heard bombs fall, many of them. One didn't forget these things. 'Unfortunately yes, during the war. Why do you ask?'

'Because I'd like to insert that sound into a piece of music I'm composing. It must be something unexpected that comes suddenly. It must shock,' he added enthusiastically. 'How would you describe it?'

Lina closed her eyes to remember that distressing sound that for years had marked her, followed and awakened her with a start.

While waiting for the answer Micky observed her and his smile faded, as different expressions followed each other on his grandmother's face.

'Before the bombs dropped we would hear the sirens,' she began. 'Then, depending on where we were, we ran to an anti-aircraft shelter. I was a child in those days. I was four when the war started and nine when it ended.'

Micky looked at her in fascination and didn't interrupt her.

'We always hoped that the bombs would fall somewhere else and we, your great grandparents and I, were lucky. One day one fell not far from our house, in a neighbourhood where Giovanna lived. She was one of mother's friends whom we were going to see that morning. I don't remember why, but we were late. Your great grandmother took me by the hand and we ran all the way to the street where Giovanna lived. There wasn't a single house standing, they had all burned to the ground, smoke was rising from the ruins.'

'And Giovanna's house?' Micky's face revealed a mixture of excitement and concern.

Lina shook her head: 'It was gone. Destroyed.'

'And the friend? Dead?' he asked tentatively.

Lina nodded with her head.

The boy wanted to know more things. Had she seen dead people?

Of course she had seen them. You could see body parts, a woman's arm with a torn sleeve, a child's leg wearing blood stained short trousers; there were body parts all over the places.

'And what did you do? Did you look away?' Micky spoke a little more calmly now.

'No, we looked, we saw, and then moved on, kept going. Sometimes, when someone tells me that they are suffering for one thing or another, it makes me think that today's young

34

people don't know what suffering is.' Lina spoke in a quiet voice. 'If they had seen those things, everything else would seem a lot less important.'

Downstairs in the kitchen it was time to organize dinner. Lina wanted it to be ready, to surprise Sofia when she came back from work. Her daughter had been up since early in the morning and would be tired. Micky showed her what was in the fridge. They found all the ingredients for a 'Bolognese' and, while her grandson returned to his room to study, Lina got to work.

Claudia arrived home at around half past six and sat in the living room talking on the phone. The conversation was with Tom, her fiancé, and after a while it seemed to turn into a heated discussion. Still arguing, her granddaughter climbed the stairs and went up to her room, her mobile phone attached to her ear, an expression of despair on her beautiful tense face.

Chapter 4

SAD AND STRESSED SOFIA

Sofia arrived at seven, bursting with nervous energy. Her dark hair windswept, her blue eyes quickly darting around the room. 'No one has lifted a finger around here, as usual,' she muttered out under her breath, but loud enough to be heard by Lina. 'Hi Mum! I bought some chicken breasts to do tonight.' She put the shopping bags down and walked to meet her mother who was quickly taking off her apron, and embraced her.

'It's good to see you; you look well!' Sofia said, quickly glancing at her. 'Who's home?'

'Steve, Micky and Claudia...'

'She's home too?'

'Yes. They're all here. Claudia is in her room on the phone. She looked tense.'

'Mmh,' Sofia commented, picking up the shopping bags and moving toward the kitchen, her face darkened.

'I prepared spaghetti with Ragu for tonight, so you have nothing to do and can relax.'

'Relax? If only! Have you seen those boxes? They're all full!' her daughter blurted out. 'If you move out of the way I'll put the chicken breasts in the fridge; we'll eat them tomorrow.' Seeing her mother's perplexed expression, Sofia tried to calm herself. 'Thank you for preparing dinner, but there's a mountain of things to do to fix this house and, apart from me, no one else seems to care. Everyone does what they want and nobody worries about a thing. And... actually... this can't wait,' she added, openly worried. 'I must speak to Micky, and Steve.' Sofia walked past her mother out of the kitchen and rushed up the stairs.

Lina heard her open Micky's door and question him: 'The graffiti on the bridge, was that you?' The door was left ajar. 'How did you get up there? Did you climb?'

Lina could not hear what Micky was replying, but she could hear Sofia's voice getting louder. 'You leaned over the top of the bridge?'

Micky must have been saying something to reassure his mother, but it wasn't achieving the desired result, quite the opposite in fact.

'Who were you with?... Are you crazy? *Alone*? You're lucky you didn't fall and kill yourself!' Sofia was shouting now.

Steve opened his bedroom door. 'What's happening?' he asked standing on the landing

'Come in and listen to this,' Sofia demanded.

Lina couldn't help listening from the bottom of the stairs, her heart held in a grip of distress. How she suffered hearing her daughter so upset.

Steve had closed Micky's door, but Sofia's voice was cutting through. 'I don't care about the marijuana leaf, I care that he doesn't get caught, or kill himself,' she was saying. After a pause, an even more distraught Sofia was shouting: '*Me*? *Controlling*? So now it's me who's the problem. What if he'd fallen? Don't you care about your son?'

One more pause during which Steve said something that Lina couldn't hear and then it was Sofia's voice again: 'I can't do this on my own. If you don't support me... I give up.' There was a painful pause when the door opened, followed by 'Micky...' Sofia implored, 'please, for me... stop being so reckless... I can't cope. It's driving me insane.'

Lina heard Micky's door close. Steve was still in the bedroom with him. Not wanting to be caught listening, she went quickly back into the kitchen, but Sofia didn't come down the stairs. Sighing deeply, Lina took the cork off the bottle and poured some red wine into two glasses, to which she added some sparkling water and a slice of lemon. Carrying them carefully she took them into the living room.

Just then she heard the bathroom door open and Sofia making her way down the stairs.

Lina gazed at her. Two lines between her eyebrows revealed the tension she was carrying inside. Slim and quick on her feet, Sofia moved, thought and talked quickly and efficiently, but was not able to relax. Lina understood her, but living like this wasn't good for her, quite the opposite in fact.

'Has something happened? Let's sit down for two minutes, until the water boils,' she suggested, trying to direct her daughter towards the sofa.

But Sofia stiffened and – clearly upset – moved out of her mother's way. 'I can't sit on the bloody sofa,' she said morosely. 'I don't have time for such luxury, do I?'

Shocked by her reaction, Lina stood in the middle of the room, glasses in hand, speechless.

Sofia bit her lip, a helpless expression in her eyes: 'I'm sorry Mum. There is so much to do and...'

'But... if you relax for a few minutes you'll feel better. I'm here to help you!' said Lina falteringly.

'Thank you Mum, but you didn't come here just to work.' Sofia plopped herself down, leaning heavily against the cushions. Looking guilty and confused, she accepted the glass Lina was handing to her, rested her head on the back of the sofa and sighed. She brought the glass to her lips. 'This is lovely,' she murmured after the first sip. 'Sorry Mum. I don't seem to be getting anything right these days. I'm always doing the wrong thing, saying the wrong words, upsetting everyone!' She stared at the ceiling, blinking fast to fight back the tears.

'I'm sure you are doing your best,' Lina reassured her, sitting on the armchair holding her own glass. 'You look upset,' she said, hoping Sofia might open up.

'I was almost home, stuck in a huge traffic jam,' Sofia started. 'I was listening to the radio, looking forward to seeing you and, as I raised my eyes right before the bridge, I saw a huge green marijuana leaf sprayed right at the top of the bridge. I recognized it immediately as the type of thing Micky does.'

'Are you sure he did it?' Lina enquired.

'Yes, because Micky has his own tag, almost like a signature, and there it was, next to the leaf. So, no doubt about it.' She sighed and her shoulders dropped. 'It's not so much doing the graffiti, though he could get into a lot of trouble...' her voice quietened as her nervous energy turned into exhaustion. 'It's the fact that he put himself in danger to do that. As I was looking at it – the traffic was stuck for a long time – I started to wonder 'How did he get up there?' I thought he must have climbed. But now he told me that he leaned over the side of the bridge, and did the drawing hanging down... and he was on his own. What if something had happened to him... He could have fallen.'

'How worrying...' Lina agreed. 'Do you want me to talk to him too? Maybe I can persuade him to be more careful.'

'Yes please, Mum. Talk to him. He seems to listen to you.' Sofia's eyes were full of concern. 'Steve doesn't realize how serious this is. He thinks I'm over reacting... and that I just want to control everyone.' She frowned, clearly distressed. 'Fortunately Micky seems to have understood the danger he put himself in, and he was sorry. At least I hope so.'

'I will talk to him, darling. We understand each other well. Luckily nothing has happened. And you... try to relax. Are you working too much?'

'I always do. If I don't get on with things, they simply don't happen.' As Sofia glanced at her mother, a few tears ran down her cheeks. Brushing them surreptitiously away with her fingers, she took a deep breath and agreed: 'But you are right, nothing has happened, thank god for that.' She took a long sip from the drink. 'Ah! This is really good; just what I needed.' She sighed deeply. 'Now... about you. Tomorrow you are going to Charlie's.'

'To Charlie's?' Lina couldn't hide her excitement. 'Oh, how wonderful! Did you organize it?'

'I called her to let her know that you were coming and she's booked you.' Sofia took another sip of wine. 'I'll go to the shop at around one, so that in the morning I can make some progress on the house. We'll leave around noon and I'll drop you off there. Is that all right?'

'It is absolutely fine,' Lina exclaimed, sheer joy making her eyes shine. 'Charlie and I go back such a long way. I can't wait to see her again. Thank you Sofia. You are so thoughtful!'

Sofia managed a smile: 'You deserve it Mum, you are very thoughtful yourself.'

As she heard Steve coming downstairs, Sofia swept her disorderly fringe off her forehead. She ran her fingers through her hair and her hands over her face, trying to dissipate the lingering upset. She avoided looking at him directly when he came to sit next to her on the sofa.

Lina went into the kitchen to leave them alone. She could hear Steve's voice; he was speaking in a calm but firm way. He spoke for quite a while.

Then it was Sofia's turn to vent her frustration – Lina could hear her words. She was upset at Micky's daredevil behaviour, but more upset still at her husband's lack of understanding and support. Despite her complaints, it didn't sound as if Steve was getting any closer to agreeing with her, and Sofia was clearly very unhappy. Steve spoke some more, quietly. Eventually Sofia's voice became lower, calmer.

Lina walked back into the living room as she heard Micky open his bedroom door. He ran down the stairs without holding onto the railing, jumped down the last few steps and landed with a thud. 'I'm sorry Mum!' He rushed to kiss his mother and gave her a clumsy affectionate embrace. 'I didn't think! I don't want to upset you.'

'I just care about your safety. I don't want anything bad to happen to you. Do you understand?' Sofia pleaded.

'I know Mum. I love you!' He hugged her and kissed, extracting a tired, reluctant smile from Sofia's lips. 'Shall I set the table Gran?' he bellowed although it was not necessary since she was right there, but he was bursting with energy and somehow it had to escape.

Claudia was the last one to come down. Her eyes were red and, though she tried to hide it, it was obvious that she had been crying. Everyone pretended not to notice it to avoid embarrassing her. She seemed keen to ignore the argument that had gone on just outside her bedroom door.

They all sat around the table and the bottle of Chianti Classico did the rounds. Lina pretended not to see Sofia gulp down the first glass and promptly refill it, starting to sip the second glass straight away. Steve did the same. Soon the bottle was half empty, but the atmosphere had finally relaxed. She told them of her train journey and the gentleman she had met. Through talking to him, she had realized that she didn't contribute much to society and felt she ought to do more.

'But you are helping us Nonna,' Claudia objected. 'And we are part of society.' And with those words Lina felt somewhat soothed.

Sofia told them about a customer who had bought five pairs of shoes in the afternoon and the employee who was three months pregnant. In a few weeks she would have to start looking for a replacement and it took a lot of time to train a new person. She didn't mention the graffiti on the bridge.

Micky was happy to move on to a completely different topic and shared with them that his college tutor, whom he saw even during the holidays, complimented him on the musical composition that he had almost finished: 'Gran likes it, too,

41

don't you Gran?' he urged her enthusiastically.

'Yes, it's interesting,' Lina confirmed with an encouraging smile.

Steve was friendly but was saying little. When Claudia asked him how he had spent the day, they found out that he had come across a big problem with the program he was designing, but was beginning to understand how to solve it. A lively exchange with technical terms on programs, anti-virus, downloads, back-ups and the likes began between him and his daughter. Lina could see that her granddaughter understood as much as her father about computers and he was very proud of her.

Sofia and Micky started talking, discussing music and college. He was full of enthusiasm. His mother listened with interest and, taking advantage of the outpouring of words from her son, leaned back on her chair and chewed more slowly.

Lina noticed that there was no direct dialogue between mother and daughter. They avoided looking directly at each other and Sofia only glanced at Claudia when the young woman was talking to someone else. Her granddaughter did the same toward her mother. The uneasiness was clear to a careful observer.

After some fruit to finish off, one by one they all disappeared, except for Claudia who was clearing the table.

'Where have they gone?' Lina asked.

'To the garden... to smoke.'

'Sofia too? I thought she had stopped.'

'Sort of... After dinner she smokes, and not just cigarettes,' her granddaughter revealed, putting the dirty dishes in the dishwasher.

'What does she smoke if not cigarettes?'

'Grass, of course.'

'Who? Your mother?'

'Yes, luckily! At least she calms down a little.' Claudia looked at her from low down, while loading the cutlery into the appropriate basket. 'Don't say I told you, otherwise she'll tear me to pieces, okay?'

'Okay… okay,' Lina reassured her. She was astonished. Her daughter smoked marijuana! This was a surprise. Let's hope she won't become addicted – she thought with apprehension. She knew she couldn't say anything. It was better to keep quiet. Sofia was almost fifty years old and an intelligent woman. Lina sighed and shook her head. Her daughter smoked 'spliffs' – as Micky called them. Who knew how many years she had been doing so… and she had never suspected anything. Lina saw them in the garden from the kitchen window.

Steve was walking holding Sofia's hand and stopped every now and then to point to the bushes. He gestured with his arm as if to explain some ideas to plant something; perhaps he was talking about the flowers Lina had mentioned. Sofia raised her face to look at him and he bent down to kiss her. Lina was relieved to see that they seemed to have got over the earlier disagreement.

Micky had climbed one of the pines and suddenly jumped to the ground next to his parents, startling them. There was an exchange of loud comments and they all laughed like children. The boy had the energy of an erupting volcano. Fortunately, when he composed music or played it, he put his headphones on and the house remained fairly quiet.

'Why don't you talk to your mother?' she asked Claudia. 'I'm sure she's suffering because of your coldness.'

Her granddaughter stiffened: 'I have a lot of problems, Nonna. I don't know what to do with Tom. I don't have the energy to face my mother with her neurotic moods, too,' she blurted out. 'She has to sort them out herself. As for Tom, I asked him if he was coming over to say hello to you tonight and he replied that he couldn't because he was visiting a friend, he didn't tell me who, to watch a football match and have a beer. He sends his love, by the way. I feel terrible, as if I'd lost an arm, and he couldn't care less.'

Lina didn't know what to think. She could tell that Claudia was gripped by confusion and insecurity. She would have liked to be able to reassure her that everything was going to be fine but, if she was honest with herself, Tom's behaviour – Lina had known him for many years – made her think that he was looking, perhaps unconsciously, for a way out. She recognized a fading relationship, and understood the girl's torment. It was going to take time, but in time Claudia would understand, let it go, and get back her freedom. 'You're not sure you want to marry him, though,' she said, to feel the ground and help her granddaughter understand.

'At this point I'm not! I feel humiliated and full of anger. He has no right to treat me like that.' Claudia's voice trembled with indignation.

'Why don't you talk with him and cancel the wedding? You would both feel better and get rid of this pressure.'

'It would be the end of our relationship.' The young woman was looking lost.

'Maybe it would and maybe not. It depends on how strong your love is,' Lina pointed out. 'But for the moment it seems the only sensible thing to do. If you're not sure you want to spend the rest of your life together, marriage is not for you, not now.'

Claudia gazed at her wide-eyed: 'Maybe you're right, Nonna. It sounds so simple the way you put it. I'll call him back to talk.'

At that very moment they heard voices climbing up the stairs from the basement. The kitchen door opened and Steve's, Sofia's and Micky's smiling faces went past them, one by one.

'Feeling relaxed?' Lina asked.

'Yes, thank you!' they all answered.

Claudia looked at them but her mind was elsewhere, her gaze far away. Mobile phone in hand, she rushed out of the kitchen, up the stairs and locked herself in her room.

Chapter 5

CLAUDIA'S WORLD

Claudia turned off the engine, lowered the sun visor and studied herself in the mirror. Then she rummaged through her bag till she found her hairbrush. She adjusted her hair and repositioned the clip over her ear. She put on a touch of pearly pink lipstick and slid her lips against each other. Lifting her cool hands to her face she felt her hot cheeks and smiled. Her heart fluttered in her chest.

She approached the office with a confident step, hanging her pass around her neck. Each time she slid the rigid card along the automatic system's groove Claudia felt the gentle comfort of belonging. She pushed the glass door open and found herself in the familiar entrance hall that smelt of vanilla. She steadily climbed the iron stairs, conscious of the loud metallic noise under her feet, and stepped into a narrow corridor flanked by offices on both sides. With five long strides she reached the photocopier, straightened her back and pushed open one final door.

The desks were arranged in islands of four throughout the large and bright office. Her colleagues raised their eyes; their smiles and greetings welcomed her.

She felt herself deflate a little as she passed Danny's empty chair but continued to her desk, hoping to hide the slight slump of her shoulders. Some of her colleagues followed her with their eyes while others stared at their screens as if there were nothing more important in the world. A couple of employees talked to each other, discussing customers, alterations to be made and orders to be dealt with. The spontaneous grin was still on her lips and so she offered it to Sarah, her colleague and friend, sat at the desk opposite. Only a low parapet divided their work stations, enough to hide their hands but not their faces. Her colleague responded with a sad smile. Sarah was not pretending to be happy. She was worried about her health, about a lump that they had found in her left breast and wanted to 'investigate'.

Claudia turned on her computer and asked her how her son was. Sarah had a bright cheeky toddler and a husband who had been acting strangely for some time. Her answer 'not too bad' meant that things were not going well. Her eyes began filling with tears. She stood up quickly to ward them off and headed for the kitchen to make them both a tea. Claudia thanked her with a smile full of affection and started to count the messages in her inbox. There were at least thirty. She was glad to have lots of work to do; the more the better. Keeping busy might give her a moment's respite from her overactive mind. She opened a customer's email: 'Dear Sirs, in reference to my letter of 10/07/2011...'

She was already beginning to question whether she had done the right thing. When she suggested to Tom that maybe it was better to postpone the wedding, he seemed genuinely shocked. But... how come? Why? Don't you love me anymore? She tried to reassure him, told him that of course she loved him, and when she said it she meant it. By the end of their conversation, though, she was completely confused and no longer grounded in any idea of what she did or didn't want. Her heart was in turmoil and she ended up telling him not to worry, that maybe they should keep the date after all, not make any changes. One minute she felt pulled in one direction and a moment later in the opposite. But she knew that now, also for Tom, a seed of doubt had been planted and with it questions were inevitably going to form. Unsettled looks, anxious uncertainty would wipe away Tom's open, childlike smile that endeared him to everyone. While she had kept quiet she had been able to pretend that everything was fine, distracting herself with fantasies of joining Danny at the Paris show and of picnics together on the grass, or walks along the river, talking about this and that; they never ran out of conversation. Danny came into her mind quite often lately... In fact, he was there when she woke up in the morning and often as the last thought before falling asleep, with a smile on her face. He seemed to be vaguely present almost every minute of the day. And she was grateful for that; thoughts of Danny were a safe thing, like a welcome escape valve that allowed her a break from the urgent, uncomfortable worry about Tom and his behaviour, his distressing project to emigrate and the alarming heartache that was tormenting her. If she could run from all the decisions, closing in on her like a cage of confusion and expectations, how fast she would run! But unfortunately she couldn't just slip off and hide, sneak away without being noticed. If only!

At least now she had begun to express what she was feeling, even if she was feeling messed up, lost and tangled up inside. From now on she would no longer be able to pretend that everything was fine. On the one hand this made her feel better, clearer, but on the other it filled her with stifling anguish. Everything was changing. She was changing and the need to be honest with herself was pushing her towards decisions she would rather not have to make.

It had been good to talk to her grandmother. She was an exceptional woman - though she didn't know it - with her feet firmly on the ground and a wise, kind heart. Claudia was happy to have her staying at their house. They would have many opportunities to talk. Her stubborn confusion usually gave way to clarity when listening to Nonna's advice. Also, she was acting as a buffer between herself and her mother, and god knew how much that was needed.

Claudia could no longer remember who started the suffering, whether it was she, saying something spiteful, or her mother expressing judgements that she should have kept to herself. The truth was that everything was going in the wrong direction. She missed being able to confide in her, but she couldn't even look her in the face. There wasn't ever any real time. She had a lot of things to do and her mother was always on the run. It wouldn't be easy to find the right moment to talk, even if she tried. And if her mother was avoiding the opportunity as vigorously as she was, well... then they might wait a whole lifetime. If Mum could just be less neurotic, kinder; if she understood that unsolicited advice was not welcome, maybe they could try to start talking again. Unfortunately she insisted on playing her role as know-it-all mother, even when it was no longer necessary. After all I'm twenty-five years old, I'm not a child – Claudia said to herself – I'm a woman who has decided to get married and instead, perhaps, is about to destroy everything.

Sarah was back with a cup of tea in each hand. She walked to Claudia's side of the desk and placed her mug on the cat coaster next to her screen. Claudia stroked her hip in an affectionate move and smiled. 'Are you very busy?' she asked her.

Sarah had a lot to do and, like herself, was happy to keep her mind occupied with orders, changes and the inevitable problems relating to the new collection. Anything was better than thinking about her own life, apart from her child who was her ray of sunshine.

As Sarah went back to her desk, Claudia stared at the email on her computer screen: 'Dear Sirs, ...', but she couldn't concentrate, her mind was spiralling and she fiddled with the keyboard, pretending to work. The idea of just doing whatever she wanted, living for today, without plans, a compass or a destination, was becoming attractive... very much so. She was not used to thinking of herself; on the contrary, she found it more natural to think about what other people wanted.

But now... to see what life had to offer, take it with both hands, enjoy the present without thinking of anyone else, abandoning herself to her destiny. Who knew what was in store for her? She had never thought like that before. Normally she liked to plan, to know what came next, tomorrow and the day after. But people change, don't they? Couldn't she? Start from scratch, choose a new style, new clothes, cut her hair short, maybe leave home and move in with a friend. But wouldn't she just be running away? And hurting other people? Perhaps she ought to fix what was broken first. But could it be fixed? Or was it broken forever? Her eyes burned as she held back her urgent tears.

She clicked on the email again and tried to concentrate on the job, 'Dear Sirs, in reference to my letter of 10/07/2011...', sipping her hot tea. The words on the screen blurred in front of her eyes. Did she love Tom? She cared about him, no doubt about that, but was she still in love with him? She didn't know, and her stomach stiffened, felt tangled and hurt. What was the difference between love and friendship? She loved her female friends and even some of her male friends, but she wouldn't marry them. Did she really want to spend the rest of her life with him? She had believed so, then she hadn't known what to think and now, at times, the idea just seemed a bit absurd.

What about all the plans they had made? The dress, the guests, what would she say to them? I'm sorry, but I've changed my mind, it's all off. The groom wants to move to Saudi Arabia and I want to stay here with you, my friends, my family, my colleagues. How embarrassing, and how much would he suffer, poor Tom? And his parents who loved her like a daughter, and she them. And the idea of being alone, how did that make her feel? Afraid. She was afraid of being alone. Free? If she replaced the word 'alone' with 'free' it sounded better. It didn't scare her so much.

The door behind her opened and she recognized Danny's step. The office seemed to spring to life. Her colleagues smiled, compelled by the excitement that entered with him like a spring breeze. She turned around and met his bright blue eyes, which were already looking at her.

He smiled promptly and gave her a wink. Her heart swelled with excitement and she laughed. She always felt like that when he was in the room.

Danny crossed the office with his fast and assured step, sat at his desk and began to lean precariously on the back legs of his chair – which he always did – while listening to his assistant rattle off the report: The Italian tailor who was manufacturing the men's suits for the autumn/winter collection recommended minor alterations to the finish of jackets and trousers, but this would push the cost up a little; the company that made the shirts wanted to know the exact quantity, forty or sixty? The artisan company that made men's footwear needed them to confirm the order by the end of today if they wanted the shoes to be ready in time.

Three questions and three telegraphic answers. Danny made decisions rapidly. He seemed to have all the answers at his fingertips: Talk to the designer, let her decide what to do about alterations, but we can't spend even a penny more, the budget can only be reduced at this stage; maybe they can try to engineer a cost reduction on something else. Fix me a meeting for this afternoon, about half past four would be fine. As for the number of shirts, Norman's office must make a decision; tell him that we meet at five so we can talk about it. See if the meeting room is free and book it for that time. As for the shoes, talk to Francis, tell him to get a move on. Why haven't they decided yet? Is there a problem? If so, tell him to let me know and we'll find a solution. Was he free this morning? This was the most urgent thing. Anything else? Nothing else for now.

Danny turned on the computer and started tapping on the keyboard with two fingers, concentrating. The peace didn't last long. One of the employees said they had to book flights to Paris and wanted to know who was going and which hotel they would stay in.

Claudia held her breath. She wanted to go to Paris at any cost, but her role wasn't essential. She was just one of the assistants. She would do anything: take notes, carry the suitcases, wash everyone's socks, a 'Jack-of-all-Trades' was always useful... surely. She turned her gaze to Danny and at the very same time he looked up. She smiled at him. He stared at her for a split second longer and her cheeks blazed. She heard him ask his assistant 'Who speaks French? and also Italian, it's always useful.' Claudia's heart skipped a beat, she spoke both languages, her Italian was better than her French but she could manage both. She could brush up on her French at night if necessary; there was still one month before the fashion show. She surprised even herself when she threw her arm in the air saying 'I speak both Italian and French.'

Danny looked at her briefly and turned to the assistant saying 'You see? Everything happens at the right time'. He instructed him to book the flights for himself, Norman, Francis and Claudia. Later on they would see who else needed to come. Claudia felt a lump in her throat. She was shaking with emotion, but succeeded in controlling herself and smiled discreetly whilst nodding her head. Then she looked down, so that no one could see the joy filling her eyes.

Her mobile phone started vibrating in her handbag. There was a message from Tom. He'd be coming to fetch her from work and wanted to take her for dinner, early, at about six o'clock, because later on he had friends coming round. She didn't know what to think; she felt mixed up, but comforted at the same time. Was it too little too late? She sent a reply message to say that worked for her, gazed over at Danny – his hair looked great, sticking up full of gel – and turned her phone off. She looked again at the email that was waiting for her: 'Dear Sirs, in reference to my letter of 10/07/2011...'

Claudia's nerves were soothed and she was able to focus on her work. The hours seemed to fly. It gave her tremendous satisfaction to get through every task and to perform it well, with professionalism. It often left her time to help her colleagues. Today was such a time. She approached Mel at her desk and asked her if she needed any help.

Mel looked at her with appreciation: 'Thanks Claudia, you're an angel. Would you take these notes and type them out for me, please; but my handwriting sucks. Will you be able to understand everything?' No problem, said Claudia laughing, she could read any handwriting, even the messy scrawl of busy doctors.

Mel had been friends with Danny for many years and Claudia had always suspected that she might have a crush on him. They had an obvious camaraderie and everyone could see that they were very close.

'Fancy going for a walk along the river to grab a sandwich?' Mel suggested. 'If the sun keeps pushing through, maybe we can even catch some rays'.

Claudia hesitated. She knew that Sarah was busy, working through her lunch hour so that she could leave early. What if Danny wanted to invite her? It wasn't as if that happened often, though. She decided that she would like to spend an hour with Mel. Maybe she'd find out some interesting things, and accepted her invitation.

The clouds had been swept away by the easterly wind and the two girls walked leisurely along the broad pavement that ran along the river, found a sheltered space and sat on the grass. Soon they removed their T-shirts and lay in their bras, hitching up their skirts a little and letting the sun warm them, feeling that it really was summer, even in London.

It wasn't difficult to start a conversation about Danny – Mel seemed as eager to talk about him as she was – and as she listened, Claudia realised quite how important he was to Mel. She talked about the gifts Danny gave her; how he opened up about the things that worried him; how much fun they had when they went to the gym. It was as if he were the centre of her life.

'And you're in love with him,' Claudia blurted out without a warning and, pretending not to notice Mel's surprised reaction, quickly added: 'I can understand you. He's a charming man, no doubt about that, and he is very funny. I think it's easy to fall in love with a man like that, mature... but quite irresistible,' she said jokingly. Seeing the shimmering tears in her friend's eyes, Claudia knew she had hit the mark and suddenly felt sorry for Mel.

'I didn't know it was so obvious,' her colleague said uneasily.

'Not to everyone, but a sensitive person can tell,' Claudia reassured her. 'Were the two of you ever together?'

Mel sighed as she shook her head: 'I've been pining for him for ten years, since well before he got married...' She put her hand in her bag and pulled out a tissue to wipe her nose. 'I was supposed to go to the wedding... and instead I ended up in hospital having a panic attack. The years went by, his daughters were born and he's never changed toward me; always affectionate, attentive, generous... but nothing more.'

'He does treat you in a special way. Anyone can see that he cares a lot about you.'

'Yup, I think so too, but nothing ever happened. Never a kiss, never got any closer... zilch, and now I have to accept it never will. He's too loyal. He's made a promise of fidelity to his wife and keeps it... unfortunately!'

Claudia felt a twinge in her heart, but brushed over her unease with a laugh: 'Indeed... unfortunately. Good of him though! And his wife is lucky. Do you know her?'

'Sure. She is a good person... and their daughters are very nice. They love me and call me 'auntie'. I'm Auntie Mel,' she concluded with sad irony.

'And instead you wanted to be the mother of his children.' Claudia felt real compassion. She leaned toward Mel and stroked her arm: 'I'm sorry for you Mel, but you have to live your life. You have to look ahead; otherwise you will be the prisoner of a dream.'

As she said these words to her colleague she had the annoying feeling they could be directed at her, but sharply rejected that suspicion. For her it was not the same. With Danny she had a special rapport, that was undeniable, but she wasn't besotted with him like Mel was, not in the least. She found him charming, and that was all. She was in a relationship with Tom, difficult and complicated as it was. However... something whispered not to get carried away by new, strong emotions, not to fall into the trap of longing for an impossible romantic love. The attraction of the 'unattainable man' had always been a temptation; she remembered similar feelings in the past. Danny was amazing and treated her in a special way. The attraction was mutual, this was almost certain; but maybe she should be wiser, careful... of what, though? She simply liked the way he made her feel, and he was helping her to get through this difficult time of her life. Now she was even more confused than before.

Opening up with her colleague seemed to be the least she could do: 'I don't know what to do about Tom.'

'You are getting married, aren't you?' Mel lifted herself on one elbow and, shielding her eyes from the sun, turned toward Claudia.

'I don't know.'

Her friend stared at her in bewilderment: 'Are you serious? I thought you were a happy couple!'

It was her turn to feel her eyes sting: 'I don't know how long it's been since we were happy. Little by little we stopped talking, being honest with each other. It's like we're estranged. He has withdrawn... and I have too. Things between us have become colder, and I let it happen... and now everything has changed. If it wasn't for the fact that I don't want to hurt him, I think I would run a mile.' She gratefully took the Kleenex that her friend handed to her and blew her nose, loudly.

Mel did the same with hers. They looked at each other and suddenly their tears turned to laughter. They went back to lying on their backs, hands under their heads, confused, united, to absorb the warm rays of the London sun. Two young women in front of the naked reality.

'So what are you going to do?' Mel asked, turning her face sideways to look at her.

'I don't know. For now, I'll just sunbathe.'

Tom was outside the office waiting for her with a small bunch of carnations in his hand.

Claudia couldn't fail to notice that it was one of those bunches they sold for a pound at the newsagent. Her first reaction was of disappointment, the second one of shame. Did she really deserve so little? But then again, at least he was trying.

He kissed her on the cheek, lightly, quickly.

They started walking side by side, a mile-long distance between them.

'How did it go today?' she asked him to break the silence laden with emptiness.

'Fine. You?'

'Good. A lot of work. I'm going to Paris for the fashion show. They need someone who speaks Italian, and also French.'

'I didn't know you spoke French.' He looked surprised and this annoyed her.

'I studied it for three years, but I'll have to brush up on it. I'll start tonight. I have a month's time and if I study an hour a day I'll get by. Maybe I should take some lessons with a teacher. What do you think?'

Tom shrugged his shoulders, his hands buried in his pockets: 'Private lessons?'

Claudia couldn't see the expression in his face, but could imagine it: 'Yes.'

'They'll cost a lot of money... and we're saving for the wedding, right?'

He turned to look at her, but Claudia kept her eyes on the road ahead. She felt an irrepressible impatience mount inside her chest, like milk boiling, rising up to the edge of the saucepan, about to overflow. 'It's an investment. Speaking a foreign language puts me in a position of advantage over my colleagues. And in any case, they've already said that I'm going to Paris, so now I can't let them down!'

She moved slightly away from him. They walked in silence. After a while he took her hand, but she felt uncomfortable. With the excuse of searching for her lip gloss in her bag she pulled it away from his: 'Where are we going to eat?'

'I don't know. What do you want to do?' Tom put his hands back in his pockets.

'Are we going for pizza?'

'Okay, but I have to be home by half seven.'

'Why? Yesterday you said you were going to come over to say hello to my grandmother. She'd like to see you.'

'Did I say that yesterday? Tonight I can't, I'm sorry. Maybe I'll pop over tomorrow. I've got Sam, Gigi and Pete coming to see the final match of the 2006 World Cup, Italy-France. It was exceptional. You'll remember it; it's the one where Zidane head butted Materazzi.'

'How can anyone forget that? It was horrible. But why are you watching a five-year-old game?'

Tom came alive: 'We decided that, once a week, we'll watch a 'classic' match. So we can study it step by step. Every player has his own technique and if we learn from the champions, we can put them into practice.'

Tom loved football and Claudia had spent many Saturday

afternoons sitting on red plastic stadium seats getting cold and watching him play. But she had stopped going a long time ago. 'Have fun then!' she said flatly.

Tom realized that she wasn't happy: 'I'll come and say hello to your grandmother tomorrow. I'd like to see her too. How is she?'

'Fine.'

'It's been a long time since she last came to see you, right?'

'Six months.'

They had almost reached the pizzeria: 'Is there something wrong, Claudia? You look angry.'

I wish I were just angry – Claudia thought. What's happening to me is an internal mayhem of seismic proportions. It scared her to witness what was going through her mind. She was so close to spurting it all out without having thought it over. Words could hurt like bullets, she knew. Hold on Claudia – she repeated frantically to herself – don't get dragged down by your instinct. Don't make a big mistake just because you feel disappointed. 'It's not that I am angry, Tom. It's not so simple!' she replied.

'So what is it? You always have a long face lately.' He didn't say it as if he wanted to understand, as if he cared. He said it as if he were disgruntled.

Claudia pushed open the door to the pizzeria, she was taking time. I wish it were just a long face – she said to herself . Let's see your face when I tell you what is really happening to me.

'Let's order our pizzas. I'm hungry... and you're in a hurry to go and see a five year old match. We can talk while we wait.'

The waiter recognized them and sat them down at one of the many empty tables

'The usual?' he asked.

'Yes, thank you,' Tom confirmed. 'A large beer and a Four Seasons for me.'

'The same for you, Claudia?' the waiter asked, notebook in

one hand, pen in the other, head tilted and relaxed smile.

'No, today I'll have a sparkling mineral water and a Margarita, please.'

Tom looked disconcerted: 'A Margarita? Don't you want a Four Seasons? It's your favourite.'

'I like it, yes, but sometimes you have to change, don't you? And try something new. Otherwise we'll get old and have tried only one kind of pizza.' She said it with sadness... and with fear. Fear of being honest with herself and with Tom.

But maybe the time had come to lay her cards on the table.

Chapter 6

SATURDAY

It was Saturday morning, the house awoke later than usual, but Sofia had been on her feet since six o'clock. She had been restless for hours, lying in bed next to Steve who was snoring lightly. She looked at his blond head resting on his pillow, his lips parted, and her heart swelled up with a painful mixture of love and sorrow. Still tired from the day before, her body crying out for more rest, she tried to go back to sleep, but was not able to do so. This had been going on for months now, being exhausted, not being able to sleep more than a few hours, and then buzzing around all day long. After more tossing and turning she gave up and decided to get out of bed; at least she would make some progress with unpacking.

Sofia moved quietly around the house, barefoot, in a white T-shirt and black leggings, her hair gathered with a rubber band in a short ponytail, a serious, concentrated expression on her face. Every now and then she would glance at the clock. By eight o' clock she had emptied eight boxes, now stacked in two neat piles under the rounded bay window. She had placed the contents in the dining room sideboard, in the kitchen cupboards, on the living room shelves. The steps leading to the first floor were almost entirely occupied with piles of towels, sheets, sweaters and clothes, leaving only the narrowest space to put one's feet. She would take those things upstairs later. The sense of satisfaction of having completed part of what she had set out to do was somewhat spoilt by how much still had to be done, while the clock kept ticking and the minute hand moved faster than she would have liked.

Seeing her mother come down the stairs, carefully holding onto the banister, Sofia gave her a quick smile. 'You are up early, Mum. Did you sleep well?'

'I slept beautifully. That room is quiet and the bed very comfortable,' Lina smiled. 'What about you?'

'So so, as usual.' Sofia placed a pile of kitchen towels on the armchair. 'I'm achieving a lot here, though.' Her eyes followed the beloved figure who was heading for the kitchen to make her first coffee of the day with the Italian coffee machine; she liked it very hot. 'Would you like some?' Lina asked from the kitchen.

'The last thing I need is coffee!' Sofia exclaimed. 'I love the taste, but it makes me very irritable.'

'Better not then,' came the voice.

'I'd love a cup of tea, though,' Sofia added, engrossed in her task, her arms full of t-shirts and trousers. One more empty carton went to join the others in the pile. She opened another box and drew out the contents with quick, measured movements.

Lina returned to the living room and lovingly handed her a cup of tea. 'Can I help you?' she offered, cup in hand.

'There's no point. You wouldn't know where to put things,' Sofia replied sharply. Then, aware of her tone of voice, she added more softly: 'You enjoy your coffee, mum. Make yourself comfortable on the sofa.' She knew that her mother liked to sip her drink sitting quietly. 'But... if you prepare dinner for tonight that would be perfect,' she added, whilst examining a piece of paper. 'You decide what to cook. We like everything you make.' Out of the corner of her eye she saw Lina get up and go into the kitchen to inspect the contents of the fridge. She hadn't meant to interrupt her mother's coffee ceremony and felt guilty for rushing her. Feeling guilty – she realized with a heavy sense of uneasiness – was a sensation that accompanied her like a shadow, uncomfortable and disturbing. Often, in moments like those, she felt like an inexperienced swimmer who had to tread water with all her might just to stay afloat.

Her mother came back and sat on the sofa to sip her lukewarm coffee.

Sofia knew she was being observed. She tried to hide the sadness that accompanied her every gesture behind the mask of efficiency, but didn't know how to recover the serenity that had deserted her, she didn't even know when. She perceived that her mother sensed it and worried about her.

'You're beautiful,' Lina remarked, 'and look younger than your age. You have a beautiful figure. You don't look fifty years old, not in the least.'

'Fifty-one Mum.'

'Incredible!' the elderly lady exclaimed, truly astonished.

Sleepy and composed Steve made his way down the stairs. He greeted them with a smile and a 'hello Sofia, good morning Lina', and went into the kitchen to make his coffee.

Sofia's eyes followed him. In the morning he found it difficult to walk straight, but pretended to be fine and stretched his back trying not to be noticed.

'How are you?' she asked him.

'As always when I get up, a bit stiff, but I'll loosen up in a while.' He gave her a forced smile while waiting for the kettle to boil. 'I had trouble falling asleep. And you?'

'I'm okay. Got up early.' She felt annoyed that he could sleep, but always complained about the poor quality or quantity of it, while she could hardly sleep at all but got on with things. Sofia looked away, burying her gaze in the box full of towels. She couldn't look him in the eye; she seemed to read disapproval, no matter what she said.

With a large cup of steaming coffee in his hand her husband climbed back up the stairs.

'Where is he going?' Lina asked when Steve's figure

disappeared.

'To the bedroom, to drink his coffee while he watches BBC news on his computer,' Sofia replied with fake simplicity. 'He likes being informed.'

Her mother's puzzled expression made her feel uncomfortable and Sofia looked away. She was painfully aware of that feeling of detachment, of emotional disconnection, that left her feeling lonely, isolated and, worst of all, misunderstood.

Then came Claudia who seemed to have slept very little. She looked exhausted and kept her gaze down. She took refuge in the kitchen, grabbed a bottle of fruit juice from the fridge, filled up a glass and drank it all in one go. 'I'm going for a run' she said without looking at anyone and hurried out, phone in one hand, a bottle of water in the other.

Sofia paused to watch the silhouette of her daughter in grey shorts, sneakers and the pink T-shirt she had given her, as she disappeared behind the door that hadn't closed properly. She felt a lump in her throat. A dull ache squeezed her heart and her face darkened, as if a black cloud had slipped in front of the sun. 'Did you see that? Not a word,' she said bitterly, her chin pointing towards the door ajar. In her eyes there was a mixture of grief and longing.

'She is not happy, even I can see that,' Lina agreed, looking at her daughter with concern.

'No. She's not happy. She has been like that for months. She suffers, and so do we all.'

Finally Micky appeared, cheerful, energetic. He ran down the stairs, skipped the last five steps and landed heavily making the house shake. 'Morning everyone! Hi Grandma! Hello Mum!' He went from one to the other, hugging and kissing them happily: 'How are you Gran? How nice to have you here! I could get used to seeing your beautiful face every morning,' he thundered, as if they were deaf. 'Can I help you Mum? You too are beautiful, in fact, you are stunning!' he said, holding her by the shoulders and looking closely at her face.

Sofia smiled in spite of herself: 'Take these piles of things upstairs and leave them on the landing. I will decide where to put them.' Then, trying to hide the irritation that had mounted inside, she warned him: 'And don't jump like that, there is already a crack on the basement ceiling.'

Micky ran up the stairs carrying the stacks of clothes and was back immediately. He came down at breakneck speed and at the last moment remembered not to jump. 'I'm going for a bike ride with Eddie, Mum. I'll be back for lunch Grandma.'

'Granny is coming out with me. She is going to Charlie's,' Sofia reminded him.

'All right. Have fun then! See you tonight, gorgeous!' He was out the door and forgot to close it.

Sofia kept going up and down the stairs carrying large piles of things. Each time she'd performed a task she crossed out an item on one of the three lists she had in her pocket. The phone rang. It was her shop assistant at work. Sofia gave her some instructions and explained where she would find what she was looking for. 'I'll be with you at around one,' she reassured her. 'You just carry on. You're doing fine.' Sighing, she hung up the phone, went into the kitchen, and started to take things out of the fridge.

Lina followed her hastily, saying: 'I'm making dinner, isn't that what we agreed?'

'Yes, but when?' There was a hint of exasperation in Sofia's voice. 'If we go out at noon we need to begin now. It's already half past ten.'

'Don't worry. I'll start immediately and everything will be ready by midday, you'll see. You go and take a shower and get ready.'

'They all tell me not to worry but, as you can see, you're the only one who's helping me. Everyone else goes about their business and then criticizes me for being neurotic,' Sofia snapped.

'They'll do their bit in the afternoon. It's easier when there are fewer people around. Have faith!'

Sofia looked at her, perplexed. 'We'll see who's right tonight, you or me,' she answered back sharply and headed up to the bathroom upstairs.

She would love to be relaxed and friendly, laugh the way she used to, and enjoy her family, but life seemed to be going in a direction all of its own. It was spinning out of control and she didn't know how to bring it back on track. She missed the trust she and Steve used to share. She knew the love was still there... but he never criticized her in the past. Now he often stood against her, especially in regard to their daughter. It made her feel cut off, ganged up on, and she didn't understand why that was happening. She had lost the closeness with Claudia that they enjoyed in the past. They used to be friends, but now her daughter didn't look at her, didn't speak to her and, whatever she said, she was always made to feel wrong. Only Micky still loved her as he had done as a child... and her mother. Lina was very sensitive towards her, but even she had noticed that something was wrong. Everything had become so complicated.

The hot jet of the shower soothed her back. Sofia massaged her head and her tears were washed away along with the shampoo. She never had time for herself. She was always in a hurry and the demands of work and family had clipped away any precious little moments of free time. She used to be creative, doing a lot of things that gave her joy. Now there was nothing left, only work, duties, the needs of others. She only recently noticed its gradual disappearance. Even sleep started to desert her. She dried herself quickly but those tears didn't want to stop. She applied a little moisturizer to her body, wiped her cheeks dry with the palms of her hands, drew a deep breath and came out of the bathroom with wet hair. It would have to dry by itself and won't look so good. The thought of it brought more tears; she felt the pressure behind her eyes but, somehow, those tears had to be pushed back. She couldn't afford the time to cry.

In the small kitchen her mother was preparing vegetarian lasagne. 'While making dinner I studied the garden from the window,' she said enthusiastically. 'I'm imagining it overflowing with flowers. We'll buy hundreds of bulbs and plant them a little at a time. They'll begin to bloom next spring. We must make some sketches to decide which colours to choose and how to match them. It's an exciting project, don't you think?'

'Yes. Thanks Mum,' Sofia smiled tightly, looking at the floor, her eyes stinging.

'I'll ask Charlie for advice. She is a master at designing a garden. What do you think?'

'Good idea. You do that.' Sofia turned her back and walked quickly to the safety of the living room.

It was midday. Sofia watched her mother at the mirror that was resting on a stack of boxes. Lina buttoned up her jacket and carefully adjusted her purple hat so that the red flowers were on the right hand side, exactly where they should be. Like most of her hats, she had made it herself. Lina had often told her how, when she was a girl, her mother used to send her to help Pearl, a neighbour and professional hat maker, and that's how she acquired the skill. She must have made at least a hundred hats in her lifetime and worn all of them with pride, and the natural elegance that distinguished her – the family always told her with a shadow of irony. Her grey hair still had shades of her natural brown, was thick and well cut. It folded beautifully in a wave under the earlobe, framing her face with its smooth, almost wrinkle-free skin. Lina put curlers in every night and her hair was always tidy. With a familiar gesture she opened the lipstick tube and carefully painted her lips a deep red, matching the flowers on the hat. She adjusted her big earrings, red like the necklace that she was wearing over her white woollen blouse. Finally she took a step back and checked her image, smiling, pleased with herself, and managed to snatch a smile out of Lina.

'Are you ready, Mum? I'm late. I have to be at the shop in less than an hour.' Lina was ready and Sofia could see she was already savouring the pleasure of spending the afternoon with Charlie. It must be at least a year since they last met up. Indeed – Sofia remembered it well – it had been July of last year, thirteen months ago, when Lina had come to London to see them in their old house.

'Time goes so fast,' her mother mused, with a hint of resentment towards time. 'It flies! The more we age, the faster it goes. It should do the opposite instead, and slow down as the years go by, to give those who walk the path of life the chance to enjoy their days in peace. But no! It runs faster instead.' She turned to Sofia, waving her skewed right hand deformed by arthritis. 'Why is time in such a hurry? It could savour the present moment, and instead it gallops like a madman.'

Sofia smiled about her mother's philosophical musing. She crossed the living room full of boxes and crates with hurried step, keys in hand, one arm inside one sleeve of her cardigan while the other tried to blindly find the hole in the other sleeve. Her shoulder bag was open, overflowing. She collected the two carrier bags near the door and, while Lina waited for her by the car, shouted towards the stairs: 'We have already organized dinner. No need to do anything else. Bye!'

Only just audible, Steve's deep voice answered from the upper floor 'See you tonight, darling. I love you.'

Those words made her want to cry. 'Darling, I love you.' He always told her so, and she struggled to answer with the same affection, whilst everything inside was torn apart by the love she felt for him. Why wasn't she able to tell him? Why that boulder of dull despair that prevented her from even breathing properly? The car lights winked and Sofia opened the driver's door.

'Every time I see you unlock the car without even touching it

I think it's a miracle,' affirmed her mother, full of admiration for the car. Then, observing her daughter, she added: 'You look lovely in that dress, Sofia. Those colours really suit you. I love flowery dresses.'

'Thank you. Come on, let's get going quickly,' Sofia urged her, throwing her handbag and carrier bags onto the back seat.

Lina spoke cautiously, attaching her seat belt: 'Steve is always affectionate towards you. He's kind... and helps you, doesn't he?'

'Yes, he helps me... a little. There is so much to do,' Sofia blurted out. 'I do nothing but run all day.' She was aware that she was driving in a brusque manner, changing gear roughly and braking abruptly. Lina didn't say anything but, out of the corner of her eye, Sofia could see her clinging to her seat belt.

'How are things with Steve?' her mother ventured.

Sofia didn't answer right away. She felt a twinge in her heart and was afraid she would burst into tears again, exactly what she did not want to do in front of her mum. Clenching her lips, she focused on the road ahead while her hands gripped the steering wheel.

'I shouldn't have asked. I'm sorry.' Lina was looking at her daughter, worrying, unsure of what she should, or should not, say – Sofia could tell.

'No... no... It's okay Mum, but it's not easy to answer. Your question touched a sore point and...' – she took a deep painful breath. Speaking jerkily she started: 'Our relationship has changed a lot from what it used to be. We were inseparable, do you remember?'

'You were always on the road together.'

'We did everything together, from morning till night. There was never any friction. He never criticized me. He liked my active personality, even if sometimes I was impetuous and rebellious...'

'You've always been like that.'

'... and for me he was perfect with his calm temperament,

considerate, attentive to others. I loved that side of him.'

'He is a kind man,' Lina said with affection.

'Indeed. We were totally different, but maybe that's why we complemented each other.' Sofia paused, not knowing what, or how much to say. She sighed: 'The problems started years ago when Claudia was a teenager. I learned to be a mother from you, parenting the Italian way. I felt it was my duty to check her freedom and stem the desire to experiment outside the home until the time she was more mature. I was afraid that something bad could happen to her. I was worried about the way her classmates threw themselves headlong into the grown up habits of drinking, smoking and experimenting with who knows what, out there in the world.'

'Claudia has always had her head screwed on the right way, I think. She's always been a wise child.'

'It's true, but I understood this as she grew up, when she was a teenager I wasn't sure. She changed so much!'

Her mother nodded.

'Unlike me, and probably because of the way he was raised, Steve saw no problem whatsoever and, instead of supporting me, he thought I was being authoritarian and openly challenged me in front of the children.'

'One should never do that; not in front of the children,' Lina asserted.

'That's what I kept telling him, but I couldn't convince him.' There was suffering and frustration in her voice. 'For me it was such a shock. I felt as if I had lost my best friend.'

Her mother turned to look at her, surprise and concern in her face: 'I had no idea. You never talked about it.'

'It was too complicated... I was very confused. You heard what happened yesterday, when I got upset about Micky's graffiti on the bridge. Instead of supporting me and telling Micky off, he couldn't see the problem... he thought I was concerned about the fact that Micky had drawn a marijuana leaf. He didn't understand I was worried about him getting hurt. And he told me I was being controlling and authoritarian. That hurt so much!'

Lina looked out the window and took a long time before saying: 'Your father *was* authoritarian and left me the responsibility of bringing you up, all four of you. Most of the time he didn't want to know about any problems. He was only interested in how well you did at school. He never raised a finger to help at home or with you children. Can you believe that he never held you in his arms, not once, not even when I was completely exhausted?'

'It's a good job that times have changed then,' Sofia burst out. 'I couldn't stand a man like that. At least you didn't have to go out to work; you were at home being a housewife and that was your job.'

When her mother started to tell her for the umpteenth time that, despite not having a recognized and paid job, she got up at five in the morning and didn't stop until midnight, Sofia was not surprised. She had drawn that clarification out of her mother with her comment on not going out to work. She'd take a nap after lunch, Lina continued and, in the intimacy of the car, she confided some new and embarrassing details. That nap was torture, because Bruno wanted to have sex every day of the year including bank holidays and birthdays, when she was so tired and just wanted to sleep.

Fortunately Lina changed the subject to the well-known story: She ended up with arthritis and a bad back because of having to wash mountains of clothes in tubs full of cold water. In her days there had been no washing machines. She loved that appliance so much! When they bought the first one, she would sit in front of the round door and watch things turn round and round in foamy water, then go through the rinsing cycle and then spin like crazy at full speed. 'Meanwhile I could drink my hot coffee. Long live progress!' Lina concluded vehemently, with more than a hint of anger. 'Let's talk about something else! What do you think about Claudia?' she asked. 'She's having a hard time, isn't she?'

Sofia knew her mother was testing the ground. 'Tell me about it! I'd like to know, too,' she commented. 'I don't understand what's going on in her head. Claudia doesn't talk with me. She used to tell me everything, but now she has shut me out... and I don't know why.'

'Children are fickle; one has to take them as they are and let them go when they want to go,' Lina consoled her. 'They are a work in progress.' She knew it well. Even now, sometimes, her children were a mystery to her. 'Do you have any idea how much I worried about you?'

Sofia took her eyes briefly off the road and looked at her mother in surprise: 'You worried about me?'

'Very much so! Do you remember when you went to India? I couldn't sleep at night from worrying. Thinking of you, alone in such a poor country... I was afraid that something could happen to you.'

'Really? You never told me.'

'What good would it have done? I couldn't have stopped you, even if I had tried.'

'That's true,' Sofia admitted, upset. 'I didn't know. You managed to keep it to yourself... it was kind of you.' The knot in the pit of her stomach was beginning to loosen and she started to listen to her mother with interest and a new awareness.

'Did you ever think about what I wanted for you when you were travelling?' Lina asked.

Now Sofia hesitated and reflected before answering. 'To be honest I didn't. I knew you and dad had found me a job in a travel agency, but for me the idea was so alien... I never gave it a second thought. I was so involved in what I was doing... it was an incredible time. It brought me a lot of good things, starting with Steve.'

'Sure! What I'm trying to say is that children have to follow their own path, we can only advise them, but the decision is theirs. For them, what parents think is not so important.'

They had reached the end of a tree-lined road, in front of them a large undulating park dotted with trees and flowers. Sofia relaxed a little leaning back on her seat; the hands that held the steering wheel softened. She glanced sideways at her mother and smiled weakly: 'I'm glad you're here, Mum. You can stay as long as you want. In fact, I would like it if you came to live with us, instead of staying in Nottingham alone.'

It was not as if she was ready to live with her mother. On the contrary, the idea terrified her, but sooner or later she would have to take that step and the fear of such a decision made her express the very thoughts she would like to deny, as if they were speaking through her, despite her.

'I'm fine where I am Sofia, I've known everyone for a long time. I have shops just a few steps away, buses right outside the door... and I like my house,' Lina objected, on the defensive. 'I hardly know anyone here... and London is too big.'

'It worries me that we are far away, now that you have reached a certain age. What if something should happen to you? I'm so busy I can hardly cope with things as they are.' Sofia indicated right and stopped on the strip that separated the two lanes.

She followed her mother's eyes out the window. There was a street market. The pavements had been turned into a bazaar of stalls selling everything from rugs to clothes, things for the home, flowers and plants and plastic bowls full of fruits and vegetables offered at one pound each. There were good prices. Knowing her mother, Sofia knew that she would have liked to take a stroll, and her words confirmed it.

'With those street stalls, we seem to be in a provincial town, not in a big metropolis like London,' Lina mused.

Driving in dense slow traffic Sofia was fidgeting. She knew she would get to the shop late. She resumed the conversation where they had left off. 'Steve is doing what he can, with his bad back. Claudia is on the verge of a nervous breakdown because of this wedding; I think it will all blow up... and Micky smokes weed, secretly he thinks. He only cares about his music and can't decide whether to remain a boy or become a man.'

Lina, who quietly ignored the comment about the 'weed', ventured: 'I am not at all convinced that Claudia will get married.'

'She's become odd, surly; you saw her,' Sofia said turning towards her. 'She goes to work all dressed up, made-up to perfection, but when she comes home she is irritable, or depressed, and at other times excited. And we see very little of Tom, not like we used to, when he was always around. He talks about going to work in Saudi Arabia, as if there wasn't enough work here. Bah! Who knows what's going on? It seems to me that Claudia is not so much in love anymore and... I suspect she is pining for that colleague she used to mention often, the married one.'

'Is he married then?' The words came out of Lina's mouth before she could think.

'Why? Has she told you something about him?' Sofia turned to look at her mother and saw that she was biting her bottom lip.

'She mentioned her boss, and I suspected there might be something, but I didn't say anything.'

'You see? She speaks more with you than with me,' Sofia blurted out with frustration. 'Not only is he married and with two children, but he is also twenty years older than her. He could be her father.'

'A forty-five years old man is still young these days, it's not like it used to be. Have you ever met him?'

'No, and I have no desire to do so.'

There was a pause in the conversation, each one immersed in her own thoughts.

'Who knows what Claudia is looking for,' Lina began again. 'It must be a transition period between a past that no longer satisfies her and a future that she can't figure out. She and Tom have been together for eight years, they were little more than children when they started to date and people change, especially the young.'

'True!' Sofia confirmed. Her mother knew something she was not aware of, and the best way to find out was not to interrupt her.

'The idea of marriage seemed like an obvious conclusion, but I think the relationship started to fade years ago,' the elderly lady continued. 'Maybe they're waking up just in time to avoid a big mistake. Claudia is afraid of the unknown and has a strong desire for security. Maybe that's why she's attracted to a man who could be her father. The fact that he is married and therefore unreachable makes the situation more exciting. Transition, that's what it is... maybe.' Turning to Sofia she advised: 'Be gentle... and patient. She's suffering a lot right now.'

'It's not easy. I no longer know how to talk to her. We haven't communicated for a long time and I'm afraid to even open my mouth.'

'Maybe she's afraid to talk to you too,' Lina ventured.

Sofia turned to look at her mother, stunned: 'Claudia? Afraid of me? Since when?'

Lina took a deep breath: 'Since you scolded her for the idea of going to Saudi Arabia.'

Sofia turned sideways to look at her, but Lina kept her eyes firmly on the road, as if she were driving. 'You don't need to look at me while you're driving,' she pointed out. 'Better to look at the road, don't you think? It makes me nervous and it's dangerous. I'm here and not going anywhere,' she said with more than a touch of anxiety.

'What did she tell you? Tell me what you know, because I don't understand anything and I don't know what to do,' Sofia begged her.

'She said you jumped at her, and that made her feel worse than before; from that moment on she didn't think she could confide in you any longer.'

A long silence followed. Sofia drove keeping her eyes on the road, her arms stretched out on the steering wheel. 'But I reacted like that because she was thinking of going over there. I know she didn't like that absurd idea at all. At least one of them must know what they want, right? Otherwise they will end up making the wrong decision... and begrudgingly, too.' She paused, full of tension. 'It scared me to think she could go to that country. They put people in jail, you know?... for things that are normal for us, like kissing your boyfriend on the beach, or drinking a beer.'

'I understand you completely, but the way you spoke to her shocked her. Maybe you ought to tell her that you're sorry and listen to what she has to say. She is no longer a child and wants to be treated as an adult.'

Sofia kept her eyes on the road, tears sliding quickly down her cheek. Her lips trembled. She drove in a silence that was bursting with emotion. She finally broke it, speaking as if to herself: 'So, do I prefer to be criticized by my daughter, or rejected?' and turned to look at Lina with a sad smile. She knew it pained her mother to see her cry, but she couldn't pretend: 'What a great choice! I prefer to be criticized, clearly, but talking with Claudia has become a minefield. Even though I'm very careful how I express myself, I always end up saying something wrong. She stiffens up and leaves the room. That's why we don't talk anymore... but it's horrible. And I am so tired! I am exhausted.'

'I know it's hard, but one of you has to take the first step... and it's easier for you.' Lina rummaged in her bag and pulled out a tissue.

'Why is it easier for me?' Sofia turned again to look at her.

'Because you are the mother, she is younger than you, has less experience...' She handed her daughter the tissue.

Sofia continued to drive, crying silently, reflecting. 'I don't know where to start...' she mumbled. 'And what if I'm wrong again and I say something out of place?'

Lina shrugged: 'Something has to change. I don't know how. I would like to know what to tell you, but I don't. Follow your heart as a mother.'

Sofia nodded thoughtfully, took the tissue she was being handed and wiped her nose. 'Thank you,' she said, her arms tense, her cheeks moist, lost in thought.

Chapter 7

REVELATIONS

Lost in thought, Lina gazed out the window, reading the street names under her breath, a habit, a game really, she had always enjoyed. Sofia knew it well. Her mother was an easy passenger, always interested in what was out there, never bored. Lina was looking at the houses for sale or for rent and, while pausing at a traffic light, she observed the people waiting at a bus stop.

Sofia followed her mother's gaze. There were two women wearing traditional Indian saris talking quietly, one dressed in red and the other one sky blue; both wore black cardigans, their arms wrapped around their bodies to keep in the warmth. Behind them was a woman dressed head to toe in grey, heavily pregnant, her head covered by a scarf. She held a little girl by the hand, her hair neatly combed in two stiff plaits. Right behind them in the queue was a striking group of five young men and women whose black clothes were decorated with chains. They looked extremely pale and pasty, had jet black hair and were waiting for their bus with a gloomy, despondent air.

'God only knows why some young people want to look as if they were seriously ill,' Lina reflected. 'If they are lucky to be healthy, why go out in such a state?'

Sofia smiled. 'It's a fashion, Mum. They are Goths, from Gothic,' she explained.

'I know, I have seen other young people made up like that. I don't like it at all,' Lina breathed, shaking her head.

'I don't like it either,' agreed Sofia. 'I am glad my children don't want to look like that.'

Behind the Goths, there was a young girl with ripped jeans and a partly shaved head and, behind her, a smartly dressed man with a small suitcase.

'In Italy the people waiting at a bus stop would look very different,' Lina reflected. 'They like to be neat and spruced up; many are positively elegant, with well cut hair. The women, of all ages, wear accurately applied make-up, and the men are well-groomed, too.'

The light changed to green and Sofia accelerated away.

'Still, although I don't agree with much of the English taste in attire and looks, I like this cauldron of humanity,' said Lina.

'Indeed. Everyone goes about their lives with their own particular style, with little judgement from others... and a good dose of politeness,' pointed out Sofia.

'Yes, true,' Lina agreed. 'From this point of view, London is fascinating, I've always thought so.'

Short bursts of sunshine warmed the air. 'It should be hot and instead it is a bit cool, isn't it? Will summer ever come?' Lina wondered... 'that kind of proper warmth when we can eat in the garden, sunbathe in a swimming costume or take care of the flowers with a straw hat on your head.'

'Yes, I'd love that! Do you have the address of the new house?' Sofia tore her away from her reflections. 'You remember you have to come back home on your own tonight, don't you? Check that you have it.'

Obediently, Lina took her purse out of her handbag and opened it.

Glancing sideways, Sofia saw the photo of her father, serious as he used to be when he was alive. The piece of paper with the address and the phone number was where she had put it.

'It's all fine. I have it here,' her mother confirmed, quickly averting her eyes from her husband's face.

As they waited at another red light, Sofia took her hands off the steering wheel and ran them over her cheeks, wiping away any memory of the earlier tears. She gave an affectionate look at her mother and smiled weakly. 'If Dad made you suffer so much, why do you miss him now?' she asked softly.

Lina opened her eyes wide, turned towards her daughter and stared at her with an astonished expression: 'Who said I miss him? What makes you think that?'

Sofia gazed at her mother, dumbfounded: 'You have his photo in your purse and...'

'I've always loved your father, but he did whatever he wanted,' Lina interrupted her. 'At home he was serious and strict with you children and with me, but whenever he went out – according to those who knew him – he was cheerful and sociable. Never once saw him laugh at home, though.'

Lina stared out the window, at a row of second-hand shops, a furniture outlet, and an estate agent that lined the road. 'There are no trees at all in this barren area. It's depressing, isn't it?' she mused. Without waiting for Sofia's response, she continued: 'Your father was such a mystery. It was as if he had two personalities. He was authoritarian at home and arrogant at work, but a charming libertine with the women with whom he had affairs, almost always older than him.' Lina spoke with a new intensity and clarity. Turning to Sofia, she went on: 'He always dominated me. He was both 'father and master'. Now I am free and, with the little pension I receive, I feel rich. These are the best years of my life. Finally I do what I want and no one rules over me. I've never been so happy!' she concluded with strong conviction and crossed her hands in her lap, hiding the deformed right hand under her left one. Sofia noticed that her wedding ring had disappeared.

Breaking out in a liberating laugh, she exclaimed: 'Wow Mum, good to know! I never realized you were so independent. So you're not sad?'

'Sad? Me? No way!' Lina retorted, defiant.

Sofia shook her head. She was amazed and amused at the

same time. She turned to her mother: 'What a shame he was like that! He loved you, you know? I remember how he looked at you when you came to visit him at the hospital. He was all wired up to the machines and you had just recovered from an asthma attack.'

'Your father loved himself,' Lina affirmed, staring at the road ahead, her back straight.

Sofia glanced at her mother. Maybe she had never understood her. She had always thought of her as gentle and submissive, but the woman talking now was determined, independent and rebellious. 'It must have been difficult for you' she said.

'I had four children to bring up. I didn't have time to think about anything else,' replied Lina as a matter of fact.

'Well, you have been a good mother.'

'I did what I could. I'm not an educated woman. I only went to Primary school, whilst he became a teacher. Didn't he half boast about that? A teacher who never taught because he didn't like children.'

'You may not have studied, but you're an intelligent woman and certainly very wise. I learned a lot from you. You taught me not to envy others,' recalled Sofia, while the car reached a tree-lined road with rows of large terraced houses on both sides. 'When Dad's rich friend came to visit us, you often told us that we shouldn't judge by appearances, that everyone had their own problems, even millionaires.'

Her mother let out a small snort: 'He had an affair with her, too. It went on for years. Do you remember that they disappeared for whole days 'to talk business'? But what business could they have to talk about? Your father was a civil servant and she had companies, factories and hundreds of apartments.' She shook her head and shrugged her shoulders, throwing behind her the humiliations she had to suffer for years on end.

'Really? I'd never have guessed, but... thinking back... now that you say it, it seems obvious. All those 'meetings' on their own. I always thought they were strange. What was their connection? She so wealthy and he...'

'Your grandmother worked as a maid in her parents' house. Her father was a famous General. Their family paid for your father's education and, in a way, the two children grew up... not quite together, but very close,' Lina explained.

'I see!' Sofia paused, reflecting about the puzzle that her father had been. 'I was intimidated by him. I didn't know him, really. But once I surprised him.' She let out a small giggle. 'Did he ever tell you that I was caught stealing? And that he had to go and talk about it?'

'*No!* You *stole*? What? When?' Lina was shocked.

Sofia glanced at her mother and smiled 'I was thirteen years old,' she started, 'and one day Rosina and I went to the department stores, to shelter from the rain. As we looked around, she stole a hair clip.'

'Rosina? But she was a good girl. I didn't think she would steal!' Lina sounded troubled.

'I know it's wrong Mum, I knew it even then, but kids do these things. They experiment. Well then, let me tell you what happened,' she pressed, peeking at her mother's frowning face.

'The next day we went back to the same store and I saw a ring in the shape of a snake. I picked it up from the counter and walked away. I held it in my hand, sweating with fear. I knew very well that I shouldn't steal. At church they taught us that stealing was a mortal sin.' She nodded and then, turning towards Lina, continued: 'I noticed a man following me, I could have plopped the ring down on any counter, I didn't even like it very much, but by then I was in such a state of confusion that my head didn't work anymore. And so, like an idiot, I put it in my bag. Immediately the man approached me and led me to the store manager's office. I was shaking like a leaf, my knees wanted to buckle and I thought I was going to faint. Sitting behind a large desk, the manager told me he wanted to talk to my father. 'Are you going to tell him or shall I?' He gave me the choice. 'I'll tell him,' I whispered, I could hardly find the breath to speak, 'but don't tell my mum,' I said. I wanted to protect you.' Sofia turned to look at her mother.

'I didn't know anything,' Lina murmured.

'And so when I got home, I phoned Dad at the office,' Sofia continued. 'Hi Sofia' Dad said, all jolly. When I told him he had to go to the store to talk with the manager, because of what I had done, I could tell he was stunned. He didn't utter a word. That night, full of shame, I took refuge watching television and he came into the living room. He leaned his elbows on the back of the chair – I could feel his breath in my hair – and asked me 'why did you do it?' Without looking at him I replied 'Children steal because of lack of affection. Please don't tell mum'. I felt him stiffen, straighten up and leave without a word. I knew you had a lot of worries and I didn't want to give you any more.'

'Did you steal again after that?' Lina uttered.

'No. It was enough of a lesson. I never took anything again without paying for it.'

Lina fell silent, but in that pause, heavy with revelations and emotions, Sofia sensed that the words 'Children steal from lack of affection' had struck her deeply. 'Didn't you receive affection?' her mother asked.

'From you I did, even if there were no kisses or caresses. But you were always present, you were kind and gave us what we needed. Dad was different. He didn't seem to care about us.'

'In his way he loved you, I'm sure,' Lina offered, 'but showing affection... never!'

'Maybe he didn't know how. After all, it's not as if his father had been a good example. Did you ever meet my grandfather?' Sofia realized she didn't know anything at all about her father's father.

'Of course I met him. He was a gentleman. The few times I saw him he kissed my hand,' Lina replied, her voice full of emotion. 'A gentleman and a libertine. He liked women, all women... like your father.'

'I don't even remember his name. We never talked about him and I don't think I've ever seen a photograph of him. So, one day he just left? Do you know what happened?'

'His name was Alfredo. He was a handsome man with thick, dark hair and slightly protruding eyes. I don't know exactly when or why he left, but your father was still a child.' Lina turned to look at her daughter and then went back to staring at the road ahead, deep in thought. 'One evening, when your dad had drunk a little more than usual, your sister Anita asked him what he knew about Alfredo. He recounted an episode that had remained engraved in his memory. His father had already been gone for years when one day he saw him. Your grandfather was on a bicycle and when he saw your father with his mother, well, he turned round and pedalled away in the opposite direction, to avoid them, do you understand? So he didn't have to face them.'

Sofia's heart sank. 'It must have been terrible,' she exclaimed. 'I can't imagine what it must have been like for Dad to see his father again, and then to watch him run away like that... Like being abandoned all over again, I guess. Poor Dad! Maybe this is why he was cold with us. How can you learn to show love, if you never received any?'

Her mother fell silent. Sofia could see that she was thinking. Perhaps Lina had never thought of it that way. Eventually she started talking again, as if to herself: 'Once, many years later – you were already older and at school – Alfredo showed up at our house. I opened the door and at first I didn't recognize him. He looked unkempt... tired... he was already ill at the time. Your grandmother looked at him and said 'Your hair is dirty. Come in, I'll wash it for you'. She washed his hair and then she cut it. He was there, sitting on a chair, limp, in silence. Your father was present but didn't say a word. He went out and came back half an hour later. He had found Alfredo a room in a guest house and showed him the door. All without a word. Basically he sent him away, after which he ordered his mother to have nothing more to do with him.'

'And where did grandfather go?'

'He must have stopped a few days in the guest house and then I heard he'd left. He went back to Brescia, where he had been living for years. He had another woman there. We never saw him again. A few years later we learned that he had died.'

'So much suffering!' Sofia's voice was heavy with sorrow. 'And Grandma? Was she affectionate with Dad?'

'Your grandmother wasn't affectionate with anyone,' Lina stated in a sharp manner, her voice laden with bad memories. 'Your grandmother was an angry woman, full of resentment. She forbade me to cuddle my babies. When Anita was born, I wanted to hold her, kiss her, but your grandmother ordered me to put her down. She said that children grew up spoiled if you held them too much, that they'd have no respect for their parents. And so, every time she saw me holding Anita, she made me put her back down. That's why you didn't get many cuddles. Your grandmother was so authoritarian and criticized everyone, she was a real gossip.'

This time it was Sofia's turn to fall into a painful silence. For the first time she felt compassion for her father. She saw him as a rejected, abandoned child, full of pride and anger. And she felt so much sorrow for her mother. How hard their times had been.

Lina was silent. Sofia wondered what she was thinking.

'Do you have any nice memories of Dad? A gesture of kindness, a gift, a sweet word.'

Lina was trying to remember. Finally she replied: 'No. I have no good memories, no kindness and no compliments.'

Sofia was shocked. 'But he did give you some gifts, for your birthday at least. I remember he gave you presents.'

'Yes. He gave me some jewellery, to apologize when he felt guilty; a broach, a pair of earrings. Gold was an investment, in case one day we should need to sell it.'

Her mother's scepticism was disconcerting. Was she a realistic woman or just full of bitterness? Sofia didn't know what to think.

Lina started talking again: 'He took me to beautiful places, this he did. We travelled a lot, especially the last ten years of his life. We went where *he* wanted to go, of course. He never took note of what I suggested. I wanted to go back to a seaside village in Yugoslavia. I asked him a thousand times, but he always ignored my request.' Lina turned to look at her daughter. 'I realize I'm not giving a nice portrait of him and so I'm trying to find something positive to tell you. I liked the trips.'

Sofia nodded, indicating as she slowed down at a junction. 'One day I'll take you to that place,' she declared. 'Do you remember what it was called?'

'Yes, but now I can't think of it.'

'When you remember, write it down. We'll go together. I promise you!'

Sofia took a small road on the left, flanked by semi-detached houses with well-kept gardens and mature trees. 'Here we are, Charlie's road,' she said, glancing surreptitiously at her wristwatch. She drove for another hundred metres before stopping in front of a lush garden overflowing with flowers.

After some searching through her bulging handbag, Sofia took a mobile phone out and handed it to her mother. 'Take this Mum. If you need anything call me or Steve, the numbers are already programmed,' she explained. 'Actually, better call him, as I'll be in the shop. Hopefully we'll be full of customers. It's high time this recession ended.'

'I don't need it Sofia. I don't even know how it works. I'm too old for these things,' Lina shied away.

'Then keep it in your handbag. If I need to call you at least I know how to find you. Answer it like you would a normal phone,' she insisted. 'Just press this key and then talk. Like this... look. Do you understand?'

'Yes yes, I understand,' Lina replied impatiently. She put the phone in her handbag and opened the car door to get out.

'And when you want to come home, call a taxi, okay?' Sofia was leaning over the empty passenger seat and talking through the open car door. 'I can't come and get you. We close at six and then I'll stay at the shop to do the stock take and sort out the till. I'll see you at home, all right?'

'All right, all right!' Her mother nodded her head and, as she walked towards Charlie's gate, Sofia saw her huff, thinking she was out of sight.

Honestly! – Sofia laughed to herself. Sometimes Lina behaved like a daughter, not like an elderly mother. When she rebelled like that she liked her even more. Her mother was a very special woman, full of surprises. Sofia was getting to know her a little better every time they talked.

She glanced in the rear view mirror, indicated and pulled away quickly. There was no doubt she would be late arriving at the shop.

Chapter 8

CHARLIE

Lina was almost relieved to get away from her daughter's instructions and suggestions. Sometimes Sofia seemed to forget that she was a seventy-five year old woman who had no idea about those modern gadgets young people were so fond of. Computers and mobile phones weren't of any use to her – Lina mused. She had lived her whole life without them and was perfectly happy to continue to do so. Instead, she loved people, they were her 'thing', especially dear friends, like Charlie. Lina's heart rejoiced at the idea of seeing her again.

As she covered the few yards that led to the house, Lina felt as if she were shedding sixty years, back to the days when Charlie urged her to rebel against everything and everyone and do things her own way. They used to spend whole afternoons talking about their dreams, their suitors, their fears, (or, to be accurate, her own fears, because Charlie wasn't afraid of anything) and their plans for the future.

She rang the doorbell and adjusted her hat while an irrepressible smile curled her lips.

Immediately Fidel began to bark hysterically and scratch the door in a frenzy. Despite the racket, Lina could make out the sound of firm steps approaching and her heart fluttered.

Charlie threw the door open. 'At last!' she exclaimed, with her strong confident voice.

She hadn't changed at all. Charlie was tall with short white hair and looked stunning in her black trousers and tight red sweater. Despite being seventy-five years old she was still a very attractive woman, openly sensual, with an enthralling personality. She held out her hand and helped Lina climb the step. Fidel was bursting with joy and jumped on her, scratching her legs with his tiny long nails. He had a very loud bark for such a small dog.

'I couldn't wait for you to arrive! I've prepared a pot of tea and some snacks in the garden, and another little thing, a surprise.' Charlie spoke with her customary assurance. 'You have to see the roses, they are a marvel! Let's make the most of today's sunshine. You never know what to expect, even if we are in the middle of summer.'

'How wonderful to see you Charlie!' Lina stood on her tiptoes and hugged her happily. Then, studying her closely she added: 'You look very well; beautiful. How are you?'

Unable to ignore the little dog, Lina bent down and attempted to stroke Fidel. He kept deafening her with his bark, turning on himself at full speed and leaping into the air trying to bite her hand with those small sharp teeth. Charlie had to yell at him to shut him up. He calmed down a little and wagged his tail happily, running back and forth.

'Not very well, I've got a knee that hurts during the day and a shoulder that hurts at night, so sleep evades me like a bloody nun on the run.'

Lina smiled. 'Some pain at our age is normal. I have a little arthritis in my feet and hands,' she shared.

'I don't want to compete with you,' Charlie replied firmly, 'but I'm much worse than you. You have no idea what a pain in the fucking arse this knee and this shoulder are.'

Lina burst out laughing. Charlie still expressed herself like she did when she was a young rebel and organized marches for the CND, the Committee for Nuclear Disarmament. She had always been a revolutionary and would never change. She read the Guardian from top to bottom every day and had an opinion about all matters of politics. To this day she marched for equality, civil rights, feminism and against anything that was unjust in the world.

Lina noticed that she walked steadily, kept her back upright and didn't limp at all. But she knew Charlie well: nobody could compete with her, not even when it came to arthritis, rheumatism or joint pains. Hers were always better than everyone else's.

They crossed the living room and the kitchen with Fidel happily wagging his tail, trotting by their side. From there, a few steps took them down to the garden.

It was not just a garden; it was a work of art!

Facing south-east it was sunny throughout the summer and was cared for with obstinacy and devotion by Charlie, who was the best gardener Lina knew. Patches of red, purple and pink next to each other stood out against the bright green of bushes, low trees and the trunks of the tallest and most mature trees. The colours blended into each other with nuances that seemed curated with a paintbrush. And indeed Charlie painted.

A climbing plant full of bright green leaves and large pink flowers covered a tall arch which framed a rosemary bush in full bloom, a few yards away. It stood next to a big stone shell supported by a short column, used to collect rainwater for the birds. Low round shrubs were covered in white flowers.

'Your garden is beautiful, Charlie. What an artist you are!'

'Yes, thank you,' agreed her friend, who had never been overly modest. 'I'll show you the newest part, come!'

Charlie walked ahead of her. She climbed down a few steps to lower ground where there was a table and three benches, sheltered by a wooden roof. She stopped, placed her hand on Lina's arm and, pointing toward a stone fireplace with a grill, said: 'Do you remember the barbecues? We had them all the time, as soon as the sun showed up.' She squeezed Lina's arm and dropped her hand. 'But... since Douglas has gone I've never used it.'

'Is it difficult to light?' Lina asked. 'I've never tried. When Bruno was alive I couldn't even get close to it. It was his territory.'

'It's not difficult, but you must want to do it and I, on my own, don't even think about it. Follow me. I want to show you my new feature.'

They descended another set of steps and, in the lower area of the garden, covered by a healthy shiny lawn, Lina noticed a grove of vibrant saplings. She recognized everything else: lanterns dangling from the branches of the more mature trees that sheltered an armchair here, a little seat there, a rough table with two benches and, at the end, a large doghouse that Fidel diplomatically ignored.

'Apple trees, pear trees and plum trees,' Charlie announced proudly, pointing out her six new trees, short but laden with fruit.

'So small and already full. How incredible!' Lina was seriously impressed.

'I have already eaten the first pears,' her friend exclaimed enthusiastically. 'They're exceptional. I plan to make jam, cakes, and I soak them in liqueur, the way your mother taught me.'

In the shade of a big chestnut tree there was a round table and two comfortable wicker chairs with floral cushions. On the table was a flask, two porcelain cups, potato chips and a bowl full of salted peanuts. There were also two liqueur glasses and a beautiful, familiar looking bottle.

'Look what I found at the Italian store... *Marsala*!' Charlie declared, triumphantly raising the Sicilian wine. 'I bought it especially for you, I know you like it. Come on. Let's drink to your visit!' She opened the bottle assuredly and filled the glasses to the brim.

'It's a bit early,' Lina hesitated. 'I'm not used to drinking on an empty stomach. It'll go straight to my head... but I'll have a little drop gladly.'

They toasted by raising their glasses and began to walk around the garden.

With pride Charlie showed her the flowers. Lina was not an expert, but she could recognize the daisies: white, yellow and purple, three plants had intertwined and formed a small flowered mountain.

'These are begonias,' Charlie pointed her finger towards a multicoloured mound of white, pink and purple, 'and geraniums,' she added, pointing to a sea of vermilion red, burgundy and white.

'So many flowers!' Lina exclaimed, impressed by the vast expanse of colours. Her gaze moved to a vibrant yellow patch, which emanated an unmistakable fragrance.

The scent of those yellow roses reminded her of her mother who grew the same variety. She remembered her as if it were yesterday, bent over the shrubs to remove the ageing leaves, peering at the stems for insects.

Her mother lived with her parents in the little hamlet of Pianzano, a quiet village in the plains near Treviso, a stone's throw from the hills. On a clear day they could see the mountains of the Alps in the distance, their peaks covered in snow even in the summer. On their street, each year the neighbours held a competition for those who grew the largest and most fragrant roses. Her mother won year after year with that particular yellow variety. Those months of May in Italy when she was still a child... so many memories.

'My mother...'

'... always won the street competition with the yellow roses.' Charlie finished the sentence for her.

Lina looked at her in amazement: 'Had I already told you?'

'At least ten times,' her friend replied with irony. 'You repeat yourself, dear. It's your age!' And she burst out laughing in such a way that - if Lina she hadn't known her so well - would have seemed almost coarse.

Charlie proceeded to bring the glass to her lips and with a quick movement of her elbow emptied it in a single firm gulp. 'Jolly nice this Marsala!' She smacked her lips loudly, licking them voluptuously. 'Mmmh... What a good idea to buy it! Come on, drink up,' she encouraged Lina with a slight nudge. 'I'll get the bottle. Wait here. They are tiny these glasses,' she remarked as she walked to the table, bringing her glass eye-height and turning it round and round as if she were seeing it for the first time.

It was incredible how a scent could awaken so many memories, so many emotions. Lina felt her heart squeeze, as an unexpected longing for her mother suddenly washed over her.

During the war they had been displaced and had moved to her grandparents' house in the countryside, to escape the bombing. Even there, in addition to raising chickens, rabbits and pigs, her mother had managed to cultivate those beautiful yellow roses.

One day the doorbell rang. Lina – who was only seven or eight years old then – went to open and there stood a boy, his shirt sleeves rolled up above his elbows, a grey backpack on his shoulders. 'I'm a friend of your grandparents' he said nervously, 'I have to put this rucksack down for a few hours. I'm coming back in the morning to pick it up, okay?'

Lina moved to let him through. The boy entered urgently – he seemed familiar with the house – and headed to the space under the stairs. There, he took his backpack off, carefully laid it on the floor and covered it with a pile of blankets. 'Tell your grandfather that Dante was here and that I'll come back tomorrow, all right? He will understand.'

He went for the door and, after looking around scrupulously, walked with a resolute step along the path that crossed the fields. She stood there watching him – a tall handsome boy, in dusty trousers, a dirty shirt and a checked cap on his nearly shaved head – until he disappeared over the mound.

Her grandfather was out in the fields and her mother wanted to know what was inside that backpack. Nobody could be trusted. She tried to lift it, but it was very heavy and wouldn't budge. So, she opened it there and then, where Dante had left it. 'Dio Mio!' she cried out in a choked voice, staring in disbelief at a heap of hand grenades. Turning to little Lina her mother warned her 'You haven't seen a thing and you don't know anything, understood?' She closed the rucksack with shaky fingers. Then she took her young daughter by the hand and led her to the shrub of yellow roses. 'Smell these roses, they are wonderful' she urged the child, and brought a large yellow flower towards her by bending it at the stem. 'Look how beautiful it is!'

Her face raised to the rose, Lina had sniffed it, filling her lungs with that sweet, velvety scent.

'What madness war is!' her mother had whispered, shaking her head. Nothing more was said about the backpack, but the next day, when Lina went to look under the stairs, it had gone.

A few days later – it was early afternoon after lunch – while her grandparents were resting, Lina went looking for herbs in the woods close to the house. She knew how to recognize wild herbs, the edible ones and those used to make medicines for a cough, a temperature or for a good night's sleep. She picked them and saved them in her apron, held up like a sack. She was anticipating the great satisfaction she would feel in showing them to her grandmother. The old lady would proceed to wash them, divide them carefully and prepare them for supper. But that day Lina found much more than herbs.

She was walking, methodically scanning the ground when, for some reason she could no longer recall, she looked up. Above her, in front of her eyes, hanging on the branches of a big tree, a parachute was trapped and a young soldier was dangling from it. She had never seen a dead man before. For a few seconds she stood there, petrified, and then started running towards the house, fighting against her weak knees that didn't want to hold her, crying inside her bursting chest, breathless, unable to release any sound from her dry mouth, dumbly moaning and sobbing without tears.

She found her mother near the yellow roses and spluttered what she had seen.

'It will be an American' murmured her mum, wiping her hands on her polka dotted apron and preparing to follow her. Hastening her way to the woods she said something Lina had never forgotten: 'Enemies or not, every soldier is a son and every son has a mother.' She said it in a voice that wasn't her own, with a tight throat, and Lina felt scared, with an urgent need to cry.

They paused for a minute or so watching the hanging soldier, his face grey. 'He's not even twenty years old' her mother sighed, her eyes full of tears. 'Poor woman! She will suffer so much when they tell her!' She took Lina by the hand and they left, but after a few steps her mother stopped, knelt down and suddenly held her very, very tight. They walked home in silence, holding hands, trying to hide the anguish they both felt.

That time too her mother took her to the yellow roses. 'Look at them Lina, every petal. Touch them, don't they look like velvet? Breathe deeply their wonderful scent. Life is beautiful, Lina. Life is sacred. Never forget it. There are no enemies. Only men and women, boys and girls, like us, who want to live in peace.'

'I remember your mother well.' Charlie woke her up from her daydream. 'I planted this variety of roses thinking of her.'

She raised the bottle, urging Lina to finish the Marsala left in her glass.

'Er... I don't know...' Lina hesitated, bringing the glass to her lips.

'Come on girl! Can't you see how small these glasses are? They're *miniature*!'

'Go on then, just a drop.'

'Cheers!'

'Cheers!'

'I was thinking about the war,' Lina said softly. 'I told you of the day I found a dead paratrooper, didn't I?'

'You did, I remember it well. He was probably one of ours. You were against us during the war, if I'm not mistaken...' Charlie burst out laughing loudly.

Lina smiled and rolled her eyes. She had heard this comment from Charlie – who thought it was very funny – a thousand times before. The 'you' she was talking about referred to the Italian army and the 'us' was the British army, which were fighting against each other.

Then, more serious, Charlie added: 'War is a big business opportunity for a few and a lot of suffering for everyone else. Here in England we suffered too, you know? We had a bomb shelter in the neighbour's garden. I wasn't afraid, but I was a little girl and didn't understand. In fact, quite the opposite! It seemed like an adventure to me, because in the shelter we were all together. Our neighbour used to tell us stories to pass the time. I liked going down there, and we were lucky. Other areas of London were hit by the bombing and so many innocent people died.'

Urgently she took a sip of Marsala, licked her lips, dried them with the back of her hand and continued: 'What did scare me were the gas masks. They were horrible and we had to take them with us at all times. As soon as the sirens sounded – or sometimes it was a policeman in the street with a whistle – my mother would put it on and be transformed into an unrecognizable monster. Whenever she did, I would cry out in terror and weep until she took it off. I should have worn one too, but *no way*. They never managed to persuade me to put my head inside that rubber thingy. How horrible!'

'Let's hope we never see a war again, and that our grandchildren don't have to suffer what we suffered... and our parents above all!'

'Thank goodness we won and not that madman Hitler and

his little friend, your Mussolini. Things would have been very different if they had won.'

'Indeed! But what a price we paid for the democracy we enjoy now, even if it isn't perfect. Without all those young people who died fighting, we wouldn't have the freedom we have.' And, with a thoughtful expression, took a little sip from her glass.

'It's not perfect because people don't care. If we want to have a functioning democracy, people need to inform themselves, get involved, instead of turning a blind eye. Otherwise politicians can do whatever they want and end up corrupt. Bah! If it had been *their* sons who died in the war, perhaps they would have more of a conscience, they might defend this society,' Charlie asserted, before gulping her Marsala.

She paused for a short while, staring ahead. Then, as her memories overtook her once again, she recalled more lightly: 'I liked the ration book. We had it until I was ten or so and I went to buy sweets. Two ounces a week I could buy. It wasn't much, but what a joy to go home with that handful of boiled sweets. We ate less sugar in those days and we were healthier.'

'We were happier when we had less,' Lina added thoughtfully. 'People today waste so much. They work like crazy and then spend their money on useless things. But at least there is no war. How precious peace is.'

'Mmmh... there are problems here in London,' Charlie remarked, deep in thought. 'Since the police killed that young black man a few days ago, the situation has been tense. I expect it will boil over soon. Without justice, things won't calm down. Besides, this is not the first time. People don't forget. And they can only stay silent for so long.' She raised her glass and with one last swallow finished the wine completely. Smacking her lips, she observed her empty glass and with ironic surprise remarked: 'Oops, all gone. Do you still have some, Lina?'

Lina had emptied hers and was feeling its pleasant effect.

'No! Mine is finished, too. It was good.'

'Good indeed!' Charlie raised the bottle, unscrewed the cap and filled her glass. 'Pass me yours,' she ordered, nearing the bottle to Lina's.

'I don't know if I should...' Lina protested without much conviction.

'Oh come on! What do you care? We haven't seen each other for ages,' Charlie urged her. 'You can nap later if you feel sleepy. This will loosen our tongues.'

As if they needed it!

Chapter 9

WHICH BUS?

'Do you remember Andy Thompson?' asked Lina. 'The tall boy who worked at the garage across the road from your grandparents' house.'

Charlie's grandparents used to live in the Sneinton area of Nottingham and Charlie spent most of the summer with them. Lina's parents' home was just around the corner and the two young girls had become friends the day they met. Quite naturally Charlie became an honorary member of the clan of teenagers that gathered every afternoon in the church square.

'Of course I remember him. How could anyone forget such a good-looking boy?' her friend replied without hesitation. 'He was completely in love with you and would've happily married you. But you weren't interested. Too besotted with Bruno. Well, how is old Andy? Still alive?'

'No, unfortunately. I heard he died last month,' Lina answered sadly. 'I wonder what my life would have been like if I had married him instead.'

They stopped to admire a bush strewn with blue flowers. 'It's a California lilac,' Charlie stroked the rich flowers. Then, pointing to two armchairs covered with bright cushions, she invited: 'Come. Let's take the weight off our feet.'

They sat on the wicker chairs, in the shade of a tree decorated with white metal lanterns.

'I remember a time when Bruno decided to go to Leicester,' recalled Lina. "I'll come too,' I said to him. He looked thoroughly surprised and at a loss for words. He fumbled for an excuse, something like he was going for work, but I knew it wasn't true, he was all dressed up, stinking of aftershave.'

Charlie sniggered: 'Ooooh, even the perfume, the irresistible Bruno. Definitely not going for work!' Her voice tinged with anger and cynicism.

'Quite! But I insisted,' Lina continued. 'Being at his wit's end he agreed that I could go along. We caught the train and when we arrived in Leicester he led me to the station café and told me to wait there. I'd been waiting over two hours when Andy Thompson strolled in. He recognized me immediately and blushed to the roots of his hair. I hadn't seen him for years. He asked me what I was doing there, and got very upset when I told him.'

'And rightly so! If Bruno was here I'd punch him on the nose,' her friend exploded. 'You never told me.'

'No, I never told anyone. I was ashamed.'

'You ashamed? *He* should have been! So rude! A philanderer... and rude, too!' Charlie was as outraged as if the slight had been that very morning.

Lina sighed: 'Going back to Andy, he said that Bruno was crazy to treat me that way and that a woman like me deserved better. In those days he was already married and had two children. He confessed that he had always loved me and that perhaps he still did. He stayed with me for over an hour, until Bruno came back.'

'What an asshole! Three and a half hours he made you wait. Good job he's not here now, 'cause otherwise... I'd show him...' declared her friend, waving her fist in the air. 'He's lucky to be dead,' she concluded.

Lina nodded: 'I suppose so. Well, Andy looked at him without even trying to hide his contempt, and Bruno just glared at him. If looks could kill... You remember how jealous he could get. That was the last time I saw the dear Andy!' Lina concluded with longing.

'The brooding Bruno. He tried it on with every woman, but

if a man just looked at you he lost it,' recalled Charlie, clearly hostile to the deceased Don Juan. 'And you had plenty of men who wanted you, you know?'

'Who? Me?' Lina asked, astonished.

'Yes, you! You didn't even notice them. There was Davide Ferrazzi, the one with the bicycle – what a luxury. He was completely smitten, but you... right over your head...' Charlie swept her hand over her white hair.

'I had no idea. I never realized...'

'And the other Italian, Tommaso Sforza, he loved you so much!'

'That, I had noticed. He courted me in such a polite way. He came to the house with flowers for my mother,' Lina remembered with a fond smile. 'And what about you? Men went crazy over you... and you weren't shy like me.'

Charlie burst out in her tomboy laugh: 'I've never been shy, that's for sure. I've always liked men, and I like them even more now.' She placed her hand on Lina's arm and leaned over the armrest to confide: 'Last month I was in hospital and got a bit of a bollocking for touching some of the male nurses.' She chortled even louder this time and was clearly enjoying herself. She bent over, grabbed the bottle of Marsala resting on the grass and quickly unscrewed the cap.

'You touched the male nurses?' Lina was shocked 'But... where did you touch them?'

'Well... Pass me your mini-glass.'

This time Lina posed no objection, stretched her arm out and gladly received another dose of the delicious wine.

'Cheers, to us!' Charlie touched the glass with hers.

'To friendship! Cheers!' Lina responded enthusiastically and reached out to her friend, curious to hear the rest, her eyes bright.

'I touched the nurse's arse, of course! And if I could, even there... in front.' Charlie's mischievous smile went from one ear to the other.

'Nooooooo! But how can you?' This time Lina was downright stunned and took a sip to recover from the scandalous revelations.

'Well... it was easy! When they were standing next to my bed, all I had to do was stick my hand out and their penis was right there, close at hand.' Charlie broke in a fit of laughter. Wild, rebellious and completely inappropriate. Not much had changed over the years!

'But why did you do it?' Lina was visibly upset, but also interested.

'I was *so* bored, Lina, you know what hospitals are like,' Charlie chuckled. She gulped down the remaining content of her glass, popped her lips and wiped them with the back of her hand. 'Divine!' she exclaimed. Then she resumed: 'It was very funny to see their faces. They were so surprised! Besides, it helped me to remember what the 'thingy' is like... otherwise I'll forget completely.' She guffawed, holding her belly and wiping the tears that streaked her flushed cheeks.

'And the nurses? What did they do?' Lina was more and more intrigued.

'At first they scolded me saying that these things are not on.'

'Well... quite! It is harassment,' Lina observed.

'I suppose it is, but it was so *dull* there! Eventually one of them told me to keep my hands in place, under the sheets.' Seeing Lina's dumbfounded expression, Charlie split her sides laughing. Her laughter was contagious, but she hadn't finished yet: 'And then one of them made a formal complaint against me.'

'Nooo. Well, I guess you did deserve it! And then what happened?'

'I said it was probably due to the meds they were giving me. No-one took it any further after that, but they kept at arm's length from my bed.' Charlie laughed with gusto, amused by her own audacity and concluded boldly: 'I'm an old woman, Lina. At my age I can do what I want... and I get away with murder!'

She had always done what she wanted. Lina remembered moments from their past. Charlie was the wildest among all the girls, but that was one of the reasons she enjoyed her company so much. She, who was shy and reserved, admired the daring nature of her friend who wasn't afraid of anything and – it seemed – had no limits. Towards her, however, Charlie had always been loyal, never allowing Bruno to get too close – although Lina suspected he had tried. A few weeks after meeting Charlie, Bruno had begun to take his distance, seeming almost afraid of her.

'You haven't changed at all,' Lina remarked affectionately, and proceeded to guzzle the last drops of liqueur left in her miniature glass.

'Come, I'll show you what I've painted this year.' Charlie picked up the bottle and they headed for the little wooden house under the trees where she kept most of her paintings. She had painted many new beautiful ones. There was a big canvas of a vase with yellow flowers. She had used a spatula and so much paste that some parts were in relief. There was another, of a dancer resting with an orange shawl draped over her shoulders. Lina studied it for a long time.

'You're very good,' she stated admiringly and then, pointing at the two pictures that had stirred her, added: 'I really like these two.'

'Really?' For once Charlie seemed unsure but pleasantly touched by her friend's sincere compliment. She was such a confident woman in everything, often too much, but for her skills as a painter she doubted her talent. 'I have lessons three times a week and I'm learning a lot,' she said, with a touch of humility.

She refilled their glasses with Marsala and they toasted happily once again.

Lina stopped worrying. She felt warm inside and was enjoying this precious time.

Walking unhurriedly through the garden, Charlie told her

about her son in Australia. He was doing very well in his job and had married an Australian woman. He didn't let her know until after the ceremony, and they now had a six month old baby boy. She saw him once every two years and hardly ever heard from him. Her other son, the younger one, lived on the outskirts of London. However, despite being so close he was very busy and didn't show up often. When he dropped in he was always in a hurry and, on the rare occasions when he phoned, he could spare no more than a couple of minutes. Luckily there was Fidel who kept her company and loved her unconditionally. Charlie bent down to caress the dog, who looked at her in adoration and wagged his tail. He seemed to have understood they were talking about him.

Charlie continued to open up. After Douglas died she had managed to save a little money, but gave most of it to her sons, in times of need. Now she had very little left and her tiny pension didn't stretch far. She rented out a room to foreign students who came to London to learn English, and this way she could put aside a little every month. Maybe she could go to Australia to see her grandchild, or on some other trip. But travelling alone wasn't great. It would be much more fun with a friend. 'Douglas always spent more than he earned, as you well know,' she said, talking about her late husband. 'We never had a penny set aside, but he didn't worry. He was sure that his charm would open all the doors and solve every problem,' she affirmed, with a note of resentment.

Douglas was right in a way, Lina reflected. He was an attractive and charming man with a big smile and his warm personality ingratiated him straight away. He was the ideal friend and everyone was willing to help him. Charlie had always been very jealous, and suspicious. She thought he would betray her with every woman he met, but Lina could see that he was loyal and had always loved her deeply.

It was getting cool and damp in the garden. 'Let's go inside.

I'm hungry,' declared Charlie, 'I want to prepare something to eat.' Once again, she refilled the little glasses that they quaffed like nectar from the gods. The lovely Marsala ignited a fire in their empty stomachs which propelled them onto their feet.

Lina went from room to room and looked at the many paintings on the walls. Charlie had filled her house with colour and made it warm and welcoming. One of the rooms on the ground floor was her atelier. It overflowed with easels, canvases, palettes smattered with patches of colour, brushes in jars full of water or dry ones in large bunches in empty cans. Colours and brushes never contradicted her, Charlie often stated. Lina studied two unfinished paintings and could only admire the choice of colours. She found that the yellow ochre warmed her heart and the harmonic lines relaxed her.

She popped into the downstairs bathroom, eyed herself in the mirror and marvelled at her sparkling eyes and pink cheeks. She felt like a girl. You're a young woman, she thought to herself, observing the smiling image that looked back at her, 'a young woman of seventy-five,' she said out loud, and smiled broadly.

She went upstairs to see if anything had changed and took a look at the three bedrooms. The one with red curtains was Charlie's. Then there was one with yellow curtains and a third one with flowered ones. The bedspreads, the cushions, the small armchair and the accessories were all in matching colours. A large lamp was placed on each desk. In every room Charlie had created a relaxing and intimate environment and Lina could only admire her friend's good taste.

When she peeped into the bathroom she noticed that the tub was gone. It had been replaced by a walk-in shower with an ergonomic shower seat. A handle on both the right and left hand side had been positioned to help Charlie stand up, for when she couldn't do it on her own. Lina felt a twinge in her heart. Age did not forgive.

Meanwhile her friend had put on a record by the Beatles. Lina went down the stairs to the sound of Obladi Oblada, inhaling the aroma of grilled fish. Charlie was an exceptional cook. Their meal was ready and Lina prepared the table, taking the mats, napkins and cutlery that awaited her in a small pile. Charlie opened the fridge, pulled out a bottle of Chablis, uncorked it with ease and filled two glasses with which they toasted. As Lina listened to the music, she found herself dancing, shaking her shoulders and swaying her hips.

Charlie joined the dance and sang at the top of her lungs, her blue and white striped apron tied at the waist, a ladle in one hand and a glass in the other. They smiled to each other, happy and carefree. One tall with white hair, the other short and plump with grey hair. Lina hadn't had such a good time for ages. 'I think I'm a little tipsy,' she giggled.

'What do you care?' Her friend replied boldly. 'Carpe Diem! Enjoy the present 'cause life is short.'

After draining the bottle of Chablis, the hours flew by. Coffee followed their meal and, before they knew it, it was already half past five. Time to go, Lina realized. Sofia had insisted that she call a taxi to come back home, but it seemed a little extravagant. God only knew how much it would cost.

Charlie encouraged her to catch the bus: 'Taxis cost an arm and a leg and then, with the traffic, it'll take a long time... and you pay them by the minute as well as by the mile. Buses have their own lane; they're not too slow and much more economical. Let me get my tablet.'

Lina had assumed it was time for Charlie to take her blood pressure tablet, but had to chuckle in surprise when Charlie pulled out an iPad from under the armchair.

Her white-haired friend slid her finger across the screen – as Claudia and Micky often did – pressed the screen a few times and declared: 'You take the 38 to Clapton Pond, then change and get on the 212. Dead easy!'

It seemed easy to her because she knew the area like the back of her hand, but for Lina everything was new and she hesitated: 'I don't know... what if I get lost? It seems a bit complicated.'

'Not at all!' Charlie reassured her. 'I'll take you to the bus stop and put you on the 38. When you get off at Clapton Pond, you don't even have to cross the road. The stop for the other bus is right there... and if you're not sure ask someone. You'll save at least twenty quid. That's nothing to sneeze at, is it?'

As they were getting ready to leave, from the turntable the Beatles serenaded them with Penny Lane. Charlie knew it by heart, every last word. Lina had never learned them properly so she hummed along to the music, joining in loudly on the last word of each line.

Fidel had understood that he was going for a walk and wagged his tail excitedly, waiting with trepidation for the leash to go around his neck.

Lina put on her jacket and her hat, carefully arranging the red flowers, and pushed her hair behind her ears.

Charlie buttoned her long cardigan and grabbed her stick. It seemed superfluous because she walked perfectly well, which Lina pointed out. 'I don't need it for walking,' her friend confirmed, 'but it's useful to stop the cars. You'll see when we cross the road. I just have to raise it in the air and look fiercely at the drivers. They stop immediately,' she declared with an excited giggle.

Fidel was ready to go, unable to hide his joy.

Charlie locked the front door and took Lina by the arm. They walked with a light step, warmed by the conversation, memories, Marsala and Chablis. Charlie began to sing a song knowing very well the reaction she would stir in her friend. She had a clear sonorous voice.

'When the night has come and the la-and is dark, and the mo-on is the only light we see. No, I won't be afraid, no, I won't be afraid, just so lo-ong as you sta-and, stand by me...'

Lina knew the Italian version and started singing it in her

native language: 'Pregherò per te, che hai la notte nel cuor, e se tu-u lo vorrai, crederai...'

Charlie raised her stick and twirled it like a baton leading a band. Raising her voice by a tone for the refrain, she resumed her singing: 'And darlin, darlin, darlin, sta-and by me, o-h now stand by me, stand by me, stand by me...'

Lina echoed her voice, free and passionate: 'Io t'amo t'amo t'amo, oh oh oh oh, questo è il primo segno-o che dà la tua fede nel signo-or, nel signor.'

One arm linked to Charlie's, the other one thrust into the air to direct the imaginary orchestra, Lina advanced with her friend along the pavement. The music had whisked them back more than fifty years and though their bodies had aged, in their hearts they were still twenty. It was not their first duet and it brought them so much joy that, without realizing, they were attracting people's attention.

Veiled mothers pushing prams, people riding their bicycles, men in overalls, turned to look at them smiling, but the two women continued obliviously.

'Volare, oh oh, cantare, oh oh oh oh,' Charlie intoned.

'Nel blu dipinto di blu,' Lina joined in. 'Felice di stare lassù', and together: 'e volavo volavo felice più in alto del sole e ancora più su' – this time Charlie couldn't remember the Italian words and Lina continued alone, bold and confident – 'mentre il mondo pian piano spariva lontano laggiù, una musica dolce suonava soltanto per me' and together again at the top of their voices: 'Volare, oh oh... cantare, oh oh oh oh...' Ahhh, so satisfying!

They arrived at the traffic lights and Charlie told her that now it was time for an Elvis Presley song. She started to sing 'It's now or never,' with that stick in the air for emphasis.

Lina recognized the tune and hummed it by herself until the words in Italian opened their way through her fuzzy memory. 'But this is O sole Mio' she protested, 'not Elvis Presley!'

Charlie claimed with great bravado that Elvis wrote it and the Italians copied it.

Lina didn't noticed Charlie's smirk, nor remember the times in the past she had fallen for this little trick. She puffed up with passion. 'You must be joking, dear!' she stated emphatically, and argued that it was a Neapolitan song of many years ago. She raised her voice to prove it to her, and belted out: 'O sole mio! Sta in fronte a me, o sole mio, sta in fronte a me, o sole, o sole mio, sta in fronte a me, sta in fronte a me'. She hurried to add that it spoke of the Neapolitan sun, not of the American sun. Everybody knew that!

But, enjoying the drama, Charlie continued and the race escalated between Elvis's version and the Italian one. Their voices could be heard across the two lanes of traffic.

They were coming to the bus stop for the 38 and Charlie finally admitted: 'All right, I know it's an Italian song.'

'Neapolitan!' Lina insisted out, her cheeks flushed. 'Why didn't you say so right away, instead of dragging it out?'

'So that we could play,' Charlie replied, and stopped at the back of the queue of people waiting in a line. She hugged Lina and looked at her with shining eyes. 'What a good time we had today, hey?' she said. Then she paused and, thoughtfully, added: 'Come and live with me, Lina. I have a big house and we'd have so much fun. You can sell your house and move in with me. We can help each other and save a little money. With what's left we can go travelling. Say yes!' she pressed and, after a moment's hesitation – which was not like her – she admitted: 'I'm lonely.'

The invitation took Lina by surprise but, in that moment, it seemed like a brilliant idea. 'Yes, all right!' she answered with enthusiasm. Just then a red double-decker bus with number 38 displayed on the front approached the stop.

Charlie reminded her to stay on till the last stop, Clapton Pond, and from there she would catch the 212 that would take her straight to her daughter's new home.

It seemed all very simple.

Chapter 10

THE THIEF

As soon as Lina got on the bus, a young man sitting near the door stood up and offered her his seat. One of the advantages of being an elderly lady – Lina chuckled to herself. She thanked him with a smile and a nod, and sat down comfortably. Looking out the window she waved to Charlie who had picked up Fidel. Her friend's eyes looked sparkling. Lina felt happy and full of life.

As the bus left, she hummed under her breath 'O sole mio, sta in fronte a te, o sole mio sta in fronte a te, o sole, o sole mio, sta in fronte a te sta in fronte a te...' and whistled the tune as quietly as she could.

The passengers sat nearby smiled, amused.

The beautiful afternoon had filled Lina's heart with joy. The Beatles' Obladi Oblada still rang in her ears and her smile widened when she remembered Charlie dancing, shaking her hips in that blue and white striped apron, glass of Chablis in one hand, ladle in the other like a conductor's baton.

She was such a dear friend; with her Lina could be herself. Actually it was even more than that; when they were together Lina felt more audacious, almost defiant. Charlie's company awakened a part of her that could be defined as... what was the right term? Ahhh, her memory... it did play funny tricks... Intrepid! There was the word she was looking for. 'Intrepid' Lina whispered to herself 'I am *intrepid*'. She struggled to hold back the giggles that were rising spontaneously, lowered her head and covered her mouth with her hand so as not to be seen laughing alone, amused by her own humour.

She would love to see Charlie more often. When she was with her she felt twenty years younger. She was definitely very fond of her rebellious unconventional friend.

If she was not mistaken, Charlie had asked her to go and live with her, or had she dreamt it? What a surprise to hear those words! Not that she would go, hey? ... although she seemed to remember having said yes. It would be too big a change moving to London. Lina had been living in Nottingham ever since coming to this country. She had a nice little house there; her local streets and shops etched in her mind in a comforting map. She had her consolidated habits; the neighbours, like Mavis... Mavis and her tea leaves. What had Mavis said? 'I see tears.' Lina has seen a few tears - that was true - but wasn't that normal? Life and tears went together. Mavis had said other things too, but it was all nonsense! Dear Mavis, with that raven black hair and her shuffling steps.

The idea of living in London... she was too old for things like that. Better the security of familiarity. This last thought reassured her and Lina lost herself looking out the window. Houses and streets followed one after the other. There were FOR SALE signs staked neatly outside houses and FOR RENT indicating apartments, rooms or dark basements hungry for occupancy. The latter must be sad inside – Lina mused – and damp too, but many people brightened up the windows with pots of cyclamens or geraniums.

However... it was also true that sometimes she felt lonely. She had a tiny back yard and her neighbours were cordial, but they were acquaintances who knew her as a pleasant old lady; they were not friends she had known since their days of uncertainty and youthful adventures. With Mavis it was different, it was a warm friendship, but Lina saw very little of her.

And how did she spend her days? – Lina reflected . She went to the supermarket, to the greengrocer. She did some window shopping, popped into charity shops where sometimes she found a real bargain. She took a walk in the nearby park, almost always alone, and in the evening watched television until her eyes closed. To describe it like this her life seemed a little... how could one say... dull? ... empty? She felt real enthusiasm only when she thought of going to visit her children and doing something for them, or with them. On the other hand, whilst living in Nottingham she was independent, had her own space, her freedom. This was something that she wouldn't want to give up. Nevertheless... now that she had admitted to herself that she felt a little lonely, a hint, a suspicion of solitude had crept into her head and had nestled there, like a worm inside a peach.

The loudspeaker announced the stops the bus was about to make and finally she heard Clapton Pond, where she was supposed to change. Handbag on her lap, Lina adjusted her hat and smoothed her hair by pushing it behind her ears. Her feet ached a little, but she tried not to think about it. As soon as she'd start walking the pain would pass and, holding herself close to the pole, with a little effort she stood up and prepared to get off. She was delighted to see that, right behind the bus stop, there was a little park with beautiful trees, a pond, two little bridges and some benches. Lina decided to stop five minutes while she waited for the next bus. Was it 121? Or the 122. Could it also be the 12? She didn't quite remember.

With the Beatles' merry song still dancing in her head, moving lightly to the rhythm of the music that only she could hear, Lina walked towards an empty bench. She sat down, breathing deeply through her nostrils to fill her lungs. She couldn't stop smiling, still savouring those hours just gone by, full of warm friendship. She watched the weeping willow languidly swaying in the breeze. The tips of its low branches caressed the water of the pond, creating trails of light that rippled and expanded. Shades of warm green and golden yellow shimmered under the rays of the six o'clock sunshine. It was still day time; in August there was light until almost ten. Long days were beautiful. Lina felt vibrant, more alive.

Youngsters rode their bicycles on the paths; others slid on their skateboards performing rather hazardous acrobatics, ignoring the sign that clearly explained such activities were prohibited. Gentlemen walked with dogs on a leash and a bag in hand, to collect the poop their pets would surely drop. It was the very reason they had been dragged out of the house. A young couple sat, laughing, on a nearby bench, the girl perched on the boy's lap. They couldn't have been more than fifteen years old.

Lina was not thinking of anything in particular. A tender mental fog pervaded her. The soft wadding woven by the alcohol lulled her into a relaxed and satisfied state. She felt just fine, observing, listening, while the weeping willow's sinuous branches swayed calmly.

A young man with reddish-blond hair and a milky, freckled complexion approached listlessly. Without consulting her, he sat down on her bench, casting an elusive glance in her direction. Lina nodded at him and, trying not to be too obvious, continued to watch him out of the corner of her eye. He wore a stained T-shirt; his jeans were grey with dirt and grease. Even from a yard away she could smell the stale sweat he emanated.

Suddenly a tune started playing, bringing a smile to Lina's lips. She looked around. Where was the music coming from? The boy turned to look at her, as if expecting something. The tune suddenly stopped and everything returned as it was: the tree tops undulating elegantly in the breeze; the children on their bicycles; the couple on the bench, now sharing a cigarette.

The music started again. It was near her... in her lap. Her eyes fell on the boy's fingers. He had tattoos, with one letter per finger: W I L D on one hand, W O L F on the other.

Now he stared at her, and this time he spoke. 'Your phone is ringing,' he said, a note of critical urgency in his husky voice.

111

Her phone? What phone? Suddenly Lina remembered: Sofia had given her a mobile phone. As she opened her handbag the music became louder. She stirred the contents, pulled out a folding umbrella, her purse, a bottle of water, a scarf, her address book and – finally – the noisy, unfamiliar gadget. As soon as she grabbed it, it stopped ringing. Lina turned to the boy. Hesitantly she remarked: 'It will be my daughter.'

He glanced at her with a blank disinterest.

'I don't know how to answer. I'm too old for these things,' she justified. She was feeling a little tired now.

He looked at her again. She could almost see him thinking. He asked: 'Why don't you call her back?' as if that was the most obvious thing to do.

'How do I do it?'

'Give it to me,' he said, holding out his hand.

Lina handed him her phone. He turned it over and over, pressed some keys. Then, without looking at her, got up and walked away.

Lina didn't know what to think. Where had he gone? Bah... he'd come back soon, she guessed.

She didn't worry and went back to looking at the passersby. The green-yellow of the willow had become darker and the gold that had made the branches sparkle had disappeared, like the sun, obscured by a grey cloud. The air had lost its warmth and suddenly she could feel a damp breeze rising. She tightened her jacket around her, crossed her hands and rubbed her arms to keep warm. Soon she would have to go and wait for the second bus. What number was it again? 112, 212, could also have been 21. Now she was really confused. She waited... and waited.

Eventually, the blond-haired boy reappeared on the left entrance to the park, a bag hanging from one shoulder. This time he was accompanied by a young man, small and stocky, with pale skin and dark curly hair. A friend who knew about mobile phones, no doubt – Lina mused, curious and trusting –

as she watched them approach. When they sat on her bench, she smiled at them, but they didn't smile back. Suddenly... a disturbing feeling clouded the joy that made her heart sing. Lina began to feel uncomfortable, anxious. She ought to get up and leave, but now a numbing fear paralyzed her. Mavis's words suddenly came back to her, 'They'll take it off you'. She clutched the handbag on her knees. Too late! With a tug, the dark haired boy pulled her handbag out of her shaking hands and quickly passed it to the fair one. The latter roughly pushed it into his own bag and ran towards the entrance of the park.

'No... no... my bag, my pension,' Lina moaned, trying to get to her feet.

But the thief stood up and, pressing her shoulder with a steady hand, forced her to remain seated. With his other hand he lifted his sweatshirt, just enough for Lina to see the flick-knife held in his trousers belt. 'Shut up!' he ordered, keeping his voice low. 'No use screaming. As if you had much in that bag,' he added with disdain. 'We'll find two quid, if we're lucky.'

Lina looked in the direction where his accomplice had escaped and collapsed on the bench. Her legs, her hands... everything trembled. She couldn't scream if she wanted to. She was dumbfounded with shock, stunned by the alcohol, a bitter taste in her dry mouth.

The young man ordered her one last time to keep quiet and then ran away. She followed him with her eyes until he disappeared from sight. Disheartened, with an empty feeling in the pit of her stomach, Lina gazed at the swaying willow that had turned a dull green, and shivered in the cold breeze.

She sat motionless, upset, but at the same time relieved. She didn't know what that boy was going to do to her. Seeing that knife had almost made her faint. At least now she knew she was safe, even if she had lost her handbag and everything in it. There wasn't all the money from her pension, fortunately. She had taken forty pounds with her and that was all those two criminals would find, she thought angrily. She was shaking from head to toe and suddenly felt exhausted.

She closed her eyes, leaned heavily against the back of the bench and drew a deep breath. And now? She had to do something, she couldn't sit there forever... Besides, she was dying for a pee. She would have to go to a cafe and ask if she could use their toilet. She didn't like to pee in public places, but couldn't resist much longer. Fighting her growing exhaustion, Lina got up and started to walk.

One step after another, walking would help her clear her mind. She'd have to remember how to get back to the bus stop, otherwise she'd get lost. But she was already lost, wasn't she? With no idea where she was going, Lina walked till she reached a large roundabout. At the pedestrian crossing she pressed a button, waited for the red man to turn green and crossed the road. She was looking for a cafe, but the few along the road were already closed. Meanwhile, she peeked at the shop windows, but very few shops were still open. Her belly was like a balloon; she was almost bursting.

There was a pub with a black door. She'd never entered a pub alone and, even in the company of other people, she had been only a few times, she could count them on the fingers of one hand. She felt like turning back, but couldn't afford to; if she waited any longer she'd be wetting herself. Despite her shyness Lina pushed the door open.

Inside the pub, the dim lights gave the impression that night had already fallen. The stale smell coming from the alcohol-impregnated carpet assaulted Lina's nostrils. The door swung closed behind her, blocking out the street noise and amplifying the patrons' talking and laughter. Some were standing with an elbow resting on the counter, others perched on high stools. They turned towards her with a vaguely interested look. Lina looked around awkwardly, searching for the toilet sign.

The woman behind the counter was in her fifties; fluffy

blond hair gathered in an elaborate way; eyes heavy with makeup and lips painted red. She addressed Lina: 'Can I help you Madam?'

'I'm looking for the bathroom,' Lina replied, bashful and embarrassed.

'The bathroom is for customers. Do you want to order something?'

'I'd love to, but I have nothing. I've been robbed. They stole my handbag,' Lina said. The realization of her situation was beginning to sink in. 'But I have to go to the bathroom... urgently,' she insisted.

The barmaid studied her briefly then, with a gesture of the arm, pointed to the right. 'The bathroom is downstairs, love,' she said.

Lina rushed in the direction indicated and heard the barmaid's voice urging her: 'Careful down the stairs love, they're steep. I don't want her to kill herself,' the woman added, talking to the patrons.

Lina went down as quickly as she could manage, holding firmly to the handrail. Finally there was the toilet. It was not exactly a bathroom, but this was not the time to be choosy. She rushed into the cubicle, her skirt raised, knickers already half way down her knees and at last... *Ahhhhhh!* Elbows on her knees, supporting her chin on her fists, she took a moment's rest, shielded by those four walls. She liked this habit they had in London of calling people 'love'. Although she knew it was a turn of phrase, it made her feel cared for, surrounded by affection. While washing her hands she studied herself in the mirror, carefully tidied her hair behind her ears and adjusted the purple hat so that the red flowers were exactly where they should be. Holding the handrail, she slowly climbed the stairs.

In the pub hall everyone seemed to be waiting for her, wanting to know what had happened. The barmaid looked at her kindly. 'Would you like a cup of tea, love?' she asked.

'Thank you, but I have no money, I've lost everything.'

'Don't worry love, it's on me. Please sit down.' The blonde pointed to a table near the window. 'I'll pop the kettle on.'

One of the patrons asked Lina if she needed anything.

She didn't know what she needed, except that she wanted to go home, to her daughter, her son-in-law, her grandchildren, but had no idea how to get there. If only she had their address...

The fair barmaid walked around the counter holding a cup and saucer. The tight-fitting, low-cut top highlighted her abundant bosom. The skirt — too tight at the waist — squeezed rolls of fat on her hips and stomach. Looking at her more closely, Lina realized that she must have been older than fifty and a smoker, from the opacity of her skin. The woman's cheeks were covered in foundation and powder, but the heavy make-up highlighted the wrinkles it was applied to conceal. She put the steaming cup of tea on the table, sat on the edge of the chair opposite Lina and, looking at her with sympathy, covered the elderly lady's hand with her own, the long manicured nails painted bright red. 'Tell me everything, love,' she said in a gentle manner. 'What happened?' The customers present didn't hide their curiosity and Lina found herself in the centre of a small audience.

And so she told them about the afternoon spent with Charlie — omitting the detail of the half bottle of Marsala and the full bottle of Chablis — of the first bus and the garden at Clapton Pond, of the first thief and then the second one. Now, without her handbag, she hadn't got her daughter's address. She was completely lost and didn't know what to do.

'That is a problem.' The barmaid was thoughtfully racking her brain over how to help her.

One of the patrons suggested that she go to the police and explained what happened. One by one, the others — all men — concluded that it was definitely the best thing to do: She should go to the police station and they'd find a solution, no sweat. They'd be able to trace her daughter's phone number. But she had just moved house. So maybe her friend's number. Yes, that should be easier; she had been living in the same house for thirty years. There you go, it was not so difficult.

But where was the police station? Another discussion ensued on which police station was the nearest. Tottenham? Hackney? Tottenham's was the best, they decided after a general consultation. Was it far? Yes, some distance, it would be better to take the bus. But Lina had had enough of buses. Besides, she had no money and a walk would do her good. Maybe she'd sober up. They said to her, when you leave the pub, go right and keep going straight ahead. You might have to ask someone when you arrive at a big crossroads. You'll know it is the right one when you see a bank on the left.

Lina buttoned up her jacket and didn't notice that the buttons didn't match, until the barmaid pointed it out. She thanked her with a smile and buttoned it up once more paying more attention. She adjusted her hat one last time and then, heartened by the tea, the rest and the attention received, she set off. She would go to the police and they would sort everything out. They would find Charlie's phone number, who'd give them Sofia's number, and from there they'd find the address. They'd probably take her home in a police car, no sirens of course, and Micky would tell all his friends. He might even turn it into a song, knowing him! The sky was pale blue. It must have been around half past six by now. She forgot to ask those kind people the time.

There was something really special about England – Lina reflected – that she hadn't known before coming to live here. It was the kindness with which English people treated perfect strangers. They had a way of talking to people they had never met before, as if they were acquaintances, or friends. There was such familiarity in these brief exchanges, such human warmth... it had impressed her from the start. What beautiful people! She walked with renewed energy, confident that before long she would be able to stop worrying. Surely, this afternoon, which had gone a little bit skew whiff, would end in the best possible way.

She walked along a road with wide pavements on both sides, shaded by large leafy oaks. Yards and yards of dazzling green grass, almost a park, separated the pavements from the rows of houses. She noticed that the passersby all dressed the same. Despite being August the men wore a black coat, trousers of the same colour – too short, showing their ankles – a white shirt and a black hat with a hard brim. Not only did they all look the same, but they all walked quickly and seemed to be very busy, as if trying to do two things at once, squeezing as much as possible into their time.

Upon reaching the crossroads, Lina was pleased to see there was a bank on the left, confirming that she was on the right track. She turned right and continued on a pavement flanked by countless shops, peeking into the windows as she moved along. There was a large church on the left, a solid building consisting of a central facade with arches, a rose window at the top and two bell towers, one on each side. She reflected that it was indeed a long way, but she had to carry on, putting one foot in front of the other. The sky had darkened and heavy grey clouds had dimmed the light, now the colour of ash.

To her great relief the shabby road soon gave way to another green area. Wide gardens flanked the pavement and a beautiful fountain sent a strong gush towards the sky while more weeping willows swayed pleasantly in the light breeze. The name of an underground station made her smile: it was called Seven Sisters. Who knew where it came from. On a high pedestal a beautiful statue of a tall angel with its wings spread out reminded people not to forget. It was a monument to the Tottenham people who lost their lives during the First and Second World Wars. Now she knew that she couldn't be too far from the police headquarters. Thank goodness, because it was much farther than she imagined. One more church with a severe facade, three large sober arches that made her feel almost in awe, a turret on each side and a kind of minaret, probably a bell tower.

There were few people on the street. Maybe it was because of the time of day and everybody was at home having dinner or watching television. Another shopping area where ethnic shops had signs in different languages. They were almost all closed.

Chapter 11

THE RIOTS

The red double-decker buses were the only flashes of colour that enlivened the wide, grey duel carriageway, barren of trees. If she couldn't find the police station soon, she would have to ask someone. In the distance a large group of people crowded the pavement – there seemed to be many hundreds of them – and some were shouting. Her curiosity awakened, Lina forgot how tired she was, hurried her pace and soon reached them.

At the edges of what seemed to be a protest stood a tall black lady with a large bosom, a reassuring matronly feel about her. Next to her was an older lady, also black, wearing thick rimmed glasses, her dark dreadlocks with streaks of white carefully wrapped in a scarf.

Lina approached her and, speaking loudly to be heard over the shouts of the crowd, asked if she knew where the police headquarters was.

The woman looked at her. 'Are you kidding me?' she exclaimed and, with a gesture of her chin, pointed at the building right opposite them. 'It's that one!'

'Ah... right, there it is, Tottenham Police Station,' Lina uttered. Then, apologetically, gazing at the simple two-story building, she added: 'I was looking for a grand imposing structure, but instead it's quite small.'

Pricking up her ears she could make out the slogan the people were shouting: 'We want justice', and asked the lady:

'Has something happened?'

At first both women studied her with a surprised, slightly critical eye, but soon they relaxed and spoke in turns.

'You bet something has happened. The police killed a black man for no reason. And they didn't even have the decency to come and tell his family.'

'Have you not heard about it? It has been on television for the past two days.'

It rang a bell. Lina thought hard... ahhh... maybe it was the one that Charlie had mentioned. 'Yes, I heard about it,' she replied. 'Did he live nearby?'

'He lived in the neighbourhood. The members of his family are at the head of this protest,' the large lady said.

The woman with greyish hair added: 'He was my friend's nephew, although I didn't know him personally.' She shook her head, pain and consternation written all over her face.

'We've asked and asked for a dialogue, but they've simply ignored our requests,' the taller woman explained. 'They told us a high ranking officer would come and speak to us. We have been waiting more than five hours and now they tell us he can't make it, and that we must clear the street.'

'We want to talk with the head of police. Why did they kill an innocent man?' the shorter lady questioned. 'We want the truth, and justice.'

'How sad, I'm so sorry!' Lina could feel the grief and confusion in the air. She then added somewhat awkwardly: 'I wanted to go into the police station to ask for help... my handbag was stolen with everything I had, money and addresses. I don't have my daughter's address, she's just moved house. I don't know what to do. Do you think I may be able to go in?'

'I think you have chosen the wrong moment love,' the older lady replied, 'because, instead of you going in, they're now coming out.'

'Look,' said the other, pointing to the police station with her chin.

And indeed they were. Rows of policemen dressed in black, wearing helmets of the same colour, carrying batons and holding shields of transparent plastic, were coming out at that very moment. They started to line up outside the police headquarters. Solemnly, powerfully. They looked quite scary.

For a short while Lina forgot about her own problems. She stood, staring at the officers and at the upset mourning crowd. She could hear louder shouts of 'We want answers, we want justice!'

The focus of her attention was momentarily distracted by a young couple approaching, a man and a woman, white this time, both strikingly good-looking. They were walking fast, talking animatedly and definitely in a hurry. They stopped close to Lina and watched what was happening across the road. She heard them talk; they were worried about the situation, and rightly so. The atmosphere was becoming more and more charged. The young man noticed Lina looking at them. He smiled in a friendly manner and said good evening.

Good evening, she replied, pleasantly surprised. Maybe she ought to ask them for advice, but they seemed to be pressed for time and, before she could think of what to say, they were on their way. What a shame! The two ladies she had been speaking with had moved further into the crowd and Lina was alone again. Hesitantly, she took a few steps back and leaned against the side of the building. How she would love to lie down, close her eyes and sleep... and forget all about her problem! What should I do? She asked herself, feeling worn out.

On the pavement opposite hers, a slim black girl with plaited hair approached the police cordon. She was wearing a black dress and white sandals. From where Lina was standing she couldn't quite see what the girl was doing, but suddenly the young woman was surrounded by policemen. Were they hitting her? It seemed that way. Lina couldn't see clearly, but she was too tired to get closer. And besides, it looked dangerous.

From the crowd of demonstrators, bitterly enraged by this latest development, a group of five or six young people broke away and headed for one of the wheeled waste containers. Within minutes it was on fire, high flames spilling out of it. They ran with it towards the row of policemen and thrust it hard, right in the middle of the officers. Pulling scarves up over their mouths and hoods down over their foreheads, the angry faces became anonymous. Some of them were holding something – the elderly lady sharpened her sight. They were wielding sticks. Stones were being hurled at the police, but the officers blocked them with their shields. As the stones bounced to the ground some youths ran to pick them up and threw them again, aiming better, with fierce determination.

Within a few minutes, the dozen or so fighters had multiplied and now there were many more of them, flinging stones, even bricks, at the policemen. Others ran along the pavement where Lina was standing and angrily began to pull a trash container from its pole, until they managed to detach it. Using it as a weapon they hit the windscreen of a police car parked a few yards away until they smashed it. Meanwhile others kicked the windows in, causing them to fragment into hundreds of pieces. The noise of shattering glass was accompanied by exultant yelling. The youths laughed and sent victorious screams. Lina saw them run, shouting loudly, towards the police station. Rioters were now holding iron bars. Lina had no idea where they had found them. Focusing better, she realized they were road signs that had been ripped up. She would have liked to take shelter somewhere, but the few shops still open were hastily closing their shutters. Where can I go? The electricity in the air made her hair stand on end.

The attractive couple that had gone past earlier were coming back, carrying two shopping bags each. Slowing down their pace, they watched with concern what was happening on the other side of the road, only a few dozen yards away. The girl recognized Lina and, with a nod of her head, acknowledged her.

Lina wanted to say something – perhaps they knew what to do, maybe they lived nearby – but, before she could find the words, they had already walked away. Apprehensively, she followed them with her eyes. She should have stopped them, but now it was too late. Lina leaned heavily against the wall. Her head was getting a bit clearer, but now she was feeling exhausted. Her hands clasped in her lap, she was on the verge of tears, from the fear she had felt when she was robbed, and the fear she was feeling now. She was quite overwhelmed.

Suddenly the girl was right in front of her, looking concerned. 'Excuse me, are you all right?' she asked.

Lina stared at her as if she had been a mirage. Her heart welled up with relief and she felt tears prick at the back of her eyes, out of relief this time. It might have been the most inappropriate time, but she couldn't fail to admire the beautiful features of the girl's face, her smooth skin and big eyes. It was like finding a life buoy in the middle of high waves. 'I had my handbag stolen... I wanted to go to the police, but now...' she mumbled. Her head was empty, she felt bewildered. 'I've lost everything, money, addresses, phone numbers... I don't know what to do, or where to go,' she stammered.

'Oh, no! I'm sorry!' the girl exclaimed. She checked the time on her small wristwatch and bit her lower lip, reflecting. 'You can't stay here. This is getting out of control,' she declared. She hadn't even finished her sentence when the ransacked car suddenly filled with flames and a gust of hot air pushed both of them backwards.

'Let's get away from here. That's the most urgent thing,' the young woman stated, coming closer and touching Lina's arm with her slender hand. 'You can come to our house. We live just around the corner. At least you'll be safe. Then we'll do something. We'll call the police and ask for help.'

That was just what she wanted! Lina was immediately heartened, as if a ray of sunshine was warming her, and felt she could trust. With a faint smile she nodded: 'Yes, thank you dear, let's go, let's go' and, encouraged by the young woman, started to walk as quickly as she could.

As if sensing her tiredness, the girl took her arm. Together they hurried along the pavement and reached her partner, who was waiting for them. 'The lady is coming with us; she can't stay here,' stated the girl.

The young man nodded and smiled at Lina – he had an open face and a friendly smile. 'Of course! It looks wild out here,' he remarked, and placed himself at her side, so that Lina was between the two of them and felt protected.

They were much taller than she, two solid and secure columns. It made her think of the churches she had seen coming here; the young couple were like the bell towers and she, much shorter, the church in the middle.

The sound of cries made it hard to hear each other speak. Walking quickly they moved away from the immediate danger and towards safety.

As soon as they were some distance away and the noise had died down, Lina described what had happened to her. The couple listened carefully, without interrupting, nodding while she spoke. They openly shared their concern about her situation.

The girl, Beverley, worked in a nursery and her boyfriend Josh was a secondary school PE teacher. Whilst covering the last few yards to their house, they explained that they were hosting a meeting at their home and were expecting a dozen people to arrive shortly.

'We'll try to call the police station straight away, to let them know about the theft and that you don't know how to get home,' Josh reassured her. 'Under normal circumstances, I'm sure they would spring into action to find where your daughter lives. Perhaps right now it'll be a bit harder, but don't worry. You'll get home tonight.'

'Are you hungry?' Beverley asked her gently.

But Lina didn't want anything, except to rest her weary legs somewhere safe.

Beverley and Josh's house consisted of a small apartment on the second floor of a building on the main road – High Road – above a shop that had already closed. The girl invited her to make herself comfortable on the sofa, while she went into the tiny kitchen, returning moments later with a small plate of biscuits.

Josh sat down next to Lina and put an arm around her shoulders, as if he had known her for years. 'Poor lady,' he said with affection. 'Fancy a cup of tea?'

Another tea. English people solved all their problems with a cup of tea.

Beverley started to search for the local police phone number, found it and called, but it was engaged. She tried a few more times but to no avail. 'I don't even get the answer phone,' she said. 'I'm not surprised, considering what's happening out there!' She gave Lina a perplexed look: 'We'll try again later. I'm expecting people to arrive any minute now.' At that precise moment the doorbell rang and Beverley hurried to open it. From the entrance hall Lina could hear concerned voices.

With a charming smile, Josh handed Lina a cup of steaming tea. She took it gratefully and, with trembling hands, brought it to her lips.

Josh went back to the kitchen, where he had prepared a tray with a jug of water and a dozen glasses. He placed them on the table next to her.

The doorbell rang a second time. Meanwhile a white woman with silvery hair entered the living room, accompanied by a black man with long ringlets. Both greeted Lina warmly and shook her hand, introducing themselves: Jane and Nelson.

More overwrought voices surged in from the entrance hall, discussing what was going on outside. The newcomers, a young man and a young woman in their twenties, said they had seen hundreds of police officers in combat uniform, with raised batons, outside the police station. Pavements and streets were full of people with their faces covered, hurling stones and bricks at the officers. Angry people managed to force open a parked truck and pulled out wooden planks with which they were attacking the police. Others had ripped open the shutters of shops, as if they were made of cardboard. The two young people introduced themselves to Lina: Carlo and Sandra; Italian, but living and working in London.

Lina was very happy to meet some Italians and wanted to know from which part of Italy they came from. Sandra was from Trieste and Carlo from Naples. They looked surprised when Lina told them she was from Nottingham, but their short exchange was side tracked by the conversation about the escalating riots.

The doorbell rang once again and more people arrived. Soon the room was packed and everyone was exchanging information on what was happening outside. From her seat on the sofa Lina listened and observed everyone with curiosity.

There was a tall slim gentleman with white hair and a tanned complexion. A very tall girl with copper-red hair and freckles across her milky cheeks was talking to him. A dainty Chinese girl in a short sky-blue dress and matching sandals stood smiling, listening to their conversation. An Asian woman wearing jeans and a red top was accompanied by a little boy of around three years of age. He donned a long thick fringe over his beautiful brown eyes, rimmed with long eyelashes. The whole world appeared to have gathered in this room and they all seemed to be friends.

Beverly introduced her to the newcomers. Everyone made her feel welcome. The young woman explained that they would soon begin to 'chant' a kind of mantra, which might seem a little strange. She wrote some words on a note pad, then tore the small sheet of paper and handed it to Lina. 'If you wish, you can join in,' she said. 'We'll chant for half an hour and then start our meeting. I'm sure you'll like it,' Beverley assured her. 'If you prefer to rest, you can lie down in my bedroom,' she added warmly.

'No, no, I prefer to be here,' Lina declared, even if the tiredness made her eyes feel as heavy as lead.

The participants found themselves a place to sit, on a chair, on the sofa or on cushions on the floor.

In front of a cabinet Lina had noticed a beautiful jug full of lush green leaves and a tray with some fruit. Josh sat on a stool and opened the cabinet doors, revealing a parchment with some sort of Chinese symbols. Then, he picked up a wooden stick and struck a large black bell with it. A beautiful vibration resounded in the room. Josh slowly intoned some words that Lina recognized as the ones Beverley had written for her. Suddenly all the other people in the room joined in the chorus and began to chant rhythmically this song without music.

The room was filled with a deep resonance that became faster and faster, penetrating, mesmerizing. It made her head and body vibrate and almost took her breath away. Lina inhaled deeply and leaned more heavily against the sofa. She observed those people so different in age, skin colour and style of dressing. The tall girl was very elegant and looked like a model. A man in his mid thirties had probably just finished work because he was wearing blue overalls. The elderly lady seemed to be more or less Lina's age and wore a simple blue skirt and a grey jersey. The Asian woman's child moved around the room, curiously looking at and touching everything he could lay his hands on. The person nearest to him kept an eye on him, smiled and sometimes stopped him.

Lina closed her eyes and allowed herself to be pervaded by that peculiar sound that made her feel more alive. She absorbed it through her skin and the rhythm of her breath. Her head was clearing a little more thanks to all the tea. Charlie and her paintings came to mind, Sofia and the boxes in the doorway. Claudia who blushed when talking about her boss, pulled in opposite directions between an old love and a new one... and she, Lina, who was lost in such a big city and found herself with these new people who welcomed her warmly. Soon Sofia would be home and begin to wonder where her mother was. She would be concerned, no doubt; as if she didn't already have enough worries of her own. But – Lina told herself – as soon as the meeting was over, they will be able to get in touch with the police and in a couple of hours she'll be home. She relaxed and allowed herself to be swept away by this sound and pleasant vibration. She closed her eyes and, overwhelmed by fatigue, fell asleep.

When the bell rang again Lina woke up with a jolt. Trying to be discreet she dried the dribble from her mouth. Embarrassed, she wondered whether anyone had seen that she had fallen asleep; maybe she had even snored. At home they told her that she did. But no-one seemed to have noticed. The chanting had stopped and the people present thanked each other. Lina could hear a lot of thank you, thank you. They smiled and settled more comfortably in their seats. Two more young men had arrived, a skinny blond one and a slim one with darker skin, handsome features and black hair.

Josh thanked everyone for attending after a long day's work and despite the disturbance going on outside. Since there were people who didn't know each other, he invited everyone to introduce themselves.

The girl with red hair went first: her name was Tracy, she was a model – Lina rejoiced because she had guessed that much – and lived fifteen minutes' walk from here.

Then it was the turn of the man in overalls: John was a builder and lived a few roads away. He apologized for wearing his overalls, but his clothes had got wet at work and he had nothing else to change into.

The older lady's name was Jane; she was happily retired and lived in a nearby street.

The gentleman with white hair was called Alex and was a photographer.

The young slim man with a handsome face and dark hair who had arrived late was called Tony, studied at University and, to support himself, worked as a car mechanic.

Then Carlo spoke, he was twenty-five years old and was doing an internship at an architects' studio.

Sandra, the other Italian, was attending a course to become a choreographer and taught modern dance.

The pale and skinny young man in his early twenties was called Jim; he was unemployed but worked as a volunteer.

Then there was Suki, the young Chinese woman from Singapore; she was twenty-six years old and studied law at university.

The young lady with the child was called Navine, was Indian and worked as a part-time secretary.

The black man with long curls, called Nelson, was thirty-eight years old and was a social worker.

Then Beverley introduced herself saying she was twenty-eight, followed by Josh who was thirty-two.

It was now Lina's turn to say something and, shyly to begin with, she introduced herself: 'My name is Lina, I'm seventy-five and I'm here because I'm lost.'

Some of the participants smiled and this made her smile too. Others looked at her with surprise. They were all intrigued and wanted to know more.

She continued: 'I'm Italian but came to live in England with my parents and my siblings when I was twelve. I have always lived in Nottingham, where I married an Italian man – Bruno – and had four children. The oldest one died five years ago, the second lives in Boston, in America, the third lives in Lisbon and the youngest one lives in London... but I don't know where, because she has just moved house and I've lost her address... and everything else that I had in my handbag.'

All the attention was focused on her and the questions started to flock about what happened.

And so Lina told them of the afternoon spent with Charlie, the half bottle of Marsala they drunk on an empty stomach and the delicious Chablis which went down like fresh water with their dinner. As everyone laughed, she started to see the funny side of things and felt encouraged to tell about their sing along down the street and how Charlie had easily persuaded her to take two buses instead of the taxi. Then she recounted what happened at the Clapton Pond garden. As she continued with the story, the laughter faded, turned into concerned listening and then into a collective jolt when she described the theft. There was a general sigh of relief when she told them about the pub and the owner offering her a cup of tea. She felt their concerned sympathy when she explained that she witnessed the beginning of the rioting outside. Everyone was captivated by her story and had a question, or several, to ask her.

Jim, the unemployed boy, asked her to describe the two men who had robbed her. He nodded when she told of the blond man with WILD and WOLF tattooed on his fingers, as if he had understood who he was. The man sitting next to him whispered something and Jim approved with a nod of his head.

The conversation soon slipped onto what was happening outside and from time to time someone went to the window to check the developments. Would they be able to leave after the meeting and go home? Instead of calming down, the situation appeared to be getting worse.

A discussion began as to how to reunite her with her family and suggestions came from all those present: Phone the police. Yes, but they were not answering. They are busy with everything happening outside, no doubt. Call Charlie. But Lina didn't have her phone number and didn't remember the address – it was a street with a difficult name. Eventually they decided to start the meeting whilst one of them kept trying ringing the police every five minutes. The topic of the Buddhist discussion was 'The things that stop us from being happy' and a very particular figure in Buddhist mythology: The devil king of the sixth heaven and his ten troops.'

To her great surprise Lina realized she was among a group of Buddhists. Unlike the traditional image of shaved heads, orange robes and placid, imperturbable people, every single person present was lively, they were all different from each other and looked just like 'normal' people.

Chapter 12

BORN TO BE HAPPY

Sitting on a stool slightly higher than the chairs, legs apart and a big smile lighting up his face, Josh opened the meeting: 'Welcome and congratulations for having made it despite everything that's happening out there.' The expression on his face showed concern about the mayhem. 'We'll talk about that too, I'm sure, but for now let's make the most of this precious hour we have together, and exchange our life experiences on a very special theme.' He shuffled on the stool. 'Buddhist philosophy tells us that we were born to be happy and to help other people become happy. We were not born to suffer, but to enjoy life. For me, this means that I strive to live in a way that creates happiness for myself, for the people around me and the people I come into contact with. Fifty-fifty: my happiness is as important as the happiness of others.'

Lina pricked up her ears and sat more upright on the couch. She had always been told that life was full of suffering, a valley of tears. She had never heard someone say we were born to be happy; in fact, it seemed almost heresy. Maybe 'heresy' was too strong a term, but wanting our own happiness was selfish... wasn't it? We had to atone for the original sin and that's why even good people suffered. That was the norm.

'What is happiness?' Josh looked around. 'A definition in Buddhist philosophy says that happiness is, literally, 'having the strength we need, when we need it'. He took a small pause to give them time to consider this.

Lina reflected on this last idea. It seemed completely new and even a bit awkward. What did strength have to do with happiness?

Josh resumed: 'When I heard this definition, during a lecture a few years ago, I remember being very impressed. I thought it contained the essence of what I was looking for. I kept repeating it in my head, to take it in properly. Happiness and inner strength went hand in hand; indeed, inner strength was essential to be happy. I felt as if I had found a treasure!'

Ah, inner strength – Lina reflected – not the strength of strong people, like Bruno for example. He always seemed so strong, but was he happy? He certainly never made *her* happy. Even Charlie gave the impression of being strong – and she was a strong person – but inner strength was something else; even she could understand that.

'Buddhism tells us that each of us has immense capacity. We can't even imagine how big it is. We are endowed with a potential for compassion, wisdom, courage and life force just like Shakyamuni Buddha himself. He was a man of flesh and blood like us, not a God with supernatural powers. He was simply a man, with a big heart, trying to understand how to overcome the sufferings of life and create joy and harmony.'

This was all new to Lina. She liked what she heard and paid full attention so as not to miss a word.

'So, if we develop these qualities, we too will definitely become strong and happy... and we'll create happiness around us. It sounds simple, doesn't it?' Josh looked at those present with an amused smile. His eyes stopped briefly on Lina and she felt warmed by his attention. 'However,' he continued, 'like all beautiful and important things, we don't achieve them without effort. And once developed, we must consolidate and deepen our compassion, our wisdom and our courage, because life changes constantly and presents us new challenges all the time.' He pulled his shoulders back and sat up straighter on the stool: 'Now, I'd like to talk to you about my grandfather who is a passionate gardener.'

'Your granddad is lovely,' Beverley interjected, with an affectionate smile.

'Oh yes, he is a great man,' Josh agreed enthusiastically. 'Every day he goes to his garden and observes his plants and flowers. If they need water, he waters them. If there are insects eating the leaves, he removes them. If he sees snails, he takes them somewhere else. Thanks to this constant loving care, his garden looks like a paradise, full of lush plants and flowers of every kind and colour. I have the visual proof here.' He pulled some photos out of a folder and handed them out. 'These are pictures I took a couple of weeks ago when I went to visit him.'

As the photos went around, murmurs of admiration confirmed that everyone was very impressed. Josh's grandfather posed proudly near an apple tree, his elbow resting on a rake pole, straw hat on his head and a satisfied smile on his face.

Josh continued: 'Our life is like a plant. If it gets enough sun, water and the right nutrients it will bloom, but if we neglect it and leave it prey to 'parasites' – he mimed quotation marks with his fingers – it won't develop, and sooner or later it will wither. Are you with me? Easy, isn't it?' He chuckled. He had a beautiful open smile and listening to him was a real pleasure.

Lina smiled. She too felt content.

'Buddhist philosophy also tells us that good and evil coexist' Josh resumed, 'and it goes as far as saying that they are inseparable, like two sides of a coin. So, inside of us, in addition to this beautiful nature that we possess, there is also another side, much less pleasant, which is defined by the term 'fundamental darkness'. He shuffled on his stool and straightened his back. 'In the Buddhism of a thousand years ago it was described in a graphic way. To make it memorable and understandable, even to less educated or learned people, it was called the Devil King of the Sixth Heaven. This powerful king had nothing less than ten armies, or troops, at his disposal.'

'He's always scared me this Devil!' Sandra interrupted boldly '...and now you tell me that he's also got ten troops. *Blimey*, better run for cover!' She spoke in English, but her pronunciation came with a strong accent typical of Trieste. It sounded funny and made them laugh.

'The term Devil comes from the Greek,' Carlo addressed her. 'It meant a 'spirit', not necessarily evil as we automatically think, but simply a spirit. It was halfway between the human and the divine, and influenced our state of mind.'

'Quite right!' Josh confirmed. 'But in our case, the Devil King of the Sixth Heaven is not at all kind. It is said that he sends his armies to attack those who are trying to attain enlightenment, in order to hinder, indeed to prevent, this process. Now, centuries later, we talk about 'fundamental darkness' or 'negativity' instead of Devil King of the Sixth Heaven. However – no matter what we call it – it's not a force outside of ourselves. We must always remember this. It is part of who we are.'

'And the ten armies?' Carlo asked, glancing at Sandra with a wry smile.

'They are the different ways in which negativity manifests itself,' Josh explained. 'They were called 'thieves of life', or 'thieves of benefits'. They rob us of the life force we need in order to live in a positive way. They steal the benefits we have already accumulated. Every time we manage to defeat these troops, we take another step toward absolute happiness, enlightenment, and we accomplish our human revolution.'

'And if sometimes they defeat us, we get up and start fighting them again,' Navine added from the cushion where she was sitting with her little son on her lap. She had a clear strong voice: 'Determine to improve. If you fall, get up again and then re-determine. The important thing is to always react against negativity.'

'True!' Nelson confirmed. 'The founder of this school of Buddhism – he was called Nichiren' he said looking at Lina –

'always reminds us that it's 'the heart that's important'. In the end, what do we want? Our happiness and that of others, or their unhappiness? Do we respect ourselves and others, or do we despise them? Do we feel indifferent to them? Maybe we want to use them? The values we hold in our hearts determine all our actions.' He had a warm, deep voice and Lina was happy when he started speaking again. 'However, we must keep in mind a really important thing.' He paused briefly before concluding: 'When we do something really positive, we can expect an attack of negativity.'

'And why is that, 'scuse me?' Sandra asked, waving her hand in the air with the index raised.

'I don't know exactly why,' Nelson turned towards Sandra and smiled at her, 'but I found it to be true in my own life, many times. It's the way our mind works, isn't it? Positive and negative, competing with each other. Once we understand the workings of our mind we are so much more prepared. We won't be taken by surprise so easily. Now, when negativity raises its head, I use it as an opportunity to become stronger, clearer, more determined in the course of action that I am following.' He looked around, hands on his thighs, a broad smile lighting up his face. 'The ancient Buddhist mythology said that the world was the territory of the Devil King of the Sixth Heaven. When he saw that someone was emancipating, he worried because he didn't want to lose his hold over people's hearts. So, to hinder his progress, he'd send one of his armies.'

'What a pain in the ass!' Sandra snapped and made them laugh again.

'Er... sorry but the pain in the ass is yourself, remember?' Carlo pointed out.

'Ah, that's true!' Sandra looked annoyed. 'Damn!'

With a smile, Josh resumed the discussion: 'We can't be intimidated or defeated in this internal struggle to change ourselves and become a better person. This is our mission as Buddhists: to become free and happy, at the same time helping those around us in their process of spiritual growth. Are you ready?'

'The ten armies!' said Tony – the mechanic – intrigued. He took out pen and paper and prepared to take notes. 'I want to write this list down!' he said.

A black cat with white paws made a shy entrance into the living room.

'That's Moocat,' Beverley said to Lina. 'Everyone here knows her. I hope you don't mind cats.'

'Oh, I don't. Don't worry about me,' Lina replied with a smile.

'She is quite nervous around people, so I don't think she will come too close. Just ignore her. She prefers it that way,' Beverley added.

Lina nodded and watched the cat, who had become the centre of attention. She stood at the bottom of a bookshelf, looking up, focused.

'She is getting ready for her act,' Josh commented, making everyone laugh.

To Lina's amazement, with one swift movement, the little cat jumped vertically in the air and reached the top of the bookshelf, to everybody's delight. She then settled near the ceiling, her green eyes observing the participants from a safe place.

'Thank you Moo, good show!' said Josh, looking up at the cat with an amused smile. 'She'll be happy up there and we can now start on the first obstacle: Greed, or being dominated by desires. Does this remind you of anything? It does to me!' He laughed again in a light-hearted way.

'I think I know something about that.' Alex glanced around to make sure no one else wanted to speak; then he crossed his long legs and dangled his hand over his knee. 'I have a tendency to be dominated by desires. I've been like that since I was a child. I always wanted what I didn't have and it really bothered my mother. 'You're never happy', she used to say in frustration. As an adult I hadn't changed much, and my endless desires meant I worked hard, earned a lot of money but spent even more. So I ended up in a lot of debt.' He looked around with an expression as if to say 'how stupid was that'? 'Unfortunately this tendency also led me to three marriages and three divorces. After the first period of falling in love I'd find something I didn't like about my wife and started to feel dissatisfied. My first marriage ended because I started a relationship with a woman who became my second wife and the second marriage, guess why it ended?'

'Because you started a relationship with the woman who became your third wife?' Jane suggested, a shadow of teasing in her voice.

'Exactly!' Alex gave her a knowing look. 'And then that finished too. The same thing happened with work. I kept changing jobs, always as a photographer and constantly wanting what I didn't have, frustrated, critical and – I realized later – very difficult to bear.'

'How hard to live like that!' Beverley commented. There was understanding in her voice.

'Indeed!' Alex confirmed. 'Eventually I found myself exhausted, alone and with nothing. Even my children found it hard to tolerate me – I have three children, one from each marriage – and I can't blame them. I was impossible. At the age of fifty I met this Buddhism and began to observe myself objectively... and it wasn't pretty. I saw that I was a selfish immature man. This caused me a lot of pain. It's not nice to realise that you've wasted your life, living like a weather vane... you know?'

'What's that?' Carlo asked.

'It's one of those devices that people fix on their roof and rotate according to how the wind blows,' Alex explained.

Carlo nodded strongly: 'Ah yes, I know! *Una banderuola*, in Italian.'

'Well, I was just like that. I would jump at any new

opportunity, dropping what I was doing and grabbing everything I could, as if it was owed to me. I was so unhappy, though. Now, a little at a time, I am turning my negative destructive tendencies into positive traits.'

'For example?' Sandra queried. She was sitting on a cushion on the floor with her elbow on one knee, her chin resting on her balled fist, absorbing every word.

'For example,' Alex turned to Sandra, 'when the first symptoms of dissatisfaction start to emerge in a job I'm doing, my tendency is to think: this job is so boring; I want to do something completely different. Or in a friendship, at the first obstacle I start to say to myself: this person is hard work; he wasn't like this when I met him.' But then, as if a light was being turned on, I become aware of my negative thoughts. I feel so excited, and victorious, in this moment of awareness. I think 'Aha! Here you go again, I caught you!'

He laughed and everyone joined him, some nodding in identification.

'At that point my new response becomes: What can *I* do to make this work as exciting as it was in the beginning?' or: how can I contribute to this friendship and take it to a deeper level? Everything changes!' Turning to Sandra once again Alex added: 'Now I think 'what can I give' instead of, as I did in the past, 'what do I get?' Am I being clear?'

'Very clear, thank you,' Sandra nodded her head with a satisfied smile.

'And this attitude makes you happier?' asked Jane.

Both with white hair, sitting side by side, it was beautiful to see the friendship and closeness between them.

'Oh gosh yes! *Much* happier!' Alex answered with conviction, turning to look at her. 'There is no comparison. Now I feel so grateful. Gratitude makes us happy,' he affirmed, looking around. 'Finally, after fifteen years of practice, I like myself. I'm not saying that I don't need to improve any further – the process of growing continues throughout our lives – but I appreciate every step of the journey, and enjoy the challenges.'

His face lit up with a beaming smile.

The little boy stood up from his mother's lap and began to wander around the room, touching everything he could lay his hands on, until he started to fiddle with the electricity socket under the table.

'Don't do that, Connor, it's dangerous,' Navine called out to him. 'Sorry guys, I forgot to bring any toys and he's getting bored.'

'Hold on, I'll get some colours.' Josh went to open a cabinet, out of which he extracted a bunch of felt tip pens and some sheets of whiter paper.

'I'll play with Connor,' offered Suki, the Chinese woman. 'Come darling, let's do some drawing together,' she said with a child-like voice. Her welcoming sweet smile persuaded the little boy to go and sit next to her. One sheet of paper on the floor and one felt tip pen each, they started to draw quietly.

'Thank you for what you said Alex; how encouraging!' Back on his stool, Josh once again took the reins of the discussion. 'Let's move on to the second obstacle, shall we? It's called 'discouragement'. It can manifest as sadness, or worry, or even depression.'

'Oh well, if we start on that one, we could go on forever!' Tracy – the model – exclaimed, waving her manicured hand in the air. Everyone laughed, including her.

She went on: 'I suffer from depression at regular intervals. It's awful. When I am prey to one of these periods, I feel like I'm in a dark alley, with no hope or energy. I don't want to get out of bed and I could unhappily stay there all day long. I really struggle to drag myself to my feet and do something.'

'I am familiar with it too, unfortunately,' Beverley joined in. 'They say it's the sickness of our times. In my case it's mild depression; it comes and goes but, all the same, it's very unpleasant. When it is more serious, I think it's important to seek help. I take herbal medicines and I deal with it through this practice.' She paused for a moment and then resumed in a more concentrated way: 'Depression influences the mind, our thoughts, the way we perceive reality. It's no use saying to those who suffer 'pull yourself together' or even worse 'get on with it' because, in the midst of depression, the way you perceive reality *is* your reality.'

'Absolutely! Mine is clinical depression, and is an illness,' Tracy declared. 'Those who say things like 'pull yourself together' have never suffered from depression. They're lucky!'

'Indeed!' Beverley agreed. 'To try to keep my spirit buoyant, every morning when I'm chanting, I vow to myself that I will be an active force for peace and happiness in my environment. Then I do my best to put it into practice. I decide: Whatever problem I have to confront, is part of my mission. I will use it to create value and to make this present suffering the cause of my future happiness. Indeed, I believe that I have chosen that particular problem in order to become stronger and happier. Once upon a time I could have seen it as my karma, but, in this new light, it becomes my mission. Instead of thinking that I'm a victim of my circumstances, I feel that I am in charge of my life. This gives me incredible strength,' she declared with powerful conviction.

'Oh Beverley, you're awesome!' exclaimed Tracy, clearly inspired.

'Bev is great, because she remembers to put the philosophy into practice,' Josh intervened. 'I often forget to do that, and sometimes I feel overwhelmed by my difficulties, especially at first, but not Bev. At the crucial moment she remembers it and uses it!'

Everyone laughed, including Beverley who added: 'I do also sometimes feel overwhelmed, but not for too long. When I confront reality in this way I am filled with hope and self-confidence; my physical energy increases and everything becomes not only easier but also exciting.'

Suddenly Moocat jumped off the bookshelf – it seemed as if

she could fly – and landed with a thud just next to Tracy. With a hand over her heart, she shrieked: 'Bloody hell cat! You give me a heart attack!' Her cry frightened the skittish pussycat, who fled towards the bedroom, making them all laugh.

John took advantage of the break and went to get a glass of water from the jug. 'Does anyone want water' he offered?

'Yes please... me too,' a few voices said. He filled several grasses with water and passed them around.

'Thank you,' said Jane, taking a sip from her glass. 'I am struck by the word 'sadness',' she continued, in a quiet but firm voice. 'Discouragement and sadness almost destroyed me. When Ricky became ill with cancer he was twenty years old. He was my only child.' She looked at Lina, knowing that she too had lost a daughter. She spoke with a steady voice. 'During his illness, to overcome the anguish that plagued me, I kept telling myself to live in the present, that none of us can foresee the future. Thanks to this I have beautiful memories of trips we made, afternoons spent at the park, picnics with friends and moments of true hilarity between us. When he died, at the age of twenty-five, I wanted to die too. But I couldn't. I was sadness personified. I used to tell myself that Ricky would have hated to see me like that. It was with the encouragement of my friends, you and others, that I overcame those difficult times. I have so much gratitude for the support I received.'

Everyone was listening, almost holding their breath.

'I realized that through Ricky's illness I had developed so much wisdom, compassion and courage that I was overflowing with them. I had more than enough to share with others, and I did just that. I started dedicating myself to people with cancer and their families. As I gave back what I had received I became stronger. I found more clarity and eventually felt the desire to open the door to a glimmer of light. I was feeling my life force grow, at last. It became more and more powerful, until one day I realized that I had defeated the darkness. I had transformed the overwhelming sadness that had threatened to annihilate me.'

She paused. No one broke the silence. 'I missed Ricky a lot, and I still do. He taught me so much. Thanks to him I'm the person I am now... and I can say that I'm happy.'

Lina would have liked to tell her that she too had suffered greatly from the loss of her daughter, and still did. She had to make an effort not to get up and hug her, but sensed that Jane could feel her emotion.

Looking at Jane with affection and admiration, Tony said: 'You're phenomenal, Jane, and a great inspiration for all those who know you.'

'So true!' Navine agreed energetically. 'You are a wonderful example.'

Hearing his mother's voice, Connor abandoned his felt tip pens on the floor and rushed back to sit on her lap.

Lina couldn't take her eyes off him; he was adorable in his tiny blue jeans and white top. Eventually Connor met her gaze and gave her a broad charming smile. She wished she could hug him tight.

Navine settled with him on her crossed legs and, turning to the group, continued: 'For me, sadness also has a positive aspect because it's part of the process of transformation. Sometimes we feel sad to leave a part of us behind, even if we are happy with this change. Like a snake that sheds its skin, we let go of those aspects of ourselves that we no longer need. For a short time, we go through a little mourning. It is the destruction of the old for the creation of something new. In Hindu mythology the god Shiva represents this process.'

'That is so true. Thank you Navine!' Josh smiled at her. 'Are we ready for the next one? The third troop is represented by hunger or thirst. Fortunately, I don't think any of us suffers from these two things, at least I hope not.'

The young thin man who introduced himself as Jim shyly raised his hand. He must have been Micky's age, maybe a little older.

'I suffered from them until recently,' he revealed candidly. 'I'm new to this group, but some of you know that I spent more than a year homeless. I had no work or money. I never thought it could happen to me, but it did.' As he looked around, purple patches began to appear on his neck. 'I was working for a construction company. Then, with the recession, things went from bad to worse and I, who had been the last to be hired, was the first to be fired. With no savings I soon ran out of money to pay rent. Maybe I could have claimed housing benefit, but I didn't know the system well enough and didn't even try. Eventually I was evicted and quickly found myself homeless. For a while I slept on friends' sofas, a week here, a week there. When I no longer had the courage to ask anyone, I ended up on the street. If you don't have an address, you can't apply for benefits. I was hungry, cold, thirsty... and ended up begging.'

The reddish patches had spread to his smooth cheeks while he nervously wrung his white skinny hands. 'When you're begging, you have this feeling of being invisible. People don't look at you. They look the other way... not all of them, but most. One day, out of desperation, I stole and got caught. I ended up in jail for two months. At least I had food and I wasn't so cold, but losing my freedom was horrible. I hated every day and every night in that cell and I swore to myself that I would never go back.'

There was a grave silence.

Navine broke it: 'You poor thing! So young! And what happened after that?'

'A new friend, a colleague of the social worker who looked after me' – Jim glanced gratefully at Nelson and nodded at him – 'told me about this Buddhist practice, over a cup of coffee. He encouraged me to experiment with it. As soon as I did, I began to feel calmer, more confident, although I couldn't explain how it was possible. After only two days, with Nelson's help, I found a room and from that moment I could claim unemployment benefit. Then I began to work as a volunteer for a charity and a month later they started to pay me a little... it's not much but at least it's a job. I am rebuilding my life. I am regaining confidence in myself and developing my self-esteem.' Jim's expression lit up as he looked at Nelson with an amused smile. 'I had never heard about self-esteem until Nelson explained what it was,' he chuckled.

Lina's heart went out to him. He was so thin and vulnerable, yet there was such strength in him, a determination that aroused in her a feeling of wonder.

Jim continued: 'Last month I enrolled on a course to become a social worker and decided that I will never again find myself in a situation like that, destitute and homeless. If I hadn't met him and this practice I don't know if I would still be alive,' he concluded, looking at Nelson, who was smiling, his eyes glistening with tears.

Lina gazed intently at Nelson. There was such a huge contrast between his muscular shoulders and arms – he looked like a wrestler – and the moved expression on his face.

'I didn't know you had such a hard time,' said Navine, a wrinkle of sorrow between her eyebrows.

'Hardly anyone knows, but I'm not ashamed,' Jim replied. 'In fact, I'm even glad that it happened, because it made me change direction. I no longer feel as alone and insecure as I did before. Now I want to do a job that is good for society, as well as for me, and this makes me feel a lot stronger. I know I'll be able to overcome any difficulty that comes my way.'

For the first time he smiled openly, showing a gap between his front teeth, and looked even younger, just a boy.

Chapter 13

AT SOFIA'S HOUSE

Looking pale and drawn, feeling exhausted, Sofia sat down on the couch, the portable phone resting on her lap.

Micky came down the stairs whistling a tune and sat down next to her. 'What's for dinner Mum?' He put his arm around her shoulders and planted a kiss on her cheek.

'I don't want anything. Are you hungry?' Sofia leaned back on the sofa.

'What a silly question! I'm *always* hungry!'

'It's true... you're still growing. I don't know anything Micky, I can't think straight. I am really concerned about your grandmother.'

'Don't worry Mum. Gran will be fine and in a little while she'll be home, you'll see.'

'I hope so, love... but I am worried. Where is she? She's not answering the phone. Charlie said that she took her to the bus stop at about five-thirty. She should have been here by six, half-six at the latest – Sofia glanced at her wristwatch, frowning – 'and now it's gone eight...'

She dried her clammy hands on her summer dress, staring at the flowery pattern without seeing it. 'There are terrible riots out there... Maybe she's found herself caught up in some way... I have a bad feeling. I told her to call a taxi and instead she got the bus. Why?' Sofia wondered in a tense voice, her hand clenched in a fist around a tissue. 'I should've just gone to fetch her. I bet she got lost.'

'Gran's smart, Mum. She will have made friends with

someone on the bus. You know how she loves to talk to everyone,' Micky loudly reassured her. 'Maybe I'll go out and look for her. But first I have to eat. I'm so hungry I could gobble up a whole buffalo.'

'You are not going anywhere... we'll end up losing you too,' Sofia objected, brusquely sitting upright on the couch.

'Come on Mum, I'm not a kid, you know? I wouldn't get lost.' Micky sounded insulted. 'What do you think? That I am a complete idiot?'

She had managed to upset even her son, who never took offence at anything – Sofia thought, with a squeeze in her heart. 'Yes, all right, but you are not going out while those crazy people are burning everything,' she said with dismay, pointing her chin at the black TV screen. She let herself plop once more against the sofa cushions. 'Have you seen what they are doing? They set fire to a pub; they're smashing windows and looting the shops. They're out of control.'

Micky brought her back to the here and now: 'I'm as hungry as a wolf.'

'I couldn't eat a thing, I'm tired and don't feel like cooking.'

'Then I'll put some water on for pasta and prepare something tasty.'

'Are you able to?' Sofia looked at him askance.

'Of course I'm able!' That upset sound in his voice again. 'You'll see! Pasta and pesto, is that okay?'

Sofia brought the tissue to her nose and nodded with a tired smile. 'Where's your dad?' she asked, looking around.

'In the garden shed, with his plants. Where else? Do you want me to turn the television on?'

'I don't know if I want to see what's happening.'

'Maybe we'll see Gran on the telly,' Micky said with real enthusiasm and rushed to turn the television on.

Sofia tried to reflect. Where was her mother? On the phone Charlie confessed that they had drunk 'a little'. Knowing Charlie, that 'little' could have been a bottle or two, and her mother usually only drank a glass of wine at dinner time. God knows how much she had drunk today... and where had she gone?

On the television they weren't talking about anything else. The camera framed an old three-story building with a turret at the top. It was burning violently. It was a carpet shop on a street corner and the flames devoured it as if it were made of cardboard. Shocked onlookers milled around on the street below.

Rows of policemen in black uniform wore helmets of the same colour with the visor lowered over their faces. They were standing to attention, holding see-through shields and long truncheons, observing the scene, motionless.

A journalist interviewed the tenant of one of the apartments above the burning shop, who – with that incredible calm indignation that distinguished the British – complained that no one was doing anything to extinguish the fire. Meanwhile his flat was going up in smoke in front of his eyes.

The image moved onto two burning cars next to the pavement. It then moved and framed a double-decker bus on fire. The flames were as high as the buildings that flanked it.

The camera captured looters ripping up shop shutters by hand and kicking the windows in. They came out carrying televisions bigger than themselves. Some, with their faces uncovered, were carrying armfuls of clothes taken in bulk. Others had filled trolleys with food and looked exultant, their eyes frenzied, pirates at the boarding. Bystanders stood transfixed, phones in hand capturing every moment.

There were boys on the pavements with their faces covered by sweaters or rolled up scarves. Some were in the middle of the road ready to improvise. Gusts of black smoke rose towards the sky. What was happening to these people? Sofia stared at the television screen, watching the broadcast, speechless, incredulous.

She heard Steve's steps coming up the stairs. She couldn't find the strength or the courage to look at him. She held her breath.

He approached and sat down on the sofa next to her, encircled her shoulders with his arm and kissed her hair: 'Still no news?'

She shook her head, but that little gesture of tenderness from her husband eroded her unsteady self-control. Her nerves on edge, tired, confused, Sofia felt she was falling apart, like a sand castle overwhelmed by a strong wave, and melted into tears. 'Where is she? How has she disappeared?' The words came out broken, her voice hoarse, she struggled to draw her breath. She felt guilty for not having spent more time with her mother. She hadn't even given her a hug since her arrival, too busy with her things, her worries, her misgivings. These feelings gnawed at her.

Steve reassured her: 'She'll be stuck somewhere and, with these riots, she probably doesn't know how to get back home.'

'But why not call, at least?' she muttered.

'Maybe she doesn't have the number.'

'But I gave her a phone!'

'Has your mother ever used one?' Steve was a practical man.

'No, and she has no idea how to use it,' Sofia admitted. 'I tried to explain it to her, but she wasn't listening; she was in a hurry to see Charlie.'

Steve was reflecting in silence. After a while, he spoke in a calm voice: 'Your mother is a wise woman. She wouldn't get into trouble... so we can imagine that she's somewhere safe, waiting till she can come back. She probably can't call, or doesn't know how to, and will be concerned about you. I'm sure she knows you'll be terribly worried.'

Steve was right. Her mother was a prudent person and wouldn't put herself in a dangerous situation. With his rational way, her husband managed to show her things from another perspective, reassuring her a little.

But they couldn't carry on doing nothing for much longer.

He seemed to read her mind: 'Let's wait another half hour and then we'll call the police. Maybe in the meantime Lina will ring the doorbell and walk in with that purple hat of hers.'

For a moment he managed to make her laugh, but the image of her mother's hat shook her deeply, and Sofia started to feel tears pushing again behind her eyes.

'I'm going to prepare some dinner,' Steve patted her hand and prepared to stand up.

'Micky has already started, he's in the kitchen.'

'Then I better go immediately, before he blows the house up,' he joked. 'But...' he suddenly recalled, 'didn't Lina make dinner this morning?'

'Ohhh... yes, she made lasagne, I'd forgotten,' Sofia stuttered, 'but... I don't want to eat it if she's not here.' She added the last sentence after a hesitant pause, afraid Steve might object – they seem to disagree all the time, even on the small things. But this wasn't the case.

'Quite!' her husband replied thoughtfully. 'We'll prepare something simple then, and we'll eat the lasagne together when Lina is back.'

Sofia looked at him as he walked towards the kitchen, her heart heavy.

Chapter 14

PLEASURE, COURAGE AND FEAR

'Wow! What a powerful experience.' Josh looked at Jim with affection and admiration. 'Thank you Jim. Now... let's move on to the fourth troop: attachment to pleasures.' He looked around. 'The first things that spring to mind are sex, good food and a cold beer, or two.' He winked and laughed.

Lina really liked Josh. She felt as if she had known him forever.

'Also watching a good movie, taking a walk in nature, or by the sea,' said Jane.

'Climbing a mountain, reading a good book,' added Tony.

'Dancing!' declared Sandra, who shimmied and giggled.

'Talking with friends about my dreams and determinations,' said Tracy.

'Spending an afternoon with my children,' Alex declared.

'Buddhism tells us that there is no problem with pleasure in itself,' Beverley remarked. 'It's when desires control us that the alarm bells should ring. When pleasure comes to the detriment of our balance, when it hurts us instead of doing us good, then it becomes a problem.'

'In a way, when we are in control of ourselves, pleasure is in perfect harmony with life, isn't it?' Tony observed, tilting his head of shiny dark curls. 'There's nothing better than enjoying beautiful things. It's a way of rewarding ourselves after having worked hard. It's the attachment to pleasures that is a problem, when we never have enough and want more and more.'

'Welcome to pleasure then, and let's curb the excesses!' Josh settled on his stool and grinned: 'Let's turn to the fifth troop, which is represented by tiredness, lethargy or indifference. Perhaps even the terms 'passivity' or 'apathy' can express this state of mind.'

'Passivity is dangerous, and so is indifference,' Tracy said forcefully, raising her perfectly defined eyebrows. 'It may seem harmless to just keep my head down and mind my own business, but in reality when I don't inform myself and don't get involved, I play into the hands of those in power. I know people who don't even vote when there are elections, as if it had nothing to do with them.'

'Maybe there isn't a party or a leader that appeals to them,' said John.

'Okay, in that case choose the one that is nearest to your beliefs,' retorted Tracy. 'But not voting at all is crazy. If we don't assume our responsibilities as citizens, we'll lose all the progress and benefits that we have earned in years of democracy.' She was heating up and gesticulating. 'What I really dislike here in the UK are the tabloids. They are terrible. They come out with these huge exaggerated headlines. They use words like WAR, THREAT, DANGER, chosen to manipulate emotions, to create fear, division and hatred. They stoke up conflict between one group of people and another.' She ran her restless fingers through her thick wavy hair and irritably moved a tuft from her forehead. 'They're responsible for many of the problems of this society,' she stated vehemently.

'But people can choose to read other newspapers if they want to, can't they?' Sandra objected, looking up from her cushion.

'True! But a lot of people choose the tabloids, I've never understood why,' Alex observed calmly. 'Maybe it makes them feel superior. When we criticize others, we feel better about ourselves, for a minute. Don't we? And less alone, like we're part of a group and therefore stronger... safer.'

'Like a pack!' exclaimed Tracy.

'Or a flock,' Alex observed.

'Aren't we doing the same here, now, by talking like this about the readers of those tabloids?' Navine asked pointedly.

Sandra laughed. Carlo smiled. John nodded his head.

'I think it's important to keep an eye on reality, all the time,' observed Alex, replying to Navine. 'I enjoy having dialogue with people who think differently to me, who have different perspectives. When I'm willing to really listen, I leave the exchange feeling like I've grown, and they do too, I think. But when a person or the media, in order to manipulate public opinion, intentionally distort or fabricate facts... that's a different thing and we should speak out against it.'

'I think it should be an offence for newspapers to make false claims, don't you?' Jane commented. 'If, for example, the manufacturers of a washing machine make false claims, they can be taken to court. Shouldn't it be the same for the tabloids... and for the politicians?'

Tony nodded: 'Well, there are libel laws, aren't there? But whether they are enforced is a different thing. Some newspapers seem to get away with publishing whatever they want!'

John lifted his index finger to indicate he wanted to speak. 'What worries me is how easy it is to be indifferent towards injustices that don't touch us directly. For example, if we see someone being bullied and we look the other way, we are accepting and even validating that behaviour.'

'I know what you mean, John.' Beverley pushed her long fringe to one side. 'However I think there are times when people are not aware of that injustice. For example, I can feel when I am treated unfairly because I'm a woman. But I may be less aware of how people of other races, with a foreign accent or a disability are discriminated against, because I don't live their reality.' She paused. 'Sometimes it's not easy to understand what it's like to live in someone else's skin.'

'Then we need to become more conscious,' Tony pointed

out. 'We need to listen to people who say they are being discriminated against. And we must watch out for it.'

'But there are so many injustices all the time, and we can't get involved in all of them,' Sandra observed, shifting the position of her legs on her big cushion.

'It's true! We are bombarded with news from around the world,' Alex agreed, 'and can't take on everything at once. However, we can have an influence on our direct environment, if we take responsibility for what's nearby and touches us closely. This is how we start, from ourselves and what surrounds us.'

'Shouldn't we be out there, then? Protesting with everyone else?' John asked, pointing his chin towards the window.

'I only found out about the protest on my way here,' Tony observed, 'and it was already out of control so... I'm glad I'm not there, actually.'

'There are many ways of getting involved and making a difference,' Nelson noted. 'When we take part in local activities, in the neighbourhood committee or the like, we are taking responsibility. Being here, as we are now, sharing and learning from each other, we're making a difference. When we go back out into the world, with hope and confidence, we are more powerful.'

'What a big topic!' Josh exclaimed, straightening his back on the backless stool. 'We could discuss each of the ten armies for a whole meeting, and maybe we'll do so, eventually. This time we'll have a general look at all ten.'

Navine's little boy had disappeared and his mother glanced around nervously. 'Sorry to interrupt, but can anyone see Connor?' she asked. 'I worry when he is too quiet.'

The discussion came to a halt.

'I'll have a look.' Beverley stood up and went into the kitchen. They heard her say: 'Oh darling, that's not what you do with flour. Come with me, sweetie.' She came back into the living room holding the little boy in her arms. His hands and face were streaked white with flour. 'He's just strewn half a pack of white flour onto the floor,' she said with an amused smile.

'Oh Connor, you naughty boy!' Navine scolded him, taking him into her arms. 'Why did you do that?'

'I want to make chapatti,' the little boy replied.

They all burst into loud laughter.

While Navine took him into the bathroom to clean him, Josh quickly nipped to the kitchen to sweep the flour off the floor.

Finally, the discussion started again, with Connor sitting quietly in his mother's lap.

'A few minutes ago Tracy mentioned fear, which is in fact the sixth troop,' Josh said.

'I was afraid earlier,' Lina ventured bravely, feeling involved in the discussion, 'when I was standing opposite the police station. Those people started breaking everything and then they set the police car on fire. It seemed like war. It brought back some bad memories.'

'I was scared too,' admitted Beverley, 'for me, for Josh, for you Lina, for the people who were there to protest peacefully. It was getting completely out of control. But we must remember that those people are not the only aggressors. They were protesting because a young man, who was my age, was shot dead.'

'What is the opposite of fear?' John asked, uncrossing his legs. 'Is it courage? When I am afraid about something I chant to draw out courage. Since I started my own business I'm always nervous of not having enough work. I have some debts and the interest is very high. If I'm unable to pay the monthly instalment I'll end up owing even more.' He rested his hands on his knees: 'I take all the work that comes. I often have more work than I can handle, but my fear remains a constant in the background.'

Nelson addressed him warmly: 'For me, trust is the opposite of fear. It's important to develop trust, I believe, because sometimes it is precisely what we lack. If I feel anxious about the future, I tell myself that it is much better to have confidence in the future. When I make an effort to chant with confidence everything changes in here,' he touched his chest with his index finger. 'I carry on chanting until the feeling of being overwhelmed subsides and hope, energy and optimism start to bubble up.' He shuffled on his cushion and continued: 'The effect of this shift is incredible, both mentally and physically. My Buddhist practice teaches me to decide what I want. When I determine to challenge myself, I do it with conviction that I will succeed. We are often defeated by our insecurities. So, the first thing to do is win over our doubt, our fear. Real courage lies in facing reality head on. Then we can clearly see what we have to do.'

'I like this!' exclaimed Sandra.

Nelson smiled: 'One of my great goals is to narrow as much as possible the gap between who I want to be and who I am. Between the values I believe in and the actions I carry out. To combat my self-doubt, every morning I chant to praise my life. This reminds me that my true nature is strong, wise and full of compassion. I connect with the rest of the universe and I really feel this connection, it's such a strong energy.' He put one hand on his belly and the other one over his heart, to express where the energy was coming from. 'From that moment on I have no more hesitation. The fear vanishes, leaving me strong, free and happy. When I am in this state of mind I recognize the potential of the people I come in contact with – quite naturally – and I am able to express great affection for them.'

'Very nice for the people you work with, especially if they have big problems of their own,' Josh commented.

'All my clients have big challenges. My role is to encourage them to believe in themselves, to act wisely and with courage, because many of the problems that people face are caused by fear. That's when we make decisions that are not what's best for us.'

Suki raised her index finger and, addressing Nelson, asked: 'You said the words 'praise my life'. I am not sure what that means. I am sorry, my English is not very good.'

'I don't know what it means either,' said Sandra, waving her hand in the air, keen to understand. 'And you Carlo?'

Carlo, who was repeatedly ringing the police station waiting for someone to answer, shook his head: 'No, I don't know exactly what it means.'

'It means to feel profound reverence for my life, and life in general,' Nelson replied. 'Is this a little clearer?'

Suki tilted her head slightly. 'A little,' she said, but didn't look convinced.

'Yes, I understand that,' Sandra declared. 'It's the same word in Italian, reverenza,' she said turning to Carlo, who nodded strongly.

'It means to have deep respect and feel gratitude for our lives and all life,' added Tony, turning to Suki.

'To venerate life,' suggested Beverly, at which point Sandra confirmed once again that she understood, but Suki still looked dubious.

'To cherish it... How can I explain?' Beverley scratched her head trying to find a way Suki would definitely understand. In a flash of inspiration she added: 'With each Nam-myoho-renge-kyo that I recite I, symbolically, bow to my life,' and she bowed her head, her hands clasped in front of her heart, 'to the essence of my life, and all life.'

Suki's eyes opened wide and she beamed. 'Oh yes, I understand,' she stated, nodding happily.

Beverley smiled and enthusiastically added: 'That's when my Buddhahood comes out, even with all my faults and imperfections.'

Lina was listening attentively and taking on board this last dialogue, whilst still thinking of what Nelson had said about fear and making wrong decisions. Did she have fears? Her first instinctive answer was that she had many.

'That was such a good explanation for praising our lives; thank you so much!' Alex spoke with a soft voice, his hands resting over his crossed legs. 'I want to say something more about fear, if I may. As a photographer I'm very much aware of what fear makes us look like. It makes us ugly. Think of the facial expression we have when we are afraid. And what are the thoughts that go through our minds in those moments? We build walls. We think about how to defend ourselves and how to attack. We live in the grip of mistrust and suspicion.'

'Yes, we start to shut down,' Nelson agreed. Then – unexpectedly – looking at the group with candour he added: 'Sometimes I'm afraid of death.'

'Your own or that of others?' Sandra asked promptly, her eyes full of curiosity.

'Both.'

Lina felt great fondness for this big strong man who showed all his vulnerability without a shadow of shame.

'I'm not afraid of death,' declared Navine addressing Nelson, 'because I grew up in a culture where we accept death naturally, as we accept life. Unlike Western culture, where death is not spoken of and is feared, we Indians often talk about it and therefore live more consciously.' Connor settled more comfortably on his mother's lap, his big brown eyes intelligent and alert. 'I also have fears though, but these are mainly to do with my child; fear of him getting seriously ill, for example and... Yes, although I am not afraid of my own death, I hope I will never have to witness the death of my son.' She stroked the child's back whilst gazing thoughtfully at Lina and then Jane. 'So I chant every day for protection and I also chant to improve myself. Every morning I think 'Today I want to become a little better than I was yesterday, and to have a harmonious accident-free day. Then, every evening, I remind myself to chant with gratitude, because... think about it: if I'm driving and almost have a serious accident, when I chant in the evening I express gratitude that nothing has happened, right?' The others nodded in agreement. 'But if that day everything went smoothly and I didn't have a near-miss, I often don't remember to feel gratitude. And instead I should, don't you think?'

Lina was thinking about this last thing and failed to notice that she had been asked a question and all the eyes were on her.

Beverley repeated the question: 'And you, Lina, what are your fears?'

Surprised by the attention, but also flattered that they wanted to know her thoughts, Lina sat more upright and addressed the whole group: 'My greatest fear is to become a burden for my family.' She didn't expect such a clear answer from herself. Maybe she had never acknowledged her fear. She looked at Beverley, Nelson, Josh, and continued: 'My daughter wants me to move to London to live with her because I'm getting old, but I don't feel old. On the contrary, I feel young, especially after a day like today with Charlie. But the years go by and one day I won't have anything to offer. When I won't be able to do the housework or cook I will become a burden and I'm afraid of this.' She felt proud at how well she had expressed herself.

Navine spoke with warmth: 'Each of us has a lot to give, but older people have even more.' She looked at Lina with kind eyes. 'In the Indian society elderly people are considered real treasures, for their experience and wisdom. Older people have a vision of the present rooted in the past. They know how things used to be, so they can appreciate what we have today. Young people can't possibly have that awareness yet.' She smiled when her little son turned around and stroked her cheek with his little hand.

Beverley joined in: 'I think you have a lot to give both to your family and to society, Lina. With your experience and wisdom you can help younger people put their problems in perspective. You can support them to make wise decisions, for example. If you see that your children are stressed because of work, money, difficult relationships, you can listen and empathise. It's not just a question of what we have to contribute materially. Your presence in itself is an enormous contribution to the well-being of others. This is especially true for a positive person like you. Don't underestimate that. We often measure ourselves for what we have, what we give. But others love us for who we are,' she concluded gently.

Lina smiled gratefully at her: 'I had never looked at it that way. Thank you.'

The black cat made a surreptitious entrance into the living room and advanced shyly, keeping close to the wall. Connor spotted her immediately and stood up to go to her.

'Leave her alone, Connor,' Navine warned him. 'She might scratch you.'

'Be gentle with her,' Josh instructed the child, '... if she lets you anywhere near her.'

As soon as Moocat saw the child approach, she jumped onto the window sill, as far away as possible from him.

'Come and sit here,' Alex encouraged the little boy to sit on his lap, 'at least you'll be near her. She may warm to you, if you stay quiet.'

With the child on Alex's knees and the cat right behind them, the discussion continued.

'I don't think that fear is some bad thing we need to get rid of all together... it can actually teach us a lot,' Beverley reflected, her slender hands moving in rhythm with her words. 'In fact, when I'm afraid and keep going anyway, those are probably my most courageous moments. Sometimes my fears show me what I want. It shows me the desires hidden in my heart, that I perhaps haven't had the courage to acknowledge.' She crossed her legs and clasped her knee. 'For example, at the moment I'm looking for a new job. I have lots of fears around the idea of change. I wonder whether I'm good enough for the roles I'm applying for. At some point my anxiety got so intense and confusing that I just felt stuck. So I wrote a list of my fears. One of the biggest ones was that, if I did find a new job, I wouldn't get on with my colleagues. I was afraid that it might be a strained environment... that I'd try too hard to fit in. What this showed me though, is that one thing I really want is to work somewhere where I can freely be myself and build a harmonious and joyful workplace. So I wrote that down as a determination. I did that with all my fears and then I threw away the first list and just kept the list of the determinations.' She paused, looked at Connor who was twisting to stroke the cat's tail and smiled, showing a dimple on each cheek. Then she resumed: 'I imagine that fear is like the wind. When the wind is very strong, like the 'bora' of Trieste for example,' – she glanced at Sandra, who came from Trieste, and grinned – 'and it blows in our face, it makes it so difficult to walk, it can stop us completely. But if we turn around so that the wind is behind us and pushes us, it becomes a force that helps us move forward and grow. Then the fear becomes my friend and even helps me!'

Lina really liked that example, because she had experienced the strength of the wind called 'bora'. The idea of having it blow from behind rather than in front seemed brilliant!

'That's great Bev. Thank you!' said Tony, who always spoke very politely. 'I think that courage can also be the constant and discreet effort to do what we think is right.'

'This is a nice concept Tony,' noted Suki, with her timid voice and strong Chinese accent. She was definitely struggling to speak in English, but striving to do so. 'Can you give an example, please?'

'Of course! For me, right now, it means talking to my colleagues at work about respect and self-care.' He smiled at her. 'Basically, I get quite upset when I hear them brag about drinking till they black out. Hearing the things they do when they're smashed makes me cringe. I could easily walk away, or pretend I don't hear them, and keep myself to myself. But I actually like these people and have nothing against having a drink together sometimes. And so, I risked becoming unpopular and started to talk about drinking in moderation, eating healthily, respecting your body, thinking about the causes they make and the effects on their life.'

'And are you popular Tony?' teased Josh.

Everyone laughed, including Tony, who replied: 'Actually, you might be surprised, but they did listen to what I had to say. At the same time, they are teaching me to be more light-hearted. Jokingly, they call me the philosopher' – he giggled heartily – 'sometimes they even ask my advice! It's strange, because I'm the youngest of them all, but they treat me as if I were the eldest.'

'Because you're young but wise,' Suki commented nodding repeatedly.

'I had a similar experience at work.' Nelson spoke with enthusiasm. 'For a long time I had noticed that nobody paid any attention to the emotional wellbeing of our young social workers. Our job is emotionally very taxing. We are in contact with people who are struggling with big problems. Our role is to help them, but who supports the social worker? When someone is at the beginning of their career, still inexperienced, he or she can only draw from the knowledge accumulated during the years of training. It's not easy to be the 'rock' that others can lean on, the 'pillar' that supports, reassures, gives confidence.' He shook his head full of curls, recalling the past. 'I remember the anxiety I felt at the beginning when I heard my clients' stories of poverty, abuse, injustice, domestic violence, bullying. It was as if I was being hit in the face, but I couldn't show how much it affected me.'

Lina noticed that Josh smiled at Nelson as if he knew him well. Beverley looked at him with affection, too. 'My role required for me to remain calm, attentive and to discuss the situation in a rational, even detached way. You can imagine! Many times I felt the need to ask for help for my own mental state. But there was no one I could turn to. I had to manage by myself. So, one day I decided that things had to change.'

'What did you do?' John's eyes shone with interest.

'I put forward the case for support for all young employees. I spoke to the director, the deputy director and anyone who was willing to listen. Some of them understood, but didn't do anything. Others told me that everyone just had to get on with it, budgets were stretched to the limit... things had always been that way... and that I worried too much. But I didn't give up. I was determined to change the situation. Young colleagues were taking sick leave because of stress – they were falling like flies – and for those left working the pressure became unbearable. I kept writing letters and petitions to the Ministry of Health, trade unions, my city councillor and my MP.'

'You are a force of nature Nelson!' Jane exclaimed, impressed with him.

Nelson laughed and nodded, as if to say 'wait till you hear the rest'. 'Finally, just last week, I got an appointment with the general director of social services. He listened to me very carefully. When I finished talking he said: I fully agree with you, Nelson. We need to take care of the new staff. It takes so long to train them, we don't want to lose them. Would you be willing to set up the support service?' Nelson opened his eyes wide and pointed his forefinger on his chest: 'He asked *me* to set up the new department, which is called Support Service for Young Social Workers... the structure, the programme, the whole curriculum basically.'

A spontaneous loud applause arose from all the participants – including Navine's child who clapped his hands and laughed happily – followed by congratulations, cheers, whistling and cries of victory.

Jim looked the happiest of all and his eyes were wet with emotion.

Lina burst out laughing, infected by the unexpected euphoria. Her heart was full of joy and excitement for what Nelson had achieved.

'And do they pay you more Nelson?' Josh shouted to make himself heard over the din.

'No! It's voluntary,' Nelson shouted back.

They all burst into a deafening laughter, including Nelson who was howling, throwing himself backwards and repeatedly hitting his thigh with his hand. As soon as he could speak again he explained: 'There are no funds for this year, but if it's successful, next year they'll ring-fence a budget.'

The mirth continued for a while, accompanied by pats on the shoulders for Nelson.

To Lina he looked the happiest person she had ever seen in her life.

Suddenly a loud noise from outside made them jump. It sounded like an explosion.

'Mamma mia, what's going on?' Carlo wondered, rising from the cushion he was sitting on. He went to the window and moved the curtain: 'There is black smoke everywhere. Can I open it for a moment?'

Chapter 15

BREAKING THE ICE

Claudia approached with a hesitant step and looked at her mother with an unsure expression in her green eyes. 'Everything will be fine, Mum. They'll find her safe and sound, you'll see,' she declared.

But, under her daughter's apparent confidence, Sofia could perceive the quivering vibration of fear. She looked up, nodded and went back to look at her hands. 'We have to start calling the hospitals.' She struggled to pronounce the words. 'Are you stopping here or going out?'

'Are you kidding? I'm staying here with you. Until we find Nonna I'm not going anywhere.'

Claudia grabbed the phone book from the shelf near the rounded window and started leafing through the pages looking for the hospital section.

Sofia raised her eyes and noticed that her daughter was wearing a turquoise skirt down to her knees – it had white lace at the bottom – and a white lacy top. She was looking very pretty. Her clothes must have been new, because she had never seen them before. In the past she would have paid her a compliment, but this time she said nothing.

Claudia took pen and paper and began to make a list of hospitals and their respective numbers. 'What's Nonna's favourite dessert?' she asked while scribbling the first notes. 'It's carrot cake, isn't it?'

'Yes,' Sofia replied with a faint voice, unsure as to how to react to her daughter's offerings.

'Do we have the ingredients?' Claudia spoke casually, without looking at her.

'I think so.'

'So, first we ring the hospitals and then we'll make the cake, all right? You and me.'

Sofia felt as if she were on a raft tossed by waves. Great confusion overwhelmed her. Her heart was in turmoil. After months of silence, distance, resentment and consuming pain, her daughter was trying to encourage her. But she didn't know how to answer. She was no longer used to her kindness, let alone her closeness. A combination of anguish and embarrassment, a tangled loneliness and the disquiet of always saying something wrong, were mixing in her stomach and forming a sickening knot.

Robotically Sofia passed her the requested phone and Claudia began calling the first hospital: 'Excuse me, we lost my grandmother. Can you tell me if by any chance she is there?'

Sofia's heart stopped while she listened with trepidation. Her daughter was answering the questions, giving name and surname: 'Lina D'Angelo'. She waited, apparently calm. Then she thanked the hospital operator. 'She is not there. Good sign!' Claudia looked straight at her mother.

They hadn't looked each other in the eyes for months. Sofia turned hers away. The uneasiness was too strong.

Claudia dialled another number, waited patiently for the answer and then asked a question similar to the first one: 'Excuse me; we're looking for my grandmother who hasn't returned home... Yes, Lina D'Angelo... seventy-five... yes I'll wait... are you sure? Thank you... thank you very much.' 'She is not there either.' Her eyes paused on Sofia's face, before drawing a line over the second hospital's name. She continued in this way, more and more confident.

Sofia observed her. Claudia was a young woman now, poised, well-spoken, kind and polite. She yearned for the time when she was little. She was an intelligent, beautiful child, generous and full of enthusiasm. Those years had gone by quickly. Did she pay her enough attention? Did she help her grow up? Was she a good mother, or did she neglect her children, too busy with work? She always did her best, but maybe she could have done more, or differently. Now she couldn't go back. In her heart, she apologized to her daughter for all the things she hadn't been able to give her.

Claudia had called four hospitals. 'Nonna isn't in any of them and that's a good thing,' she said assuredly.

'So where is she?' Anger bursting through Sofia's words.

'Don't worry! She'll be home soon, you'll see.' Her daughter spoke lightly from the opposite side of the living room.

'Easy for you to say! But she is my mother and I can't help but worry.'

'She is not just your mother, she's also my grandmother and we all love her,' Claudia scolded her. Then she softened her voice: 'Let's try and face this situation together, Mum. Don't shut yourself away. We are all worried.' Hesitantly she approached the sofa and stood in front of her mother.

'You can sit down for a moment... if you want,' Sofia invited her in a subdued voice.

Claudia sat down awkwardly, as if the sofa were stuffed with fresh eggs.

'I shouldn't have talked to you so abruptly when you told me about Saudi Arabia,' began Sofia, staring at her knees. 'I was afraid... and it came out all wrong.'

Her daughter looked at her in silence.

'I was terrified that you were going to go to a dangerous country... and I reacted badly. You're a woman now. You're not a child anymore.' She spoke in a jerky fashion, squeezing the tissue into her fisted hand. Her eyes were fixed on the window with the curtains still open, the light of dusk turning a muted grey. 'I'm sorry.'

Claudia sat at an angle, looking just as uncomfortable. After a long pause she sighed: 'I felt awful. From that moment I didn't feel I could confide in you... and I distanced myself.'

Sofia sagged. The tension that had kept her going until now was deserting her and she felt exhausted, a deflated balloon.

'I don't want to go to Saudi Arabia,' Claudia continued in a soft voice. 'I want to stay in London. I thought about it a lot, and when I spoke with Nonna, she gave me some good advice. I have all my friends here, my job... I'm happy here.'

With a squeeze in her heart Sofia acknowledged that she was not part of the equation. The words 'and the wedding?' were on the tip of her tongue, but she was afraid to pronounce them. Besides, she hadn't got the strength to risk another snappy reaction from her daughter.

Claudia sighed again: 'For now I don't want to think about marriage. I'm not sure about anything anymore. We'll see.'

Sofia wanted to ask her if she had talked about it with Tom, what he thought about it, but even this didn't seem appropriate. They were no longer as close as they were months ago, and maybe it was better that way. She had to cut the umbilical cord that held them too close. She had to let her daughter fly, free to live her life. This thought made her chest swell and she wanted to cry again, but she also felt a small surge of relief and gratitude. At least now she knew that Claudia didn't want to go to Saudi Arabia.

'You'll see that everything will work out.' Claudia approached slightly.

Sofia extended her hand, took a cigarette from the packet and lit it.

'No smoking in the house!' her daughter reproached her, imitating her manner of speaking.

Sofia snapped a little smile: 'I know... I need an ashtray.'

The young woman stood up quickly, went to the kitchen and came back with a saucer. Then she took a cigarette from the packet and put it between her lips.

Sofia stared at her in amazement: 'But you don't smoke! You don't even know how to!'

'Neither do you!' her daughter replied and – for a blessed moment – they laughed together.

'I spoke with Tom.' She drew from the cigarette without inhaling the smoke and exhaled it through her mouth in a messy disorderly cloud. Waving her hand in front of her face she tried to sweep it away. 'I told him we have to postpone the wedding... indefinitely.'

Sofia held her breath. She didn't know if she could ask what Tom's reaction was, or if she should be quiet.

'Don't you want to know how he took it?' Claudia shifted her thick dark hair from her forehead with her slim fingers and pink-enamelled nails.

'If you want to tell me... What did he say?' Sofia looked at her daughter's hand. For a brief moment they looked into each other's eyes. Overwhelmed by a perturbed emotion, she pulled a new tissue from the packet and blew her nose.

Claudia gave her a summary of the conversation they had had on the phone. She told her that Tom had gone to fetch her at work with a bunch of flowers – he hadn't bought her flowers for years – and they had gone for pizza. She had told him she wasn't happy, that the idea of going to Saudi Arabia was his alone, that he hadn't even thought of asking her opinion. 'He was surprised. In his head it was obvious: we get married, go to work there for a few years and save a lot of money. When I told him that the idea scared me, that I was happy here, he was shocked.'

For a long time Sofia had been wondering what they had in common. In the beginning there had been enthusiasm, perhaps love, but she had always thought that the love was coming from Claudia, who was helplessly romantic. Tom had responded to her as a mirror reflects an image. She sighed: 'Sometimes I think he doesn't know you at all, even if you have been together for a long time.' She paused, charged with trepidation. Should I ask or is it better not to ask?... 'Do you love him?'

Claudia didn't stiffen as she had feared. On the contrary, she rested her back on the sofa and seemed to relax. She was reflecting, searching for the right words: 'Yes, I do love him... but not enough to give up everything and go with him to a place that doesn't attract me at all.' After an uninterrupted silence, she added: 'Maybe I love him like a brother.'

Sofia turned to her daughter and this time looked straight at her: 'That's not enough to get married. You do know that, don't you?'

There was a long silence, followed by a deep sigh. Then Claudia returned her mother's gaze and nodded, in her eyes an expression of imploring bewilderment.

Chapter 16

DOUBT, REGRET AND ANGER

'It's crazy! There is a double-decker bus on fire, and there are people armed with wooden sticks... and iron bars.' Sandra was leaning out of the window. 'It's terrible,' she exclaimed withdrawing slowly. When she turned, there was a stunned expression on her young face. 'I didn't think anything like that could happen in London,' she muttered.

'The anger and hurt that have been brewing for a long time have now exploded,' Tony remarked.

'Come on, close the window,' Carlo urged her. 'Smoke is coming in. They have only just started out there. Who knows when and how it will end.'

From the street below gusts of smoke and rage rose up polluting the air, saturating it with a disturbing sick energy. There was a sense of disbelief in the room.

'Let's hope no one gets hurt... or killed,' said Alex as he headed back to his chair.

'The best thing we can do right now is to chant for everyone's safety and get on with the meeting,' Tony added, going back to his place.

John poured a glass of water for himself and offered some to the others, while everyone sat down again.

Josh perched on his stool and took up the reins of the discussion. 'I'm sure we'll talk about what's going on out there in a little while. One of the next topics is anger. But for now, shall we carry on? We have the seventh troop, which represents doubt and regret,' he explained. 'Doubts block us, don't they?'

'They are also very useful, because they make us check that we did the right thing or that we did it well,' Navine declared. Little Connor put a hand on her mouth trying to shut her up. Navine removed it and spoke to him firmly in Hindi, to which the child went quiet. She continue: 'but we have to resolve them as quickly as possible, because they take away our confidence and when we're not sure, we can become paralyzed.'

'You're so right,' Sandra agreed. 'For me doubts are unbearable. When doubts assail me, it's like torture. I feel like I'm being split in two. I no longer know what is true and what is false, what's right and what's wrong.'

'What is the opposite of doubt?' Josh asked. 'It's conviction, isn't it? I always think 'What is the opposite of a feeling that makes me uncomfortable'?'

'We acquire conviction when we overcome our doubts, and in this sense doubts are very useful because they make us consolidate, or change, a decision,' affirmed Alex.

'In our practice, the opposite of doubt is faith,' Tony remarked. 'It is not blind faith, quite the opposite. It is knowing that I can reach the same state of absolute happiness that the Buddha achieved, after a whole life dedicated to the search for truth. His great desire and conviction were that we too could achieve it.' He looked at Lina, smiled at her, and she smiled back at him. He turned to the group: 'They called Shakyamuni Buddha 'the Enlightened one' because he understood that our true nature is that beautiful part of us we were talking about before. An enlightened person is a human being full of compassion, wisdom and courage. He, or she, has a strong life force and can overcome all the attacks of fundamental darkness that manifests itself with its ten armies. All I need to do is believe it; have faith, precisely. When I believe in the power of this enlightened nature of mine, I will recognize it in myself and, consequently, I will know that all other human beings possess it too.'

Beverley smiled and nodded. 'It's easy to believe when we see a person doing a good deed. It it's much harder to accept it when people show the uglier sides of their nature, especially when I see my own,' she observed.

'You? I don't believe it!' John exclaimed.

'Ask Josh! He'll tell you!' she promptly replied, and laughed along with them. 'This is why faith is important. Because, even in those circumstances, we can remember the positive potential we have, and relate to others from Buddha to Buddha.'

'I don't understand.' Sandra butted in, stirring on her cushion. 'What do you mean?'

Beverley turned to her and smiled: 'Let's say that I am faced with a person who, for his own reasons, is very angry and talks to me rudely even though I spoke to him in a polite manner. If I react instinctively, I might retort in an aggressive way, if only to defend myself from his attack. In this case my ego responds to his ego.'

'Okay!' Sandra was very attentive, her back straight.

'If instead I'm able to remember that behind that anger there is suffering, I will look at that person with the 'eyes of the Buddha' and perceive his unhappiness. In that moment of perception, my Buddha nature connects with his Buddha nature. In other words, the goodness that we all have inside us, mine and his, recognize each other and, symbolically, shake hands.' She tucked her hair behind her ears and shuffled on her chair. 'The strength of my compassion and wisdom will be greater than the strength of his anger. And the result of that exchange will be very different. Certainly I will feel better than if I had reacted from my ego, and I am sure that person will feel a great difference, too.'

'But it's not easy!' Sandra reflected.

'No, it's not easy,' Beverley giggled. 'It's a question of developing compassion and practicing self-control. This can be learned, little by little, by doing it. It becomes ever easier, more natural. Then, every time we put it into practice we find ourselves happier and stronger inside. I have experienced it many times and it's incredible to see how an unpleasant exchange can be turned into a satisfying experience.' She leaned over to Sandra and spoke to her as if she were the only person in the room. 'Seeing a person in the grip of anger that begins to calm down, and eventually can hear what I'm saying, creates such satisfaction that I can't explain. It makes me so happy when she, or he, realizes that we are not enemies, but two people who are trying to do something; we just haven't understood each other immediately. It gives me great strength, and every time I feel more confident about myself. It works! Sometimes we even laugh together and then we leave each other as friends. It's beautiful!'

'But how can you change a person's mood so radically?' Sandra queried. 'I wouldn't be able to. I would be ruled by my ego instead. I'd probably have an argument and tell him, or her, to fuck off,' she said bluntly.

A few people laughed, other smiled. Little Connor brought his tiny hands to his mouth and opened wide his big brown eyes. Stifling an uneasy giggle, he turned around and looked to his mother for her response.

'Oh, I'm sorry!' Suddenly aware of her swearing, Sandra apologized to Navine.

'It's okay… but we don't swear at home,' Navine replied in a relaxed way, 'so… better not, if you don't mind.'

'Yeah, sure. Sorry!' Sandra nodded, and raising her shoulders, gave Connor a sheepish smile.

Beverley smiled too and, turning to Sandra, said: 'To answer your question – how can I change someone's mood so quickly. It starts in the morning when I chant and praise the Buddha nature in my life.' She looked to Suki with an unspoken question, as if to say, do you understand? Suki nodded repeatedly and smiled. Beverley continued: 'I awaken it, reminding myself it's always there. Then, during the day, I can manifest it. The result is that it opens my eyes and allows me to see the positive potential in each person. It is so powerful. It takes away the distrust, or the fear, of the other person, and replaces it with trust. It takes away the anger of the ego and replaces it with compassion and profound respect for the person in front of you. From that trust comes the ability to establish a dialogue between equals, without any sense of superiority. Because it's not that I don't know what anger is. I know it very well but, at that particular moment, our shared connection is stronger. When we are ruled by anger, we are not strong, quite the opposite.'

'That's true!' Tracy butted in. 'I always get into trouble when I get carried away by anger. Beverly is right when she says that self-control is something we learn.' She glanced from Sandra to Beverley, aware that her friend knew her anger well. 'Since I started practicing Buddhism I have improved, fortunately, but I still have a long way to go.' She laughed out loud and leaned back on her chair. 'So, if I can do it, have faith guys, you can do it, too! Just try your very best.' She threw her fist in the air and laughed with gusto.

'Changing our tendencies is probably the most difficult challenge we can take on,' Alex declared, addressing Tracy with a smile. 'But, if we chant with a strong desire to create peace and happiness, for us and others, then even our most difficult character traits, our past or our mistakes, don't control us any longer. We are not shackled by them. We can choose, and use every difficulty as a cause to make a positive change.' He paused, tilting his white head slightly. 'For example, instead of chanting to get rid of my anger, I chant to use even my anger to create peace and happiness. The result in my heart is immediate. A change happens. My anger gradually transforms into a strong sense of justice. It feels so good that I am encouraged to make this shift in my head and heart over and over again. Little by little I turn any negative tendency of my character into a positive feature, and I become a little happier. How wonderful is that?'

'That was very well said Alex. Quite brilliant!' exclaimed Jane, and patted him on the leg.

'Inspired! Thank you Alex,' confirmed Josh.

Jim shyly raised his hand. 'I have a question,' he started. 'Earlier on – Tony – you said that the good side of us is our true nature. But it seems to me that even the bad side of us is our true nature. So how can you say that the good part is the real one? If anything, the opposite seems true to me. Look at what's going on out there' – he pointed his smooth chin towards the window. 'And this was also my personal experience when I was sleeping rough.'

Tony, who had been nodding while listening to him, smiled and nodded. His brown eyes shone with vitality. 'Your question is very important, Jim, thank you,' he said. 'Our negative side is part of who we are, absolutely. It is the 'fundamental darkness' we were talking about earlier, which tends to envelop our Buddha nature.' – He moved his hands as if to embrace something – '...if we allow it. It's a very strong instinct. In a certain way, our Buddha nature must *extricate* itself from this tendency towards negativity. Buddhism says that every day within our hearts we undertake a great struggle between good and evil. This is really an internal dialogue. In this fight we can either win, and our enlightened nature wins. Alternatively we lose, and our fundamental darkness gets the best of us. There is no middle ground. The important thing, Buddhism tells us, is that we win.'

Everyone laughed when he said this last thing.

Turning to Jim, Tony resumed: 'We decide what we want to be, how we want to live. We choose between being selfish, angry and swayed by everything that happens to us, or... we choose to awaken to the greatness of our lives. We choose to live in an altruistic way, with contentment, fullness and strength. I know how I want to live. I want to create value every day of my life. This gives me great joy and endless energy. I'm also aware that when there are more of us who live in this way – the more the better – we will create a society based on respect for people, the environment and animals. Instead, if most people live in the grip of fundamental darkness, we have to live in an unjust, violent or even cruel society. This is why we share our philosophy with those around us, so that the humanistic values will gradually inspire the society in which we live. Regardless of whether people actively practice Buddhism or not, when they live in a conscious way, society will definitely improve. It is our behaviour as human beings that matters. This is Buddhism's teaching.'

'Can you clarify what you mean by humanistic values?' Sandra asked, changing position and sitting crossed-legged on her cushion. 'I hear this expression often, but I couldn't explain what it means... exactly.'

'It means putting human beings at the centre of our thoughts, of our attention,' Josh replied. 'Not economic profit, not religion or progress per se, but the person. Think about it. Look at how we are being used in our society, how people are exploited... People are manipulated as a means to an end... for gain, for the profit of the few at the expense of many, for political or religious agendas. These things – economic progress, religion, scientific discoveries – should be used to improve the lives of all living beings that form society. And when we talk about living beings, we include the environment around us, animals and plants. Because we are all connected to each other.'

'So true,' confirmed Jane. 'When the environment is destroyed, or polluted, everyone suffers, people, animals, plants. We see it all around us.'

Looking at Tony, Jim – who looked hesitant and embarrassed – put his hand up again. 'Sorry, but I still have my question,' he said. 'How can you say that the good part of us is stronger than the bad one?' His neck was developing purple patches rapidly spreading towards his adolescent face.

'That's something *you* ought to explain to us!' interjected Nelson, who was looking at Jim with affection, and laughed as if he had just said something funny.

Lina liked Nelson. He made her feel safe, comforted. She was mesmerized by the cascade of ringlets – some with black shiny beads woven into them – that framed his handsome face.

'Me?' Jim was clearly confused.

'Yes, you indeed.' Nelson's smile was warm and wide. 'You could have continued down a path that would have taken you back to jail, petty crime, hustling, surviving, like so many others. And yet, despite overwhelming obstacles, you fought to get out of all that, and create something beautiful with your life. Your experience is the testimony that the positive part in us is stronger than the negative one.'

'But without your help I couldn't have made it,' Jim objected, flattered by Nelson's words, a light of unexpected pleasure in his eyes.

'I only helped you. You made the decision. It is thanks to that decision that you have revolutionized your life. On your own it would have been more difficult, it would have taken more time, but you would have done it. Once you decided what you wanted, even the environment started to move in helpful ways. The positive part of you has won over the negative one,' Nelson declared. 'I behaved like a good friend, and now you can be that good friend for someone else.'

Jim nodded with conviction. 'Without a doubt,' he declared. 'That's what I want to do.'

Moocat was stealthily walking across the tops of the sofa cushions, just behind Lina's head. Her white paws made her look as if she was wearing socks.

Lina turned around and tried to stroke her, but the skittish pussycat ran away. With a vertical jump, she reached once again the top of the bookshelf. From her safe place she looked down on them, her green eyes half closed.

Tracy quickly stood up: 'I can't sit here now. If Moo jumps down again I'm gonna have a heart attack!'

'Let's swap places,' Navine offered, standing up from her cushion with her little son. 'I could do with changing position.'

Connor scanned the room and his eyes stopped on Lina. She smiled at him and patted the place next to her.

Without hesitation the little boy walked over, climbed on the sofa and curled up next to her.

'You know Jim, when we live dominated by fundamental darkness, or negativity – however we want to call it – it's not a nice way to live,' Alex intervened, looking at the young man. 'It's not comfortable, or pleasant, because inside us we have a conscience and, as much as we try to ignore it, it won't stop talking to us. It is like a worm, truly! Our conscience is probably a close relative of Buddhahood,' he suggested jokingly.

'Buddhahood is a high state of consciousness,' Tony confirmed, 'and what you just said, Alex, shows how strong and rooted the Buddha nature is in human beings; how deeply part of our nature it is.'

'Wow, what a beautiful discussion!' Josh remarked. 'This is also a topic to be explored more in depth. Shall we now move on to the next troop? Regret, or even remorse. What a heavy word, isn't it? Buddhism is clear on this. What has happened cannot be changed. However, sometimes we are full of regret for not having done something, or remorse for having done it,' he reflected. 'Both emotions are directed to the past, to what has been. Maybe we said something we regret, we offended someone, were rude to a loved one. We keep thinking about it and, if we could go back, we would do things differently. Regret and remorse stop us from being happy. The thought continues to torture us and can become an obsession.'

'Buddhism tells us not to be dominated by guilt,' said Navine waving her hand. Her golden bangles stood out against her beautiful amber skin. 'Guilt, by itself, doesn't change anything. Instead, Buddhism encourages us to remedy the damage caused.' She looked around and smiled at Lina who had her arm around Connor's shoulders. 'I really like this concept. It is so liberating! If I offended someone, I apologize. If my apology comes from the heart, from the desire for this person's happiness, my words will touch her. If I have done something that I repent of, I have to redress it. And then I apologize to myself, to my life, which I have offended by doing something that goes against my conscience.'

'This concept of apologizing to one's life touches a deep note,' Alex observed. 'I find it really moving. As Navine says, first of all we must remedy the damage caused, or apologize to the person in question, but afterwards? It's important to forgive oneself for the mistake made, and to promise ourselves, not someone else, not to repeat the same mistake and improve from now on.'

'Another wonderful concept,' Tracy added with passion, her blushing cheeks matching her thick red hair. 'We always start again from this moment, having learned from our experience. It means that I look forward, instead of going over what I've done, again and again, beating myself up. It means that I encourage myself to become a better person, as I would encourage my best friend. In this way I can become free from that heavy sense of guilt that is so oppressive and prevents me from advancing. I say to myself 'Next time I will be better, I'll do the right thing.'

Josh stood up from his stool, went over to the table and filled a glass with water. Holding the jug, he looked around, to see if anyone wanted a refill.

Jane nodded enthusiastically and held out her glass, as Alex did.

Josh walked carefully among legs and cushions over to them and poured some water into their glasses. Then, as everyone else was signalling they didn't want any, he went back to his stool, and drank from his glass.

Leaning towards the group Beverley joined in: 'The function of the ten troops is precisely to confuse and weaken us with respect to what our conscience tells us. When we apologize to ourselves we dig inside our soul.' She gestured with her slim hands as if digging into the earth. 'We touch an open nerve and suffer for what we have done or have been. At that time, we can chant to change. We can look to the future with confidence in ourselves – again the concept of faith. This way we bring forth wisdom, and from there will flow the joy and enthusiasm to start all over. We will have grown, and transformed our karma. As a result, throughout this process we change ourselves, but we also affect the person to whom we have done wrong, because to hear someone apologize honestly, sincerely, is an experience that makes us feel humble and unites us.'

Lina looked at her with admiration. This young woman had a way of talking that touched her. She could actually feel her heart squeeze with emotion. Despite her awkward situation, Lina was feeling quite relaxed. Momentarily, she could push her worries at the back of her mind, waiting for a telephone call from the police to arrive. Carlo had finally managed to leave a message on their answer phone and they were now waiting for the police to call back. Connor had slowly but steadily climbed onto her lap and Lina was now holding him.

'What you've just said is so beautiful,' Jane pointed out. 'Humility is such a wonderful quality, and it's used so little these days. It is rare, almost out of fashion, for someone to recognize their limits. Many people act like they know things they have no idea about. Humility brings us closer to others. It unites us. It's so true!'

'It feels good to live with humility,' Alex added in a quiet voice. 'We have no desire to be superior to others, but we don't feel inferior. We don't try to prove anything. When I live with humility I am simply myself. I don't compare myself with anyone else and human relationships become so much easier. It's wonderful when I manage to live like this!'

'So many interesting things are coming out. Thank you very much!' Josh declared. 'Are we going on to the eighth troop? Anger, rage, wrath.'

'That's what it feels like out there now!' said Tony, pointing at the window with his hand. 'In a way I'm not surprised. There has been a lot of hurt, distrust and anger simmering for a long time. Each time local businesses are forced to close because of the gentrification, trust between the government and local people is eroded. Each time a person of colour is stopped and searched aggressively, whether on their way back from school or work, or dies in police custody...' – he paused and took a deep breath – 'the trust between the police and those communities is destroyed. When young people are treated like dangerous animals to be feared rather than listened to, their faith in our society fractures. We are not living in a society that works together at the moment. We have forgotten how to treasure each other. Perhaps we never knew.'

'I agree,' Nelson concurred. He looked from one person to the other in turn as he spoke. 'Even within the busy mixing pot of London, I still regularly experience moments where I am discriminated against, because of my colour. It's hard to talk about. Sometimes it can be as subtle as someone being surprised by my level of education, that I'm well spoken, or that my name sounds English. I can't ignore the persistent gentle suggestions that I am an outsider. Sometimes of course it's not so subtle. When I'm stop-searched or pulled over in the car, which still happens a lot, I behave with respect and try to keep my frustration to myself. At times the police officers respond respectfully. Other times, instead, I have experienced rudeness, attempts to humiliate me and even downright abuse.'

There was a grave silence in the room.

He continued: 'This relationship with the police is a

particularly difficult one. These are just my experiences, but I hear many stories from the people I work with as well. More often than not they are not treated as equals. Consequently it's hard to believe that there can be justice for them. Based on their past experiences they don't feel safe with the police. They don't feel they can turn to them for help. If the norm for a white man is to be presumed innocent until proven guilty, for a black man it can often feel like it is the opposite. There are exceptions, of course, but this happens time and time again. In such a context, when something big happens, like this latest killing, it's not surprising... but it's deeply, deeply painful.'

'It's not clear whether he was armed. It seems he wasn't,' John added. 'What is known is that he was going about his business, in a taxi, when he was stopped, for no apparent reason. A few minutes later he had been killed.'

'How sad!' Suki looked at Nelson with sorrow in her eyes.

'I didn't know England was like this,' Sandra said, thoughtfully. 'Did you, Carlo?'

'No. I thought that, in London at least, the different races had found a way to live together, with respect. On a superficial level it seems to work,' he replied.

'If you are white you don't realize what the reality is like for black people,' Tony observed. 'As Beverly pointed out earlier, you may not be aware of the problems faced by some minorities, if you don't feel them on your skin.'

'Let's really chant for this young man who got killed and his family. I feel so much for them,' said Jane with empathy.

'Indeed,' agreed Suki, with her sweet voice.

'This started as a peaceful protest though,' Tracy observed, 'but now it appears that other people have jumped in and are using it as an excuse for violence. It feels like anger is flooding the streets!'

Navine interjected: 'Many people are clearly very unhappy, but it's too easy to explode and destroy what is outside of us, without looking at what's inside.' She paused, reflecting.

'There's such a lack of respect, and that starts from here,' she said, touching her chest. She looked at Jim, who was listening carefully. 'Taking care of external causes is not enough. We must also take care of the internal causes.'

'What do you think those internal causes are?' Jane asked.

'Lack of respect for ourselves and for our own lives,' Nelson intervened with confidence. With a glance he consulted Tony, who nodded with conviction. 'Not realizing the enormous potential that everyone has within. Many people think they'll never be able to get out of the vicious cycle in which they are born. It's a real challenge to believe in the greatness of your life, if you're poor and growing up in a society that worships wealth and greed. Difficult not to be angry. Some people feel they have nothing to lose and no future. Actually it *is* difficult to get out of this spiral. But what's going on out there, this outpouring of anger and greed, it's not just the less privileged. We all have the potential for those emotions and to behave in that way. That's one of the reasons why we chant: to appreciate, to cherish our lives and cultivate a deep respect for all life, starting with our own.'

'But what can we do? What should society do?' John asked.

After a moment of silence Tony offered: 'Education – of all members of our society – is the first step, isn't it? We have to work together to transform the discrimination, our lack of belief, our pain. Young people need values that our culture doesn't provide. Above all they need to feel respected, and this doesn't happen at the moment. We give so much importance to possessions, to appearances, and not enough to what we are, and what we can be. We need to educate ourselves, our children, young people, to live together and respect each other, to learn to appreciate differences. Educate ourselves to the fact that, although our challenges may be different, from the point of view of our humanity, we are all equal. We must teach the importance of contributing to society, each person in our own unique way. With our work, intelligence, creativity and, above all, we need to understand how important we are, how precious, unique, irreplaceable our life, and life in general, is. Wouldn't it be incredible if this was the main concept of education?'

Alex nodded with conviction: 'Indeed! Teaching young people to believe in themselves, in their immense potential. Helping them understand that they count, so they can become stronger and happier people. This way we can create, all together, a better society.'

Chapter 17

SHOCK HORROR

Sofia looked at her daughter and spoke slowly, clearly: 'Living together can be beautiful, exciting, but it requires effort, compromise, constant generosity and a lot of love. If there is enough love you can face any difficulty. If there isn't, everything seems difficult, even the small stuff.'

She thought about her relationship with Steve. They had overcome mountains of obstacles: problems with money, health, jealousy on both sides, differences in values and clashes on how to raise their children, how to treat them. She and Steve were very different, but the love between them had always been solid, stronger than anything else, even depression. In that case though, she had reached rock bottom and had questioned everything, including their marriage. Suddenly she had found herself alone, frightfully, desperately sad and lonely, even – and especially – when she was with him. She had been so disheartened that she could no longer see the point of getting out of bed and facing another day. The memory of those months still filled her with anguish. Would she ever be able to forget them completely?

'What would you do in my place?'

Claudia surprised her with that question. Did she really want to know her opinion? Sofia had to be honest with herself and take the risk. She put the cigarette out on the saucer, taking some time. 'I found myself in a very similar situation when I was about your age,' she revealed, somewhat reluctantly. It was not easy to open up after months of having shut her heart, of building walls within, trying to protect herself from the harsh pain that besieged her, from the lethal cut of all communication. It felt as if she had dried up emotionally and was a mother, but only in part. Could she start to trust anew? What if she said something wrong again?

'Were you going to get married? I didn't know.' Claudia turned to her and her knee touched that of her mother's.

This contact made Sofia quiver with discomfort. She tried to control herself, but couldn't. After a few seconds she crossed her legs to escape the thorny closeness, her hand on the flowery dress. 'No, we were not planning on getting married, but we had been together four years. Basically, I 'fell out of love' with him... It happened a little at a time. At first my enthusiasm to see him, to spend time with him, began to fade.' She spoke without looking directly at her daughter, focusing on the window that was letting in the last glimmer of daylight, the dark of the night pushing steadily forward. 'I started to feel embarrassed and irritated by things he did, things he said... Then I began to find excuses not to see him... and then I fell in love with someone else.' She held her breath, knowing she was touching a delicate point.

Claudia didn't speak immediately.

Sofia could almost hear her think.

'And... did you start a relationship with the other one?' her daughter asked with a dry mouth.

'No. He was about to get married.'

'Ahhh.'

'It was hard to end the relationship,' Sofia continued, 'not for me; for me it was a huge relief, but I felt sorry for him... It's painful to know that you're causing suffering to a person who, until recently, was everything for you, and you for him.'

'Did you ever regret it?'

'No. Never.'

There was silence. It had been ages since they had talked together, woman to woman. Maybe for now it was enough. Big rips and tears needed to be mended slowly, little by little.

'Well, I'm happy about it. If you hadn't left him I wouldn't be here... I wouldn't exist,' the young woman realized.

Sofia turned to look at her daughter and Claudia smiled at her. 'It's true,' she said, 'you wouldn't be here... and that would be a great shame,' she added, returning Claudia a faint smile.

Micky came rushing down the stairs holding onto the handrail and sliding down the carpeted steps.

'Can't you walk down the stairs like everyone else?' his sister scolded him. 'You'll be wearing the carpet down rubbing it with your shoes like that.'

But Micky didn't seem to take any notice of her and burst out: 'I'm writing a rap about Gran. It's coming on really well. I'll play it to her when she comes home. I'm sure she'll like it. I've also used some classical music, as she suggested. I wasn't keen on the idea when she said it, but I thought I'd do it to make her happy and, as it happens, it sounds really good. She was right. What a modern little granny she is... my Gran! Any news of her yet?'

'No, nothing at all. What time is it?' Sofia asked, deep lines of concern marking her tired face.

Reluctantly Claudia looked at her wrist watch: 'Ten to nine.'

'We can't wait any longer. We need to call the Police... now!' Sofia decided. 'Can you get me the number Claudia? Or shall we call 999?'

'Let's call 999. It's easier,' the young man suggested.

'No Micky. That's for emergencies only, and this is not an emergency,' Claudia reproached him. 'They'll be very busy with what's going on out there. They don't need our call, too. We should call the local station, surely. I'll get you the number, Mum,' Claudia declared. Then, turning to her brother: 'Were you not preparing pasta and pesto?'

'Dad's doing it,' Micky replied absently, his eyes peeled to the television screen which was reporting scenes of the riots, the volume down to zero. 'He said it was fine...' Suddenly he stopped short. 'Look at that!' he exclaimed, mesmerized, watching the television broadcast. They were showing the start of the riots outside Tottenham police headquarters.

He and Claudia saw her at the same time. They exchanged a look of open-mouthed incredulity that didn't escape Sofia.

'What?' she asked alarmed, looking from one to the other. 'Why did you look at each other like that?'

'Nothing!' Claudia replied hastily, but it was obvious that what she had seen had taken her breath away.

'Granny was there!' Micky couldn't take his eyes off the television. 'I saw the hat with flowers. It was her, I'm sure. You saw her too, didn't you?' He turned his eyes away from the screen for a split second to ask Claudia for confirmation. Then he went back to staring at it, looking for validation. 'I'm sure. It was her on the pavement. No one else has a hat like that.'

'Are you trying to give me a heart attack?' Sofia begged, sitting rigid on the edge of the sofa.

Claudia could not lie. She had seen her too. 'It's a good sign Mum,' she mumbled the words that sounded unconvincing even to her. 'At least we know where she is. And that she's alright.'

'She's *alright*? In a place like that? Shout to your father and get on the phone. '

Sofia stood up and started pacing aimlessly around the living room. She grabbed the packet of cigarettes. Trembling visibly she took another one out and lit it with shaking hands.

'Madonna santissima, mamma... where the hell is she?'

Chapter 18

FAME AND ARROGANCE

'Thank you so much. Amazing contributions! Shall we move onto the ninth army? Obsession with fame and wealth. I don't know if there is anyone among us who has had to fight this troop,' Josh chuckled. 'For me it has never been a problem. If only!'

'It has never been an obstacle for me either,' John sniggered.

'I never had to deal with this difficulty in my life,' said Navine laughing. 'I only wish!'

After a visible hesitation, Tracy waved her manicured hand. This time she was not as bold as before and spoke in a quieter way: 'Those who have known me for some time know that I've been modelling for a few years now. I became quite well known, even famous, I suppose... and wealthy.'

Jane and Alex nodded, and so did Nelson and John, Beverley and Josh.

She had seemed a familiar face! Lina suddenly realized that she had seen her before, many times.

'I started with fashion magazines. I was earning so much money that I didn't know what to do with it. I was very young and my father managed my business. He was good. He left me a good sum and the rest he invested in houses and apartments. We were well off and happy as never before. Then the big contracts arrived, with weekly and monthly magazines, and the sums increased in proportion to the fame of the publications.' She looked around and shuffled uncomfortably on the cushion she was now sitting on, crossed legs.

'You were in all the fashion magazines, now I remember!' exclaimed Sandra. 'Were you in Vogue, too?'

Nervously Tracy moved a strand of her copper hair from her forehead and nodded: 'I was everywhere: magazines, billboards, television, fashion shows. I was twenty years old and started to believe I was important... and infallible. After a while, instead of following my parents' advice, I rebelled and decided to go it alone. That's when the big problems started. I compared myself to actresses, to princesses. The admiration I received always seemed inadequate. I never had enough. I wanted to become more famous and richer. I began to feel ashamed of my humble origins and tried to hide them.' Her cheeks were beginning to flush. The earlier fiery attitude had disappeared and was replaced by a humble, almost embarrassed tone. 'In those days I used to hang out with extremely rich people. They took all kinds of drugs, but mainly cocaine and heroin... and alcohol of course, a ridiculous amount of alcohol. I began to use them too. Before I knew it, I was spiralling downwards. I hardly slept, I ate little and badly, I was late, or didn't show up at all for jobs. I became unreliable and... unpleasant, I must say.' For a few seconds she exhaled deeply through her nose, staring at the floor, lost in thought.

All eyes were on her. There was complete silence in the room.

'Within a few months my descent turned increasingly steep and I was more and more dependent on heroin. Without makeup I was ugly. Inside I felt like I was nothing. I saw friends die from overdoses.' She paused again, overwhelmed by emotion, and swallowed with difficulty. With effort she continued: 'There were a couple of times when I wanted to die too and... I tried to commit suicide.'

Everyone was holding their breath and Lina perceived a wave of compassion in the room that was almost palpable.

With her long fingers Tracy wiped the tears that were running down her cheeks. She drew a deep breath. 'I wanted to stop so much, but I couldn't do it on my own... Eventually, an old friend, an ex drug addict who had succeeded in becoming clean, persuaded me to enter a rehabilitation centre. There, with lots of help and love, I did it.' She looked around, a little calmer, more positive. 'When I came out I started to attend NA meetings – I still do – and that's where I met the person who became a dear friend and introduced me to this Buddhist practice. I have never looked back since. I am so grateful to all the people who helped me, and to my parents. How I made them suffer! But they never gave up on me, thankfully.' She pulled a tense smile. 'My father, who is a very wise man, managed to save part of my estate, but a lot less than what it was. I had spent most of my money on drugs.'

'But you made it out of drug addiction,' Beverley declared, easing the tension that had built up. 'Well done Tracy! We are very happy to have you here among us.'

'Indeed! It's not easy to do what you did,' Josh looked at her with admiration.

'Thanks in part to you all, who supported me in the most difficult moments, without judging me,' Tracy acknowledged. 'Meeting this practice has opened my eyes to how precious my life is, and to how much I have to give.' The emotion was transforming her face, showing a hidden vulnerability which made her look younger.

Lina liked her much more than before. She felt like hugging her, but couldn't. Instead she simply smiled at her and Tracy – who must have perceived her feelings – looked at her and returned her smile, gently, her eyes still wet with tears.

'I bet you're happier now, without all that money, than before, when you were trapped in addiction,' John remarked.

'Without a doubt,' Tracy agreed. 'That wasn't happiness. It was an illusion, completely. It concealed the immense confusion... the dismay that I felt inside. Although I was raised with strong principles, once I was in that environment I lost myself. I believe that my education was good, but not strong enough to resist the charm of fame and wealth. At the crucial moment I chose not to think about what my parents had taught me. I threw those values out of the window and I adopted new ones. Unfortunately they were unhealthy and almost destroyed me.'

'They have done studies on happiness,' Alex observed. 'The results show that, once we have what we need to live on, the rest doesn't increase our happiness... it can even be an obstacle.'

Jane nodded firmly, whilst following Connor with her eyes. Having left Lina's lap, the child was now climbing on Nelson's back, making everyone smile.

'Connor, don't be naughty,' Navine scolded him.

'He's fine,' Nelson reassured her, helping Connor get a good grip of his shoulders and settle on his back. 'I like him climbing on me.'

'Okay then, if you're happy... I wanted to say that, if our self-esteem depends on our financial situation, then we are definitely on the wrong path,' Navine declared. She uncrossed her legs and leaned forward on her chair. 'With such mentality it is inevitable to experience existential problems. On the other hand, if we value wisdom, generosity, good human relationships, we can build a solid identity and be much happier, no doubt about that.'

'For me, human relationships are the determining factor,' Tracy agreed. 'Now I am much more aware of the importance of being surrounded by people who want what's best for me, for my happiness.' She looked around, more relaxed and at ease. 'This practice has taught me to desire the happiness of others, even those who make me suffer. This was a revelation. Before, I didn't really think of other people's happiness, it never even crossed my mind. I gave little importance to my own happiness too, come to think of it. But when I started to chant things began to change. I am so glad that I did. I never thought I could become as happy as I am.' She put her palms together and bowed lightly.

'This is probably the most important benefit of practising Buddhism,' said Beverley, looking at Tracy with fondness. 'Little by little we transform the beliefs, doubts, lies about ourselves that have guided us until then... and we begin to discover that we are so much more than what we thought. We become stronger, more independent, creative, cheerful and connected to the rest of life.' Her gaze went from Tracy to Jim and she gave him a big smile, causing him to blush to the roots of his hair.

'At that point we notice how the 'protective forces' of the universe get together to help us,' Josh hinted, smiling with anticipation. 'I'm sure each of us has an experience or two about this that they could share.'

'Ah yes, the Buddhist gods! I'm dying to tell you what happened to me!' Navine jumped in, fidgeting and waving her hand in the air. 'Last week I was on a plane, coming back from Mumbai, and the flight was late. I was worried as to how I'd get home. I explained to one of the flight attendants that, if I missed the last train from Birmingham, I would have had to wait all night, until five o' clock in the morning.' She chortled at the memory of those moments.

'This young man began to keep me informed regularly of the progress we were making. Twenty minutes before landing he moved me to a seat near the exit and, as soon as they opened the aircraft door, he said: follow me closely. He preceded me down the steps, walking fast. Meanwhile the other passengers were still waiting to get up from their seats. We entered the airport at full speed. Peter – that was his name – was almost running ahead of me, opening all the doors with his magnetic pass.' She giggled like a little girl. 'He got me through passport control on the lane reserved for the flight crew and then guided me to the exit for the station. At that point I kissed him!' She laughed aloud, leaning back on the chair, and then added: 'on the cheek, of course. I arrived at the platform ten minutes before the last train left. Unbelievable! That flight attendant was truly a 'protective force of the universe'.'

Lina joined the participants applauding spontaneously among exclamations of cheers and congratulations.

Navine resumed, excited: 'I even told him... I said... in Buddhism we don't worship a god, but we have Buddhist gods. These are the people around us who support and help us. Today you are my Buddhist god. He was very pleased... a bit surprised, but moved. I also told him that I would write to the airline to let them know how much he had helped me.'

'And did you?' Jane asked.

'Sure! The next day!'

'What a beautiful experience!' Josh remarked, smiling broadly. 'When so-called coincidences begin to happen, we're amazed at first, because they are so unexpected. Then, little by little, we get used to them. They don't surprise us very much anymore, don't you find?'

'Indeed! 'Alex confirmed. 'But I always notice them.'

'But... why is it that they happen?' Sandra moved restlessly on her cushion. 'It happens to me, too, but how does it work?'

'They happen because the environment reflects our life state, our vibrations – whichever way you want to describe it,' Tony replied, his eyes brimming with excitement. 'So, when you are positive, open, giving... the environment responds in kind.'

'So true! It's like a mirror,' Josh agreed. 'And we have now arrived at the last army: arrogance and contempt for others. Perhaps the ugliest of all. I can just imagine hundreds of soldiers armed with hatred and disdain for others. Truly frightening.'

'An arrogant person often treats other people harshly, offensively, with insolence. It comes from an attitude of superiority,' said Alex. 'I know it well, because I was like that, and now I'm ashamed of how I behaved. I thought I was important; instead I was nothing but a fraud. I caused a lot of suffering for others and ultimately for myself, too. It took me losing everything to understand... but it was worth it.'

'And what about contempt? Isn't it the same thing?' Sandra queried him.

'Very similar. Contempt is a magnified manifestation of arrogance and it comes with a desire to dominate others,' Alex explained. 'When we feel contempt we consider other people to be inferior, unworthy of our respect. I remember this feeling well. How horrible!' he shuddered.

'It's a sort of inflamed ego, isn't it?' Tony observed. 'When the ego feels challenged it reacts violently. Its nature is to divide, dehumanize. When we label someone we deprive them of their humanity and justify actions that are unjustifiable. The moment we generalize – even if we do it superficially – we fall into the devious trap of contempt. How many people were killed because they were different?'

'Or part of a group of 'others', such as Jews, Armenians, gays, gypsies, disabled, slaves?' Beverley stated strongly. 'Or hundreds of thousands of women burned at the stake, labelled as witches because they knew about medicinal plants.'

'We must be very careful not to fall into this trap,' Suki warned timidly with her childish voice, her small hands clasped in her lap. 'It is the most destructive of all.'

Lina looked at her a little bit too long. She was very sweet, with that oval porcelain face and kind eyes.

Suki noticed it and smiled at her.

'I felt the contempt of others when I begged.' There was a note of rancour in Jim's shaky voice. 'I clearly perceived that I was judged to be a 'waste of space', a slacker or, worse still, invisible. I was going through the hardest time of my life, but I was not the beggar. I was Jim and I needed help. The contempt that was so easily dished out intensified the shame I felt. What I needed instead was a hand out of the quicksand.'

No one dared to interrupt him.

Lina perceived an atmosphere of compassion for him, but also a feeling of discomfort. Perhaps those present were questioning themselves.

'That's why I want to become a social worker and help as many people as possible who are in a similar situation.' Heating up, the purple patches on his neck rising toward his face, Jim was visibly struggling with his shyness, but pressed on. 'Now I want to ask a question...' he paused and glanced at Connor who was happily sitting on Nelson's shoulders. '... If you see someone picking up a piece of... poop,' – he turned the colour of a tomato – 'and throwing it at a weak person, does this action tell you more about the person who throws the poop or the person who is hit by it?' He looked around for an answer, red faced but feisty.

There was a moment of hesitant silence, broken by Jane who responded calmly: 'It tells me a lot about the person who throws the poop, but it doesn't tell me anything about the person at the receiving end.'

'Thank you!' Jim nodded once firmly, feeling vindicated.

The uncertain pause that followed was interrupted by Sandra who, raising her index finger, candidly asked: 'Err... 'scuse me, but does the poop represent contempt?' and made everyone smile.

'Evidently dear,' confirmed Carlo, ironically patting the back of her hand with the tips of his fingers.

'So, how do we defeat the attacks of these armies?' Alex asked. 'From what we've said, they are not a small challenge.'

'We have to be stronger than they are,' Josh replied with confidence. 'When we know what we want, what our mission in life is, we become strong. Day after day, looking inside ourselves, listening to our conscience and the voice that comes from the heart, we give life to a vision for the future that respects and expresses our uniqueness. That's why our daily practice is so important. Through the chanting to praise our life, – he smiled at Suki – we seek to understand how we can most contribute, with all our unique aspects, just as we are.'

'I agree!' Tony declared. 'I'd change my mind every few minutes if I let my desires – fickle as they are – determine the direction of my life. If I react instinctively to whatever life throws at me I'd never become strong, let alone achieve anything of value. But when I believe in myself I will be able to visualize what I want for my life. It's very much like painting a picture of my future. I keep adding more and more details, pushing aside any doubt about my unlimited potential. I chant to become a man rich in wisdom, courage and compassion. I can feel my enthusiasm and energy growing by the day and, quite naturally, it becomes easier to see the same potential in others.'

'This is so good! Thank you Tony!' Josh was beaming, his eyes shining with enthusiasm. 'And when we see people's potential, we can see their inner beauty. When I do a good chanting session in the morning, I go out and look at people thinking 'you are my brother, you are my sister'... The feeling is *fantastic!*'

'That's my experience too,' declared Nelson. 'My daily practice is an exercise that reconfirms my real nature.' He looked around and stopped on Jim with a smile in his eyes. Nelson put his hand out, palm up: 'Think about it. If it wasn't true I couldn't experience it, could I?'

At that moment Beverley's phone rang. She looked at the screen and, raising her eyes, turned to Lina: 'It looks like the Hackney Police!'

'I left your number on their answer phone, as you asked,' Carlo hurried to explain.

'That's perfect. Thank you Carlo!' Beverley stood up, answered the call and, waving her hand, invited Lina to move to another room.

Lina's hesitant hands were damp with sweat as she took Beverley's phone. Fortunately the policeman was kind and she was able to explain her situation and provide the information he was requesting. There wasn't much to tell, because she could only give her name and surname, her daughter's name and Charlie's. She didn't remember their addresses or phone numbers. Then she was asked to describe the two boys who robbed her. She answered the detailed questions posed by the officer, having to repeat the same things a few times. The telephone call seemed to last an eternity.

The policeman explained that, due to what was happening outside, all their resources were being used and they could only provide emergency services. They would certainly be able to track down her daughter and her friend, but Lina would need to be patient. He wanted to know if she was safe where she was. Having received her affirmative answer, he asked to speak again to Beverley. Could she, should it be necessary, host the lady for a few more hours, maybe even overnight? 'Honestly,' he explained, 'out there the situation is serious and at the moment it's engaging all our officers. It could deteriorate further and I can't say when we will be able to track down the lady's family. They may also contact the police to report her disappearance – he noted – and now that we know where she is, it will be easier to reunite them.' He encouraged her to be patient and reassured her that it was only a matter of time.

Beverley put the phone down. 'This could take a few hours, Lina,' she said. 'From what the policeman said, it might even be tomorrow morning before they can trace your family. Don't worry though, you can stay here tonight.'

'I'm so worried about my daughter. She will be beside herself with anxiety,' Lina moaned, '... as if she didn't have enough problems of her own. Poor Sofia!'

Beverley put her arm around her shoulders and heartened her: 'Everything will get sorted. It's just a question of a few more hours.'

In the living room everyone wanted to know the latest developments.

Looking at Josh, as if to ask him for confirmation, Beverley said: 'You can sleep in our room Lina. Josh and I will settle in here. That's a sofa bed.'

'I have a spare room. She can stay at my house.' Jane turned to Lina and added: 'I live just a short distance away. I would be very happy if you came to stay. We can have something to eat and talk a little more. What do you say?'

'You are all so kind,' Lina wanted to apologize, looking from one to the other. 'I am sorry to cause so much trouble.'

'It's no trouble at all,' Josh affirmed. 'We are glad we can help. It's a difficult situation and you're being very brave.' He put his arm across her shoulders and held her affectionately.

'It's dangerous out there,' Beverley hesitated, shifting from one foot to the other.

'We'll take them,' Nelson looked at John, who nodded decisively. 'In any case, we can't stay here all night. Don't worry Bev, we'll see them home safe and sound.'

They discussed the best route to take. Jane suggested they went along the back roads in order to avoid the clashes; the way was longer but certainly safer. Jim decided to go with them.

It was time to get moving. Everyone wanted to say goodbye to Lina and they approached, waiting patiently for their turn to speak to her.

'It was a great pleasure to meet you and talk with you,' said Tracy, bending down and shaking Lina's hand. 'I'd like to see you again.'

'Thank you so much for what you said.' Alex, the white-haired photographer, held Lina's hand between his own.

Suki gave her a smile and a bow and, holding out her small, pale hand, said in her shy English: 'I hope to see you again, Mrs. Lina. I'm very happy to have met you.'

Navine picked up little Connor. The child leaned over toward Lina. She laughed, flattered by that gesture and welcomed him, holding him tenderly in her arms. He hugged her tightly and kissed her, before returning to his mother's secure arms.

Lina had buttoned her jacket but – as often happened – the

buttons didn't match and one side was lower than the other.

Suki smiled and pointed it out to her and, at exactly the same time, Navine said to her: 'You've done your jacket up wrong.'

'It's always best to start with the lowest button,' Jane advised gently. 'That's what I do and it works.'

'I always do it up wrong,' Lina exclaimed, and she almost expected one of them to help her. Instead they all looked at her smiling, waiting for her to do it. And so, under the amused look of her new friends, she unbuttoned the jacket and started from the lowest button.

'Take responsibility for the buttoning,' Jane declared in jest.

Lina approached Carlo and Sandra to take her leave of them, but the young man surprised her, declaring: 'I'm coming with you. I want to make sure you get home safe and sound. Are you coming Sandra?'

'Sure!' she answered brightly. 'I wouldn't want to miss this opportunity for a little walk,' she joked.

They decided to leave all together. Alex and Tony would walk with Tracy, Suki, Navine and Connor, while the other group would escort Lina and Jane.

Chapter 19

JANE AND LINA

When they arrived on the threshold of Jane's home, a ground-floor apartment in a block of low-rise council flats, Jane already had her keys in hand.

Nelson, John, Carlo, Sandra and Jim were standing around, waiting for her to open the door. To Lina's delight, Nelson bent down and placed a kiss on both her cheeks. He told her that it had been a pleasure to meet her and that he hoped to see her again at the next meeting. John also kissed her, keeping a little distance, afraid that he might dirty her jacket with his work overalls. And then Jim approached timidly, as if he didn't dare.

Spontaneously Lina stood on her tiptoes, placed a kiss on his smooth cheeks and stroked his face. Jim blushed, but looked pleased. She felt real tenderness for him and wondered why, being so young, he was alone, without a family. When their turn came to say goodbye, Carlo and Sandra gave her a special hug, an embrace between Italians. It felt as though she had known them for a long time and, when the group started to walk away, she paused to look at them, touched by their warmth.

Jim turned around and raised his arm in the air to wave. She smiled and responded, to which he sent her an unexpected kiss on the tips of his fingers.

In the hallway, Jane removed her shoes and Lina did the same.

'This way there is less cleaning to do,' said Jane and handed her a pair of slippers. 'I don't have the energy I used to have.'

Lina could identify with that. 'Oh, I know!' she empathized. 'When I was young I used to clean all the time, I even liked it, but my enthusiasm on that score has definitely waned over the years.'

'Absolutely! It only gets dirty again,' Jane agreed with a chuckle. 'I have some vegetable soup ready. Do you feel like eating? It will take me two minutes to warm it up.' She walked ahead of Lina down the narrow corridor.

'I didn't think I was hungry but, come to think of it, hot soup sounds perfect, thank you.'

Lina followed Jane into the small kitchen. Like in her own house, everything was rather old – the cabinets, the pots, the window curtains – but clean. When Jane opened the fridge, Lina was surprised to see that it was almost empty. Her own fridge was always full, even excessively so, and often she would find mouldy vegetables in the bottom basket.

While the soup was warming up, Jane showed her to the spare room. It felt uninhabited, there was a cold quality about it, perhaps because it was already late in the day and everything felt damp.

'It was my son's room. I hardly ever go in,' Jane revealed. 'Let's leave the door open and let some joy and friendship in. This room needs it,' she observed, as if she had read Lina's mind. 'You lost a daughter, too,' she added simply, looking directly at her.

Lina nodded: 'Yes, unfortunately.'

'I'm sorry.' Jane made her way back to the kitchen. 'It took me years to get over losing Ricky. He was my only child. His father and I were separated and so I found myself completely alone. Life lost all sense of purpose. I wished I could have died. But we can't, can we? We must go on.'

'That's right, life goes on' – Lina often repeated these words to herself – 'but now you seem to be happy.'

Jane pondered those words. Eventually she tilted her head and nodded: 'I'm fine... yes, I can say I'm happy. Ricky was a

Buddhist and after his death I wanted to keep his Gohonzon, the same scroll as you saw at Beverley's.'

'It's beautiful.'

'Yes, it is. It reminded me of him. Whatever mood he was in, happy, sad or angry about something, he'd opened the cabinet and chant to it. For me it was important to keep it in the house. It made me feel as if the essence of his life was still here. The members of the group told me that he left it to me, as a sort of inheritance. It has no financial value of course. They said that, if I wanted to, I could also practice the same philosophy.' Jane put on a pink and white apron and busied herself around the kitchen. 'I began to chant in the moments of deepest dejection. It comforted me. After months, maybe even a year, I went to my first meeting and I haven't looked back since. From that time on I never felt lonely again and no longer fell into despair. I started to understand that I have an important task to accomplish. My son showed me the way and I am very grateful to him for this. And you? Was your daughter young?' Jane bent down, opened a cabinet and took out a saucepan.

'She was forty-five when she found out that she had breast cancer. She was my eldest child. She had good doctors, they helped her a lot, but there was nothing they could do to save her. Ten years ago cancer was so much harder to beat. A lot of progress has been made since then and now it has become much easier for people to recover, fortunately.' Lina tightened her lips and shook her head with resignation. She was leaning against the grey worktop, keeping out of Jane's way. 'Anita fought for five years. When she had chemotherapy she hid it from me. She wore a wig and I didn't even notice. I didn't know she'd lost her hair. Can you believe it? In Italy we say that nobody is blinder than those who don't want to see.'

Jane opened a cupboard above her head and pulled out two soup bowls: 'It's very difficult for a mother. How long is it since she died?'

'It's already been four years.'

'Still early days. Time heals the wounds, you know it too.' She gazed at Lina with understanding, opened a drawer and took two spoons out.

'This is true.' Lina went back to those days in her mind. She felt she could open up with Jane, trusting she would understand. She wished she could have seen more of Anita – she confided – but her daughter was fickle; sometimes she'd be willing to see her, other times she would flatly refuse. Lina would travel for two hours on a train to go and visit her, but often she'd have to wait a whole day, once even two, at a friend's house, before being able to spend some time together. She never knew whether to talk about meaningful things or to just have some frivolous conversation. Whatever she said it seemed to irritate Anita. Sometimes her daughter was brusque with her; other times she was generous, but always distant. Anita seemed to hold a grudge against her and Lina had never understood why. It had caused her a great deal of suffering and, even after her death, it had been hard to come to terms with it.

Once she had a dream. Lina recounted: 'I was in a station. I saw my husband – may his soul rest in peace, he was a difficult man and since he's died I've started to live – and Anita was there too. I called her – in the dream my voice was choking in my throat and I couldn't make any sound – but Anita didn't turn around... I was mortified.'

Jane was stirring the soup and listening carefully, nodding gently.

Lina continued in a low voice, absorbed in her memories: 'I don't understand why she didn't turn to look at me. I wanted to say hello... I don't think she loved me very much. I don't even think she liked me.' She said so without emotion, as a matter of fact, but Jane knew a mother's heart, and that Lina was suffering.

'Can I speak to you as a friend? We're friends now, aren't we?' Jane said sympathetically, whilst filling the bowls with ladlefuls of thick orange soup on which she sprinkled some finely chopped herbs. 'I know that for many people it's difficult to make new friends at our age, but I still feel young.'

'Of course you can. I like it. I feel young too, except when I go back to sad moments like this one.'

'I think I know why Anita didn't turn around, and it has nothing to do with liking you or not.' Jane spoke calmly, firmly. 'You have to remember that dreams come from our subconscious, so they have to do with what's inside us.' She tapped her chest and looked her in the eye, to make sure that Lina was following her. 'I have read lots of books on the interpretation of dreams and yours sounds very simple.'

'Really? Why didn't she turn around to say hello to me?' Lina's heart felt heavy, as if someone was pressing down on it.

Jane's voice was warm: 'The station is a stage of existence, in this case without your husband and daughter. The train is symbolic of our life which, if you think about it, is a journey. And your daughter didn't turn around because you're not yet ready to follow her – or your husband – where they've gone. Basically it's not yet your time to leave.' Jane tilted her head, looking at Lina with kindness. She nodded thoughtfully, then continued: 'If Anita had turned around, if she had offered you her hand and, more importantly, if you had taken it, that would have meant that you were ready to go to her,' she concluded with confidence.

Lina's face revealed the hopeful wonder her friend's words had awakened: 'You mean I'm not ready to die yet?'

Jane stopped to look at Lina, her hand resting on the open refrigerator door. 'Definitely not!' she stated, and laughed softly: 'You should look at yourself in the mirror right now. You look like a young girl!'

Flattered, Lina smiled: 'A girl with grey hair.'

'And eyes full of excitement for life.' With a pair of scissors she opened a carton and poured fresh cream around the green herbs on the orange soup, drawing the shape of a heart. She took two trays and arranged a bowl, a bread roll and a napkin on each. 'Let's go and sit in the living room, we'll be more comfortable,' she said, handing Lina one of the two trays.

Lina couldn't help worrying about Sofia and her family. They would be so anxious about her. How could they track her down?

But Jane reassured her. Beverley had promised to call as soon as she received a communication from the police. In the meantime they might as well relax. She must be tired – Jane observed – after a day like today.

Yes, Lina was very tired, and she was sorry to have lost her handbag and the money that was inside. She confessed how the boy with the flick knife had scared her to death and, once the effect of the alcohol started to wane, how confused she felt realizing that she was lost. Many kind people had helped her though and the meeting at Beverley's and Josh's house had opened her eyes to a new world. So many different men and women talking about themselves and encouraging one another; people of all ages, social classes, levels of education, different nationalities... in short, it was beautiful! Did they meet often?

Once a month for meetings like that one – Jane replied – but during the month they met in smaller groups at someone's house, depending on their needs. If one of them was having a difficult time, they would see one another more often. 'We can't solve other people's problems, but we can give each other the hope to go on. We look ahead and remind ourselves that we have an enormous potential that allows us to overcome any adversity,' she explained. Holding a piece of bread with her fingers, she mopped up the last remnants of soup left in the bowl until it was completely clean.

Lina smiled – she too wiped the plate clean with bread when she was at home. Encouraged by her friend's example, she broke off a piece of her roll and skilfully wiped her bowl with it, whilst listening carefully to what Jane was saying.

'As we grow in our Buddhist practice we learn to transform those things that make us suffer. I'm talking about our behaviour and the conditioning that makes us make decisions without reflecting whether they truly reflect the person we are now, because we change, you know? It's amazing how we become more open.' She folded her napkin neatly and smoothed it on the tray, next to the empty bowl. 'Once I used to think that I was 'like that' and would never change, but it's not at all true, we keep changing, if we want to. When I started attending the meetings I was in a state of profound grief, I felt completely lost. I began to absorb a lot of new and fascinating concepts. Those meetings became the highlight of my week and I wouldn't miss them for the world. The new friends I made were incredibly sweet and generous. I don't know what I would have done without them.'

'I really understand,' Lina said empathetically. 'I remember when Anita left us. My world fell apart.'

'Yes, it seems as if all the things that made sense until that moment suddenly collapse around you, and you find yourself totally empty... apart from the ache that fills every part of you. It feels as if your heart could burst with pain, doesn't it?' Jane shook her head.

'Yeah. A pain that takes your breath away,' Lina sighed.

Jane took a deep breath: 'When I realized that my challenge was to become happy despite this great loss, and that my role was to help others become happy, everything took on a different dimension. My life began to transform.' She leaned forward and her voice became infused with a new intensity: 'Dedicating myself to caring for other people filled me with energy... it enriched me so much... and living became meaningful again. We may think that we are helping others – which we are and it is of great value – but *we* are the first ones to gain.' She placed her left hand above her diaphragm. 'In fact, I think true happiness can only be achieved when we do something for others.'

'It shows, you know?... that you are happy,' said Lina with conviction. 'There is such strength about you. I perceived it as soon as I saw you; even before I heard you speak. And when you talk, you communicate calmness... and trust. This encourages me so much.'

'That's exactly what I want to do,' affirmed Jane. 'Thank you for saying that.'

'I would like to see the people who were at the meeting again,' Lina reflected aloud. 'I have the feeling I can learn a lot from you all.'

'Nothing could be easier! Come to the next meeting. We too would like to get to know you better.'

'They invited me... everyone did.' Lina smiled at the memory. 'I definitely want to go,' she nodded with conviction. 'Changing the subject, I'm curious to know how you spend your days, apart from the Buddhist meetings.'

Jane relaxed in her armchair: 'I work voluntarily for our neighbourhood committee. I've been elected chairperson and it's almost a daily commitment. We meet once a month to discuss the various problems – there are always plenty – and try to find the best solution for everyone. We also arrange social activities for young people, the elderly and women with children; there are many single mothers who live on the estate. At the moment we are organizing a neighbourhood party. It'll be next month in the garden right outside,' she gestured towards the window behind Lina's armchair. Then she giggled. 'But I usually start the day with aerobics.'

'At your age?' exclaimed Lina in awe. 'But isn't that something for young people?'

Jane laughed and told her that she went to a gym three times a week. 'We are a group of women that exercise to music of the eighties, or even more modern. We have this talented teacher who leads us in dancing and works us so hard we don't even have time to drink a sip of water.' From the enthusiasm with which she was talking about it, Lina could tell that she really enjoyed it. 'We use weights, big balls, hula hoops, rubber bands, and we do floor exercises for the abdominals. Every lesson is different. We sweat in abundance and have a lot of fun.' She crossed her legs and continued: 'Some exercises are named after us. For example, when the teacher says 'Jane' we all know that we have to bend our knees four times with our arms outstretched. If she says 'Lilka' we have to move our arms in a robot-like fashion while we tense our belly and tighten our ass.'

Lina burst out laughing.

Jane chortled and explained: 'She says it just like that: squeeze your bum, squeeze your bum!' and made Lina hoot with laughter. It was contagious, and Jane joined in the mirth.

'I hadn't laughed like that for a long time,' Lina confessed, still giggling.

'Neither had I,' her new friend agreed. Jane continued: 'When she says 'Claudia' everybody complains loudly, because it means doing very hard abdominal exercises with your legs in the air whilst lifting arms and shoulders.' Jane chuckled at the memory of those moments. 'And then, once we've done the hour and a half, we go for coffee. It's one of the best moments of my week. You should come too. You'd like it.'

Lina was thinking exactly the same; she would love to do something like that. 'At the moment I still live in Nottingham,' she explained. 'My daughter is insisting that I come to live with her and her family... but I'm not sure.'

'Do you have a lot of friends in Nottingham?'

'I know people, I have good neighbours, but I can't say I have many friends, apart from Mavis. She's a fortune teller, a famous one,' Lina revealed, picturing dear Mavis, her jet black hair and the artificial flowers she wore in it.

'Ohhh,' said Jane, intrigued. 'And does she tell your future? I shy away from those things; once they tell you something it sticks with you, you can't forget it.'

'So true!' replied Lina. 'I never ask her, but sometimes she insists and I let her read my tea leaves. However I don't believe in these things... although this time...' her voice trailed off. Maybe this time Mavis had said something true... she would try to remember Mavis's words, later, when she'd go to bed. Lina went back to what she was explaining: 'Most of my friends, those who are still with us, live scattered across the country. One of them lives in London; she's the one I went to see today.' She thought back to her and Charlie dancing in the kitchen to the sound of the Beatles and had to laugh. She recalled the last thing that Charlie said to her at the bus stop, 'come and live with me Lina, we're good together'. To which – if she was not mistaken – she had answered 'Yes, all right'.

She told Jane how things had gone in the afternoon, from the first glass of Marsala.

Jane laughed loudly listening to her story. She had such a joyful laughter. When it came to Charlie's proposal, she said: 'It wouldn't be a bad idea. Living alone is not always nice. I like my independence, but I also like to have company. And as I age, I think it's better to share a home, especially if it's big and welcoming.'

Lina hesitated. She hadn't thought about it. 'That idea has only just surfaced and selling my house in Nottingham would be a big step... It represents my financial independence as well as my own personal space,' she thought out loud.

'Instead of selling it you could rent it,' Jane suggested. 'Find a reliable person who pays you on time every month. This way you have more money in your pocket while keeping your house, for now at least. Later you can see. It's not that you have to decide everything now and forever. One step at a time.'

This idea made Lina think. She fiddled with her empty spoon: 'Living with my daughter and her family could be nice, but I think that after a while things would change and it would become uncomfortable. I don't want to spoil the relationship I have with them. Being too close for a long time creates frustration, irritation. I don't think it's wise.'

'There is an English proverb that says: Familiarity breeds contempt'.

'Exactly! Besides, they see me as an old woman but, apart from a little arthritis,' Lina looked at her deformed hand, 'my blood pressure... a bit of asthma... apart from that I'm fine and feel young.'

'Of course!' exclaimed Jane. 'We have a lot of energy and a great desire to enjoy ourselves. Why don't you try to live with Charlie for a few months and then make up your mind? I have a spare room too, if things with Charlie shouldn't work out.' She paused and smiled at her. 'I have a feeling that we would get along.'

Lina felt a wave of excitement mixed with fear rising in her chest: 'Thank you! Good to know. I too, think we would get along.'

She pondered, striving to remember what she had heard at the meeting, and thoughtfully said: 'Now I feel apprehensive. I am thinking of what Beverley said about the 'bora' of Trieste. What does it actually mean to turn around, so that the strong wind is behind me? How exactly does it work?'

'Don't put pressure on yourself Lina. Reflect about things, calmly,' Jane reassured her. 'It's an important decision. Give yourself as much time as you want. Maybe chant, as we did at the meeting. In this way you listen to your intuition, your heart.'

Lina nodded: 'Perhaps we could chant together? I want to make sure I do it right. But what should I think about when I say that phrase?'

'I would ask myself: what do I want? and then I'd chant, without thinking too much,' Jane replied, beating her temple with her forefinger. 'You simply chant for your happiness and for the happiness of the other people involved. Sooner or later, you'll find the right answer. It comes from the heart, not only from the head. But don't rush... and trust that you will come up with the solution that is right for you.'

They were both tired, especially Lina who had had an exhausting day and couldn't stop yawning. They decided to go to bed without turning the television on. Sometimes it was better not to know what was happening.

Jane lent her a long white nightie and a brown velvet dressing gown. She took the phone into her room, ready to answer Beverley's call, and waved her good night.

Lina went to her bedroom, lay down under the soft duvet and, as soon as she closed her eyes, fell asleep.

Chapter 20

THERE IS NEWS

Lina heard her name being called from far away. Her eyelids felt as heavy as a rolling shutter and she had to fight the immense weariness that held her still, before she could open her eyes. They stung from exhaustion. She blinked a few times and had to close them again, but not before she saw Jane place a mug on the wooden bedside table.

'I made you a cup of tea!' her friend beamed while she opened the blue velvet curtains to let in the pale morning light. 'And if you want any more, there's plenty in the pot.'

'I've never had tea in bed,' Lina murmured, running her hands over her face. It was a luxury that she'd never allowed herself and made her feel a little uncomfortable. As she slowly lifted her body to sit up, she realized she hurt all over. Her back, shoulders, legs and arms were all aching, and she leaned heavily on the pillow against the headboard.

'There's always a first time!' Jane, still in her dressing gown, gave her a wink and a smile. With loving care she handed Lina another pillow and helped her place it behind her back. Then she sat on the edge of the chair next to the bed.

'There is news,' she exclaimed, her eyes shining with euphoria.

'Did Beverley call?' Suddenly Lina was completely awake.

'No, better!' Jane spoke loudly and couldn't contain her excitement: 'Do you remember Jim, from the meeting?'

'The young man who was homeless and always blushed?'

'That's right!' Unable to hold back her enthusiasm, from under the chair Jane pulled out a supermarket carrier bag and handed it to her. 'Look what's inside. You are not going to believe it!'

With her misshapen hand Lina placed her cup carefully on the bedside table. She took the bag and peered inside. For a long moment she remained motionless, dumbfounded. She looked up with an expression of disbelief. 'It's my handbag! The one that was stolen,' she breathed.

Jane was radiant and spoke fast: 'Isn't it incredible? Jim brought it early this morning. I couldn't wait for you to wake up. You were fast asleep and I waited for as long as I could resist.'

Lina pulled her handbag out of the carrier bag. She turned it over and over. With trembling hands she opened the zip and checked the contents. 'How is it possible? I don't understand,' she murmured, shaking her head.

Jane was fidgeting on her chair, quivering with excitement: 'Yesterday, when you described the thief, Jim understood who he was. He had met him when he was sleeping rough. He came across many people who live by tricks and crimes. It was your description of the tattoos on the thief's fingers and the colour of his hair. Last night Jim tracked him down, persuaded him to take him to the rubbish bin where they had dumped your bag and recovered it. They've probably taken all the money,' Jane added, pointing her chin towards the handbag.

Lina emptied the contents onto the duvet and awkwardly moved the various items. 'Here's my address book!' she exclaimed excitedly, waving a little agenda in the air like a trophy.

'And the money?' Jane stretched her neck.

Lina opened the purse: 'They have taken all the notes... and left the copper coins. There was forty pounds. Oh well!' she said resigned, looking at the items scattered on the bed, one by one, and noticed: 'They've taken the phone.'

'Do you have your daughter's number in that booklet?' Jane pressed her.

'Yes, it's in here, I wrote it down myself,' Lina declared, raising the little book in the air, a mixture of joy and anxiety painted all over her face. 'Let's call right away. Sofia will be on tenterhooks.'

Jane stood up quickly, went into the living room and returned with her mobile phone: 'Call her now! Then we'll also call Beverley and ask her to notify the police.'

'My reading glasses are missing, too. They were in the bag.'

Without hesitation, Jane removed the chain she wore around her neck, with her reading glasses attached, and handed them to Lina.

With the spectacles resting on the tip of her nose, Lina opened the booklet and, with her crooked uncertain fingers, and Jane's guidance, dialled the number. She looked at her new friend and took a deep breath. Her hands were sweating and she wiped her free hand rubbing it onto the sheet, while waiting with anticipation for someone to pick up the phone.

'Hello?' said an anxious voice at the other end of the line.

'Claudia? It's me, Grandma!' Lina had to move the receiver away from her ear and hold it with her arm outstretched lest she would be deafened.

Even from where Jane was seated, she could hear Claudia scream with joy, her voice crying 'Mum, Mum, Dad, Micky, it's Nonna on the phone!' The young woman was laughing, asking where are you, how are you, what happened to you, all without waiting for an answer, mixing cries of jubilation with exclamations of disbelief.

Unstoppable tears began to flow from Lina's eyes and flooded her cheeks. Her lower lip trembled and her hands shook.

Seeing her cry, Jane was also moved and couldn't hold back the emotion. She pulled a packet of tissues out of her pocket, slid one out and wiped her eyes. She was laughing and crying at the same time.

Gratefully, Lina took the tissue Jane offered her, blew her nose and soaked it in a second. She was trembling. She laughed when her friend brought a small bin closer and handed her the whole packet of Kleenex.

Finally Sofia came to the phone and spoke as loudly as Claudia. Mum how are you? Where are you? We were awake all night. I haven't slept a wink. What happened? Are you okay? They saw you on television. You were in the middle of those madmen. Steve Steve! It's Mum, Sofia shouted, as if her husband could have possibly failed to understand who she was speaking to.

Lina had understood next to nothing of what her daughter had been saying, too excited to form coherent sentences. In a jumbled way she tried to explain the events of the day before and, all of a sudden, she felt thoroughly overwhelmed. The accumulated fatigue, the shock and fear experienced, were washing over her, and she felt as if someone had placed the weight of the whole world on her shoulders. She reassured her daughter that she was all right, that she had met many people who had helped her and that everything was fine. Then she handed the phone to Jane. 'They want to know your address,' she said, while with the palm of her hand she brushed away the tears from her face.

When Jane took the phone she found Steve on the other end of the line. He was calmer than his wife and daughter, and Jane explained to him how to get to her house. 'They will be here in a while, it depends on the traffic,' she declared, hanging up. 'It will probably take them about an hour. Meanwhile let's have something to eat. You'll be hungry.'

Since it was Sunday and for her it was a tradition, Jane cooked an English breakfast: eggs, sausages and bacon prepared under the grill; beans, fried mushrooms, slices of toast with butter and marmalade, and a large pot full of tea. The table was beneath the open window that looked out onto a communal garden and, from where she was sitting, Lina could see only the leaves of swaying trees and birds flying from one branch to another. A fresh breeze moved the curtains and caressed her forehead, calming the nervous excitement that made her hands quiver, comforting her heart, shaken by so many emotions.

Sharing breakfast was a lovely experience and at first they ate in silence, sitting across the table, both still in their dressing gowns, facing each other.

'What an adventure, hey?' Jane remarked after a while, whilst pouring her a cup of tea.

'At my age,' Lina said ruefully.

'All's well that ends well,' her friend stated, passing her the milk jug.

'And all because Charlie insisted I take the bus instead of a taxi,' Lina remarked with a note of blame.

Jane seemed surprised and looked at her straight in the face: 'But she didn't *make* you catch the bus, did she?'

Lina thought back to the day before and her face broke into a smile – they had so much fun! 'No, she didn't *make* me but, by telling me that it was a lot cheaper and that it was easy, Charlie persuaded me.'

'Yes, all right... But in the end, *you* decided to take the bus, didn't you?' Jane pressed on, concentrating on spreading the butter on another slice of toast.

'Well, no, *Charlie* did... and me... I suppose.' Lina wondered with a hint of discomfort as to why did Jane insist on repeating the same question. 'I always go by bus in Nottingham, I'm used to it. I never take taxis, they are too expensive. But I was in a part of London that I didn't know... and I was quite tipsy.'

Jane raised her eyes and smiled: 'Was that also Charlie's responsibility?'

'That I was tipsy? Well... *Yes!*' It seemed pretty obvious to her. 'It was her who kept filling those glasses with Marsala... and then also the Chablis with dinner... we drank the whole bottle,' Lina recalled, and chortled at the memory of the two of them shaking their hips like young girls and Charlie dancing, waving the ladle in the air. Ahhh, what a memorable afternoon!

Jane spread a light layer of orange marmalade on the buttered toast and bit it. Chewing slowly she cast a puzzled look at Lina.

'Why are you looking at me like that?'

'...............' Jane was looking perplexed.

'Do you think it was my fault?'

'I wouldn't say fault, more like responsibility.'

'That I drank too much and almost got drunk?'

'Almost?' Jane giggled.

'Okay, I was very merry. Has it never happened to you? And that I took the bus and then was robbed?'

'And whose responsibility is it, if not yours?'

'*Charlie's* of course! She makes all the decisions, all the time.'

Jane poured another cup of tea, silently, giving Lina time to ponder.

'And mine too, I suppose... partly... It's not all my fault... okay, responsibility... a little bit maybe... When Charlie decides to do something no one can stop her.'

Jane added milk to her tea and didn't speak.

'And what should I have done, in your opinion?' Lina was confused. 'What would you have done in my place?'

'I'm not sure... I probably would have got just as drunk, in that situation. From what you told me you had a lot of fun.'

'It's true! So? I don't understand what you're trying to tell me,' Lina complained. 'That I have done something wrong?'

Jane looked at her with affection: 'Lina, you are responsible for your actions. We all are. Otherwise it's like saying that we are puppets in the hands of anyone whose personality is stronger than ours.'

'So, should I have resisted? Should I not have drunk?'

'I'm not saying that. I'm just saying that if you decide to take responsibility for how things went yesterday, the next time you're in a similar situation – with Charlie or with someone else – you'll pay more attention, you'll take more care of yourself, making sure you are safe.'

'I shouldn't have caught the bus, then. I should have followed Sofia's instructions.' Lina looked dejected, unhappy with herself.

Jane was thinking. 'In your place I would have written down the number of the second bus, so I wouldn't forget which bus to take. But now it's done, and anyway... you got robbed in the park, not on the bus,' she concluded more lightly.

It was so obvious that Lina's mouth fell open. 'Yes... but you're right. I went to sit on a bench at Clapton Pond because I didn't remember what bus I had to catch.' Her hand, resting next to the teacup, slumped: 'If Charlie had written me a note...'

Seeing Jane raising her eyebrows, Lina tried a different version: 'I had to write it myself, without waiting for her to write it down... but I had no pen and paper.'

Jane smiled with understanding. 'You could have asked her to write it down for you,' she suggested delicately.

Lina was mortified. She had caused a lot of trouble for her daughter and her family. She had found herself in such a dramatic situation that could have ended really badly. She had involved the police and a lot of other people... And it was all her fault, or – as this kind new friend would put it – she hadn't taken responsibility for her actions. She was dumbfounded.

Jane stretched her arm across the small table and covered Lina's arthritic hand with hers, dry, warm and reassuring: 'It's all in the past now, and your daughter will be here soon.'

But Lina was dismayed. She didn't know how she could possibly look Sofia in the eye now. 'I'm such a mess. I've caused a lot of problems for everyone. I'm dying of shame,' she moaned.

Jane squeezed her hand and smiled warmly: 'You're not a mess. We all make bad decisions sometimes. The important thing is to learn the lesson and become wiser.'

Lina didn't know what to think. She felt so miserable that she didn't have the courage to look anyone in the face and kept her eyes low.

'Everything that happens can be used in a positive way,' Jane said encouragingly and leaned towards her, bringing her head closer to Lina's. 'For example, it occurs to me that if you're thinking of going to live with Charlie, it's important that you understand the nature of the relationship between you two. Charlie has her share of responsibility because she could, and should, have taken better care of you... but you can't unload all the responsibility onto her. After all, you've always made decisions. You're perfectly capable of managing your life.'

'Of course! I've always done it,' Lina confirmed with energy. 'It's not even as if we see each other that often. The fact is that Charlie has such a strong character... and when we are together I get carried away. Maybe it's better if I don't go and live with her.'

'If you know that you're being influenced by her personality, you can decide to change. Do you remember what was said at the meeting? We can transform any situation. Think about it! Would you be able not to be overwhelmed by her temperament?'

Lina looked up and found Jane's tender face: 'I think so. I'm not a weak person. I'm stronger than anyone thinks. I had to become strong.'

'So what happened is a perfect opportunity to show you your weakness. If you take responsibility for how things went yesterday, you can change the relationship between you and Charlie, simply by paying more attention as to how you behave when you're together. If you change the way you react, maybe everything else is fine.' Jane paused and then, taking Lina's warped hand into hers, she added: 'It seems impossible, but a little difference in the way we behave sets in motion a chain reaction all around us... and the behaviour of others changes, too. I've seen it with my own eyes many times and I promise you... it works.' She smiled encouragingly: 'Do you know the domino effect? When one piece falls, consequently all the others fall as well. It is a great friendship yours, but it could become even better... It depends on you, Lina.'

'Do you think so?' Lina looked at Jane in the eye, hesitant.

'Yes. I have no doubt whatsoever,' her friend reassured her, squeezing her hand with confidence before letting go of it.

Standing side by side, Jane washed the dishes and Lina dried them. She opened the cupboards and, following the instructions, arranged things in their place: 'I'm getting to know your kitchen.'

'Good, so next time you'll know where to find everything,' remarked Jane with a smile. Drying her hands on a tea-towel she continued: 'We'd better get dressed, before Sofia arrives. Then I'll do my morning chanting, like you heard yesterday at the meeting. You can join me if you like, maybe in the simplest part, where we repeat the same sentence.'

Lina did so happily but, as soon as she started to chant, tears began to flow down her face. She was surprised, she didn't expect it. The tension she had been holding inside, the tiredness that made her feel as heavy as a boulder, and now the realization of having behaved in an irresponsible and reckless manner, filled her with a disturbing sense of guilt.

Jane turned to look at her and briefly interrupted the prayer to say: 'From this moment on, Lina. Don't scold yourself anymore. We always start from now. Learn from the experience and look ahead. You're growing, and this always involves some pain... but it's worth it.'

Despite feeling so mixed up Lina had to chuckle: 'I'm growing now, at the age of seventy-five?'

'Of course! As long as we continue to grow we remain young. Forever young, like Bob Dylan's song!' declared her friend, full of conviction, and winked at her. She turned back to the scroll contained in the cabinet and, with a smile that was reflected in her voice, started once again to repeat that phrase, this time with more intensity and a contagious joy.

Lina joined in shyly and, after a while, she felt her heart calm down, open up and flood with gratitude. She liked this loud prayer, confident, full of strength. It made her feel good, and she smiled too.

When the doorbell rang it was as if an electric shock traversed her body. Lina gasped and suddenly felt anxious. 'They're here!' she exclaimed.

Both women stood up but, while Jane rushed to the door, Lina followed her with trepidation; she even felt a little sick.

The wide open door revealed four people. The whole family had come to fetch her.

'Mum! At last!' Sofia rushed to hug her mother and held her close, as she had never done before. 'How happy I am to see you! You have no idea how worried we were. I must have aged ten years. I bet my hair has gone white!' Her pretty face showed a lot of pent up emotion, accumulated tiredness, together with relief and gratitude.

'I'm sorry, Sofia, to have worried you so much,' Lina blurted out. 'I'm so sorry. Please forgive me, all of you.'

But nobody seemed interested in her apologies.

Claudia came forward and held her close, until Micky claimed his moment. Taller than Lina by more than a full head, Micky lifted her up and held her suspended off the ground, squeezing her a little too hard, making it difficult for Lina to breathe. He then proceeded to smack a kiss on each one of her cheeks. And lastly Steve, who was calmly waiting and smiling. He bent over, held her by her shoulders and gave her a kiss on the forehead. She could see that he was happy.

'Come and sit down,' Jane invited them. 'Would you like a cup of tea?' Having received a positive response from Sofia, she went into the kitchen to put the kettle on.

The moment that Lina had feared, the time for questions was upon her.

Sitting on the sofa and the two armchairs, the members of her family filled the small living room and wanted to know what had happened. Remaining vague as to how she had spent the afternoon with Charlie, Lina focused on the theft at Clapton Pond's garden and what had happened from that moment on. The questions overlapped, they wanted to know the why, how and when of everything. Soon Lina felt dazed by the pressure, the memories of the day before and the boundless exhaustion that came over her in waves.

She was happy to be here with her family though, and with this new friend that she liked so much. She was relieved, knowing that everything was in the past. She even felt excited by the story she was telling and that now – from this safe place – came across as a great adventure. At moments it all seemed like a dream. But now she was safe and being the centre of attention made her feel almost like a heroine.

With a cup of hot tea in her hands, Sofia thanked Jane profusely for looking after her mother. Claudia, Micky and Steve too joined in a chorus of thanks, but Jane shied away. Getting to know Lina was a great pleasure, she said. They discovered they had many things in common and she hoped Lina would go with her on Monday morning to do aerobics – they were almost all ladies of a certain age, she explained. She turned to Lina with an encouraging expression: 'You will come, won't you? I'm sure you'll love it.'

'Definitely! I can't wait!' Lina declared with a new found confidence. 'And you have to tell me where the next Buddhist meeting will be, because I want to attend. I had never taken part in a meeting like that and I liked it a lot.'

Her daughter, son-in-law and grandchildren were gawking at her. 'What Buddhists?' Sofia asked.

Lina went back to the moment when Beverley and Josh had saved her from the riots: 'Had it not been for them, god only knows what would have happened to me. A few minutes after we arrived at their house all these people started to turn up, of all ages and colours. We got on well straight away you and I, didn't we?' she said looking at Jane.

Her friend nodded and smiled: 'It was easy. Everyone liked you.' Turning to Lina's family members, Jane explained: 'It's my Buddhist group; we meet once a week. It is a lay Buddhist movement, without priests or monks. We're ordinary people who practice to become happy and help other people become happy too, and for peace in the world... in a nutshell.'

Sofia, who had held her thoughts until now, said: 'Me too, years ago, when I was in India, I met some Buddhists, beautiful people who opened my eyes to a new way of seeing life. For a while I chanted a phrase. I still remember it. After a while, I don't know why, I forgot about it and stopped. I let go of the contacts I had, too. I'm sorry I did.'

'I had forgotten about that, too,' Steve remarked. He seemed equally touched. 'It was lovely,' he said with longing.

'What's the phrase?' Jane asked.

'Nam-myoho-renge-kyo,' Sofia pronounced it clearly.

'That's what *we* do. We were chanting when you arrived,' Jane confirmed.

'*Wow!*' Sofia and Steve exclaimed at the same time, exchanging an amazed look.

'Really Sofia? You too, the same phrase? Incredible!' Lina was bursting with excitement. 'I want to know more about it and I want to see all those kind people again and thank them. They treated me like one of the family, and Jim was so kind to retrieve my handbag.' She turned to Jane: 'Did the police get in touch?'

'Not yet. I called Beverley. I told her you connected with your family. She was very happy and promised to call the police to let them know. We can trust her. When she makes a promise

226

she keeps it.'

It was time to go. Steve had reached for Lina's jacket and held it open – like the gentleman he was – so that she could put her arms through comfortably.

Lina buttoned it up and, as happened more often than not, the buttons didn't match.

Claudia approached and eagerly corrected her: 'Nonna, you buttoned it up wrongly. Come here, let me... I'll put it right.' Affectionately, she unbuttoned the jacket and started from the top, one button at a time.

As if to check that she had understood something important, Lina turned to Jane: 'I should take responsibility to button it up correctly, shouldn't I?'

'Oh yes!' her friend replied with an amused smile. 'We start with the small things and then move on to bigger ones.'

Chapter 21

SUNDAY AT HOME

Once at home, Sofia prepared some tea and then they all sat around Lina in the living room, curious to hear more details about the day before. She was given the seat of honour in the biggest armchair. Steve sat in the other armchair, Sofia and Claudia on the sofa and Micky cross legged on a cushion on the floor. They wanted to know everything, from the beginning, and warned her that she was probably going to have to repeat it all over again when Charlie arrived; she was on the bus on her way over.

'Two buses, you mean!' Lina remarked, prompting laugher. She carefully avoided talking about the Marsala-drinking afternoon and began from when things had started to go wrong, at Clapton Pond, where she should have caught the second bus.

'Oh mamma mia!' Sofia exclaimed when she heard of the thief who had stolen her phone after the first call. 'It was me, calling you to see if everything was all right.'

'And I thought music was just playing through the air,' Lina could now see the funny side of things. 'You know I have no idea of how to use a mobile phone. I'll buy you a new one to replace the one I lost.'

'Nonna, I'll give you a mobile phone for you to keep,' Claudia declared, 'and I'll teach you how to use it. It's very useful.'

'Claudia is right,' Sofia agreed. 'At least while you stay here I would like you to have one, especially if you go out on your own.'

'All right then, since I'm going to be very active,' Lina conceded, 'but I have no idea how to use it.'

'It's very easy. I'll help teach you too!' Micky encouraged her.

'Mum and I made you a cake last night while we were waiting for you to ring,' said Claudia, pointing her chin to the telephone near the front door. 'Carrot cake. It's your favourite, isn't it?'

'How kind!' Lina still felt guilty, despite what Jane had explained to her. 'I'm sorry to have caused so much worry. I knew you must have been concerned, but I didn't know what to do. At first I didn't realize how serious the situation was.'

'You walked several miles,' Sofia pointed out with concern. 'You must have been very tired when you arrived at Tottenham Hale.'

'I was, but what could I do?' remembered Lina. 'Eventually, when I got there, there was this big protest, with people shouting that they wanted to talk to the Police about that young man who had been killed. His family was at the head of demonstration. I really felt for them! While they were shouting I didn't have a problem, on the contrary, I agreed with them. After that everything changed though, and some people started to set litter bins on fire and then even a parked car. At that point I was really afraid! I was right there, next to it.'

'My God!' exclaimed Sofia, suddenly covering her mouth with her hand.

Micky butted in: 'We saw you on television. They showed the guys setting fire to a bin. I saw you first and then Claudia saw you too, isn't that right?'

His sister nodded strongly: 'Yes, I couldn't believe my eyes!'

'On TV? Really?' Lina was amazed.

'*Yes*, with that hat of yours we recognized you immediately,' confirmed her granddaughter.

'I told you on the phone,' Sofia reminded her.

'You said many things on the phone, dear, and I understood almost nothing. You mentioned television, I remember, but I hadn't realized that *I* was on television! How wonderful!'

'Yes, marvellous! I thought I was going to have a heart attack when they told me,' Sofia remarked, placing a hand on her heart.

'I'd love to see myself. I wonder if they'll show that bit again. I've never been on television.'

Sofia had to smile at her mother's enthusiasm: 'Maybe in another situation, next time.'

'They may show it again in the next few days, if they talk about how the riots started,' Steve suggested from his armchair. 'Watch the news.'

'Of course! Sure.' Then, pondering, Lina said: 'You know, now that all is in the past I'm almost glad that it happened, because I have the feeling that my life has changed. The things I heard at that meeting made me reflect... I am thinking of making some changes.'

'What sort of changes?' Sofia asked.

Lina explained that, although at this stage it was only an idea, she was considering the possibility of coming to live in London for a trial period of three or four months and... no, she wouldn't be living with them – she hurried to clarify – but with Charlie, if her friend remembered having offered and if her proposal was still valid. Later, if sharing Charlie's house worked out, she would be putting her Nottingham house up for rent and, with that income, she could go travelling, with Charlie and maybe even with Jane. She would also like to take the whole family on a holiday somewhere, maybe to Lisbon, so they could visit Marcello, and to Italy.

Steve, Sofia, Micky and Claudia were all gawping at her.

'Nonna, when you left with Mum yesterday you were an elderly lady, but now it's as if you're a young woman again... and all in less than twenty-four hours!' Claudia was stunned, but full of admiration. 'What a change!'

'Gran, I started writing a song about you and now I have to change all the lyrics,' Micky declared with deafening enthusiasm.

'No Micky, don't change what you wrote,' Claudia butted in,

'just add new parts to your song about how Grandma has 'refashioned'.' She laughed, looking tired but happy.

'You're right! Gran has just turned twenty.'

Everyone burst out laughing, including Steve and Sofia.

It was the first time that Lina heard the sound of laughter in that house. 'I heard interesting things at that meeting, and seeing so many different people confident that we can change and become happy, or happier... it was such a great experience!' Lina was brimming with enthusiasm.

'For example?' Sofia's face expressed a mixture of amazement and curiosity.

'That people love us for who we are, not for what we have to give. This concept struck me more than anything else. And Josh said that 'doing' was not a substitute for 'being'. He said that we often do too much, work too much, thinking that in this way we show our love for someone, or for our family.' Lina was waving her hands to emphasize her words, the Italian way. 'But often we become so tired that we have neither the time nor the energy to enjoy the results, especially with those people for whom we worked so hard.'

Steve looked at Sofia as if to say 'just as you do'.

She returned his look, perplexed.

'And then they told me that I'm not old, that age is a matter of mental attitude. And indeed I don't feel old. Jane, the lady who hosted me at her house, told us how her life transformed, despite her situation being very sad, she lost her only son.'

'Oh, poor woman!' Sofia exclaimed.

'Yes, indeed,' agreed Lina, who was too excited to stop on any one thing. 'And there was also a photographer, more or less my age, very dynamic, who spoke like a young man. In short, after that meeting I felt twenty years younger.'

'And it shows Gran!' Micky exclaimed.

'It's true! You've changed,' Claudia confirmed with a look of amused incredulity in her big green eyes.

'I realized that we must enjoy what we have now, without

waiting for things to change in a more or less distant future. Beverly, the girl who took me to her house, talked about how fear, in a way, can show us exactly what we want.' She put her good hand out decisively, palm up, nodding repeatedly. 'She said that when our life is trying to expand we tend to feel fear because we have to enter new territory and we are afraid of what we don't know. This idea made a great impression on me, because I was a little bit tempted by Charlie's suggestion that I go and live with her, but I felt a lot of fear even just thinking about such a big change.'

Claudia seemed struck by lightning: 'Did she say what she does when she feels like that?'

'I can't remember anything else just now,' Lina breathed, feeling unsettled and leaning back. 'My mind has gone blank. I think I'm tired.'

'Don't worry Mum; it will come to you,' Sofia reassured her. 'We were talking about fear and how to confront it.'

Micky stood up, quickly rushed to fetch a note pad and, sitting crossed legged on his cushion, started to take notes. 'Carry on Gran, you're a volcano of inspiration.'

'Oh yes!' The memory of what she had heard was coming back to her: 'A delightful black man – such a good-hearted person, Nelson was his name – said that also trust is the opposite of fear. When I heard those words I felt immediately reassured... I can't quite explain why.'

'Trust in what?' Claudia was absorbing every word coming from her grandmother's lips.

'In ourselves,' Lina declared, proud of her memory. 'He said that when we are afraid we often make the wrong decisions.'

'Ohhh!' Sofia and Claudia said it at the same time. They looked at each other and smiled.

Lina noticed the look of understanding between mother and daughter and it made her heart swell. Something good was happening.

'And then? Come on, Gran, we want more. I am getting inspiration for a fantastic song.'

'Ah yes! I loved it when Beverley compared the fear to the 'bora' of Trieste. Do you know what it is?' Lina asked turning to Micky and Claudia.

'Nope.'

'What a strange name!'

'Trieste's 'bora' is famous, because it is such a strong wind that it sweeps you away, literally.' She made a theatrical sweeping movement with her hands. 'Imagine that in Trieste – a beautiful city on the sea – there used to be strong ropes on the promenade along the sea edge, so that people could cling to them when this wind blew. Sometimes it can reach even one hundred miles per hour. I have felt it and it's really incredible,' she declared, her eyes open wide.

'What did Beverley say about fear, Mum?' Sofia brought her back to the subject they were talking about, but Lina had lost the thread again.

'Yes, what did she say?' Claudia was keen to hear the answer to this question.

'Fear?' She had to think about it... 'Oh yes! Fear is like the 'bora'. If it blows towards you it stops you from advancing but, if you turn around so that it is behind you, it will push you forward.'

'Wow!' Micky was more and more impressed and scribbled quickly, bent over the notepad he was holding across his legs.

'I'd like to understand better,' urged Claudia, who was leaning forward, elbows on her knees, absorbing this new information with great interest.

So Lina told them about Beverley's list of fears and determinations.

'Phenomenal!' Micky kept on writing as quickly as possible.

'I'd like to meet her,' said Claudia.

'Me too,' Micky concurred without raising his head.

'You'd like her, I'm sure. I've never heard anyone say the

things she says. And Nelson, who is a social worker with muscles like that' – Lina bent her arm and placed her opposite hand five inches from her forearm – 'said that sometimes all we need is to trust ourselves and what life offers us. This is what made me consider coming to live in London. Instead of being so fearful, I thought: why not give it a try? I won't lose anything, and maybe I'll like it.'

'Hurray!' Micky shouted punching the air.

'How wonderful!' Claudia was thrilled. 'So we can see each other all the time.'

'There's room for you in this house, you know Mum? You don't have to go and live with Charlie,' Sofia said, but Lina denoted the lower tone of voice, a hint of hesitation – fear precisely – and, in any case, the first solution enthused her, for the moment at least.

'I know dear, and I'm grateful, but for now I would like to try the other idea. Maybe I'll find it works very well and we would be close without being too close.'

'You'd be doing what students do, sharing a house and all the expenses,' Claudia declared.

Lina smiled: 'True! But Charlie and I have known each other for over sixty years. I don't think I will have any surprises. We are very fond of each other; we feel at ease together and can talk about anything.'

'She can be quite authoritarian though!' Steve remarked. 'She always wants to do things her own way and you're used to your independence and to doing things your way. Don't you think you'd find it difficult?' It was only the second time that Steve spoke since they arrived home.

Lina reflected: 'It's true that she has a strong character, she's always had, but she's also good-hearted... and likes things to be clear.' She took a deep breath and, looking from Steve to Sofia, observed: 'I'll have to be strong in myself, won't I? Make my own decisions, like I've always done, rather than just go along with what Charlie says.' She didn't want to falter right now. She was not one hundred percent sure and didn't have all the answers. 'We'll talk about it calmly. One step at a time, with trust,' she added, 'without fear.'

'One step at a time... with trust...' Micky wrote, bent on his notepad.

'Without fear.' Claudia looked at her grandmother open-mouthed. 'I'm learning a lot of things.'

'Why don't you go and prepare another tea and bring the carrot cake in?' Sofia suggested.

'We'll make sandwiches, too.' Steve exchanged a knowing look with his daughter. 'I'm hungry and we'll have to eat something,' he said, heading for the kitchen, followed by Claudia. With a steady hand gesture he stopped Sofia who was about to get up: 'You stay here with your mum. We'll let you know when it's ready. We'll prepare for Charlie too; she'll be here shortly.'

'I'm going to my room to work on Gran's song,' Micky announced, running up the stairs with those long legs of his. 'If the phone rings, I'll answer. It's for me!'

Lina glanced at her daughter and smiled at her. How many small but important things had changed in less than twenty-four hours.

'Come and sit here Mum,' Sofia patted the place on the couch next to her, 'so we can talk quietly.'

As soon as Lina was sitting next to her, Sofia took her shoes off, lifted her feet up onto the sofa and snuggled up close. 'I hadn't even hugged you since you arrived. I'm sorry Mum,' she apologized. 'I was so busy with things at home, in the shop, concerned about the problems with Claudia.' She kissed her mother's cheek, inhaled the smell of her hair and then leaned her head on her shoulder. 'I was so worried about you last night... I just wanted you to come home.'

Lina turned to look at her daughter's head and stroked it. It was all new to them, and a little awkward. They had never been very affectionate, not physically.

'You work too hard Sofia. You have to find some time for

yourself, rest and enjoy your life and your family. Work is not everything, nor is money.'

Her daughter didn't answer right away. The silence between them was a beautiful, calm silence.

Shyly, Lina caressed Sofia's arm.

'You're right. I'm always in a hurry... and I often feel lonely,' her daughter said softly. She raised her face and looked at her mother's profile with an uncertain expression. 'So what should I do? Work less? And what if the money is not enough?'

'You worry too much. Let *them* worry a little, too,' Lina pointed her chin towards the kitchen. 'You need to find some space for yourself. You were good at painting when you were a student. Have you done anything since? Would you like to?'

'Paint!' Sofia sighed. 'I never even think about it. Of course I'd like to. I could paint pictures for the house, to hang on these huge empty walls, but I haven't even tried for so long... I don't know if I'd still be able to.'

'Talk to Charlie about it. She attends a course two or three times a week, maybe she can advise you. You ought to see how good she is. Her paintings are beautiful.'

'It will probably cost a lot of money,' Sofia mused, '... and time...'

'Perhaps you'll find a time that suits you; after all, most adult students work during the day. You could look for an evening course... I'll pay for it. It's my gift. You deserve it.'

'But... no Mum, you don't have much money either,' Sofia protested, trying to sit up straight. Lina held her next to her and gently put Sofia's head back on her shoulder. 'I have what I need and more. I'm comfortable money-wise,' she declared. 'And I'll give you another gift. Find a cleaner who can come in for three or four hours a week and I'll pay for it. You can't continue like this... and no arguing, okay?' She squeezed her daughter's shoulder and turned towards her: 'You must learn to receive as well as to give. All you need to do is say thank you. It's not that hard, you know? Try it!'

Slowly Sofia sat up straight and, when her face was at Lina's level, she looked into her mother's eyes.

'Accept what others want to do for you. Don't always say no,' Lina advised. 'Everyone likes to give and I want to help you. Okay?'

'It makes me laugh to hear you say okay.'

'Good! So... Okay?'

'Okay, Mum. Thank you!'

Lina embraced her with both arms and put her chin on her daughter's head. 'That's the spirit. This makes me happy. Okkkay!' she said, and smiled knowing that Sofia was smiling too. 'I still remember the paintings you did when you were fifteen. You even sold some, didn't you? And you took part in an exhibition.'

'I gave two paintings away, because someone liked them. And I showed three of them at an exhibition. I'm glad you remember. I had forgotten about it.'

'You'll see what beautiful pictures you'll create when you pick up a paintbrush again.'

'You make me want to.' Reluctantly Sofia freed herself from the embrace and, turning to her mother, looked at her as if she were seeing her for the first time. 'You're such a surprise, mum. Transformed!' she declared.

'Really?' Lina was flattered by those words, even if she didn't understand why they were all so surprised. She felt excited, enthusiastic, but not transformed. 'Even the kids said the same. I don't think I have changed and I don't understand what you see that's so different.'

'I've always thought of you as a mild woman, always ready to devote yourself to the needs of others, without thinking about your own needs. I've never seen you as a woman with her own opinions, capable of making radical decisions.'

Lina raised her eyebrows. 'And how do you think I could have lived with your father and your grandmother? Bringing up four children with one inadequate salary, facing humiliations, betrayals and a slew of deceptions.' She said this with a touch of rancour, but also as a matter of fact. 'If I hadn't been strong, I couldn't have endured what I did.'

'And you used to sing! I remember how you sang while doing the housework. Even if you weren't always in tune,' Sofia laughed.

'Who me? I'm always in tune!' Lina pretended to be upset. 'I've always liked to sing. Even now I sing. I would love to listen to the old songs.'

'So you'd sing along... I always had the impression that you were happy... maybe not happy, but contented, yes,' mulled Sofia.

'Because I had you children, and I was so busy that I had no time to think about anything else.'

Sofia relaxed in her mother's arms, forgetting the uneasiness that this contact had caused her at first. She stroked Lina's hip with her hand and smiled. She was very tired after spending the whole night awake, but the joy and relief she felt now were so beautiful that it all seemed worthwhile. Compared to yesterday everything had changed. Her relationship with Claudia had unblocked and they were starting to communicate again. It wasn't like it used to be, but maybe a change was necessary. She could no longer think of her daughter as an extension of herself; she had to accept that they were two separate entities. Claudia wanted things for her life that she, as a mother, sometimes disagreed with. Her daughter had made it clear: she didn't want to know her mother's opinion about the choices she made. I'm strong – she said to her – you made me like that, you just need to encourage me. At first Sofia was shocked, almost offended, but then she realized that she had to trust the decisions that Claudia took and, in a certain way, her role became easier. She was already getting used to it. The relationship with Steve was softening, too. She appreciated his calm strength, his kindness. She knew he loved her; he told her every day. She had to believe it again, as she had before the depression, when she didn't doubt his love for her. Sofia thought back to the recitation of the Buddhist mantra that she had done thirty years ago, how she liked it and how it had opened her eyes to a completely different perspective on life. How could she have let it slip into oblivion?

Her mother seemed to read her mind. 'What a surprise when you said that you were doing that Buddhist chant. I remember something like that.'

'I was just thinking about the same thing!'

'You did it when you came back from India, am I right? Why did you stop if you liked it?'

'I don't know why I let it go,' Sofia reflected. 'Perhaps because I didn't know anyone close to me who did it, or I became interested in other things. A little at a time I forgot all about it. I also let go of those friendships. I stopped replying to their letters. What a pity!'

'I'm very interested. I've never come across anything like it. I wish I had. My life would have been different, I am sure of that.' Lina spoke with great enthusiasm. 'They meet every week; they support each other. I noticed there is a lot of respect between them... and they have such beautiful friendships!'

'I only just met Jane and she appears to be wonderful, but from what you told me, I am curious... intrigued.'

'It made me realize that many of the people I know tend to criticize others. It seems to be the normal thing to do,' Lina observed. 'This practice instead seems like a more positive way to live.'

'Mmmm... indeed...' Sofia mused, her heart open to hope.

Chapter 22

THE CALLS

Just then the telephone rang. Micky thumped quickly down the stairs: 'It's for me! I'll get it!' He picked up the receiver. 'Hello?' he shouted, potentially deafening the caller. He deflated within seconds. 'Yes, she's my grandmother... Yes, an hour ago... Yes, just a moment...' The surprise in hearing a deep voice asking for Lina exceeded the disappointment painted all over his face. 'Gran, it's a man... wants to talk to you,' he said, 'Nelson, I think. I'll bring you the phone.'

Standing next to Sofia, Micky observed his grandmother coming to life, smiling, laughing aloud and shying away from the compliments that were clearly reaching her ear. And then she thanked him, paid many compliments in turn, thanked again, sent greetings to at least four other people and promised to be present at Jane's house in a few days time.

Mother and son exchanged incredulous looks.

When Lina returned the phone – without hanging up – her eyes were full of excitement, her cheeks flushed and a big smile brightened her face. 'It was Nelson!' she confirmed, 'the one with muscles like that,' and she bent her arm, holding her opposite hand cupped ten inches from her forearm. 'He got our number from Jane and wanted to know how I was. How sweet of him!'

'Yeah, and his muscles are a lot bigger than before,' Micky joked. 'When you're done with the phone, you turn it off like that, Gran.' He bent down to show her how to turn the portable off but, as he was speaking, it rang in his hands for a second time. 'This one's for me!' he rushed to say, bringing it to his ear: 'Hello?' This time he spoke in a quieter manner: 'Yes... yes, she's my Gran.' He rolled his eyes and then stared at Lina: 'Yes yes, very well... I'll put you on to her.' He covered the microphone with his hand and exploded: 'Another man! This one's called Alex...' and with his arm outstretched handed Lina the phone.

The conversation was similar to the previous one, with smiles, thanks, compliments, giggles, some serious comments about the latest developments of the riots and a new promise to meet again. Lina was about to hand the phone back to Micky but then, remembering her recent lesson, stretched her arms as far as she could and pressed hard on the off button.

'Well done Gran, but you don't need to make a hole in it,' Micky commented with a light hint of sarcasm. 'Press lightly like this... look!'

'Did I do it right?' Lina was jubilant. 'Without my reading glasses... I am doing very well!' she complimented herself, pleased and proud.

As soon as Micky put it on the stand, the telephone rang a third time: 'This *has* to be for me!' he declared with impatience: 'Hello? Yes... yes... of course, here she is!' He looked at Lina, exaggerating his goggle-eyed expression and, approaching with the phone in his hand, exclaimed: 'And this one's called Jim. A younger man this time!'

'Ahhh, Jim!' Lina exclaimed, standing up from the sofa to take the handset. She sat comfortably back on the couch and crossed her legs. Once again her words were full of warmth. She thanked him for his kindness in having returned her bag; she congratulated him on his courage; told him twice to look after himself; asked to meet him again; sent him a hug, and a kiss, and another thank you. Then she skilfully turned the phone off and looked up at Micky, a happy smile flooding her face: 'It was Jim, the one who rescued my handbag. He's not much older than you.'

'And it looks like you need a secretary, Gran,' Micky joked. 'What do you think, Mum?'

Sofia was smiling, equally dazzled by her mother's popularity and aplomb.

'Are they all people who were at the meeting?' she asked.

'Yup. We only spent a couple of hour together, if that, but it feels as if I have known them much longer. Beautiful people!' And then she repeated: 'Truly beautiful people.' Lina's attention shifted to her grandson, who was more fidgety than usual. 'Are you waiting for an important call Micky?' She inquired.

'Err... fairly!' He was twitching with excitement while still remaining vague. It wasn't like him. 'She should call now, she promised,' he revealed, impatient to spill the beans.

'Where's your mobile?' Sofia asked.

'It broke yesterday,' Micky looked embarrassed. 'It fell into the toilet. I had it in my back pocket and when I sat down to poop...'

'Yes yes, fine, thank you, I understand,' his mother held her hand outstretched. 'And now?'

'Total disaster! I lost all my numbers,' he complained, throwing a further worried look at the home telephone.

Remembering a girl's name he had mentioned a while ago Lina threw a hook: 'Are you waiting for a call from Dawn?'

Micky took the bait: 'Noooo, Dawn is a classmate.' When he blushed they knew he was about to disclose his secret: 'It's Trish.'

'Trish... Trish...' Lina looked at him questioningly to find out more.

'McDonald,' he blurted out.

'But... your judo teacher?' Sofia looked very surprised.

'Exactly!' Micky confirmed, the redness in his face reached his ears and he was about to explode, with anxiety, excitement and the torture of waiting.

'So she's older than you. How old is she?' Lina couldn't hold her curiosity back.

'Twenty-eight!' If Micky had been a peacock, his tail would have been in full bloom. 'Ten years older than me... We are both adults,' he stated, as if he felt obliged to justify himself. 'Well... almost. I'll be eighteen in two months' time... in case anyone should forget.'

'Yes yes! I'm not saying anything! As far as I am concerned...' Sofia mumbled. 'And... are you dating?'

'I think so,' he replied nervously. 'I'm meant to be going to her place for dinner tonight. Waiting for her to confirm.' He kept buzzing around as if he had been powered by a small engine.

'Micky, can you do me a favour and sit down? You're making me sea-sick!' Sofia was trying hard to keep calm. Then a thought occurred to her: 'But why don't you just call her instead of suffering like this?'

'I can't!' Micky replied, sweating and on the verge of a hormonal explosion. 'She said 'I'll confirm by four'. If I phone her she'll think I'm desperate. No way! I'll just wait!' he declared stoically.

Lina and Sofia looked at their watch at the same time. It was three o'clock. They exchanged a look and tried to remain serious.

'Will there be many of you for dinner?' Lina asked, probing a little more. 'And... will Trish be cooking?'

Micky stopped pacing and stared at her: 'I don't know! I don't think so.' He started walking back and forth. 'I hope not!'

'Is she not a good cook?' Lina ventured.

The young man stopped in his tracks and looked at her open-mouthed. 'It's not the menu, or the quality of the food that worries me, Gran,' he spelt out. 'I hope there won't be many people. In fact... I hope it's just the two of us.' Pacing up and down again he groaned: 'Argh, this is torture!'

The doorbell rang. It had to be Charlie. Micky rushed to open it.

Charlie's loud voice boomed in from the porch and burst into the room in a flurry of words, when? how? why? She stopped in the doorway, her eyes on Lina, one hand holding her stick and the other planted firmly on her hip. 'How did you manage to get lost if I put you on the right bus?' she thundered. 'All you had to do was get on the 212 and it was done! How did you get to the Tottenham police headquarters? It is *miles* away. You were on television, you know? I was sat there watching the riots and who do I see? You! With that purple and red hat of yours. I almost had a heart attack!'

Lina laughed, excited: 'I know. Isn't it wonderful? Did I look good? I mean, could you clearly see it was me?'

'*Did I look good? Could you clearly see that it was me?*' Charlie exaggerated the Italian accent that still coloured Lina's pronunciation, as she approached the armchair on which she flopped dramatically. 'Who else has a hat like that?' she challenged Lina. 'You have to tell me what happened, without neglecting anything, I'm all ears!' Feeling observed, she shifted her gaze – partly guilty and partly reluctant – onto Sofia, who was staring at her with a serious face. 'Oh! How careless of me! I almost forgot to say hello. Sofia, come here darling!' Charlie opened her arms wide, inviting Sofia to come closer, and pouted, ready to receive a big kiss.

Sofia came forward and bent down to kiss her on the cheek. 'Before you start talking, I'd like to ask you something, Charlie.' The expression on her face showed clearly that she was not going to be taken for a ride. 'I told Mum to get a taxi back home. Why did she get on a bus instead?' Sofia had known Charlie since forever, from the moment she was born. Charlie had always been part of her life and Sofia had always liked her and – unlike many others – was not afraid of her.

Instead of answering straight away, Charlie turned to Micky. 'I am *desperate* for a cup of tea. Darling, would you be so kind as to bring me one with a splash of cold milk? I prefer English

Breakfast, if you have it, otherwise Earl Gray will do. Thank you! Ahhhhhhhhhh...' she exclaimed, and turned to Sofia. This time she was a little more humble: 'My dear! You're right, you're *absolutely* right. Your mother wanted to get a taxi but then we thought it would cost so much money... and the buses work so well...'

'They have their own lane,' Lina added to support her friend but, seeing the severe expression with which her daughter turned to look at her, she understood that perhaps – for the moment – it was better if she kept quiet.

'They work well if you know where you are going and if you're not wasted after having drained a bottle of wine,' Sofia replied, determined not to be misled.

Charlie laughed out loud. 'We had so much fun! Didn't we Lina?' she appealed to her friend for support. 'We had a fantastic afternoon. We talked about so many things, dusted out old memories, and we sang...'

'And danced,' Lina added, smiling at the memory.

'I'm sure you had a great time!' Sofia turned back to stare at Charlie. 'Do you have *any* idea how worried we were? And what danger Lina was in? We were up all night. We didn't know where she was. We called all the hospitals, notified the police.' There was no sign of a smile as she spoke, her accusing eyes fixed on Charlie and her pretty face oozing reproach.

Charlie held Sofia's stare, softened her voice and lowered it to a normal tone: 'I was worried too. And after seeing her on the news I felt awful.' She glanced at Lina with a tormented look and then went back to look at Sofia: 'I too was awake all night. Lina is the dearest friend I have. I could never forgive myself if anything had happened to her.' She paused for a long time, she seemed really upset. 'I'm sorry,' she said, looking at Lina first and then at Sofia, and covered her younger hand with hers, speckled with brown spots.

Sofia relaxed her shoulders and nodded her head. 'None of

us could have forgiven ourselves,' she remarked. Then she spoke sternly: 'You two ladies are not girls anymore. You ought to be an example for the young ones, instead of behaving like daredevil teenagers.'

'It's not just Charlie's fault... responsibility,' Lina stood in defence of her friend. 'I should have caught a taxi as you told me to, instead of worrying about the money. We just thought it was going to be easy, didn't we?' She looked at Charlie for confirmation. 'We are very sorry Sofia. I am truly... truly very sorry!'

'It's true Sofia, I am sorry,' said Charlie, glancing at Lina, grateful and relieved. 'So very sorry!'

Sofia hesitated, wondering whether she had been too hard on their old friend. In a softer tone she said: 'In a minute we'll be having sandwiches and tea.'

'Ah great! I was hoping to find something to eat,' Charlie perked up. 'I left the house as soon as I got your call and now I'm starving.' Slowly she stood up, helping herself with her cane and – limping deliberately as Sofia watched her – went to sit next to Lina on the couch.

Before leaving, Sofia stopped at the living room door and warned: 'And if you want to live together, you'll have to protect and take care of each other... and behave responsibly.' She stared at Charlie as she said this last sentence: 'If you carry on like yesterday, I'll worry a lot more if Mum lives with you than if she lived in Nottingham alone.'

As soon as Sofia left the room, with a look of amazement all over her face Charlie exclaimed: 'Did she say 'if we live together'?'

'She did,' Lina turned to face her friend. 'Do you remember that you asked me to come and live with you, when we were at the bus stop? You said 'come and live with me Lina, we'll save some money and have lots of fun. You also said that you feel lonely... I'm alone in Nottingham, and so...'

'Of course I remember, and you said yes, but we were both tipsy... I didn't think you had taken me seriously.'

'Well, yesterday I heard things that made me reflect and I started to think that, instead of rejecting the idea, just because I'm scared of change, I could at least give it a try.'

Charlie was looking at her as if she couldn't believe her ears.

'But maybe I am getting ahead of myself...' Lina hesitated.

'No... no no... not at all,' Charlie rushed to say. 'I'm just surprised... more like speechless, to be honest!'

'That's not like you!' Lina laughed and leaned back on the sofa. 'I was thinking we could try, for two or three months, and see if we get along. I would pay you rent of course. And if it doesn't work, no harm done... there might be other possibilities, or I'll go back to Nottingham.'

Charlie opened her mouth to speak, but then she closed it again without making any sound. Finally she spoke, her voice vibrating with emotion: 'I didn't expect this, Lina. I thought I'd find you in pieces after what happened to you yesterday... and that you'd scold me. I felt so guilty, you have no idea.' She placed her hand on Lina's arm and squeezed it. 'I was wondering where you could have ended up, what could have happened to you. As the hours went by and we didn't know anything about your whereabouts I felt worse and worse... all sorts of thoughts crossed my mind. I didn't know if I would ever see you again, and instead look at you! You're here safe and sound, confident as I've never seen you before and full of ideas for the future.'

'Well, and I have never seen you quite as unsettled, Charlie,' Lina admitted plainly. 'It's true that I had a pretty bad time... there were some dramatic moments, but I was rescued by some very special people. I ended up in a meeting where I heard new ideas that opened my eyes. I understood a lot of things and I have to say that, in spite of the bad moments, I'm glad it happened.'

Charlie looked stumped, lost for words.

'So, what do you think? Shall we give it a try?' Lina suggested, looking at her old friend with a smile.

Charlie spoke slower than usual: 'It sounds wonderful, but... you know me better than anyone else, Lina. I'm not easy to live with. Sometimes I think that nobody can stand me for very long, not even my children.'

'We know each other very well. I don't think we'll have many surprises.'

'I'm almost emotional... and that doesn't happen easily!'

'You can say that again! I have to think hard to remember when I last saw you touched.'

'I reserve it for exceptional moments,' Charlie conceded, looking sideways at her friend and smiling with a hint of irony. In a quieter voice she confessed: 'It's true that I get lonely. I promise you, Lina, I'll do my best not to be overwhelming.'

'I'm quite sure that it will take some goodwill from both of us. It's not as if I'm an angel, hey? I too have my hang-ups, my habits and my needs, but I think the idea is exciting.'

'It is very exciting! I can't wait. I can teach you about plants and flowers so you can help me in the garden; it's getting almost too much to handle on my own. You haven't exactly got green fingers, have you?' Charlie's boisterous self was returning by the moment.

'No, you're right. My gardening fingers are as brown and shrivelled as dead flowers,' Lina burst out laughing. 'But I'd love to learn. There are so many things new things I want to try!'

'More things?' Charlie was even more surprised.

'Oh yes! Tomorrow I'm going with a new friend to try an aerobics and dance class.'

'At your age?' Charlie couldn't help raising her voice.

'Yeah, why not? If they can do it, so can I. And also I want to contribute more to society, maybe I'll do some voluntary work. And I'm going to go to Buddhist meetings, like the one last night.'

Charlie was still in shock: 'I didn't imagine that you could make so many important decisions so quickly, from one day to the next. Either you've changed Lina, or I didn't know you as well as I thought I did.'

Lina blurted out: 'Everyone's saying the same thing! It's just that I'm starting to see now that I've always been full of fear... and worrying about what other people want, without ever thinking about what *I* want.' She pointed at her chest with her warped hand, bobbing and shaking her head: 'So, now it's time to start asking myself. If I want things to change, I will have to change first, won't I?'

'Oh! Alright then. Sounds great!' Turning to look at Lina straight in the eye Charlie asked: 'When were you thinking of moving in?'

'How about next week?... if that's okay with you,' Lina replied with ease. 'I brought some clothes with me, and the medicines I have here will last me almost a month. For now I don't need anything else and I can't wait to start my new life.' She glanced at her friend and laughed: 'Better close your mouth Charlie... if you don't want flies to get in there!'

Chapter 23

LET'S DANCE

It was Monday morning. Jane and Lina had decided to meet outside Carrot Dance Club, conveniently located halfway between Jane and Sofia's homes. Lina caught a bus most of the way and then covered the remaining distance with a ten minute stroll. Her legs and feet were aching at first – a result of the miles she had covered on foot on the Saturday – but after a few minutes the pain disappeared and she enjoyed the walk. As she arrived early, she sat on a low wall right outside the gym's glass door and waited for Jane. She was excited about dancing and, when she thought that maybe she was too old to start now, she told herself that if Jane could do it, she could do it too. She couldn't wait to see her again.

A young woman in a yellow summer dress approached. Speaking with a strong French accent she greeted Lina cordially and asked her if she needed anything. I'm waiting for a friend – Lina answered – and smiled back at the girl, who then settled herself behind the reception desk.

Lina's attention was caught by a woman in her sixties who had skilfully parked across the road and was now approaching with a confident step. She was wearing red trainers, black leggings and an 'I love London' t-shirt, with the word 'love' replaced by a big red heart. She smiled at Lina and greeted her with a bright 'good morning'. Instead of going straight in, she stopped near the entrance and started to talk to her. She was Dutch, her name was Lilka and she was waiting for a German friend; both were in the dance group. She explained that in the class they danced, but also did Pilates and yoga, and assured Lina that, although physically demanding, the lesson was a lot of fun.

One by one other women arrived – some were younger than Lina, others were older – and greeted each other cheerfully. A rush of excitement ran through her when she saw Jane from afar and instinctively got to her feet, ready to welcome her. The Buddhist meeting and the precious hours spent together at Jane's house, had laid and cemented the foundations of a great friendship. Lina didn't remember ever before talking about such personal and profound things with someone she had only just met... or of being listened to with such full attention. The things that Jane told her, with affection and understanding, had comforted her enormously and even when her new friend pushed her to reflect on her actions, she did so with great kindness. It felt as if they had known each other for a very long time.

When Jane reached the gym they hugged and then, very naturally, Jane slipped her arm under hers. Lina knew that the joy of seeing each other was mutual; there was no need to say anything. She could feel it from the way Jane looked at her, her warm smile, her thoughtful little gestures, like stroking her arm, squeezing her hand. Simple, unpretentious people understood each other easily; there was no need for many words. As they were about to enter the gym together, a woman approached with a vigorous step and followed them closely. She must have been around sixty, with a muscular snappy body and blond hair gathered in a ponytail.

'This is our teacher, Kate,' Jane said and, turning to Kate, introduced Lina to her, explaining that she would like to join the group.

Although Kate smiled graciously, Lina noticed a shadow of reluctance. Speaking amiably, the teacher hastened to explain:

'We are preparing a dance piece for a charity event organized by the gym. It's in two months time and all the different groups will perform; the salsa, tango, aerobics classes, the children. We are the 'grannies' and have already done more than a month's rehearsal.' Seeing Jane's surprised expression, she added: 'I don't know if your friend could manage to be ready in time.'

Lina hadn't expected this and didn't quite know how to react, but the words came out of her mouth, despite the surprise. 'I like dancing... and I have a good sense of rhythm...' she muttered. She could have held back and given up, but that would have been so disappointing. She had been thinking about it for the past two days and she really, really, wanted to be in it. Besides, apart from anything else, she was curious to see if she was able to do it. Her desire spoke for her: 'Could I try? Since I'm here... If afterwards you think that I'm not doing well, then...'

Jane intervened: 'I encouraged her to come. If she can't be ready for the show, she can at least join the group, can't she?' She asked gently but firmly and this seemed to convince Kate, who was wavering anyway.

'Of course! That sounds like a plan. Do come in Lina and let's see how it goes.' Kate gave her a more relaxed smile and then, in a clear resounding voice, individually greeted the women who had already arrived: Good morning Lilka! Morning Marion! Good morning Suzanne! Some women wore stretchy outfits and, despite their advanced age, had a well toned body. Others, like Lina, wore leggings and T-shirt. Some wore trainers, others were barefoot. Lina didn't have suitable shoes and anyway, if the floor was not cold, she liked the feel of it beneath her bare feet.

In the dance hall there was a large mirrored wall, four or five ballet bars and a row of exercise balls. While waiting for the lesson to begin, the women gathered in small groups and discussed the weekend. The conversation inevitably turned to the riots continuing across London. They had now spread to other cities in England, too.

Meanwhile Kate was busying herself with a computer connected to two speakers. When she heard the beginning of a song by Abba she smiled satisfied and hastened to prepare the equipment they would be using during the lesson. She laid hula hoops of various colours against a wall, placed green and red exercise bands across the stretching bars and leaned a bunch of coloured sticks against the corner where two brightly painted walls met. Accompanied by one of the women she left the room. They returned a few minutes later dragging two heavy bags containing weights, while a third woman carried a stack of mats.

In the meantime more women had arrived and now there were about fifteen all together; quite a crowd.

'Let's make a start, girls!' Kate encouraged them glancing at her wristwatch and then gazing at them all in the big mirror. 'Today we have a new lady called Lina. Welcome Lina!' The announcement was followed by a chorus of 'welcome' accompanied by many smiling faces.

Lina felt truly welcome and her heart was full of excitement. She positioned herself towards the back of the room, in the fourth row, next to Jane.

As soon as the notes of Dancing Queen filled the gym it became impossible to stand still.

The instructions reached them loud and clear: 'Let's warm-up. We march! Raise your knees, head to the right, to the centre, to the left. Check your breathing.' Looking in the mirror, Kate smiled, one by one, at all the participants. She moved with great vigour in rhythm with the music. Her body looked strong and supple and her beautiful blue eyes were shining with exuberance.

The pace was fast and Lina had no time to look at anyone else, too focused on the exercises, trying to do the best she could. Hearing Dancing Queen took her back many years. She must have been in her forties and Sofia was a teenager wearing hotpants and white boots, just like the Abba girls. Bruno strongly disapproved of Sofia wearing mini-skirts and hotpants and had forbidden her to go out unless her legs were covered at least down to her knees. But then... he objected to everything that was new and progressive; he even disapproved of Sofia wearing flairs. Lina was more permissive and knew there was no point in forbidding Sofia to dress like her friends, so she objected only mildly to her daughter showing her beautiful legs and, unbeknown to her father, the girl regularly did. She must have inherited those legs from me, Lina reflected with a mischievous smile because – not wanting to be falsely modest – when she was younger her legs had always been highly admired. Sofia had saved up to buy 'Dancing Queen' and played the record over and over again, dancing in front of any available mirror in the house, swaying her hips and prancing around, proud and thrilled with her hotpants and booties. Lina had loved watching her daughter dance and her zest for life. Eventually the song had got under her skin, too. More and more often she would join Sofia's dancing, daring her daughter's reaction – a mixture of embarrassment and amusement. Loudly she would beg Lina to stop, whilst surreptitiously enjoying the fun. Such precious memories flooded back, simmering in those well loved notes, and Lina's face broke into a happy smile.

Kate kept giving sonorous commands, checking the group's movements in the mirror.

Lina felt she was being observed but didn't mind; on the contrary, she liked it and when her eyes met Kate's, they both smiled. There were keywords that defined the exercises and soon Lina became familiar with them. She especially liked it when they used dance moves: mambo, cha-cha-cha, swing. They always started with the leg movements and gradually added the arm motions, making the progress quite effortless.

Lina found that she could keep up with all this new activity and, with the encouragement of the music, she felt exhilarated... as if she could fly.

Having a large mirror reflecting such a big group made it all look quite impressive. It sent back the image of fifteen women of an advanced age, active and happy. They were all so different: short blond hair; long hair dyed a beautiful ginger colour; beautifully cut grey hair; thick soft white hair. Some women were tall, other were short; some had skinny bodies while others were quite robust, one or two decidedly big, but all fit, toned and definitely agile. They moved in synchronicity and were clearly enjoying themselves.

Now they danced to the rhythm of Madonna's Like a Prayer – one of Lina's favourite songs – and they zigzagged, bent, stretched and hopped, following the instructions that kept coming fast.

Lina never remembered all the words of the song – although she learned them she couldn't retain them for long – but loved to sing along and was quite content to pronounce just the end of each sentence. By the time this song came out, she had become a grandmother and Sofia had opened her first shoe shop. Lina often spent a few days in London looking after Claudia, who was only two or three years old. The child adored the song too and asked for it repeatedly, saying 'sing take you there', so much so that one day Steve had come home with the latest Madonna cassette for the tape recorder and they had played it, sang and danced to it over and over and over again.

Every now and then Kate instructed 'Don't look at Lilka', or 'There's someone out of rhythm... and it's not me!' and made them laugh, in an atmosphere of unity, commitment and lightness that made Lina feel inspired and young. From time to time she noticed a glance and a smile from Jane through the reflection in the mirror and felt delighted to be there.

'Quick change, don't stop and get a hula hoop,' Kate firmly directed and, as soon as they stood ready in their place, the Refrigerator song by Dire Straits began to fill the hall. It was probably not the real title, but Lina had always called it that. Kate's strong voice rang out instructions for a mambo and hula hoop routine. They repeated it several times and each time they performed it better. The mirror didn't lie and the reflection of the colourful group proved that they moved in time and rhythmically, just like an ensemble troupe... more or less.

As soon as that exercise was over, Kate told them to get a set of weights each from the big bags. The quick swap left just enough time for a sip of water.

At first – thinking she was just a beginner – Lina chose the one-pound weights, the lightest ones, but then she changed her mind and picked up the two-pound ones; her arms were strong, she was used to working them hard.

The next track reminded her of a Fellini film, circus-like music that made her feel a bit ridiculous, but it didn't matter; it was funny and she was having a great time. Flexing the arms, bending the knees, those who could bend more did so, while those who suffered from arthritis in their knees were advised to take it easier. Lina realized that she could bend further than most and felt encouraged and proud of herself. Despite the sweat and her accelerated heartbeat she felt strong, light and couldn't stop smiling. She looked in the mirror and saw Jane smiling at her affectionately.

For the last part of the lesson they lay on mats. 'Only twenty abs,' Kate ordered, full of energy. What she really meant was: twenty forward abdominals. She seemed to have eyes on the back of her head and enjoined 'don't pull your neck, look at the ceiling' just when Lina was pulling her neck. After a hundred or so abs and a few positions with their legs raised, wide open in the air – not a very lady-like pose, Lina giggled to herself – and when they had just about reached their limit, Kate called the end.

Meditation music began to flow from the speakers. They lay on the floor, arms open with their bodies in the shape of a cross. They twisted, stretched, breathed deeply. They ended the session on all fours, arching their back like a cat, and then lowering it and raising their faces up like a cobra. Lina looked at herself in the mirror, hair dishevelled, face relaxed.

And finally, with a satisfied grin, Kate announced the end of the lesson declaring 'Time for coffee!' The announcement was greeted with cheers and a spontaneous collective applause. They had danced an hour and a half without interruption.

Jane approached; her cheeks were pink and she looked ten years younger. 'Did you like it?' she asked cheerfully.

'I loved it!' Lina smiled from ear to ear. 'Let's hope the teacher is happy with me.'

Just then Kate came over with her assured step. 'You fit in very well, Lina. I hope you enjoyed it and that you'll continue to come to class,' she said with a bright smile.

Lina felt so happy she could have burst. In the back of her mind there was a thought pushing its way to the forefront: maybe she would be able to join the dance group for the charity event? The very idea made her heart flutter. She checked herself. This morning had been good enough and, although she was quite exhausted, she felt completely satisfied.

In groups of two or three, the women started a small lively procession towards a nearby cafe. Lina had hardly ever gone to a cafe. She was not used to spending money on herself and at home she made her own coffee with the Italian coffee machine. Bruno on the contrary – may his soul rest in peace – had never given up his daily espresso at the Italian bar – the real espresso, he used to say – and his cigarettes. For those things there was always money, even if it meant eating rice and beans the last week of every month, until he got paid again. She, on the other hand, had saved all her life and thanks to that frugality had managed to put aside a nice little nest egg. Now Lina didn't have to justify to anyone how she spent her money and she felt daring as, step by step, walking beside Jane, they approached the River Cafe. They sat at a table and the circle widened as more and more women arrived. Lina ordered a cappuccino without asking the price, feeling independent and free.

Jane introduced her to the other ladies by simply saying that they were friends, without going into the details of how or when they had met. Lina was grateful for her discretion. Being the first time she met all those people she preferred to listen rather than talk. She had learnt that in life it was useful to listen and understand who was in front of us, before opening up. For each mouth two ears, said a proverb – it was probably Chinese by the sound of it – which taught her to talk less and listen more.

Lina discovered that the Dutch lady was as old as she, had been living in London for thirty years and her husband was fifteen years her senior. Birgit, the German lady was eighty years old and a widow. Today she was the centre of attention because an old suitor, from her teenage years, had made contact. The women wanted to know all the details and Birgit was happy to tell them that he was a widower, had tracked her down and contacted her after more than sixty years, and asked if they could meet. He was going to arrive in London at the end of the month from Australia, where he had been living all those years. The women shared with her the excitement of this new development and toasted with cups of coffee, cheering as if it were champagne. Lucy, a tall, elegant and well-spoken lady with short brown hair, used to be a hostess for an airline and had travelled all over the world. She wore tens of silver bracelets that jingled at every movement, smiled freely and seemed to find everything wonderful. She drank her coffee through a short straw and, noticing that Lina was observing her, explained that a year before she had suffered from mouth cancer but, after a complex operation and further treatment, had overcome it completely. The only memory was a slight difficulty in using her mouth normally. Lucy spoke with a beautiful warm voice and Lina was impressed with her relish for life; she warmed to her immediately.

After a while Kate arrived, her blond hair wet from a shower. Lina couldn't believe she was almost seventy years old. She didn't look a day over sixty. She also discovered that Kate was from Nottingham and this made her like her even more. In front of everyone Kate complimented Lina on how well she had danced and made her glow with delight.

When it was time to leave, Lina and Jane walked to the bus stop together. The air was very warm, almost stuffy, with no wind whatsoever. It was a real summer's day and Lina, who tended to suffer the cold, had to remove her cardigan and carry it over her arm. Jane's bus arrived first. She was now going to do her afternoon shift as a Macmillan nurse. She hugged Lina warmly and reminded her of the meeting at her house this coming Wednesday.

Sitting on the bus home, Lina looked out of the window and felt totally fulfilled. She had never done dancing and aerobics at the same time; it was such a good idea. It made all that hard work feel as if it was fun and she had loved every minute of it. She had never gone to a cafe with a group of women and hadn't thought that at her age she could make new friends. She was clearly wrong because nothing seemed to be easier. Her eyes were opening to a new, exhilarating reality. She thought she was going to be tired after all that physical exercise, but instead she felt lighter than before. She looked at the houses, trees, bicycles, women, men and children walking on the pavement and smiled. She would get a bus pass which, as a pensioner, would be discounted... it might even be free, and began to think that she might actually enjoy living in London.

Chapter 24

THERE IS NOTHING SACRED ANYMORE

After a sandwich and a cup of tea with Steve, Lina went to bed for a twenty-minute nap and woke up two hours later. She was a little bit slow after all that exercise, but her back was straighter and she was sure she was taller. It was silent in the house. Steve was quietly working upstairs. Lina prepared a cup of coffee and sipped it on the sofa watching television. She was hoping they would show her caught on camera at the beginning of the riots. How she would love to see herself on TV!

Unable to sit still for long Lina put on a bright apron, it had a view of the Rialto Bridge in Venice; Claudia had bought it years ago. She tidied up the living room and vacuumed the carpet. Then, with a pair of bright yellow marigolds, she cleaned the kitchen, glancing at the television screen every now and then. When the five o'clock news started, she sat on the sofa to watch it. The images being shown had been taken only a couple of hours earlier in Hackney central, about a mile from where she had been robbed. The explosive war-like atmosphere of that day – she was never going to forget it – had not dissolved. On the contrary, it had expanded and intensified across the more deprived parts London.

The news showed three police cars stopping at the end of Mare Street, the wide main road running through Hackney Central. It was a sweltering, oppressive afternoon; there was that airless mugginess that normally preceded a big storm. Even inside the house it was so hot and humid that Lina struggled to breathe properly. Ten officers had surrounded two black men to arrest them, but the men resisted. They shouted, argued, wanted to know what they were being accused of, insisting they hadn't done anything wrong; they were innocent of any crime. They tried to push themselves free, but the policemen shoved them back against the wall. A large crowd had gathered around, shouting at the officers, calling them murderers. A rising, rebellious rage was spreading through the sultry day.

A group of young men kicked and punched the windscreens of the three police cars parked under the railway bridge, encouraged by passersby who stopped to watch the action. Sticks and rubbish bins replaced fists and feet, until the windows finally shattered to the sound of cheers from the excited crowd. The spark marking the beginning of the most violent night of the London riots had been lit.

The camera focused on a group of rioters who began to pluck up the shutters of stores, pulling with all their might, till they managed to get inside and, like maniacs, grab anything they could lay their hands on. They entered a supermarket through the shattered glass windows and came out with cans of coke and bottles of water, to drink or use as missiles against the police. A mood of revolution blended with that of a big party, the chaos was spreading like wildfire. Wherever the police stood, a crowd would gather close by and begin to break, destroy or set alight anything they could find. In that boiling cauldron of public rage, resentment and exasperation, there were people genuinely angry and tired of discrimination who fought for change and justice; there were also those who craved some long awaited revenge and others who jumped at the opportunity to let off steam and take what they could. Many were determined to fight face to face with the police. The shouts and screams of the rioters, mixed with the suffocating heat, created an incandescent atmosphere.

Lina was watching in disbelief, quite unable to accept that what she was seeing was happening only a mile or so away.

Keeping a safe distance from the direct action, groups of people stood outside the shops and couldn't make up their minds as to whether they wanted to stay, or leave and go home. Men and women of all ages seemed glued to their patch of pavement, sensing that something big was building up. In the middle of the road at least a hundred policemen in parallel rows stood with their visors down, shield and truncheon in hand, Alsatian dogs on a leash. At times they moved slowly, other times they ran a few metres and then stopped. They were covered from head to toe in their dark uniform and ankle-high leather boots. They must have been boiling hot, Lina mused.

Pedestrians watched, walking by their side. A young man in a red T-shirt zigzagged on his bicycle right in front of the first row of officers. He showed no fear as he mocked them. People filmed the action on their mobiles; others phoned friends and reported what was going on. When loud, alarming bangs of firecrackers burst in rapid succession people looked startled. A clamour of broken bottles preceded the sight of a glass recycling bin that had been knocked over on the pavement, the shattered glass spilling onto the road. Shouts and screams, car and shop alarms went off all at the same time, causing an assault on the ears, acute, shrill, ill-fated. The air was pervaded by the noises of a neighbourhood exploding with rage.

Lina couldn't take her eyes off the television screen and wondered how it was possible that a city like London should descend into such mayhem. Things usually seemed to work well: transport was excellent; people behaved in a polite and tolerant manner; different races and religions seemed to coexist in peace; there were jobs for those who wanted to work and unemployment benefits for those who couldn't. The health system was not always perfect but, on the whole, it was very good; anyone who needed medical attention received it and the health workers were kind. Even now, when she went to the hospital, she was surprised to see how many different nationalities there were among doctors, nurses and support staff. She never got bored when she was in the waiting areas because she loved to people-watch. Between patients and medical personnel there would be at least twenty, maybe even thirty different nationalities: black Africans, nurses of Jamaican descent, Indian doctors, Muslim women with their heads covered and well-groomed faces, Chinese and South American, Spanish and lately people from Eastern Europe. Each had their particular way of speaking English, their own mannerism, but all addressed the patients with courtesy and Lina had been called 'love' with all sorts of different accents.

She couldn't understand why such dramatic riots should explode right now. It was so sad!

She remembered what Charlie had said about the young black man who was killed by the police, and Nelson who said that black kids were discriminated against and felt alienated. Was lack of justice, lack of respect, the cause of all this? Lina liked English policemen. They were kind, often nice, always ready to help her, but maybe they were not like that with everyone. She was an elderly white woman and had never experienced what it meant to be black. She couldn't ignore what she had heard from people she trusted; she believed what they said to be true. But then, many of the rioters she could see on the news were white. Were some people just taking advantage of the chaos?

Lina glanced at the television one last time, shook her head and clicked her tongue as if to say: what a shame.

With an effort she stood up and went back to the kitchen. She opened the fridge, checked what ingredients there were for the evening dinner and took out an onion to sauté. In the cupboard she found olive oil and a can of peeled tomatoes. With the sharp knife she started to chop the onion into thin slices and with the back of her hand rubbed her weeping eyes.

Claudia arrived home at six o'clock. 'It's boiling out there!' she stated in a cheerful voice. 'I went on the river bank with a colleague on my lunch break and it was almost too hot to sunbathe. Still, we managed. I even got a little sunburned, I think.' She hastened to kiss her grandmother.

'You are a little bit red, indeed... on your forehead. You have definitely changed colour,' Lina observed.

Trying to keep out of Lina's way in the little kitchen, Claudia perched on the red stool. She wanted to know what her grandmother had done during the day and how the dance class had been.

Lina was more than happy to share the many new different emotions she had felt and couldn't help noticing the wonder in her granddaughter's face.

'Nonna, you talk with such enthusiasm and energy that any young woman would envy you. Listening to you makes me feel like... maybe I can trust that the future will turn out ok.'

'Of course it will, my love,' Lina reassured her, while stirring the chopped onion that was frying in olive oil over a low flame, the aroma pervading the whole house. 'At the meeting the other night they said that we always start from the present moment and that it is useful to think about the past only so that we can learn from our mistakes.' Wooden spoon in hand, she turned to look at Claudia and smiled brightly: 'I also learn from other people's mistakes, to tell you the truth, not just from my own. We can see when someone does something wrong, can't we? It is often clearer to those who observe from the outside than to those who are in the thick of a situation. So why not learn from everybody? But after that, you have to look forward... which is what I'm trying to do. I'm starting to see I have much more to offer than I once thought.' She smiled again. Her face was relaxed and her eyes, which had always been full of curiosity, now expressed a new-found confidence and poise.

'I'd love to be optimistic like you, but instead I feel like I'm in the eye of a storm. I'm scared. Sometimes I think I'll never be happy,' Claudia confided.

Lina was filling a pot with water for the pasta and turned to look at her. Claudia hurried to take it from her hands, put it on the gas stove and lit the ring. Taking advantage of closeness, she bent down, hugged her grandmother and gave her a kiss on her grey hair: 'Love you!'

The elderly lady smiled and stroked her cheek: 'And so do I. I wish you happiness darling, with all my heart. This is a difficult time for you. Right now, you have some decisions to make. I know you will make the right ones.'

'But how can I be sure? I'm so afraid of making a mistake.'

'Well, first – I think – you need to understand what it is you want,' reflected Lina, slowly stirring the sauté onions. 'And to believe it might be possible to achieve it. I really liked what Beverley said about our fears helping us see what our desires are. Do you remember what I told you about her list of fears and determinations? Why don't you get a pen and paper, Claudia? While I finish dinner, perhaps you could try it?'

'I wish I had been at that meeting too. It might have done me good.' Claudia went into the living room and came back with a notepad and a pen. 'What am I afraid of? A lot of things right now. The possibility of moving to Saudi Arabia scares me to death.'

'Draw two columns and write it on the left,' Lina encouraged her, whilst pulling two large courgettes from the vegetable box in the fridge.

'I'm afraid of marrying Tom.'

Lina nodded in silence.

'Of leaving this house. Leaving London.'

'Mmhm mmhm.' Lina chopped the small bunch of parsley she had washed.

'I am nervous about how I feel about Danny,' she ventured.

Lina faced away from Claudia and hoped her granddaughter hadn't noticed that she was holding her breath. Even without looking at her, she knew that the young woman was blushing. 'What do you feel for him?' she asked without turning around, peeling a clove of garlic.

'I like him too much... Everything about him, how he talks, what he says. He makes me laugh... I like how he makes decisions, then and there, with no hesitation. I like how he walks and... how he looks at me.'

Lina started to cut a red pepper into thin strips, her head bent, her eyes focused on her chopping board: 'And Tom is different?' She heard from the intonation in her voice that Claudia was smiling sadly.

'Oh Nonna! Tom is the opposite!' With an ill-concealed note of sorrow she elaborated: 'Tom doesn't make me laugh. Maybe once, at first, we laughed together, but it's been years since we've done so. He hardly speaks to me and when he does, I'm not interested in the things he talks about. And the decisions... He made the decision to go to Saudi Arabia without even consulting me. I just can't swallow this one. And as far as looking at me... I don't think he has looked at me for months, and if he looks at me, he doesn't see me... not really.'

Lina laid the knife on the wooden chopping board and slowly turned around, her eyes full of tenderness.

'But...' Claudia hurried to add, 'I know that Danny is married and has two daughters. So I should forget all about him.'

Lina looked at her in silence for a few moments, studying her face. Then she spoke: 'You're a beautiful person, Claudia. You are good, generous, full of consideration for others. You are a smart and talented girl.' She gazed at her full of love.

Her granddaughter was absorbing every word she was saying.

'You deserve someone who appreciates your qualities, who loves and respects you. Don't accept anything less. Mediocrity doesn't suit you, it's not for you. Nor is the deception of a clandestine relationship. Respect yourself.'

Claudia was nodding sadly, biting her inner cheek.

'There is an Italian proverb that says: better alone than in bad company.' Lina looked at her granddaughter openly: 'Don't be afraid to be alone, it will not be forever.'

Claudia's eyes were wet with tears: 'Are you saying I should break up with Tom?'

Lina held her stare: 'You have to ask your heart.'

'But he loves me...' the young woman stopped abruptly, as if the sound of those words suddenly felt wrong, '...in his own way. I don't want to hurt him. And I don't want to hurt his parents, they are good to me, they love me.'

'And you... what do *you* want?'

Claudia looked at her with dismay: 'I don't know!'

'But you know what you don't want, and that's a good start,' Lina reassured her. 'The Buddhists I met chant as a way to listen to what their heart tells them, especially when they have to make a difficult decision. It works for them. Maybe it can help you. Don't be in a hurry to make any decisions and don't let anyone put pressure on you. You must be sure.'

Claudia handed her the notepad. She looked deflated, but there was a glimmer of hope: 'Can you write it down for me?... that sentence. At this point I'll try anything. It all seems a bit weird, but anything must be better than this torment.'

From her pocket Lina pulled out a card and, with her right hand deformed by arthritis, carefully copied the sentence on the first page: 'Now try to pronounce it properly. You say it like this: Nam-myoho-renge-kyo.' She made her repeat those new sounds until she was satisfied with how her granddaughter enunciated it.

Claudia looked at her in amazement: 'Just saying it a few times has calmed me down a little; but it's a bit embarrassing to say it out loud... I feel stupid.'

'Then go to your room. When dinner is ready I'll call you.'

'I can't leave you to prepare dinner all by yourself, I want to help you!'

'I'd rather you did something that might help you feel better. It's all done here. Go sweetheart... and don't worry about a thing. I am happy if you're happy.' She gave her an affectionate spank and directed her to the stairs.

'My grandmother's sending me off to chant a Buddhist mantra,' Claudia exclaimed, incredulous and amused at the same time. 'How did we get to this point?' And with a giggle she added: 'Seems there is nothing sacred anymore!'

With the gas ring on minimum the water for pasta was slowly heating up. Everything else for dinner was ready and Lina turned the TV on again. It was time for the news. They were still talking about Hackney's troubles that were escalating to unprecedented levels when, at seven, Sofia arrived home. She put her handbag down in the living room and placed two large shopping bags just outside the kitchen. 'Hi Mum, how are you? It smells delicious!'

'We have aubergines in tomato, roasted peppers and sautéed zucchini. The water for the pasta is ready and, as soon as Steve and Micky get back, I'll put the spaghetti in. How did it go today?' She stood up and turned the television volume down. 'Let's sit down a few minutes. I'll prepare you an aperitif.'

'But isn't there anything to do?' her daughter asked.

'No, everything is ready. Let's just have ten minutes and a little chat.'

Lina returned with a glass of red wine and sparkling water with a green olive inside.

'A spritz! You're spoiling me Mum.' Sofia brought her lips to the glass and sipped the drink voluptuously.

'You deserve it. You work harder than any of us. Now tell me what you did today.' Lina liked to listen to the day's stories. Sofia saw so many people. Men and women came to her shoe shop; female customers in particular opened up with the shop assistants, especially if they were willing to listen. They heard the stories of women who needed, or wanted, something new and asked for advice; some were feeling low and buying a pair of shoes made them feel a little better. Then there were those who adored a bargain or had limited resources and looked only among the sale racks. There were also wealthier customers who browsed only the newest models, which were beautiful but expensive. With every single one of them there was some sort of exchange, humanity, friendliness, a joke or a giggle.

'Every time a customer leaves the store I feel richer. I love it there, the hours seem to fly by,' said Sofia with a smile, while she twisted to place the empty glass on the coffee table next to the sofa.

'Have you thought any more about the painting course?' Lina asked. 'I heard you talking to Charlie about it.'

'Yes, I thought about it a lot, but I don't know when I would find time to paint. Sometimes I don't even have time to take a shower, let alone find half a day to do a painting course. Maybe later, in a few years time, but for now... it's not even worth thinking about it.'

'I understand... and I know you are very busy. But you need to do something for yourself now, not in a few years' time.' Lina was concerned about her daughter. 'If I move to London, I can help you find the time.'

'You have already done a lot for me, Mum. I don't want to take advantage.'

'I'm your mother Sofia, and I want you to be happy. Why don't you try doing the Buddhist chanting too? While you chant, listen to your heart.' Lina seemed to repeat the same thing to everyone but, since she had started to chant herself, she was getting a lot of ideas and inspiration. She also felt better, both mentally and physically, and full of new, exciting energy. 'Claudia's doing it now too, to clear her mind.'

'Really? Claudia? Now? In her room?' Sofia was pleasantly surprised.

'Yes, yes and yes.'

'It will do her good. I remember how much I liked it. I can't believe I forgot about it.'

'Why don't you do ten minutes now? Meanwhile I'll put the

pasta on. Steve and Micky will be here soon and then we can eat. Go upstairs love, nobody will disturb you.'

'But I want to help you, Mum. You did everything alone,' Sofia protested.

'There's nothing to do. Claudia helped me and everything's ready. Go. Disappear. Make the most of this precious little time.' And, with a caress on her arm, she directed her daughter towards the stairs.

Taking advantage of that little break, Lina prepared a 'spritz' for herself and also put a little green olive in it – why not? It was the first time in her life that she prepared an aperitif for herself.

She turned the TV volume up and, glass in hand, sat on the couch to watch the latest developments. There were people with balaclavas; others with scarves raised over their faces who threw Molotov cocktails at the police; others still hurled bricks with full force, aiming well, with the intention to hit and hurt. A lorry carrying wooden planks had been opened and looted, providing unlimited ammunition. In an area of high-rise buildings, various gangs, normally hostile to one another, had grouped together against the police, forgetting their rifts for a short time. The BBC envoy reported that a bunch of people had raged against a policeman who had found himself isolated. They could have killed him but, luckily, he had been rescued. The air was crackling with static electricity and, even watching from such safe place, sitting on a comfortable sofa, Lina felt her hair stand on end.

The violence unleashed seemed unstoppable. A stolen car was driven at full speed towards a row of policemen. Stores were being ignited, ignoring the people living in the apartments upstairs, who were forced to run away. Cars exploded. In a part of London where the riots had spread to a historic furniture store was set alight. The flames threatened to extend to a nearby tower block with dozens of apartments whose residents were evacuated. One of the people who lived in the area was being interviewed. He said that it felt like being in a war zone.

Another neighbour said that some of the rioters seemed to be having fun. 'They are in their hundreds,' he remarked. 'They go into the shops and empty them. They can take what they want. They are having fun, they laugh. They steal the spirits, they drink them and celebrate. In five minutes they destroy what others spent a lifetime to build. They are destroying our – their – neighbourhood.'

Lina sighed. She got up, turned the television off and went back to the kitchen. The water for the pasta was boiling and she threw in a handful of coarse salt. From the bedrooms upstairs she could hear the buzz of the chanting: it was the sound of her daughter and granddaughter reciting the mantra, each one in her room. Claudia's voice was hardly audible, while Sofia's voice was louder, more confident and infused with the joy of having found again something she once loved. Lina couldn't help noticing the striking contrast between the war-like atmosphere she had just witnessed on TV and the peace inside the house at this very moment.

She opened a packet of spaghetti, broke them in two and poured them into the pot, stirring them with a long wooden spoon. In a quarter of an hour they would be cooked.

The door bell rang, not once, but twice, and then a third time. It was Micky who was in too much of a hurry, or too hungry, to look for his key and hadn't enough patience to wait for his father, who was unloading boxes from the boot of the car. As soon as she opened the door, she found herself lifted off the ground, wrapped in her grandson's enthusiastic embrace.

'My beautiful granny. It smells so good in here. And I am so hungry! I could eat a whole buffalo, noooo problem. How are you? What are we eating?'

Lina laughed: 'Put me down, you're holding me too tight. You'll break me!' Once her feet were back on the ground, she asked him about the driving lesson. Micky was determined to get his driving license, hopefully on the very day of his eighteenth birthday, and Steve was taking him out to practice.

'It went very well! Dad took me on the North Circular. There was hellish traffic; it was rush hour, so we were stuck. As soon as the traffic started to move, everyone sped up to fifty miles an hour and I sped away with them, too. It was fun!'

And there came Steve carrying a big box that Micky hurried to get out of his hands: 'Give it to me Dad. Tell Grandma how well I drive. I'm great, right?'

'Very good!' Steve confirmed with a smile and bent down to kiss Lina: 'It smells great! What did you prepare?'

The family sat together at the table. A classic bottle of Chianti – one of those bottles with a round body and close-fitting straw basket – was passed around and compliments on dinner poured out, especially from Sofia, who deeply appreciated not having to cook after a long day at the shop. Steve – who loved Lina's cooking – joked that it was 'Italiano verace' – true Italian – with an unspecified accent from southern Italy.

In between mouthfuls, seemingly unaware of her recent turmoil and confusion, Micky questioned Claudia: 'So, is my little sister getting married, or not? I'd like to become an uncle as soon as possible, if you don't mind.'

Lina and Sofia exchanged concerned glances.

'Don't count on it, dear,' Claudia promptly replied. 'I'm certainly not ready to make you an uncle. What about you? And your girlfriend? If we can call her a girl! She's twenty years older than you, if I'm not mistaken,' she retorted. 'You're her toy boy!'

'Twenty years, now! She's only ten years older than me,' Micky replied, and blushed violently.

'You've gone all purple, even your ears are red, you should see yourself,' insisted Claudia. 'In my opinion she only wants you for sex.' It had been a long time since Claudia had joked like that. They were all surprised, and pleased.

Micky was quick to answer: 'Well, that's perfect, isn't it?

What more can I ask for!'

They were all laughing and only Sofia heard the phone ring.

'I'm going!' Micky snapped, jumping to his feet.

'Hello? Good evening! Yes, very well... thanks... Now I'll put her on to you.' Turning towards the dinner table he said: 'It's for you Gran, your friend.'

'Which one?'

'One of the many,' Sofia replied, laughing. 'You have more friends than me.'

It was Jane, who had received a message that had been circulating all over East London. It was a spontaneous initiative that had just begun and was spreading like wildfire. The people of Hackney, in response to what was happening, were meeting in the morning to clean up and repair the damage caused by the riots. They were all volunteers and everyone was welcome. Those who decided to go were to bring at least a broom, a dustpan and brush to sweep up the broken glass, and strong bags to collect the rubbish. Jane was going to be in front of the Town Hall at eight. Did she want to come too?

'Sure! I'll be there at eight, if not before,' Lina answered with enthusiasm. Then she added: 'Wait a minute!' Tapping the receiver with her hand, she reported what she'd just being told. 'Do you want to come too?'

'I can't unfortunately, I have a deadline to meet,' Steve replied.

'I can't either, what a pity,' said Micky.

'I want to come!' Claudia declared.

'Don't you have to go to work?' Sofia asked.

'Yes, but I'll go later; I'll stay on in the afternoon. I'm not going to miss this.'

'I'm coming too!' Sofia decided there and then.

'And the shop?' Steve asked.

'The assistant can open up. I don't want to miss this moment either. With what is happening it will be nice to clean up all together. I can get to the shop later.'

Lina drew the receiver back to her ear: 'So, I am coming with my daughter and my granddaughter... Yes, the three generations,' she confirmed with a smile. 'Thank you Jane... see you tomorrow!'

Chapter 25

TUESDAY - THE HUMAN REVOLUTION

It was seven o'clock in the morning. Sitting at the dining room table, her hands wrapped around her favourite mug, Lina was sipping her hot coffee, freshly made in the Italian coffee machine. The strong bitter taste enriched by dark cane sugar was a unique pleasure which she loved to savour calmly. She willingly got up even when she was still tired, anticipating the enjoyment of that first cup. She could hear someone coming down the stairs. By the sound and rhythm of the steps it was probably Sofia, who – Lina knew – would head straight for the kitchen to make herself some tea. Her daughter didn't like to talk in the morning until she had had her first cup. The sounds told her that she had turned on the tap, was adding a little water to the kettle and switched it on.

Whilst waiting for the water to boil Sofia came to the threshold of the dining room and greeted her mother with a cautious smile. Her face still half asleep and hair dishevelled, she was wearing a lovely dressing gown with colourful flowers.

'You look beautiful, even with untidy hair,' said Lina.

Sofia smiled. 'Thank you.'

'Did you sleep well?'

'Not really! I'll tell you in a minute.' Sofia went back into the kitchen and returned with a steaming cup of milky tea. She bent down and kissed Lina on the head - something she had never done before - then sat down and sipped her tea. 'I was awake for a long time,' she said slowly, thoughtfully. 'I kept thinking about the painting course and, when I fell asleep, I dreamt I was

276

in front of a huge canvas supported by two easels.' She looked at her mother and smiled sleepily. 'The teacher was telling me: You have a big brush stroke, Sofia. Give brush strokes... like this. He extended his arm as far as he could and made a semicircle in the air. He was encouraging me and I was happy.' She sipped her tea slowly, looking inside the cup. 'I enjoyed painting so much!'

'You were very good, gifted, all the teachers said the same,' confirmed Lina. 'I'm sure you'll be able to find some time to attend a course, you'll see. Enquire with the college.'

'I'd love to, but at the moment it seems an impossible dream, unless someone adds a couple of hours to the day,' her daughter sighed.

'Whenever you really wanted to do something, you've always found a way. You never let anyone or anything stop you. I know you little poppet,' Lina declared warmly.

Her mother had often used that phrase when she was a child, and it made Sofia smile. 'I suppose you're right. Maybe in the past I had more energy,' she remarked.

'You had more time. Now you have a job, a family, the house to manage.'

'It's true... but... while I was chanting last night I felt such a desire, a yearning, and I just wanted to paint.' Sofia looked at her mother. There was a vibrant light in her eyes and she became more excited remembering the sensations she felt. 'I could imagine myself taking a tube of bright red paste, squeezing it to get the paint out, mixing it with water and then doing big brushstrokes on the canvas... and I painted and painted. I even made the gesture with my arm, in bed. I almost hit Steve in the face,' she chuckled, while with her arm she traced a large semicircle in the air. 'And the other colours! A deep forest green and a bold gold in the middle... blended delicately with the red... ohhh! So much longing!'

Claudia came down the stairs with a firm step and poked her head round the door. She had already applied her makeup and was wearing a pair of jeans and a pink shirt. 'Are we ready to clean up Hackney?' she asked with a new enthusiasm. 'I'll have breakfast and then I'm ready. I have so much to tell you.' She went into the kitchen and they could hear her open and close the fridge door.

'We'll find a way for you to paint,' Lina affirmed, putting her hand on Sofia's arm and nodding confidently.

'That would be a miracle!'

Claudia returned to the dining room with the box of cornflakes under her arm, a cup in one hand, milk bottle in the other and sat between her mother and her grandmother.

'How did you sleep?' Sofia asked cautiously. She couldn't quite believe that the stand-off was over and they might be finding a new closeness.

'Quite well; better than many other nights. I think the chanting really made a difference.' Claudia widened her eyes as she looked at her grandmother. 'I did it for twenty minutes and I was enjoying it so much I didn't want to stop. It's like it shook me inside. I got a lot of inspiration.' She poured enough cornflakes to fill the bowl and then added cold milk to the brim.

'Has it helped you see things more clearly?' Lina asked.

'I think so. It's not so much the ideas in my head – my head is all over the place at the moment – as much as a feeling coming from deep within... here,' she touched her stomach to point where the change was occurring. 'I feel calmer and less afraid than before.' With the spoon she carefully mixed the corn flakes with the milk, but some spilled onto the table. She picked them up one by one with her fingers, dreamily, and put them back in the bowl. 'Once I stopped worrying about sounding silly, I enjoyed the chanting,' she remarked. 'It became completely clear that I don't want to marry Tom... and I don't even know if I still want to be with him. Our relationship is worn-out, there is no enthusiasm... getting married is out of the question.'

'Wow!' Sofia exclaimed.

'Indeed!' Claudia confirmed, nodding with conviction. 'I saw myself on the day of the wedding, in the morning, wearing the wedding dress, my hair being styled, doing my make-up with my bridesmaids, and I couldn't feel any happiness. On the contrary, I felt empty.' Both her mother and grandmother were gazing at her, listening in silence. Claudia continued: 'Then I visualized the moment when I was getting into the car with Dad, who was taking me to the church where Tom was waiting for me. When I imagined walking towards him, the actual moment of committing myself, making that promise of loving him and being with him for the rest of my life, the whole of myself in here,' she touched her chest, 'swelled up in protest. I felt like throwing up. At that point I had to accept that I can't do it and this, I think, is definitely a step forward. So, I will talk to him, I'll let friends and family know, because there is no alternative.'

Sofia blew out the air she had been holding in – almost forgetting to breathe – whilst listening to Claudia: 'What amazing clarity my dear, after so many months of misgivings.'

Lina said thoughtfully: 'It'll be a headache to cancel everything but, as you say, we'll just do what has to be done. The important thing is that you're happy, my treasure.' She covered Claudia's hand with hers and squeezed it. 'And, if I have to be honest, although I am fond of Tom, none of us will lose too much sleep over it. I'm glad you realised in time how you felt and that you won't marry the wrong person. You avoid a lot of disappointments later. Better alone than in bad company,' she concluded decisively, repeating the Italian proverb that she had always found very wise.

'For me, knowing that you won't be moving to Saudi Arabia is a huge relief,' declared Sofia. 'And I agree with your grandmother. We all love Tom, but... speaking frankly – oh gosh, I feel disloyal saying it, but – ... for years I've had this feeling that you have very little in common.'

'You're right Mum, and I'm glad that this issue of Saudi Arabia came up. It forced me to face doubts I think I've had for a long time, but didn't have the courage to admit, even to myself. I'm sorry to hurt him though.'

'He may not suffer all that much, dear,' Lina reassured her, patting her hand.

Mother and daughter stared at her in surprise and then burst out laughing.

Lina laughed too, realizing she had said something funny, and tried to explain herself better: 'Men are not like us women. We mull things over; ponder our feelings, sometimes for months. Men don't – not all are the same of course – but on the whole, they are less complicated; they are simpler than us.'

Both daughter and granddaughter laughed again at Lina's explanation of the difference between the sexes.

Lina smiled and waving her good hand said: 'You know what I mean.' Focusing on Claudia she made one more point: 'Also, you have to be honest with Tom because, apart from anything else, he has the right to be with a woman who accepts him and loves him for who he is.'

'This is true,' Sofia agreed.

'Yes, you're right Nonna, as always. Thank you,' Claudia nodded and smiled.

A palpable sense of liberation filled the room. The elusive, oppressing heaviness that had been hanging over them for a long time was beginning to fade and disperse, leaving them lighter, free to breathe deeply.

'I also got the idea of... maybe not now, maybe later...' Claudia kept her eyes on the cornflakes that she slowly, nervously, shuffled around with the spoon, '... of going to live with a friend, someone my age.'

Turning to her granddaughter, Lina reacted: 'You have a big house here, with your parents, your brother; you've just moved in. What need is there to go and live elsewhere? It will cost you more. You'll have to pay rent, water, gas, electricity...'

Claudia avoided looking at her while she hesitantly admitted: 'Yes, I know Nonna, I've thought about that too... but I'd like to.'

'Times have changed, Mum,' Sofia looked at her mother with affection. She spoke calmly: 'Young people want to be independent, live their own lives, without having to account to their parents for everything they do.' Her elbows resting on the table, her hands wrapped around the teacup, she turned to Claudia. She still felt uncomfortable looking directly at her, so she went back to staring at her hands. 'I wanted to be independent too when I was your age and I must say that being free and responsible for your life is a beautiful thing. If you know someone you'd like to live with, you have my support. Whatever you need, you know we are here for you,' she concluded, briefly raising her eyes to look at her daughter.

'Thank you, Mum. It's not as if I want to leave home right now, hey? For the moment it's just an idea,' Claudia specified, 'and I don't have anyone I'd like to go and live with. But later maybe...' She took a deep breath and resumed: 'Last night, in those twenty minutes, everything began to shift... a visceral reaction,' Claudia put her hand on her stomach. 'Things that have felt hazy suddenly became clear, all at the same time, like a chain reaction. It was as if, having understood one thing, everything else was revealing itself too. It all happened so fast, during the night basically, so much so that... if I think about it, it all seems quite weird, even to me. Suddenly I see my life as it is, and how it could be.' Her eyes shone, her beautiful face showed a vitality that had long deserted her.

'And how do you see your life now?' Sofia asked, her chin resting on her open hand.

'I see it with my friends, colleagues, trips abroad for work, you... my family, maybe an apartment that I share with a friend, holidays on the beach...' As her enthusiasm mounted, Claudia seemed exalted. Her cheeks were flushed, as if she had been running. Speaking without even thinking about what she was going to say, the words almost fell out of her mouth: 'I decided to work on my rusty French and improve it. I will enrol in an evening course at the college and prepare for the advanced French exam. It will be very useful for work and maybe they'll even give me a promotion and a pay rise.' Her gaze settled on her mother, her eyes shone with excitement for life: 'What about you, Mum? I heard you chanting last night. Did it have an effect?'

Sofia smiled and snorted: 'Did it have an effect?! I felt this crazy desire to paint but, as much as I'd like to, at the moment it's impossible.'

'Why impossible?' Her daughter reacted belligerently. 'Finding two or three hours a week for you seems impossible? I don't believe you, Mum. Think again and you'll see that you can do it.'

Feeling observed, Sofia shifted her gaze to her mother and in her eyes she recognized a yearning, a well of love, but also strength and determination.

'Maybe you couldn't do it on your own Sofia but, with some help from all of us, I am sure you could. It can't be that your life is just work, duties and family.' Lina put her misshapen hand firmly on the table top. 'You too have the right to do something that gives you satisfaction and I want to help you. I already told you that I'll pay for a cleaning lady, three or four hours a week. You'll see what a difference it will make.'

'What a good idea, Nonna!' Claudia exclaimed with admiration.

Lina turned to her granddaughter with a focused expression: 'And how can you help your mother find a few hours to do a painting course?'

'Me? I already have a lot to do,' the young woman became suddenly defensive. 'I have very little free time as it is and, if I start this French course, I will have even less.'

Lina observed her without replying.

'It doesn't matter Mum,' Sofia intervened, looking away from both of them, focusing on her mug. She perceived Claudia's resistance and didn't want to spoil the fragile harmony they had just found. 'It's true she's very busy.'

Lina looked back at her granddaughter, gently but decisively: 'Nobody expects much, we know you have a lot to do, but a little effort on your part will make a big difference to your mother... and if she is happier the whole family will be happier. Besides, you will feel proud of yourself.'

Claudia blushed and lowered her eyes, trying to hide the obvious reluctance. 'For example?' she uttered, staring at the empty bowl.

Lina turned to her daughter. 'What house chore takes you an hour, an hour and a half a week?'

'I don't know, Mum. Let's forget about it.' Sofia was uncomfortable, nervously shuffling in her chair while fiddling with her cup of tea.

'No, it's not better to forget it. Everyone has to contribute.'

'I can guarantee an hour a week,' Claudia said, looking up, her cheeks hot. 'Anything more than that would be difficult. Come on Mum, what can I do in an hour?' This time they could tell she had a small desire to help.

'The washing machine. It means loading two or three washing machines, hanging the laundry out and then folding things once they're dry. Usually I do it during the week. It takes about twenty minutes per wash.'

'If it's that simple, I can do it, no problem.' Now Claudia was happy. 'I can load the washing machine before dinner and hang the things out after. Would that be all right?'

'That would be fine.' Sofia seemed embarrassed and smiled shyly. 'Thank you.'

'And let's find out about evening classes for painting,' Claudia urged. 'Maybe we go to the same college, me for French and you to paint. And how can Micky contribute? And Dad? They can do something too. Come on, Mum, we can do it!'

And so, their heads together, they thought that father and son could be doing the weekly supermarket shop, maybe after one of Micky's driving lessons. He could then carry the heavy bags so that Steve didn't have to do any lifting.

'Micky won't object, quite the opposite! But Steve won't be very happy,' Sofia hesitated. 'He has a lot of work.'

'I'll talk to him, don't you worry,' Lina casually stated. 'They will both agree, you'll see.'

Her daughter and her granddaughter glanced at each other and burst out laughing.

'What's there to laugh about?'

'You Nonna, with your confidence,' Claudia's eyes were shining with mirth. 'Until a couple of days ago you were almost shy, cautious to open your mouth. You never took a position openly for fear of creating conflict, and now you're astounding. You've changed so fast!'

'You are very observant, darling. It's true that I don't like to meddle but, in this case, I am sure I can persuade Steve. We understand each other well. Just leave it with me.' She patted her hand in the air and nodded in a self assured way. 'But look who's talking. In twelve hours you have revolutionized your life,' Lina bantered.

'You've both changed,' Sofia declared, getting up and gathering the cups from the table. 'Are you still thinking about coming to live in London, Mum?'

'I think so, I'm quite excited about it now,' Lina's voice quivered with enthusiasm. 'I'm going to enrol in Jane's dance class and, if I fit in well, the teacher might even include me in the performance at the theatre.'

'*What?*' Sofia and Claudia blurted it out at the same time, and proceeded to listen in amazement at the explanation that Lina provided them.

'You'll have to practice a lot at home,' Claudia pointed out.

'Then that's what I'll do! I did theatre when I was a child and since then I've always longed for the stage,' Lina declared dramatically.

Her daughter smiled, amused and proud of her mother. 'You're the youngest seventy-five year old I know,' she exclaimed.

Lina continued to list the reasons she had found for moving to London. Besides dancing, she wanted to attend some more Buddhist meetings and do her human revolution. Also she really wanted to try living with Charlie. The idea of renting her house in Nottingham – and above all getting a small but useful income – enthralled her enormously. The possibility of travelling with her friends, and with her family, gave her shivers of excitement. She would like to take a trip to Italy with them and visit the relatives she hadn't seen for decades. She wouldn't mind going to America to see Vittorio, her eldest son, and find out how people lived there. 'When I am in Nottingham I feel quite lonely... I thought it was normal, part of getting old. But if I came here I don't think I'd feel that way. And anyway, if I don't do these things while I still have my health, when will I ever do them?' she asked with an expression of ardour in her face, a sparkle in her eyes.

Sofia smiled as she moved towards the kitchen carrying the empty cups. 'I can't believe it is my mother who's talking.' She gave a last glance at the elderly lady. 'You look twenty years younger, Mum. You should see yourself.'

'It's true!' confirmed Claudia. 'And the things you say!'

'Why? What do I say?'

'Dancing... being an entrepreneur... travelling... going to America... and then doing your human revolution... and what would that be?'

'It means becoming a happier, better person.'

'You can't get any better than this, Nonna,' Claudia laughed.

'Of course I can. I want to develop my potential.'

Sofia returned from the kitchen and smiled, amused, while wiping the table with a tea towel.

'And how do you do that?' asked her granddaughter, leaning towards her, elbows on the table.

'Don't ask me difficult questions Claudia! I've only been to one meeting and I can't explain well,' Lina placed her hands on the table top and pushed her head forward, 'but I know that when I chant and listen to my heart I discover a lot of things that I didn't know were there.'

She pushed her bottom towards the back of the chair and put her hands on her thighs. 'I wouldn't mind singing, for example. That gentleman I met on the train is in a choir. They perform in orphanages, residences for the elderly, and they also raise money for charity. I could sing and, at the same time, do something useful. Yes... I'll have to find out... Do you think there's a choir around here?'

'There's everything in London, Mum, we just have find it.' Sofia folded the damp cloth and put it on the cold radiator. 'We should get going,' she encouraged them.

Lina stood up and, as she placed her chair next to the table, she added: 'When I went to bed last night I couldn't stop thinking... I felt as if I was a river flooding with ideas, and I wanted to do many things. I struggled to go to sleep, but while I was lying there I was happy.'

'I'm happy too,' Sofia stroked her back. 'Our life is changing so much.'

'So true! And all because Nonna got lost.'

'Every cloud has a silver lining,' Lina said. Her face was lit up, full of satisfaction. She put her jacket on and started to button it up from the lowest button. 'Taking responsibility,' she muttered, glancing at Sofia and Claudia with an amused expression. 'We start with the small things and then move on to the bigger ones.'

Chapter 26

IT STARTS AGAIN FROM NOW

Sofia pressed the key fob and the car lights blinked. She opened the boot and made some space by moving the big orange blanket and a couple of boxes.

Claudia was carrying two buckets, one inside the other, two brooms and a mop.

Lina approached with two dustpans and a large roll of garden waste bags, placed them in the boot next to the blanket and hurried back to the kitchen to get a third broom, for Charlie, if case she forgot to bring one.

Both Sofia and Claudia were surprised; they didn't know Charlie was coming too.

Lina had called her late last night. Charlie had always been an activist, loved being on the front line and was very happy to have been informed. She was going to tell other friends, too.

'Let's go! Otherwise, by the time we get there, there'll be nothing left to do!' Sofia joked.

'Off on a mission!' declared an excited Claudia.

'I'm ready!' announced Lina, taking her place on the back seat.

The temperature was mild and Sofia was driving with her elbow protruding from the open window, her hair fluttering in the wind. They felt as if they were going on a holiday. 'Are you getting too much air in the back Mum?'

'No no, I'm okay, thank you.' Lina brought her little scarf closer to her neck. She enjoyed the fresh air, but wanted to make sure she didn't bring on an asthma attack. She had so many things to do.

Sitting in the passenger seat, Claudia was checking the latest news on her phone and read it aloud: 'The riots have quietened but they have left a hellish chaos on the streets of Hackney. Rubbish collectors have been at work since six in the morning and an ever-growing crowd of volunteers is flocking to the area.'

'What did they say at work when you called?' Sofia turned to look at her daughter.

'I only spoke to Mel. She would have liked to come too but, by the time I told her, it was too late to get organized. It'll be fine, I'm sure. I'll make up for the hours this afternoon and then, when I tell Danny that I'm going to enrol for the French course, I'm sure he'll be happy. There is a proverb in Italian that says 'a blow to the barrel and one to the iron' or something like that, isn't there Nonna?'

Lina laughed from the back seat. 'A blow to the rim and one to the barrel, are the correct words,' she pointed out.

'What does it mean?' Sofia's eyes looked at her mother in the rear view mirror.

'It means moving between two people, or two conflicting needs, and doing things in such a way to keep everyone happy.' Perched on the edge of the back seat, Lina leaned forward holding herself onto their backrests, her cheery face peeping between the two front seats. She explained: 'When the cooper had to put the circles around the barrel, he gave a blow to the barrel and then one to the circle, which was made of iron. He went on like this until he had placed all the six circles around the wooden barrel. Well done Claudia for remembering that proverb. My mother – your great-grandmother – taught it to me.'

'Claudia is quite a little expert in proverbs, aren't you? I am wondering how we would say it in English,' Sofia was racking her brain. 'Any ideas Claudia?'

'No, but I can look it up.' The young woman consulted her faithful phone. 'Here it gives me: Run with the hare and hunt with the hounds, but I don't know whether it's right. I love proverbs. They're so funny... and wise!' Claudia was feeling so much better today. She almost seemed a different person: 'Thank you for teaching me the Italian ones, Nonna. Do you know any more?'

Lina thought about it: 'In this case, with Danny and work, you could also say that you use 'il bastone e la carota'.'

'The carrot and the stick!' Claudia laughed.

'Yes! You hit the donkey with a stick to make him work and then, to reward him, you give him a carrot,' Lina elaborated.

'Is it not cruel to beat donkeys?' Sofia questioned as the car rolled between one set of traffic lights and the next, on a road which was unusually, blissfully, almost traffic-free.

'The fact is that donkeys and mules are very stubborn,' Lina explained and, if they don't want to move, there is no other way to persuade them. This is why the peasants hit them with the stick, to make them work. The donkeys know that after the stick come the carrot, which they like very much, so they move.'

'Better the circle and the barrel,' said Claudia. 'I wouldn't want Danny to be offended by being compared to a donkey.'

The three of them burst out laughing.

'But stubborn... yes, he definitely is!' Claudia concluded with a note of affection in her voice.

'Come on Mum, give us one more,' Sofia encouraged her.

Lina could see her smiling eyes in the rear view mirror. She didn't need to think too much: 'There's one that my mother repeated often to encourage me to start doing what I had to do. She used to say: Chi ben comincia è a metà dell'opera.'

'And it means...?' Claudia queried, while fidgeting with her mobile phone, looking it up online. 'Here it says: Well begun is half done. Is that right?'

'It sounds right. It means that once you've made a start on what you need to do, continuing and then finishing it is easier,' clarified Lina. 'I'll give you an example: it was my job to clean the chicken coop and the rabbit cages every afternoon but, since I preferred to stay at home sewing, I always found a reason to postpone getting started.' With her hands hooked to the back of their seats, Lina slid forward to be closer: 'I was always busy with something, making a hat, or a dress, for myself or someone else. So, my mother used to spur me on by saying: Prepare the bucket with water and the brush. Put them near the cages and then, when you get to work, it will be a quick job. And so I did. Once organized what I needed, cleaning the cages seemed like a quick chore, it took me only a few minutes. Besides I liked the animals.'

'I do the same at work, but also when I was studying,' Claudia turned to look at her grandmother. 'I organize everything I need and then, after an interval doing something completely different, I focus on my task, without interruption. We are the same on this,' she declared cheerfully, stroking her grandmother's straight hand, close to her arm.

'It's true that we are very similar,' confirmed Lina, returning the caress.

'Do you remember anything else that your mother used to tell you?' Sofia asked.

'I do!' Lina confirmed. 'If I continued to procrastinate – as I often did – she would lose her patience and say: 'varda ke ciapo la scova', or 'varda ke ciapo la savata'', and she laughed out loud.

'What does that mean?' Claudia asked

'It means 'watch out that I'll get the broom, or the slipper... and I'll beat you with it!' Lina revealed brightly.

'And did she?' Sofia asked.

'My mother never laid a finger on me,' Lina replied without hesitating, 'but she chased me holding her slipper, or waving the broom in the air, threatening me as a joke.'

'Your mum sounds funny,' Claudia laughed. 'I wish I had met her.'

'I never knew her, either. She died before I was born, the year before. Is that right?' Sofia asked for confirmation, looking at her mother in the little mirror.

'Yes, unfortunately... She was only fifty-four years old.'

The traffic flowed smoothly. They had reached their destination and had to go around the block several times before finding a place to park on one of the side streets.

Sofia got the cleaning tools out of the boot and they walked steadily towards the centre of Hackney. Despite having followed the events on television and hearing the latest news from Claudia, none of them was prepared for what they saw. Desolate grey skeletons of burned cars. Smashed windows of shops that had been looted. Shards and slivers of glass on the pavements. Bins miserably overturned out of which had escaped hundreds of plastic containers; colourful cans rolling with an annoying metallic noise; cartons soiled with milk and fruit juice and, on top of it all, smelly rubbish everywhere.

They had to work their way through the broken glass and the garbage, paying close attention to where they put their feet. But they advanced with a sense of purpose, armed with their buckets and brooms, exchanging glances with other volunteers who were converging and looking around, startled, upset.

As soon as they reached the square outside Hackney Town Hall, the atmosphere changed, as if a fresh gust of wind were bringing a wave of clean energy. A mixture of enthusiasm, solidarity and determination impregnated the air. Seeing brooms and brushes in the hands of the new arrivals, people winked and smiled. A union of purpose brought together men and women, young and old. In their shorts and t-shirt, one hand in the pocket and the other on the broom handle, people chatted filling time, waiting for the signal to start cleaning up their neighbourhood.

Lina looked around and recognized Jane talking to a small

group of people in front of the Town Hall. She would have rushed to her straight away, but didn't want to leave Claudia and Sofia alone, so she called her name out loud and waved her arm in the air, attracting the attention of dozens of people. It was her Italian temperament that made her shout to be heard – instead of approaching discreetly – and that even after so many years took over when she got carried away by enthusiasm.

Jane heard her but couldn't see her. She was looking around and, when she finally spotted Lina, her face lit up with a smile. With her arm raised in the air she signalled vigorously.

'Come on, let's go to Jane!' Lina was already moving decisively in that direction when Claudia caught a glimpse of Charlie. She was alone, bucket, broom and rubber gloves in her hand, her face frowning. 'I'll go and get her,' Claudia declared, and ran off to fetch their elderly friend.

'Look what a mess they've made!' Charlie's voice thundered as she approached with a determined step, observing the area with a disapproving expression: 'It was to be expected; sooner or later it was going to happen. Injustice never gets forgotten... but what a shambles! They really surpassed themselves.' She put her bucket down on the floor and, with her free hand on her hip, scouted the area with a critical eye. 'What are we waiting for? Why don't we make a start?' she asked.

Jane, who had just reached them, explained that, for security reasons, the police had asked people to wait. But she had heard that the shopkeepers would appreciate some help. They were alone trying to remedy the chaos in their shops, discouraged, angry, some even in tears, trying to save what they could. And so they all set off together.

Lina – who had quickly introduced Jane to Charlie – walked briskly ahead with them, carrying brooms, dust pans and bags, followed by Sofia and Claudia with buckets, rubber gloves and a scrubbing brush.

They reached a newsagent. The owner, a small thin Indian

man in his late fifties, was looking around with a dejected air, his shoulders drooping, when Jane asked him if he wanted a hand.

At first he didn't understand. He couldn't quite believe that they wanted to clean his shop but, when Charlie began to sweep the floor, Claudia picked up the broken pieces of glass and Jane started sweeping the pavement, the surprise and gratitude in his eyes were clearer than any words. Shuffling his feet he went into the back room and returned with two empty boxes that he handed to Sofia: 'We put the things they threw on the floor in here, what little is left,' he said, and gave her a pat on the hand to show his gratitude. He took one of their buckets, went into the back room and filled it up with water. When Lina tried to take it from his hands, he firmly refused to give her that weight. 'It's too heavy for a lady,' he declared, and carried it to the entrance, where the floor was stained and sticky because of fizzy drinks that had been spilt.

Turning then to Lina, who didn't know where to start, the man indicated the newspapers and magazines strewn all over the place, torn, crumpled or trampled. 'I can send the newspapers back. They go in a pile here,' he explained. 'The magazines instead must be put in order, if they are not ruined. Otherwise I hope I'll be able to return them. If you can do this, I'll make tea.' Before disappearing in the back room, he turned around and thanked her. He seemed touched.

A few minutes later he was back with two cups of hot tea that let out an aroma of cardamom. He brought one for Charlie, who was sweeping energetically between the rows of shelves, and handed the other one to Sofia who had already filled the two boxes he had given her. Then he returned to the back room and came out with two glasses full of the hot milky tea. He gave one to Jane, who had cleaned up the pavement and filled two bags with rubbish, and the other one to Claudia who had already washed the floor with the mop. Finally he returned for the third time with a steaming cup of tea for Lina and one for himself.

They had more or less finished cleaning and the store was almost empty of items, but had a neat and tidy appearance.

The owner insisted that they put down their cleaning tools, went to a box containing a few chocolate bars and took five. Going to each one of them in turn, he pushed a chocolate bar into their hands. 'Eat, eat,' he encouraged them, 'while we drink tea.'

They could smell the bleach that Claudia had added to the water to wash the floor and it seemed as if even the morning air was cleaner than before.

Hurrying behind the counter the shop keeper returned with a stool and insisted that one of them sit down. 'Please madam,' he turned to Lina and apologized: 'I'm sorry I only have one chair.' Then, walking more briskly, he disappeared once again in the back room and returned carrying two wooden crates, which he turned upside down so that they could sit on them. He offered them to Jane and Charlie, saying: 'You ladies already have a certain age, but don't hesitate to come here and help me clean, while people yesterday destroyed everything around them. I've spent years working for this shop, and now...'

'The insurance will repay you for all the damage, you'll see,' Charlie affirmed and, before sitting down, she gave him a friendly pat on the shoulder. 'At least they didn't burn your shop down, as happened elsewhere. Did you see the news reports?'

'Yes, yes. What a mess!' the man uttered, shaking his head.

'Unfortunately, even good people sometimes get carried away,' Lina recalled, as she unwrapped her chocolate bar. 'While I was watching the news I saw some people entering the shops where the windows had been broken and coming out with only two cans of soft drinks in their hands. They were not all young, some were fully grown adults. They could have taken anything if they had wanted to. It seemed to me that they wouldn't normally have done something like this, but got swept up in it and stole things too.'

'We need to reflect on what has happened – and is still happening in other parts of England – and remedy the injustices of this society,' reflected Jane, who sat with her elbows on her knees and the cup of tea in her hand. 'The cause of all this is the lack of respect, for life and for every human being, regardless of skin colour, culture or social position. From the point of view of our humanity we are all the same and everyone is equally worthy of respect,' she concluded clearly.

'Let's hope everyone learns from this and that it never happens again,' commented Sofia. 'I've never seen anything like this in London in my whole life.' Slowly she brought the cup of hot tea to her lips.

'It all seemed quiet until two days ago, and then, all of a sudden...' Lina said.

'This has been going on for much longer than a couple of days,' Charlie stated, waving her hand in the air. 'More often than not members of the black community are treated unfairly. Whenever something happens and black people are involved, many members of the police, and a section of the public too, automatically assume they're guilty. So, it's up to them to prove otherwise... if they're not killed first,' she added forcefully.

'I remember something that happened last week...' Claudia, who so far had been listening attentively, started: 'It was quite late and I was waiting for the train with a work colleague. It must have been after midnight and, apart from the two of us, there was hardly anyone else around.'

They were all gazing at her while sipping their hot tea.

'A quarrel between a black man and white man began on the platform. I think they were both drunk. Another black man, younger than the two fighting, intervened to try and calm them down, but the two men kept shouting. My colleague said to me: Let's wait here; we might be the only witnesses. And so we did.'

'You didn't say anything about that,' interjected Sofia with a worried look.

'I've only just remembered,' Claudia replied. 'Within a few minutes two white policemen arrived, who immediately stopped the two black men and ignored the white one. The younger guy kept saying he wasn't part of it, that he'd been trying to help, but it really seemed like the officers weren't listening. We approached them and my colleague backed up his story. Only then did they pay attention. Things turned out all right in the end, but it might have ended very differently if there had been no-one else there.'

'They would have arrested the two black men?' Lina suggested.

'It seemed very likely,' Claudia confirmed.

'What happened to them?' asked Jane.

'The policemen told them all to calm down and let them go.'

'When the police officers got there, I breathed a sigh of relief and immediately felt safer,' Claudia reflected, 'but maybe that's because I'm white. Watching those black men, I think they felt *less* safe the moment the cops arrived.'

The shopkeeper, who had been quietly drinking his tea, began speaking slowly: 'I have lived here for over thirty years. We live well together, white people, black people, Indian people and all the other nationalities. In the past there was more violence, but in recent years things have improved. Everyone lives their life and people respect each other. Until a few days ago there was peace in this neighbourhood. But this morning, when I got here and I saw what they'd done to my shop, I lost all confidence in the people of Hackney. I will be honest and confess that I cried. But then you came and, without wanting anything in return, you cleaned, swept, washed the floor and tidied everything up. With your kindness, you have helped me regain trust in people.'

'Helping you, made us happy too,' said Jane.

'This is a good way of thinking. If everyone thought like this, we would live better. There would be more peace,' said the owner, and bowed with hands clasped.

Before going to another shop to offer their help, the five women decided to return to the Town Hall to see if there was any news and, just as they got there, the communication arrived: the volunteers were soon to start helping cleaning streets and pavements.

In the meantime, journalists and photographers from the national press had arrived and, taking advantage of the waiting time, carried out short interviews and took some pictures. The three women with white hair – armed with brooms, buckets and gloves – immediately attracted the photographers' attention, who asked them to pose on the front row. Lina, flanked by Jane and Charlie, motioned to Sofia and Claudia to stand behind them with their brooms.

Claudia lowered herself to speak to her grandmother: 'What did your mum say when she was chasing you with her broom up in the air?'

'Varda che te dago co la scoa!' Lina replied chuckling, and lifted her broom in the air.

In a flash of inspiration Charlie imitated her by wielding her broom like a drawn sword and shouted: 'This is Hackney!'

'This is Hackney!' repeated the other volunteers behind them, raising their brooms in the air, proud and smiling.

'We start again from now!' Jane cried, her mop held high like a banner, her eyes bright and her smile triumphant.

'Yes, we start from now!' Lina echoed passionately, full of enthusiasm, lifting her broom even higher.

'From now!' Sofia repeated, her voice breaking up with emotion.

'From now!' Claudia exclaimed jubilantly, pushing her broom upwards, as a coveted trophy.

The clicks of dozens of cameras and the blinding light of their flashes followed one after the other, illuminating and immortalizing them forever, just like movie stars.

PART TWO

Chapter 27

CLAUDIA'S VOICE

Last Wednesday I finally did it. I moved out of Mum and Dad's house and into my new flat. When we loaded the boot with boxes of my clothes for the last trip, I suddenly felt unsure and a bit emotional. Mum had been helping me willingly and said that it was all fine, if I was happy she was happy too, but when she's sad it's written all over her face. She was clearly sorry to see me leave home, but she encouraged me to enjoy this new stage of my life. 'You're young' – she told me – 'enjoy your freedom.' However, in her next sentence, she warned me to take great care of myself, not to drink too much and not to get cold.

This thing of getting cold has been going on since I was a teenager and, in winter, I'd go out with friends on a Saturday night, leaving the house without a jacket. Mum always scolded me – every time it was the same spiel – insisting that I would catch a cold or, worse still, pneumonia. As none of this had the desired effect, she'd reiterate more and more passionately that, when I'd get older, I'd develop rheumatism (especially in my neck) and that by then it would be too late to do anything about it. Since even this got her nowhere, she would conclude with frustration that I was obviously ignorant of the law of cause and effect and throw in the towel. I was going to learn the hard way, she intimated with an exasperated frown. She never understood that the boy I went out with that particular night would only lend me his jacket if I didn't have mine.

Well, finally she can relax because when it gets really cold I even wear the thermal vest she gave me for Christmas, and I always wear a jacket now. Working for a fashion designer we're encouraged to wear the brand's clothes to represent the style of the firm, so the jacket is practically a must.

As much as I was excited about going to live with Mel, I was also sad to leave my family, especially Mum. Since we got over our gigantic crisis, we've become even closer than before and have been getting on really well. It must be the Italian side of me that's so attached to family and finds it hard to let go. However, I made them promise to keep my room for me, because sometimes I might want to go and sleep at home, and they had to swear they were not going to take my pictures down.

Micky teased me by saying it'd become a museum – or rather a shrine – and that he would go and light a few candles from time to time to honour my memory. I suspect he'll use my room with Trish instead, his girlfriend. They have this passionate relationship and, if they could get away with it, they'd have sex on a bus. Mum was a bit worried about it for a while, given the age gap. With Trish being ten years older and women being more mature than men at the best of times, she worried that Micky might get hurt – over protective of him as she's always been. However, it would have been impossible to stop that relationship once it started, out of pure lust, without a doubt. It was embarrassing to be in the same room with them, always touching or kissing. After a while it became really too much, and both me and Mum, and Dad too, quickly found an excuse to run away. However, they're still together and it seems to have a good effect on my brother. In the past two months Micky has improved in more ways than one. He's not quite as loud as he used to be; he now speaks instead of shouting and even manages to control himself when coming down the stairs. Mum made him paint the cracks on the basement ceiling and forbade him to jump four or five steps at a time. The lust story with Trish seems to be turning into a sweet love story. They care a lot about each other and we're all happy for them, and for us.

Once or twice a week Micky meets up with Jim, the young Buddhist man from Nonna's group – and mine too, for now. They are writing a song about homelessness. Jim's helping him with the lyrics and Micky's composing the music. They spend hours talking in the basement. They sing, play tunes and I think they've almost finished it. It's a rap of course, but with some nice pieces of music, from what we can hear. They have become close friends and Jim is losing a little of his shyness. He's opening up, especially with Dad, who's bought himself a new computer and is preparing the old one to give to him. He's cleaned it, installed some basic programs and an antivirus, and on Sunday he'll show him how to use it. He's excited to see Jim's face. He says that Jim is a good man and wants to help him. I left home and he has 'adopted' another child! My dad must be the kindest man I know. Without a word to anyone, he bought a CD player for Nonna and recorded two CDs with her favourite old songs. He got her to make a list – without giving away what it was for, so he wouldn't spoil the surprise – and sourced all the tracks. Grandma was so happy she did a little dance. She is doing a lot of that recently, whether or not there is someone around, and has been singing along ever since.

The trip to Paris was very interesting – although not as I expected, or hoped – and opened my eyes in a big way.

We were a group of ten from the office and arrived in Paris two days before the fashion show. Danny surpassed himself. He was nice and friendly with everyone *and* made us work twelve hour days.

I thought he was paying me a *lot* of attention, which was very flattering. During the journey he treated me in such a charming, gallant way and, although I was a bit embarrassed – everyone knows he's married with kids – I was also so infatuated with him that I believed he felt the same about me. I can see it and admit it now, no more denial on this score. I even thought that the whole thing of speaking French and Italian was an excuse to take me to Paris so we could be together. I got so carried away with the fantasy of being the true love of his life, that I even got nervous about him divorcing his wife to be with me, and started to feel guilty.

To my surprise, the second day in Paris I noticed, that a colleague – Helen –- was also flattered by his attentions. When Danny said the word 'principessa' – he says it just like that, in Italian – I saw her face light up and laugh excitedly. It took my breath away! I was astonished, and bewildered. Fortunately I hadn't reacted immediately on hearing the term 'princess', which of course I'd assumed was addressed to *me*. I felt stupid, embarrassed and – if I'm honest – ashamed, too. From that moment I took a big step back and started to observe how Danny behaves with women.

He courts them all, or better, he doesn't court any of us, but likes to be charming and seductive with every woman, young or old. He's funny, compelling, irresistible; the perfection of masculine charm. So, many of us fall for it like ripe pears from a tree, hit the ground and get squashed... swash, splatter, slop. Pathetic pears for whom a compliment paid with shining eyes is enough to make our legs shake and our hearts melt.

Ego, it's all about the ego, Beverley explained to me, and about our need to be loved, adored, but above all chosen among the many, I above all others. The ego precisely. Ufff! What a revelation! She also said that there's nothing wrong with wanting to be treated like the most special, precious, important person in the world. However, that 'someone' treating us like that ought to be ourselves. Wow! So many new concepts.

From that moment of sudden realization – literally a lightning bolt – and, despite feeling quite unsettled, I began to put my heart at rest. Actually I felt much calmer, knowing that I wasn't planning the end of his marriage and the beautiful relationship with his daughters. I started to feel freer and lighter. That same evening, chanting in the room I shared with Helen, I realized how deeply relieved I was. After that, I focused on my work. This was just as well, because the question of who spoke Italian and French was not at all an excuse to take me to Paris, it was a complete necessity. No one else spoke those two languages and I worked hard from morning till night, translating written documents, talking with customers, with the waiters at the restaurant to order food, with hotel employees to make changes to reservations and with taxi drivers when we moved 'en masse'.

When we got back to London and I went for lunch with Mel, I told her about how the trip went, trying to help her understand what I had realized about Danny, in the hope that she too would resign herself and stop wishing for a fairy tale. I think she understood and is now beginning to look to the future. I love Mel and, since I saw her cry that first time when we were sunbathing, I feel this strong desire for her to be happy. I didn't tell her right away that I chant for her happiness – it seemed too personal – but the other day, sitting outside our favourite pub on the Southbank, after the second gin and tonics, I confessed.

She became quite emotional and then started asking me a lot of questions about Buddhism, to which I didn't really know many answers, apart from the little I've learned. She thought it sounded like an interesting thing to try and decided to come to a meeting, to see with her own eyes. Of course I told her it was fine and I mentioned that since I started practicing every day – I do ten minutes in the morning and ten in the evening – my gentle idea of leaving home had turned into a goal that I definitely wanted to achieve. And she, just like that, out of the blue, invited me to go and live with her. She has this two-bedroom apartment in North-West London, which is expensive for just one person but, if shared between two people, is reasonable. So I decided to move in. The only downside is that it's quite far from my parents' house. If I want to visit them I have to cross half of London and, depending on the traffic, it can take up to an hour to get there. It also takes about an hour to get to work. I would much rather have a ten or twenty minute commute. Beverley told me I can chant for whatever I want and so I'm chanting to find something closer; after all we're renting, so we can easily move if we find the perfect place.

Talking about Beverley: I like her a lot. She's good-hearted, you can see it in her eyes, those beautiful big eyes. I go to her group's meetings, where I also get to see Nonna, and am really enjoying them. There are all sorts of people and we talk about such varied topics – big, life things – as I would do with a close friend, except that at the meetings there are ten or twelve of us. Everyone arrives with their own news, problems and aspirations, and shares them.

The practice of Buddhism is not what I'd imagined – sitting on the floor cross-legged, eyes closed, thumbs and forefingers circled together saying Ommmmmm. On the contrary, it's very dynamic. The chanting is fast and has the rhythm of a galloping horse. Day by day I'm becoming more aware of the way I think and behave, and strive to improve on that. There's no passive attitude or resignation; quite the opposite. It encourages me to take positive action and I like that, I'm ready for it.

When I found the courage to open my mouth – during the second meeting I went to – and talked of my doubts about the relationship with Tom, the response from all those present, without exception, left me in awe. In short, they told me that I had to respect myself. This phrase continued to resonate in my head and in my heart, unabated. It was as if it was coming out of speakers and at such high volume that I couldn't ignore it. When I got home I felt the need to chant some more and I went to bed with a feeling of emptiness in my head, but a beautiful emptiness, as if I had cleared out a closet which was cluttered with old things that had gone slightly mouldy. The following morning, during my ten minutes of chanting – done with the strength and speed of a consummate Buddhist – everything appeared very clear and simple. The fear of hurting Tom and of disappointing his family had melted like snow in the sun and I found myself light, with a calm but robust courage (like Nelson's forearms). Joking aside, I felt like I was a table supported by four legs, strong and stable.

With Tom it was much easier than I feared. On my initiative, we went for a long walk to the park and I told him that I loved him like a brother and thought that, both him and I, would be happier as friends than as a couple.

He was sorry – I could see – but he didn't insist too much. I think he was relieved too. When we parted, outside the house, we hugged each other and even shed a few tears. He told me that he wanted to keep in touch with me and my family, and this made me happy. I love his parents, they have always treated me with great affection and I would be sorry to sever the relationship. His mother will notify their relatives that we're no longer together and that the wedding isn't happening, and I will inform mine. When I chanted that night I cried, out of tenderness, sorrow, nostalgia and a lot of other emotions, but I was calm, I had no doubts. I went to bed with a smile on my lips; a sad smile, but a smile nevertheless.

The next day I made an appointment with Mel's hairdresser – she's expensive but very good – and had my hair cut and re-styled. It was the first time since childhood that I've had short hair. I looked through various magazines with the hairdresser and explained how I felt. In the end we chose a cheeky style, shorter at the back and a little longer at the front, with a fringe. I hadn't had a fringe since I was ten. I was, and still am, very happy with how it looks. Every time I step in front of a mirror I am pleasantly surprised and feel like greeting myself, as if I was saying hello to a friend. Hi Claudia, you look pretty today!

Both Mum and Nonna pushed money into my hands and

sent me off to buy myself something new, and so I did. Mel and I went shopping and I deviated from my usual classic style. I bought a pair of faux leather trousers and a pair of cowboy boots. Mel gave me a couple of her T-shirts, one of which was torn (she bought it like that). The other day I cracked up when I saw Nonna sitting on the sofa with needle and thread, mending every little tear. I explained to her that it is the current fashion and she laughed too, even if she doesn't understand why I want to go around dressed like that. According to her, it doesn't come up to standards – Italian standards, she meant – of which I ought to be a proud representative.

Since Nonna arrived in London, my life has changed completely, to the point of being almost unrecognizable. I remember how I felt when I went to fetch her from the station: full of fear, anguished and lost, like a little boat without its anchor, tossed here and there at the mercy of big waves. I no longer knew who I was or what I wanted. It's only been two months since that day and now, when I look back, I can't quite believe that my life has transformed so totally. I'm 'single' and it doesn't feel as scary as I feared, quite the opposite. I love doing whatever I want, without consulting anyone. I'm planning a holiday to Barcelona with Mel and going to college for French lessons is so invigorating. I'm becoming free from my obsession with Danny; it's not instant, but it's getting easier. Every day I feel calmer, wiser, lighter and I also chant for his happiness, whatever that means to him.

I'm opening my eyes and my life to my potential and this is very exciting. I believe in myself, like I've never done before. Every time I go to a meeting I have this feeling of my horizon opening up more and more. I'm discovering new ways of looking at situations, of facing problems, and am learning to enjoy life, the present moment and the little things. I'm less worried about myself and this gives me an incredible sense of freedom and an inner strength that I didn't know I possessed.

Beverley and Sandra, the Italian girl, are great. I like talking with them, because they never say obvious, trite things. They consistently surprise me with their point of view, although sometimes I would prefer if they didn't tell me that I'm responsible for whatever goes on in my life. They *love* this concept of taking responsibility. Sometimes it's a lot easier to blame others, but it's also true that when I take my responsibility I can make a step forward, indeed my steps are gigantic!

I'm also learning to recognize how my ego works – my smaller self, we say in Buddhism – how it affects the way I think and how I perceive and interpret what people around me say and do. I've started to notice when my smaller self has the upper hand and makes me feel dissatisfied, unhappy, in a bad mood. In short, I am learning to know myself deeply and I'm beginning to understand that living is an art, an art that I'm learning.

I must work at it, as with all the arts, and follow the advice of a good teacher, and that's great. It's a journey – says Beverley, with her open smile – an endless journey to achieve happiness for myself and for others, and on this journey I'm the driver. Wow! So, I'm taking driving lessons to get my happiness license!

Chapter 28

SOFIA'S MIND - EVERYTHING CHANGES

There is a song in Spanish that says 'cambia, todo cambia'. It is sung by Mercedes Sosa and always touches a key in my heart. It goes like this: 'Superficial things change, but also deep ones do, the way we think changes as do all things in this world; the light of a diamond changes according to who wears it; birds change their nest, lovers' feelings change and, since everything changes, it's no wonder that I change too. The sun changes, from day to night; the plants change from barren to green and so, if everything changes, it's not surprising that I change too.'

Every time I hear it I get a lump in my throat. The music and the instruments that play it, the lyrics and the voice singing it move me deeply, because it is true that everything changes constantly and when it does it is the end of something, a little death. That's why it hurts. But it is also true that when one door closes another one opens. I must say that lately, in my life, there has been a great deal of coming and going, a lot of changes, doors have closed and others have opened. Lots of emotions all around.

Claudia left home and that was hard for me, especially the first few days. At home we have this evening custom of throwing dirty socks and underwear onto the second floor landing. In theory, the first one to go downstairs collects them and takes them down to the first floor. From there, they get tossed down the stairs leading to the basement and the laundry area. Eventually, someone puts them in the washing machine and starts it.

So far this system has worked reasonably well, as long as I am the one who collects, takes, throws, loads and gets the washing machine going. This way the dirty clothes don't accumulate in the children's rooms – in this I include Steve too – and get washed regularly. Every morning for the last twenty-five years I found Claudia's knickers and socks on the landing and, suddenly, one day they were no longer there. It might seem ridiculous, but I burst into tears. I cried and cried and couldn't stop.

I ended up crying in the shop and a client with whom I often exchange a few words consoled me. She was very sweet and told me that, just as Claudia acquired her freedom, I was getting my freedom too, and encouraged me to appreciate it. She also advised me to take drops of St John's Wort, a herb that helps lift the mood. I bought them that same afternoon during my lunch break. I took the first drops as soon as I returned to the shop and began to feel the effect very quickly. What happened was amazing.

Within a few hours, to my great wonder and delight, I perceived once again that magical source of life force that lies somewhere deep in my head. I was beginning to feel upbeat again. Ideas and enthusiasm came back and I decided it was time to create a promotion for the shop, which needed a bit of a boost. I told the shop assistant we were going to do so and, in the back of my mind, I felt a smile surfacing and thought 'This is who I am!'

At the same time I had the distinct impression that a veil of sadness that had been hanging over my face for a long time was gently being removed, leaving my vision sharp and clear. I found myself looking at the customers who came into the shop with a sense of connection I had long lost. I recognized the power of my mental energy, which had weakened so much I didn't even remember I possessed it. Even physically I felt more alive.

Within a few days I noticed a great difference in my emotional state and realized that, while for months, even years, I believed I had got over 'mild' depression, in truth I was still immersed in it and it was much more serious than I had thought. I was lost in a troubled swamp shrouded in darkness, convinced I was a heavy, embarrassing nothingness.

Now, looking back, I can see that I was struggling to stay afloat without realizing how dangerous the waters were in which I floundered. Since then I have been taking the drops faithfully and every day that goes by I am rediscovering myself a little bit more. I finally regained the desire to 'swim' and I think the seed of change began to sprout and grow when my mother arrived in London. Having her close by, with her discreet sensibility, unassuming wisdom and the affection that she offers in her simple way, marked the beginning of my climbing back.

The evening of the riots, when she disappeared, I hit rock bottom, but it was also the moment when – symbolically – I used that very bottom to give myself a push and swim back to the surface. I re-emerged, gasping, weak and tired, but in front of me I found a raft. All I had to do was reach out, cling to it and make it mine. That wonderful philosophy of life I had met in India, which had given me so much joy and then – I don't know why – I had forgotten, was exactly what I needed and the most beautiful thing I could find. My mother brought it back into my life and from that moment on I started a new journey, the second part of my adventure in this world.

As the days pass I reflect and realize that over the last twenty-five years of my life, despite endeavouring to take care of my body, I have often abused it with too much work, smoking and wine. I tried to take care of my intellect, filling it with information, knowledge and culture. I travelled a bit, amassed notions and opinions, explored different points of view. Now I see that I stuffed my mind, I fattened it; I made it grow in quantity but not in quality.

At first I had nurtured myself with creativity and, as long as I was creating something, my life had a certain, precarious balance. However, I often endangered it with sudden decisions, or the wrong words or a poorly-thought action. Then, as my free time was nibbled away by work and family obligations, I stopped dedicating time to the little things that I loved doing and that gave me satisfaction.

I thought I was strong, but I was only active, determined, I moved quickly. In the meantime I forgot, completely pushed to one side, the other part of me, the one that feeds my soul, that makes me understand why I'm alive now, in this historical moment. I forgot what my life is for, as a woman and a mother, what mission I have in this world. It is this part of me, deep, essential, that works like an engine and creates my life force, my enthusiasm, my will power and my true energy.

One day I read a sentence that struck me. It said: 'We are not human beings living a spiritual experience, we are spiritual beings who live a human experience'. It resonated so much and felt so true that it made me smile, rejoice and silently shout Eureka! For me it was the very crux, the heart of the matter. My spirituality is my base, my roots, and gives life to my humanity, it nourishes it, inspires it and makes it grow. It fills it with warmth, strength and dignity, a sense of justice and compassion, of appreciation and respect. Everything seems clear to me now, it all adds up: if I take care of my spirituality everything else comes naturally; mind and body work in harmony. I put it into practice every day and I feel so much happier.

It also makes it easier to accept that Claudia is not here. I miss her presence, but she calls often to ask for advice on how to cook a chicken in the oven, how to wash delicate things, or simply to hear my voice, or that of her dad or her brother's. I will get used to the fact that she doesn't live with us anymore. I know this is the way it needs to be. I must remember to be grateful that she won't be going to Saudi Arabia and lives only an hour away from here and that, if I want to, I can get in the car or catch the tube and go and see her. That's exactly what we'll do on Sunday. We're going to her place to take her some things for the house and then we'll go out for lunch, all together.

Mum did what she had planned and went to live with Charlie for a trial period; it has been almost two months now. Everything seems fine and the two ladies are doing well. They do squabble at times, but mainly about small things, such as Charlie complaining to Mum about putting the sugar bowl in the wrong cupboard, or Mum complaining about Charlie's behaviour when she watches the news. Charlie is very vocal about the expenses scandal and when Cameron, the Prime Minister, comes on television she swears like a trooper and throws whatever is in her hand at the television screen. One time Mum complained about it and Charlie told her to fuck off. However, their disagreements never last more than a few minutes. Mum has such an accommodating personality that it is impossible to argue with her for too long.

They invited us for dinner two weeks ago and it was clear that they were happy. Charlie seemed to have softened; she was calmer and appeared to be content in Mum's company. A few times she said how she disliked being alone and how much this has changed. Mum has her lovely room and everything else they share. They are like sisters. Mum also loves living in a house with a big garden. It's a new thing for her, who only had a paved yard in Nottingham with a few scraggy plant pots. She is learning from Charlie how to care for shrubs and flowers; she talks about it with great enthusiasm and when the weather is good they spend hours together out there. I'm very happy that she made this decision and I hope it will last, because it means having my mother nearby but without living together, which worried me a lot. Being the only one of her children who lives in England I have always felt responsible for her, even more so now that she is getting older. Maybe one day I will want her to move in with us, but just now I am not ready for it.

I must say, however, that instead of growing old Mum seems to be getting younger and, with all the activities she has taken on, I have to make an appointment to see her. I am not joking. Between the choir, which she attends once a week, her Buddhist group, the volunteer work for the Cancer Research on Monday and Thursday mornings, the group of women she dances with on Tuesday and Friday, and the new friendships she strikes up every time she goes anywhere, Mum is more socially engaged than me and is a transformed woman. Sometimes she even looks like another person. She has lost some weight and wears less traditional, more modern clothes; she loves tracksuits and trainers and I even saw a pair of jeans in her wardrobe. Her hair is always impeccable though, and necklaces and earrings are still the order of the day.

A Nottingham estate agent has put her house up for rent and Mum is very excited about getting regular money in from the rent. I never expected her to take such a radical decision, or that she could change so much in such a short span of time. I have a feeling that more surprises will be coming. Who knows what else is in store?

As promised, she is paying for a cleaning lady who comes every Friday morning and is a tornado of energy. She throws the windows wide open (apart from Steve's, who keeps his office door tightly shut and complains it's freezing cold), vacuums the carpets, including the stairs, cleans the bedrooms, living room, bathroom and kitchen. In the evening, when I come home from work, the house smells fresh and clean. It is real luxury.

I am also grateful to Mum for having pushed me to take on painting. On Wednesday afternoon I leave the shop at five o'clock and let the assistant close up. I stop in town for a quick bite to eat and then I go to college, the same as Micky's, not far from our house. The lesson is from six to nine; we have a live model and work very hard. The teacher is young and full of enthusiasm. He goes from one easel to the other giving advice and encouragement. At the beginning, those few times I went to look at other people's work, I felt dejected because they were all better than mine. Of the people coming to class there are many who studied graphic design; others qualified from art school and come to class to practice drawing with a model. I have almost no formal background instead, I'm learning now.

One evening I apologized to the teacher for not being very good but he, with great conviction, said that I am growing faster than anyone else, and this encouraged me a lot. Incredibly, he repeated what my teacher had told me at school at the age of thirteen and I remembered when my mother sent me to chant. 'You have a big brush stroke,' he said and made that gesture with his arm, like drawing an arch. And then he added 'buy a big canvas Sofia; you can put it on two easels, next to each other. You'll see what beautiful things you'll create.'

I bought a large canvas, five foot by three, placed the easel in the basement near the French window overlooking the garden and I paint on Sundays. At this very moment I'm doing an abstract painting with the colours I had imagined on that sleepless night: green, red and a lot of gold. I will put it in the living room on the wall above the sofa. I felt an urgent need to use those colours and followed my instincts. They say that colours are therapeutic and I think it's true because when I paint, despite being hard work, I fill up with a joyful kind of energy. I am already planning the painting I will do after this. The house is big and, apart from a few posters, the walls are bare, so I have a lot of opportunities to give expression to my imagination.

With me painting and my son making music our home is

imbued with creativity. Micky is working on a rap piece about a homeless young man, inspired by Jim's experience. He has included a short piece from one of Beethoven's symphonies – this will please his grandmother – and, from what we can hear, it's very catchy.

Jim comes over a couple of times a week, stays for dinner and sleeps here. He and Micky have taken two mattresses down to the basement, where they make music and talk until dawn. I feel an enormous tenderness towards Jim. He is so young, skinny, almost frail, but has an iron determination regarding his future. He commits one hundred percent to everything he does and I am convinced that his dedicated attitude is a good influence on my son.

Micky often stops at Trish's, with whom he is living a relationship of great passion. When it started I thought she would soon tire of him because of his young age. I was afraid he would end up getting hurt, but this couldn't be further from the truth. She adores him, admires and respects his talent and his kindness. He, on the other hand, doesn't seem at all concerned about the age gap and is confident in himself. I watch in amazement how he is changing: from the boy he used to be until a couple of months ago he has become a man... and, since being with her, he hasn't been out once to do graffiti. Fortunately he hasn't lost his joyful and loving side and still hugs and kisses me with great affection, as he has always done. These shows of fondness are good for me; they are like transfers, payments into a love bank. I have an open account of warmth and tenderness with Micky, to which he contributes generously.

With all these changes, Steve and I often find ourselves at home alone, for the first time in many years. We talk about our children who, even if not physically present, are a central part of our life, but we are getting accustomed to being a couple again, because over the years our relationship has changed a lot.

I had always been protective towards him, from the very

beginning, despite him being much bigger than me. I often thought I was physically stronger than him, which sparked many raised eyebrows over the years. I have memories – that now make me smile – of when we were travelling and, if I believed he was struggling, I'd insist in carrying the heavier of the two rucksacks. I probably had a lot of nervous energy, but the strength we find, even on a physical level, is incredible when motivated by our love for someone.

When Claudia was born, we settled in London and dedicated ourselves to parenting with great enthusiasm. We were not a traditional couple: Steve used to go out with Claudia in the pushchair while I painted the house. It worked for us as we gave expression to our natural inclination. Years later, when Micky was born, parenting became much more intense, but we were well organized and did a good job of it. Then, when the kids started school, I opened the first small shop and spent many hours outside of the house, whilst Steve began working from home.

The problems started when Claudia became a teenager and Steve and I discovered we had very different ideas about our role as parents. There were painful clashes and arguments. The support and approval I had always received from him started to falter and at times I was being challenged by his open disapproval. The chemistry and harmony that until then had glued our family together began to break down and show cracks. My world, my strength, did the same.

Something changed in my head, which I could not understand, let alone control. It felt as if I were walking not on ground, but on a slippery slab of ice. An insidious uncertainty about who I was in relation to my husband, my daughter and my son, gradually took possession of my thoughts, my emotions, the way I perceived their words, the way they looked at me, even the sound of my own voice. I felt more and more isolated, misunderstood, useless, perhaps even detrimental in my role as a mother. I didn't know anything anymore. For many endlessly long, dark, sick months I struggled with the anguished feeling, the mortifying tormenting suspicion that perhaps they would have been better off without me. Now I understand that my descent into depression began in those days.

I fought against despair and self-destruction by throwing myself headlong into work, moving faster, filling my life with activities, travel and things to do. Every free moment was occupied by commitments, dinners with friends, bottles of wine and a few stiff joints so that, for a while, I didn't have to think, or feel. Meanwhile, the children grew up surprisingly well, I survived and we are still together.

Today I look at those years to learn from what I experienced, and I realize that I can help people who find themselves in a similar situation; opportunities abound. In a sense, having waded through depression, however soul-crushing that was, is one of the most precious and important experiences of my life and for which I am deeply grateful. I never thought I'd say this. It gave me the gift of a new sensitivity, which makes me understand when someone is going through a difficult time. The perception of reality is altered when you are in the grips of depression and it is often someone else who notices that something is wrong. Now I am one of those people.

To be able to reassure a friend, to tell her that the dark time will pass, that it is a painful but incredibly useful and significant period which will make her a better person; to tell her not to be afraid because I am the actual proof that you can win over it and come out stronger than before. I can do this only because I've been there too.

It is true what the words of the song say, that when things change around me I change too, but it is even truer that when I change, everything around me changes and this is what is happening now. My core, what I hold in my heart, is changing. External influences are being replaced by inner mastery. I choose the values that nurture me and these determine my mood, my words and my actions. I am no longer like a weathercock on a rooftop, changing direction according to how the wind blows. Now I am firmly rooted to the fertile soil of my humanity.

The other evening at the meeting of my Buddhist group, one of the participants suggested we think of our life as a tree with deep roots. Every morning and every evening, when we nurture it with our chanting and the deepening knowledge of this philosophy, we are giving the tree of our life the water and the nutrients it needs to grow well. In this way the tree is healthy; its branches are thick and full of flowers and fruit, which are the benefit of this practice. This is necessary for the quality of my existence, just like water is necessary for a plant to thrive. I really liked this example, because my experience confirms that it is exactly so.

The spiritual part of me is now the centre, the basis of my life and I rediscovered how much it enriches me, how hungry I was for a solid foundation, a sense of direction, the clarity to distinguish between right and wrong, what's important and what is not. I realize that I am changing. Day after day the tree that was sick is healing, it is becoming healthy and strong. Now I feel confident in myself, in my life, and I am happy.

Chapter 29

LINA – THE LIMELIGHT

The applause for the street dance performance was fading and the group of teenage boys and girls was moving off the stage. After a scene change in the blackout, the spotlights came up again, illuminating ten little girls in polka-dot dresses, two each of red, yellow, emerald green, pink and electric blue. The poofy dresses with a tight-fitting corset and black-edged frills filled the big stage with bright colours. Eyes heavily rimmed in black, lips painted red, a rose in the hair and a fan matching the dresses, the ten little girls seemed miniature women.

The audience, largely made up of friends and families of the children, teenagers and the few adults who performed in the acts, were watching with nervous affection. The little girls were preparing to carry out the complex flamenco movements to the best of their abilities.

Announced by a robust start of stringed guitar, the music swiftly flooded the theatre, crept into every corner and crack, penetrating under my skin and giving me goose bumps.

The brightly clad mini-dancers on stage were bending, crouching and stretching upwards, raising their arms in an arch over their heads, lowering them in front of their chests, pushing them behind their backs. They were swaying chest and hips to the right and to the left, forward and back, moving resolutely and striking the beats with the heel, toe and sole of their little feet, clad in black flamenco shoes. The young performers were giving their all to express the strength, pride and majesty of such passionate and challenging dance. Their wrists rotated – even the fingers were dancing – and the vivid fans were waving to flap in rhythm with the music.

After the little girls it was our turn. There were twelve of us, sitting in the back row of the audience, waiting for the signal to stand up. The black leggings and t-shirt we wore made us almost invisible in the darkness of the theatre. I was excited – we all were – but not as apprehensive as I had feared. We had rehearsed on the stage the day before and Kate had decided where we were to stand. Luckily I was in the second row. I wasn't feeling insecure, nor did I think I wasn't as good as the others, but I was glad that in the front row were the women who had been part of the group for many years and had more confidence with the dance routine. During rehearsal the volume of the music had surprised me. I didn't expect it to be so loud. It had distracted me and I found it more difficult to remember the sequence of movements, which worried me a little. I really hoped it wouldn't have the same effect during the show. As the minutes went by I was jittering and giggling inside.

At last, following the agreed signal, we stood up. We moved with discretion, so we wouldn't be noticed, and went down the steps leading to the stage, careful not to stumble. Kate guided our line of black-clad ladies with her usual assurance. I was penultimate and Jane was behind me. Hot pink was the colour chosen by the group for the sequinned chokers we wore round our necks, the bracelets on our wrists and the band around the hats. Birgit's white hair stood out particularly well under the Borsalino hat, as did Mariolyn's, the other lady in her eighties. In my life I wore hats of many colours, but this was the first time I ever donned a hot pink one. Each of us held a stick covered in golden glitter and, hanging from our right shoulders, an equally glittering hula hoop.

'How are you feeling?' Jane, who was one step above mine, bent forward to speak next to my ear.

I leaned backwards, not quite turning my head: 'Excited... but quite confident. I've practised so much at home... I hope I won't make any mistakes.'

Jane chuckled: 'We'll all make mistakes, but it doesn't matter. What's important is that we enjoy this moment. If we have fun, the audience will have fun too.' With her hands on my shoulders she made me twist towards the back of the audience, saying: 'The local news is filming the show. Look at the cameraman, over there.'

I turned and, sure enough, a man was moving , holding a camera on his shoulder. 'Are you sure it's the news?' I asked. A sudden flutter of excitement made my heart quiver.

'I am,' Jane confirmed. 'See the logo on the side of his camera? This time you might finally see yourself on screen.'

'Do you think they might show our dance?'

'There's a good chance. We're unusual... older women, but groovy.' Jane giggled and added: 'The Carrot Club is filming too so, one way or the other, you'll definitely see yourself on a TV.'

I was very excited about that. 'How many people are there?' My eyes swept over the audience.

'A thousand. It's full.'

'Madonna santissima. Holy Mother Mary!' I burst out, while my hand flew to my chest.

'Don't worry.' Jane patted me on the shoulder. 'Dance for your friends, and especially for your family.'

I turned to look at the rows of people on my right hand side. 'They're all here!' I murmured in disbelief. It was true, my whole family was there.

Peering through the spectators I spotted Sofia. Next to her was Steve, who at that very moment was leaning towards her, whispering something. Sofia laughed and nodded strongly in agreement. She has changed so much in the last two months; she seems like a new person. It happened almost before my eyes. She was like a shrivelled flower that, after being watered, gradually recovers, is able to stand up straight and eventually glow. She has finally shaken off the invisible weight she had been carrying on her shoulders. That grey veil of sadness that blurred her eyes has finally disappeared and my heart can relax at last. I have been worried about my daughter. She tells me it was depression, and I take her word for it. Luckily I never had to go through that, but I could tell that she was troubled. Little by little, day after day, she is becoming herself again, the Sofia I knew. The difference is stunning and I can see that she is happy at last.

Sitting to her left was Marcello, my second son, who came from Lisbon. I hadn't seen him for months but, when he heard that I was going to dance, he booked himself a flight and got here the night before the performance. Fortunately he had warned me, so I was ready for his arrival. I was so excited to see him and it was great to be all together in London. When I lived in Nottingham he used to come and visit me there and, while Sofia and her family were living in a much smaller house, there was never a chance for us to get together. Now instead we have a lot of space. At Charlie's there was a free room and she invited Marcello to stay with us. The night he arrived we talked until late and, when he asked me to visit him in Lisbon in the spring, I said yes straight away. I'd like to go with someone else, because during the week he works and can't be with me all the time. We'll see who wants to accompany me. We have plenty of time to decide, but I am thrilled at the idea of this adventure.

Claudia was sitting next to Marcello. Since she and Tom broke up she has been much happier, much lighter. After coming back from Paris she started to look younger, livelier and even more beautiful. Then she took a big step and went to live with Mel. She told me that, although she likes to be independent, she misses her family. The other day, at the Buddhist meeting, she said that from the caterpillar she used to be she was turning into a butterfly and made everyone laugh. There is some truth to it though, and I am delighted for her.

Tom came to see the show, too. He was sitting just one seat further down the row. He said he considers me his adoptive grandmother, loves me and is proud of me. I am very fond of him; after all, he was part of the family for ten years. In a month's time he will leave for Saudi Arabia. I wish him all the good things in the world and I hope he'll find a woman who loves him just as he is.

Vittorio, my eldest son, was sitting between Claudia and Tom. He arrived from America two days before the performance. What a surprise that was! I thought I was going to have a heart attack. We were in the dining room, having Sunday lunch, when the doorbell rang and Sofia rushed to open. I thought all that hurry seemed odd. When she returned to the room, by her side was Vittorio. At first I didn't recognize him, or rather, I knew very well who he was, but I couldn't believe my eyes. And when I realized it really was him – Vittorio – I dropped my fork, burst into tears and couldn't stop crying. I had to drink all the champagne that Steve poured into my glass to begin to recover.

I've never understood this passion that young people have for surprise parties. It might be a great idea for them, but for someone my age it's a big shock. I was so happy though. I hadn't seen Vittorio for two years. We hugged tight, I don't know how many times.

He said that, when Sofia confirmed that I had been chosen to dance at the theatre, he requested two weeks holiday straight away. He wasn't going to miss it for anything in the world. He kept saying that he was proud of me, and that the family was reunited after more than two years thanks to this 'so-called human revolution' that I am doing. I was so excited I could hardly sleep that night.

Next to Tom was Micky, and Trish was sitting next to him.

They were holding hands and I saw them kissing twice in a row. They are so sweet, full of passion and the joy of life. Perhaps because he felt observed, Micky turned towards me and our eyes met. He sent me a kiss on the tips of his fingers and struck his chest repeatedly, meaning that his heart was beating with love for me. He made me laugh. I waved my hand at him and reminded myself that they, and all the friends sitting in the back row, were my audience.

Charlie was sitting next to her son Ernesto (named after Ernesto Che Guevara, of course). She has changed, too. She has always been good-hearted, but her abrupt manners kept the family at a distance, sometimes feeling offended, but lacking the courage to express it. Conversely, my grandchildren and their friends seem to like her blunt ways and giggle at her swear words. Since I moved in with her, she has become less harsh and now it's easier to see her generosity. Before she seemed to hide it, as if she didn't know how to express it without feeling embarrassed.

Within a few weeks, both she and I noticed how Ernesto, who lives in the outskirts of London, became closer. He stopped over for dinner several times and on a Sunday he even invited us to a lovely restaurant. He is a fairly introverted man, clearly very sensitive. He always talked little, but lately he tells us about his work and is opening up in regard to his partner, with whom he has been living for a few months.

When I told him that I was going to dance, he immediately accepted the invitation to accompany his mother. Charlie was on cloud nine. She adores him and is very proud of him. For a rebel like her it is an honour to defend the rights of her gay son. The other day she asked him if he'd be getting married to his partner, when they eventually legalize same sex marriage. She has no doubt that in the future it will become possible. Always a step ahead of everyone else, Charlie. She doesn't miss any news, any change in the culture of society. Now, all she needs is a rainbow flag to wave in the air.

Next to Ernesto, with her jet black hair enlivened by red artificial flowers, was Mavis. I saw her when I went to Nottingham to pick up my things. She remembered perfectly well the reading she'd done for me, before my eventful trip to London, and pointed out that she had been right in every aspect. I had to admit it was true: my life has changed completely and I am going to be dancing in a theatre. When I invited her to come down, she accepted straight away and arrived in London by train the day before the show. She stopped with a friend of hers – one of her clients – who was only too happy for her to stay in exchange for a Tarot reading. Dear Mavis, I do miss her. She has offered to put me up whenever I go to Nottingham, if my house is rented out. She is such a good friend!

Beverley and Josh were there too, in the same row. They are expecting their first baby and both looked glowing. They have a special place in my heart and I will never forget what they did for me. Meeting them has literally changed my life. From that evening in their home, nothing has been as it was before. That day I wasn't just lost in London, I was lost in another sense too. I thought I had little to give, less and less as the years went by, and that I was slipping into old age against my will. I believed the future was written, that growing old meant becoming a burden and fading like a candle... and that it was normal to feel that way. Since the day of our encounter I understood that I have a lot to give and many things to do. I rolled up my sleeves and started to contribute to society, loving every minute of it.

The idea of having my 'mission' in this world, which only I can carry out, gave me an impetus and an inner strength that I don't remember ever having had, not even when I was young. They said that I was ready to welcome a new perspective and I think they are right, because I find it all very easy and I really like the chanting of our mantra that I do twice a day (it is not exactly a mantra, they patiently keep telling me, but the title of the Lotus Sutra). In the morning I focus on praising my life, having a constructive day and enjoying the present because, at my age, you never know when it can end. In the evening I chant for ten minutes and I feel so much gratitude towards those around me, for what they do for me or for others. When I experience that gratitude in my heart, I feel clean, fresh, satisfied and I don't stress like I did before, when I did much less than I do now, but worried a lot more.

I am happy, as I have never been in my life. In fact, I don't think I have ever uttered this word: happy. There have been times with my children when I felt joy; other times, when I travelled, I felt contented, but this is more than contentment and only the word 'happiness' can describe this fullness and delight I feel inside, as if my heart was smiling.

Alex was there, too, with a big impressive camera. He moved around the theatre and took many beautiful photos of us. Navine came with little Connor who sat next to her, looking gorgeous in a white Indian-style shirt and trousers. Then there was Jim, and next to Jim was Nelson. He was sitting next to Mel, Claudia's colleague, and they seemed to be leaning against each other. Mel had come to a couple of meetings, had liked them a lot and she had liked *him* too. They got on straight away. I think I was the first one to notice the attraction between them – I am very perceptive about these things. Who knows, maybe the spark to make them fall in love has already been ignited. They are both generous and selfless, but alone and shy. There is nothing more beautiful than seeing two good people come together and become happy.

John came too, and so did Suki, the delightful girl from Singapore, and also Tony, Carlo and Sandra. They were sitting all together behind my family. The only one who couldn't make it was Tracy, because she was abroad for a fashion show, but she sent us a text message to inspire us. All the people who were at the meeting on the evening of the riots were at the theatre on the night. Of course they came for Jane, who has become a dear friend of mine, but also for me – they told me so.

The Flamenco music was ending with a crescendo of intensity and passion. Jane put her hand on my shoulder and squeezed it.

I grabbed her hand and held it tight.

Kate turned to us and gave us a big smile of encouragement. Her eyes were bright with excitement.

Jane spoke in my ear in a loud voice to make herself heard: 'In a moment it's our turn.'

'I know!' I shouted. My heart was so full of emotion it could have burst. I glanced at the row where my family was sitting. Sofia turned to look at me, she raised her hand with her thumb up as if to say 'good luck' and at the same time my two sons and my grandchildren, turned towards me. Charlie and all those sitting in her row did so too, smiling at me and Jane.

For a moment I thought that maybe I looked ridiculous in the hot pink I was wearing, but I decided I didn't care. I was so excited that I felt as if an electric current was flowing through my body.

The audience cheered the flamenco girls, who bowed twice and left the stage. Kate turned around and loudly – to be heard over the applause – announced 'Let's go!' The lights went out. We couldn't see anything in the pitch black but, knowing where the steps were, one by one we climbed onto the stage.

My legs were shaking, my arms and hands were trembling too, but I got into position. I was the second from the left, next to Birgit. We looked at each other and smiled. We rested the sticks on the floor, one metre in front of our feet, and took the hula hoop with both hands. I looked at Mariolyn, who stood on my right, and we both grinned. From her place in the centre of the front row Kate turned around, smiled confidently and nodded her head. We were ready!

When the opening words of 'Born this way' burst upon them, the audience recognized Lady Gaga's latest hit and gasped in surprise.

The lights came on. They shone on us so strongly they almost blinded us. We raised the hula hoops to frame our faces. The thumping beat of the music and the first notes of the song exploded at full blast. The audience roared in response.

I didn't expect it and laughed, trembling and giggling inside.

One step forward with the right, raising our knees high and lifting the hula hoop above our heads; we lowered it and repeated with the left. Hula hoops in the right hand and, shifting the weight from side to side, we swung them four times, facing the audience who started clapping to the beat of the music.

And then I don't remember exactly, but I know that we moved as a harmonious group, with the hoops flying in the air, catching them again and earning a thunderous applause.

Mambo with the right, pushing the hoops away from the body and bringing them back with arms bent. Marching forward, turning them clockwise, walking back turning the hoops counter clockwise.

After placing them on the ground, we stood inside them, marching on the spot and moving our arms in a robotic fashion. The audience cried out in wonderment. We followed it by a swaying our hips in a seductive move. This movement, performed by seventy and eighty year old women, made everyone laugh.

Stepping outside the hoops, we picked them up once again, spinning and rotating them whilst dancing, marching, jumping and turning around, performing full heartedly for our audience.

I was trembling with joy, my heart vibrating with the music. For a moment I glanced at the people and lost concentration. I made a mistake, turning to the left instead of the right, but I didn't panic. I recovered immediately, getting back into the dance routine.

The piece with the hula hoops was about to end. Placing them on the floor we began to clap our hands energetically at a fast pace, in rhythm with the music. The public took it as an invitation to join us and everyone began clapping with irrepressible enthusiasm.

We bent to pick up the glitter-covered sticks, knocking them on the ground, raising them in the air and twirling them in all directions. This part of the choreography was easier and we executed it to perfection. We were a close-knit, fast group. Professional majorettes would have been envious of our performance.

With the song about to end, we picked up the hoops and, at the rhythm of mambo we marched, spinning them, throwing them into the air and catching them again. I could hear the cries of admiration from the audience and my head felt light. At the beat of cha-cha-cha we moved towards the final position. All in a single row, our lowered hoops overlapping the sides looked just like the Olympics rings. And then came the finale. Raising the twelve interconnected hoops in the air we stood united, victorious, with triumphant smiles and hearts beating fast.

The theatre broke out in a tumultuous applause, accompanied by shouting and whistles of appreciation. Bowing twice, we took our hats off and waved them in the air.

The applause didn't stop, instead of abating it increased. The people sitting in the first row began to stand up, clapping raising their hands. The infectious enthusiasm took over until the whole audience was on their feet, the vigorous applause becoming rhythmic and continuous... going on, and on, and on.

My body was vibrating, my heart was swollen, full of exultation and joy, my smile was as big as my face. Never before had I experienced such incredible, exhilarating feeling of euphoria, excitement and pure happiness. It was, without a doubt, the most beautiful moment of my life... so far.

THE END

ABOUT THE AUTHOR

Born in Treviso (Italy), Emanuela Cooper studied foreign languages in Venice and Political Science at Padua University. She lived in India for six years, travelling and getting to know the Indian culture and traditions. She then moved to England with her husband, living and working in Nottingham as a teacher and translator for twenty years. She now spends her time between London and Ibiza.

Emanuela Cooper is a member of the Soka Gakkai International (SGI), a lay Buddhist movement for the realization of peace through culture and education.

Her first novel, Made in Nirvana, has been beautifully received, with an average of 4.8 stars out of 5. Some reviews below.

5.0 out of 5 stars
A whole new perspective on life
By Miss C Kleanthous on 13 June 2015
A highly recommended read! Emanuela Cooper writes in such a way that allows the reader to be swept away with Maria, experiencing the character's fascinating journey from start to end. The detailed and vivid images of life in India and beyond help you to clearly visualise what Maria sees, feel what she feels and dream when she dreams. Made in Nirvana has given me a whole new perspective on life and will undoubtedly continue to influence me in many ways. Thank you.

5.0 out of 5 stars
Couldn't put it down!
By Nicole on November 9, 2015
I stumbled across Made In Nirvana by chance. Upon reading I found

myself completely locked into the story and unable to put it down! A wonderful story full of romance, humour, friendship and spirituality. I learnt so much about Buddhism and have since started chanting myself. This book has literally changed my life! Can't recommend it enough :)

5.0 out of 5 stars
<u>Read this and go to sleep with a smile on your face!</u>
By <u>Jean H.</u> on 13 February 2015
A refreshingly positive novel providing a fascinating insight into the Indian way of life from a young westerner's perspective. Anyone who has travelled around India on a tight budget should be able to relate to the experiences in this book. Emanuela Cooper keeps the pace flowing with a balanced mixture of descriptive detail, light humour and thoughtful analysis of human behaviour. The respect that the main character feels for the people she meets on her travels shines through and illuminates the reader. If you read it at bedtime you'll go to sleep with a smile on your face.

5.0 out of 5 stars
<u>'Made in Nirvana is a beautiful Book. It is utterly 'charming' in all various ...</u>
Made in Nirvana is a beautiful Book. It is utterly 'charming' in all various meaning of this word. Magical, Poetic, and deeply Moving. The characters are friends we come to know, feel for, identify with. India's verdant beauty - vivid colours, sounds, smells, tastes. Realisation and respect for humanity awoken by those with 'materially so little' yet who share appreciation of 'true treasures within'.
I think Made In Nirvana is a Healing Book. I travelled to exquisite and challenging places. Inside and out. The writing is so vivid - the images imprinted in my memory like sensorial paintings.
Finally, I came to a place of rest. A good place in my self. One of Hope.
Thankyou so much Emanuella Cooper

5.0 out of 5 stars

I have enjoyed every minute of reading this book and would recommend ...

By Derek Andrews on 16 August 2015

I have enjoyed every minute of reading Made in Nirvana. You have this overwhelming feeling that you want to step into the book, join Maria and Franca in their travels and experience the dangers, the trials and tribulations which they encounter on a daily basis, but also the love, the building of friendships and the amazing places they visit, India becomes this place you have a urge to visit and the people come across beautifully.

5.0 out of 5 stars

A fantastic read!!

By jonrty on 13 February 2015

An amazing 'coming of age' story, set within the beautiful country of India. Beautifully written with incredible attention to detail. A real page turner. I loved it and would highly recommend this book.

5.0 out of 5 stars

Peaceful and uplifting reader

By Luna on 7 July 2015

As I was lucky to buy the book directly from the author after a public reading in Ibiza, I expected a diverting lecture. But reading 'Made in Nirvana' has given me much more than that: I constantly had to smile, once or twice I was crying a little bit (due to the beauty of the situation described) and I really enjoyed the introduction into buddhism, which is never missionary but very interesting! Afterwards I found my self chanting with joy - and wanting to go visit India again… ;-) Even for me, with a German mother tongue it was easy to read, although it is written with eloquent style. In conclusion, I can say this is a very uplifting book! Looking forward to read it again!

5.0 out of 5 stars

A Great Read

By Mrs. C. Myers on 18 October 2015

A wonderful, very readable book. I couldn't put it down. I have been to India, years ago and it brings it all back... meeting strange people who open your eyes, the vibrant colours, the smell of food cooking, the drugs, the poverty, the laughter and the tears of a great adventure are all brought to life in the pages of this book. I particularly found the author's awakening to Buddhism very interesting and she explained it all in a way that I finally understood.

Five Stars
By S Star on 23 November 2015
Fantastic book. Was sad to finish it!

Printed in Poland
by Amazon Fulfillment
Poland Sp. z o.o., Wrocław

52945333R00202